The Privateer

S0-AFI-432

DAWN MACTAVISH

LEISURE BOOKS   NEW YORK CITY

*For DeborahAnne MacGillivray, whose friendship
and support is appreciated beyond words.*

A LEISURE BOOK®

January 2008

Published by

Dorchester Publishing Co., Inc.
200 Madison Avenue
New York, NY 10016

ISBN 10: 0-8439-5981-9
ISBN 13: 978-0-8439-5981-9

10 9 8 7 6 5 4 3 2 1

Visit us on the web at www.dorchesterpub.com.

The Privateer

One

"In ya get, me lady," the slovenly turnkey at Lark's elbow barked. Without ceremony he handed her over the threshold of a tiny, dingy, cell-like quarter collecting shadows in the bleak half-light that lived in such places on the edge of darkness.

"There must be some mistake," she murmured, taking in her new surroundings. "Surely you can't expect me to *live* here?"

"No mistake, me lady," said the man, perusing the open ledger in his dirty hands. "Lady Lark Eddington, number six. You be her, and this be number six." He snapped the book shut. "This here be one o' the better ones, ya know. Up a flight, ya won't get too many rats like they do below, just flies and spiders. You'll want ta eat up all o' what food ya get, or you'll draw 'em, though—the rats, that is. Have ya got any more blunt ta spare?"

"Blunt, sir?" she blurted. "You've taken it all! If I had any more money, I wouldn't be in here, would I?"

"No need ta take a pet. Blunt'll get ya extras here at the Marshalsea is all—aye, and the necessities, too, come down to it. What ya already give has bought ya a few days' food and clean water, and this fine room here. When it's gone, you're on your own. There's plenty o' vendors in here, but they don't give credit. I'm only tryin' ta help ya, me lady. Folks who don't pay garnish—and them that's a rougher sort, if ya take my meaning—live in the cells below all crammed in together. They sleep on the floor, where the straw don't get changed too often, if ya get my drift, and scrounge for their food how they will. You've got a nice mattress there that only two has died on, filled with fairly clean straw, and it'll stay that way unless ya soils it."

"Well, I haven't any more . . . 'garnish' for you, so you may as well take yourself off and leave me be."

"In due course, me lady," the turnkey said, expanding his posture. "Got ta read ya the rules first; 'tis the order o' things here at the Marshalsea."

"Get on with it, then," Lark snapped. Extras, indeed! What was that supposed to mean? She raised her handkerchief to her nose. There was a fetid stench about the place that turned her stomach; she'd noticed it the minute the gated doors swung open to admit her earlier. It seemed stronger now, what with the jailor's unwashed odor added. How would she ever stand it shut up in the debtors' prison?

"You'll get used ta the stink," the man replied to her cough. "We've got strict rules against it, but some o' the folks in here don't have a care where they empty their chamber pots. Ha! Some o' 'em in the better cells like yours don't even have the decency ta holler '*guardie-loo*' when they dumps 'em out o' the windows. But you won't have ta bother 'bout that up here above stairs, just watch yerself when ya go down for a stroll. You'd best not stand too close ta the buildings. Any o' the guards'll show ya the proper place ta dump your pot. You'll get no maid service in here."

"Please get on with your rules," Lark snapped, repulsed by the discourse and the prospect of being entombed in such a foul and filthy place.

"Ya can have guests, but no gentleman callers, unless they be relatives; that's strictly enforced. Ya can go down for a stroll whenever ya like, during the day, that is. After lockup, you're in for the night, and ya can never go beyond the gates ta the outside, o' course—ever. There's guards ta make sure o' that. This is a jail, remember, not the Grand Promenade.

"The coal is in the cellar below the communal cells. It's a long way down, and you'll fetch it yerself in that scuttle there," he said, pointing to it beside the small black stove in the corner. "One scuttleful a sennight in summer, two in winter—unless, o' course, ya want to pay garnish for more—and ya can have whatever wood and paper bits ya can scrounge hereabouts free o' charge, but I wouldn't count on none o' that if I was you. Folks in here would kill for such, especially in winter. Me name is Tobias, me lady; I keep this section. If ya have any issues, ya bring 'em ta me."

"I was told that I might work to pay off my debt," Lark said. "How might I do that if I cannot leave this place?"

"That's your coil ta unwind, now, ain't it?" the jailor chided. "If yer lucky, some kind benefactor'll pick ya up. We get 'em come in here from time ta time, lookin' over the ladies for one thing or another. Keep yourself up, and mind your manners, and ya might just attract one o' 'em. Can ya sew or write or do sums, and the like?"

"I can."

"Sometimes folks have need of such services, and they come here with their piecework to get it done cheap." The jailor flashed a wry smile and his small eyes, like two raisins in the wrinkles of his face, gave a sly twinkle. "If ya was to happen ta scrape up a bit more garnish, I could steer such folk as might inquire your way."

"I've already told you—"

"Oh, aye, ya told me right enough, and I'm just telling you, is all, that's how things go here in the Marshalsea. It's better'n the Fleet, or Newgate, come ta that. If ya have a special talent, somethin' that can be taught for a price, ya can turn a pretty penny just amongst the 'guests.' You'll see shingles on the units all along out there advertisin' the trades o' folks tryin' ta make their way. Ya need ta be enterprisin' ta survive in here, me lady."

"Is that all, then?"

"You'll find a tinderbox in the drawer in the table. I've left ya a candle. Don't waste it, ya only get one a sennight, unless—"

"Yes, yes, I know, unless I pay garnish for more," she snapped.

"Now you're gettin' the drift," Tobias returned. "What food your blunt bought is in the cupboard—potatoes, a cabbage, a turnip, a bit o' bread, and some hard cheese. No coffee, but there's a bit o' used tea. The vendors dry it out and sell it again. Don't use it all up at once. You won't get nothin' but slops when it's gone—not without garnish, just so's ya know. Now, if ya want that coal, ya better step lively. Ya won't get nothin' after the closin' bell rings. That about covers it." He ambled toward the door. "I'll be leavin' ya ta get yourself all settled in."

Lark closed the door behind him and sank into the rickety chair in the corner, thankful that there even was a chair after the odious turnkey's oration. She untied the ribbon that secured her wine-colored bonnet, and set it aside with the bundle of belongings she was permitted—a plain dove gray twill frock, a pelerine for when the weather turned colder, a warm pelisse for winter, a shawl, and her whalebone comb to order her cap of naturally curly ringlets that defied taming in normal circumstances. How they would behave in these conditions? she shuddered to wonder. Aside from the wine-colored traveling frock and spencer she wore, and the underthings she had on beneath, that was the sum total of her worldly possessions. All of her fine silk frocks, ball gowns, jewelry—even her portmanteaux—had been confiscated with the rest of the contents of Eddington Hall when the house and grounds reverted to the Crown, and still there were hundreds of pounds in debts outstanding.

It was no use. She would never be able to pay what was owed by taking in sewing and doing sums in the ledgers of some cheeseparing miser who came only to have his work done cheaply. She was only twenty-two years old. She'd been robbed of her come-out, orphaned, left without a feather to fly with, and now this. It didn't bode well for her future, but she would not cry. Lark Eddington was no watering pot, though she certainly had every right to be, alone in her dark, dingy cubicle, too exhausted to eat and too frightened to sleep, though she must do both if she were to wake with a clear head and some semblance of a plan.

Even though it was still some time before dusk, it was dark in the room. Should she light the candle? Better not. She would have to make it last. She did need to fetch her ration of coal, however, and she took up the scuttle and decided to begin with that.

When Tobias described the coal cellar as being "a long way down," he wasn't exaggerating. It took Lark some time to descend the rickety stairs past the communal cells to the dimly lit bins and fill the scuttle; a guard keeping watch on the landing above made certain the coal was level with the top before he let her pass to return to her cubicle. Halfway up, she set the heavy scuttle down and leaned against the dank wall bleeding with moisture, brushing the tendrils back from her moist face. Her body ached. She wasn't accustomed to hauling coal up three long flights of precariously open stairs. She looked at her hands. They were black with coal dust, as was her frock, come to that. Had she wiped it on her face just now when she'd pushed back those dratted tendrils? She must have, and she hadn't seen soap anywhere. No doubt she would have to pay garnish for that luxury. Hi-ho, what did it matter? She shrugged, took up the scuttle, and resumed her climb.

She had almost reached the top when the sound of raised voices drifting downward from the open door of her cubicle nearly stopped her heart. Had she left it open? No. She was certain she hadn't. Her breath caught. Three women burst through the gaping door fighting over her belongings. Tugging on her spare frock, her pelerine and pelisse, they tore past, flattening her against the wall in their haste, and knocked the coal scuttle out of her hand as they fled. To her horror, it tumbled after them, bouncing off the steps all the way to the bottom as the coal rained down between the open slats in a dusty black shower to the landing below.

Lark steadied herself against the shaky wooden banister. Staring over the edge, she watched the coal she'd gathered and carted up three long flights scatter over the landing, where others were scooping it up in their hats, their pots, and their aprons, rejoicing over the precious find. She scarcely blinked and it was gone. Groaning, she slouched against the wall, but that reaction was short-lived. The coal notwithstanding, how dare they take her things?

Anger charged her with new energy, and she spun on the step, raced down the stairs and out into the courtyard, where the scuffle was still in progress. A crowd of inmates and visitors had gathered around the three women wrestling with each other over possession of her clothes. There wasn't a guard in sight. Where were they when a body needed them? They were visible enough when garnish was in the offing. Enraged at that, she joined the foray of flailing arms and flying fists in a desperate attempt to take back her belongings, but her education hadn't included instruction in the art of fisticuffs. While she held her own for a time, encouraged by the spectators' cheers, she soon was knocked off her feet, landing hard without ceremony in the dust of the courtyard. When it settled around her, the women had disappeared with her belongings, and an outstretched hand came into focus. She stared, her eyes following it up the length of a man's indigo superfine sleeve to modest shirt points held in place by a flawless, Oriental-tied neckcloth, so fashionable that season. He doffed his beaver hat, exposing a crop of dark wavy hair burnished with deep mahogany glints in the light of the setting sun. She almost gasped. A mysterious-looking black patch covered his right eye.

After a moment, she took the hand, and he raised her up with ease, then bowed from the waist over the fingers he'd captured, taking longer than she deemed proper to release her. She did gasp then. It was like holding on to a lightning bolt for the startling effect his touch was inflicting on her most private regions. Tall, and well proportioned, he looked too prosperous for a prisoner—too meticulously groomed. There was a provocative masculine scent about him, of pipe tobacco and leather, and wine recently drunk. It was pleasantly dizzying, or was that from just having the wind knocked out of her? She couldn't be sure.

"Are you hurt?" he said, his voice deep and resonant as he took her measure and finally let her go.

"N-no, I don't think so," she murmured, gazing into his exposed eye, dark and penetrating, shimmering like obsidian beneath the thick lashes that gave him a sensuous seductive look. The eye patch didn't detract. It was almost a blessing: Looking into two such riveting eyes would have been more than she could bear, considering the effect the one was having upon her. She had never experienced the like. This man seemed to see into her soul.

"What occurred here?" he queried. "Were those things yours?"

"Yes," she murmured.

Tobias pushed his way through the crowd, his bark preceding him. "Don't trouble yourself, me lord," he said. Snatching Lark's arm, he began leading her away. "I'll deal with this."

"Let go of me!" Lark cried, looking back toward the gentleman who was still staring after them as the jailor propelled her along the courtyard, steering her toward number six. "Where were you when those harridans were robbing me?" she demanded.

"This ain't no way ta start out in here, me lady," Tobias said, shoving her up the stairs.

"They took my things! They spilled the coal I'd just gathered, and others below stole it all before I could retrieve it."

"You've got ta look sharp in here. I don't know what got inta them. Folks don't steal from the other guests."

"Hah!"

"There's a code o' ethics here in the Marshalsea. Ya musta provoked 'em some way."

"*Provoked?* I wasn't even in here. I was in the cellar gathering coal for the stove, like you told me to. They knocked it out of my hands fleeing with my things, and now everything is gone. Well? Do something!"

"I'll look inta it."

"When?"

"In due course, me lady."

"What about my coal?"

"Ya get a scuttleful a sennight, like I told ya."

"But they took it!"

"So you say."

"Do you see any lying about here? The guard below checked the scuttle. He'll tell you. He made me put a handful back. The scuttle is still down there. They've probably got that too by now. Don't just stand here—go and see for yourself."

"In due course, I said. In the meantime, you'd best stay right in here. You've caused enough trouble for one day— yer first day, ta boot!"

"In due course, *in due course.* Is that all you can say?"

"I'll look inta it," he repeated. "Now you just settle down or I'll lock ya in here till ya do! I've got important prison business ta attend."

This was another dream, another nightmare—it had to be. She would wake soon in the mahogany sleigh bed in her spacious bedchamber at Eddington Hall, and all would be well. Her father, the Earl of Roxburgh, would still be living, not buried in shame outside the churchyard fence—that awful spiked iron fence with its high arched gates, so cold and forbidding. Such fences had terrified her ever since she was a child in leading strings. Could that terror have been a premonition of her dire circumstances now, some sort of strange foreshadowing? She was open to that sort of thinking. Could that iron fence, those forbidding gates, really keep the redeemed souls in and the lost souls out? The vicar was convinced of it. Was there indeed a designated army of invisible celestial beings standing guard, arms linked around it to enforce such things? And if there was, how could she bribe them? What must she suffer to ransom her father's poor damned soul? This nightmare? But it wasn't a nightmare, was it? It was all too real.

She hadn't been all that truthful with Tobias. She still had a little money put by—a very little in a small embroidered pocket sewn into her corset. She would have to use it wisely, however, and it would be best if he didn't know she had it. These were desperate people: inmates and jailors alike. Imagine, forcing her to spend what little she had—and should be trying to save to pay off her debt—upon life's bare necessities just in order to survive; it was insidious. It was *evil*. But there it was.

She prayed she'd wake from the dreadful dream, but then a bell pealed; loud, rasping, and final. After a few moments of shuffling, murmuring noise as a stream of visitors literally fled lest they be locked in for the night, the clang of the iron-barred doors set in the high brick wall that surrounded the prison slammed shut. Lark gave a start at the sound echoing through the narrow courtyard below. She was trapped. Shut up in the Marshalsea debtors' prison, in Borough High Street, without a prayer of redeeming herself.

She eyed the dubious mattress on its crude wooden frame in the corner that was supposed to suffice for a bed. At the very least it would have fleas. She dared not speculate as to what else it might have. There was a tattered blanket at the foot, and while she could still see, since the light was fading, she crawled underneath it. Maybe in the morning it wouldn't be real. Maybe she would wake to find that the terrible mistake had been rectified—that someone had come to rescue her, but who? There was no one. Still, she had to believe. It was all too terrible not to believe. And though she had never been one to cling to false hope, even though she was prone to believing in things unexplained and unexplainable, she beat back the face of cold reality just this once, and slept.

Basil "King" Kingston, Earl of Grayshire, thrust his walking stick under his arm and tugged his gloves on as he paced outside the prison keeper's office waiting for Tobias. Where was the gudgeon? Now the bell had rung, and he would have to be let out. That meant he would have to pay a tribute, or spend the night. Damn and blast! This was the last place he wanted to be, but there was nothing for it. He'd given his word, and he would see the dashed chore through to the bitter end—he had to, if he were to get on with his life with a clear conscience.

Taking impatient, long-legged strides in the dust of the courtyard, he wondered about the scene he'd just witnessed, about the attractive, well-spoken young woman with the petal-soft hand—too soft for an inmate of such a place— who had been cast down literally at his feet. Yes, attractive. For all he knew, she might even be pretty underneath all the coal dust and courtyard dirt that obscured her true image and dulled the cap of sun-painted ringlets that framed her dirty face. The startled—almost desperate—look in her eyes settled uneasily in his memory for some reason, along with their color: an odd luminous shade of blue that bordered on violet. What was such a creature doing in the Marshalsea of all places? That alone was enough to pique his interest, and a number of questions came to the fore when Tobias finally joined him.

"Sorry 'bout the ruckus, Lord Grayshire," the turnkey grumbled, tugging the wrinkled lapels straight on his plain black frock coat, and slapping the dust away that sullied it. "This ain't the most peaceable place in the realm, ya know."

"Who was that young woman?" King queried.

"A fine lady, ta hear her tell it. Lady Lark Eddington, o'

Yorkshire. Her father done for himself and left her in the suds."

"Ahhh," King returned. "Roxburgh's daughter, of course. Do you mean to say that none among the *ton* would stand for her?"

"Evidently not, me lord. You know how the *ton* loves a juicy scandal. She's done for amongst the gentlefolk now. Her father owed half o' England when he turned thief, and hanged himself after he got caught—that was her inheritance. Dead or alive, it don't matter none ta them holdin' the vowels. Blunt is blunt, and folks want satisfaction. She come in just this afternoon, and already she's a troublesome sort."

"Hmmmm," King mused. "How much is her debt?"

"Upwards o' five hundred pounds. Why? Ya ain't thinkin' o' settlin' on *her*, are ya? She ain't fit for nothin'."

"She's fit enough for what I have in mind," King said tersely. The softness of her hand in his came without bidding, and he tugged at his gloves and flexed his fingers, but the action did little to cure the tingling her touch had left behind.

"And what might that be now?"

"None of your affair."

"I can't just hand her over," said the turnkey. "You'll have ta take it up with the magistrate."

"Very well. I will need her particulars—the magistrate's name, her docket number, and the like."

"Aye, me lord, if yer sure ya know what yer doin'. I still say—"

"Yes, well," King interrupted, "I shall be the best judge of my needs. Now, if you don't mind, I'll have the lady's specifics if you please. The legal aspects are going to take time, and I am already behindhand as it is."

Two

A *cheerless dawn mist was ghosting in off the Thames* when Lark woke. It pressed up against the one small, barred curtainless window that looked out on the courtyard, or would, once the fog lifted. The room seemed even shabbier in dreary daylight. There was a scarred wooden table beside the wall, with a pewter trencher and beaker, fork, knife, and spoon stacked on it. A two-drawer cupboard stood alongside. The food Tobias had mentioned—scarcely fit for provender—was in the bottom of it along with a pot, a kettle, an old crazed teapot with no lid, and a chipped cup. No saucer; so much for "extras." It didn't matter. She wouldn't be entertaining.

Since she had no coal for the stove she couldn't have tea, but the bread, to her surprise, wasn't too stale, and Lark cut off a wedge that the cockroaches hadn't nibbled and gobbled it down. Then, slipping on her bonnet, she unlatched the door and ventured below for a look at her new domicile, wishing she had her pelerine to throw over her shoulders, for the mornings were cool as September approached, especially when there was no sun to burn off the morning mist. It was a far cry from the velvety rolling green—the patchwork hills and splendid gardens—that hemmed her beloved Eddington Hall in Yorkshire.

What met her eyes first was the vastness of the gray stone, a dingy brick high-walled city within a city, already teeming with life. Both prisoners and visitors milled about dilapidated carts and stalls and rickety tables set up in the courtyard. Those who could pay, bought. Those who could not stared longingly at wares forbidden them while light-fingered urchins made off with what they might.

Lark shuddered. It was indeed worse in the light of day—a grimy, filthy place reeking with the foul stench of rotting food and raw sewage, threaded through with sugary, spicy bakery smells and the tantalizing aroma of roasting meat. There were chickens and sausages skewered on spits, their rendered fat dripping and hissing into live coals. The unlikely combination of smells threatened to make her retch.

The strident sounds of milling voices calling, shouting, laughing and cursing bounced from building to building across the courtyard. The strange litany echoed from the patrons, from the vendors hawking their wares, from the high barred windows, where inmates too infirm to come below to collect their purchases called out their orders and cast down their coins. Lads pushed and shoved in a mad scramble to deliver these in hopes of a halfpenny reward at the end. They came and went, spending their meager tributes at the baker's table, and their more substantial awards on the fat greasy sausages.

What shocked Lark most on first appraisal was the presence of the children amongst the prisoners. A boy of about twelve years, and a girl, who looked to be eight—obvious siblings—were engaged in a dispute over the ownership of a tin hoop, gone slightly out of round for the tugging, when a woman's hand on her arm and a voice close to her ear spun her around with a jerk.

"Oh, la, my lady, I didn't mean to give you a fright," the woman said. "I meant only to welcome you into the Marshalsea. My name is Agnes Garwood. I was a . . . I mean, I *am* a milliner. Being shut up in this rattrap for nigh on three years tends to make a body forget who or what—or even *if*—she ever was."

"Forgive me," Lark gushed, still swallowing her rapid heartbeat. "You startled me. I didn't see you there."

"I saw old Toby bringing you in last night. Watch him. He's a sly one. He'll weasel what blunt you've got right out of your pockets before you can wink if you aren't careful."

Lark studied the dark-haired woman, who might have been attractive once—pretty even. She couldn't be more than thirty, but her pale face was lined and her posture apathetic. Her clothes hung awry on her slender frame, suggesting that she'd lost weight, and her gray eyes were bloodshot, the skin around them spread with shadowy stains. Was this what Lark herself would look like after three years in the Marshalsea?

"Is there something amiss?" said Agnes.

"N-no, I beg your pardon for staring," Lark murmured. "How rude of me. Please forgive my want of conduct. My mind was a million miles away just now."

"Nothing to forgive," the woman replied. "You must be quite overset, a fine lady like yourself being shut up in here. How did that ever happen, if I might be so bold as to ask?"

Lark hesitated. Should she say? She had always been a private person. But she was so alone now . . . so dreadfully alone. It would be so good to have a friend, someone to talk to. What harm to tell it? What did it matter? What would it change?

"My mother died when I was born," she began. It was still difficult saying the words. But maybe that's what was needed to purge the nightmare. "My father raised me at our estate in Yorkshire. I loved him very dearly, but he was a compulsive gambler . . . a dreadfully unlucky one, I'm afraid, and he didn't make sound business judgments. Little by little, he frittered away our fortune until he'd put us in Dun territory. I wasn't aware that we were sailing the River Tick until it was too late . . . until after he . . . died and I was set upon by creditors, merchants—an endless parade of his gambling associates demanding satisfaction for the hundreds, thousands of pounds in outstanding vowels he had out all over the Realm."

"Oh, la, my lady! He just up and died and left you dipped?"

"He was caught stealing from a . . . friend. Rather than face prosecution, he committed suicide—hanged himself—in prison," she said, low-voiced. It was the first time she'd spoken it aloud. "With no male heir, and none to even designate, I was put out, and the estate reverted to the Crown. I sold everything I possessed—my clothes, jewels, and my personal belongings. But it wasn't enough to satisfy the outstanding debts, and so they put me here for the few hundred pounds remaining."

"Was it the creditors or the gamblers holding the last?"

"My father's gambling partners, and the friend from whom he stole."

"And they wouldn't do the gentlemanly thing and let you off—a lady like yourself, bereaved and all, with no fault in it?"

"Oh, they had ideas on how I could redeem myself to their satisfaction, if you take my meaning. I came here gladly."

"I'm so sorry for your trouble," Agnes breathed. "I didn't mean to bring up bad memories . . . oh, la, I only meant to offer friendship. You looked so forlorn standing here, and I saw what happened to you yesterday, when those three bawds took your things."

"No, no, I needed to tell it," Lark reasoned. "Such things fester if kept inside. I needed to say the words aloud to someone in order to face it, leave it behind, and move on. Even so, I doubt I will ever be able to put it behind me completely. Not after this," she added bitterly, glancing around at the inmates with a shudder. "And I could certainly use a friend. I'm glad you took the initiative."

Being reminded of the skirmish brought the mysterious man of yesterday to mind. His evocative scent threaded through her nostrils, overpowering the courtyard smells. She relived the touch of the strong hand that had lifted her up, and the spell he'd cast over her with his obsidian gaze. There was no other way to describe the effect the man had upon her.

"You've got nobody, then, who'll speak for you?" Agnes said, interrupting her reverie. "What of the *ton*? Surely somebody among them—"

"My father's thievery—not to mention the suicide— put paid to that," Lark cut in. "That and the fact that many of his gambling cronies were *haute ton* and held the largest vowels. Most of his peers suffered great losses staking him over time. After his death, I was shunned by all of our so-called friends, and I've already told you what the less familiar in their number had in mind. There were many who might have come to my rescue—if only to offer moral support—but none willing to risk even that for fear of more loss. I became a pariah, and I can hardly blame them."

"It must have been hard, all alone and all."

"The worst of it was I never dreamed . . . It all came as such a shock to me. I wasn't equipped. I made bad judgments just as Father did, sold holdings and possessions far too cheaply. I was ill-advised by solicitors who were only interested in gouging—taking their shockingly padded fees straightaway. They made certain of that, and let the rest go by the wayside. They took advantage of me when I was addled with shock and grief and shame over the scandal. I could have realized so much more if I'd had decent counsel."

"I know how bad advice can do a body in," said Agnes. "I was married, you know, doing my millinery work from our home in Shropshire. Then, my husband's advisors persuaded him to take out a mortgage on our farm and cottage and set me up in business proper. I was afraid to take the risk, but Timothy, my husband, thought it a fine idea, since the farm was turning a profit and all. One year later, Tim was dead of typhus and I was encumbered. Now, I'm trying to work off my debt fashioning hats for the *ton*'s elite in here. La! Not a one of them would be caught dead admitting their fine headgear came straight out of the Marshalsea. They'd swallow their tongues first. I get some satisfaction out of that."

Lark was only half listening to Agnes's tale. A threadbare dandy was watching her from the doorway of number four across the way. He was staring in a rude and vulgar manner, a man she took to be in his early thirties, darkly handsome in an unkempt sort of way, and certainly no gentleman, judging from the ungallant way he was taking her measure. It made her uneasy, and after a moment Agnes turned toward the man also.

"Oh, *him*," she grunted. "I wondered what had taken your notice all of a sudden. Don't pay that one any mind, my lady. Don't let the pretty face fool you. That's Andrew Westerfield, the second son of the Earl of Stepton, from Cornwall, to hear him tell it. Be that as it may, he's a regular rake, and he's tried to have his way with every gel in here over the age of fourteen. You'd best steer clear. His own father wouldn't even cover his vowels and bail him out. He's nothing but trouble, you can take it from me."

"I quite intend to," Lark murmured. "He makes my skin crawl." She looked away then, cupped Agnes's elbow in her hand, and steered her toward number six. "I know what let's do," she said. "I haven't any coal for a fire to make coffee, or some of Tobias's 'used' tea, but I do have some bread and cheese. We can take our nuncheon together. Will that suit?"

"That will suit fine," said Agnes. "I have a bit of coal I can spare. I'll just run on and fetch it. Thank you, my lady."

"Lark," she corrected. "If we are to be friends, you must call me Lark."

"Like the bird?"

"Like the bird," she agreed.

Even though her back was turned, Lark was aware of the dandy's eyes following them; her peripheral vision had caught him turning as they did, and she shuddered. The hairs on the back of her neck stood on end, flagging danger. "Don't make it obvious, but is Westerfield still watching us?" she asked in an undervoice.

"Yes, the cheeky gudgeon. Don't pay him any mind, my la—*Lark*. I saw him just this morning with the three who took your things, jawing away as cozy as you please. Just remember what I said. Don't you trust him."

By the time Agnes came with the coal, Lark had set a respectable, albeit shabby, table. They had just started a smoky fire in the dirty coal stove when a knock at the door they'd left open to draw off the smoke turned them both around with a lurch.

It was Andrew Westerfield.

"I believe these belong to you, Lady Eddington," he said, stepping over the threshold from the shadowy hall into the shaft of light streaming in through the window. With unabashed insolence, he held her stolen garments to his nose and inhaled deeply.

He was even shabbier in close proximity, and Lark's breath caught as she snatched her clothing from him and hugged it to her. The frock was wrinkled and distressed, the pelerine was stretched out of shape, and the pelisse was covered with the dust of the courtyard. They weren't in much better condition than the torn, coal-stained dress she wore, but they were hers, all she possessed.

"Thank you, sir," she breathed. "I am in your debt."

"Which is just what he wanted," Agnes snapped.

Tobias burst through the door, breathless. "I seen ya come up here, Westie," he said. "What do ya think you're doin'? You know the rules. Out!"

"I am merely returning the lady's belongings," said Westerfield.

"I might have known you was in on it," Tobias returned.

"Quite to the contrary, my dear man," Westerfield said. "'Twas Alice and Maggie and Maud who stole them. I am simply returning them."

"Out, I said!" Tobias barked, taking the man by the arm.

"Your servant, my lady," Westerfield said, clicking his heels in a bow from the waist. Then both men were gone, and Lark barred the door after them and sank down on the mattress still clutching her things to her breast.

"Is that everything?" Agnes asked, nodding toward her clothing.

"Yes," Lark replied. "All but my whalebone comb. What did you mean before when you said it was just what Westerfield wanted?"

"I told you I saw him and those three with their heads together. I saw him ogling you when Tobias first brought you in here yesterday. I'd bet my last halfpenny that he planned that little brouhaha—bribed those lightskirts to take your things—just so he could save the day and put you right where you said you were . . . 'in his debt.' He never does anything without a reason, that one. I told you not to trust him. Mark my words, you'd best watch yourself."

For the next few days Lark stayed in her cubicle, fearful of another incident. Her window faced the courtyard, and Andrew Westerfield, who had stationed himself in the doorway across the way, was watching, always watching, whittling aimlessly on some anonymous scrap of wood with his penknife as he leaned there, his gaze never seeming to leave her window. At least it was always fixed there whenever she glanced below, which was often.

The only bright spots in her days were her visits from Agnes, who called often and even brought more of her own coal, which Lark knew she couldn't spare, so that they could heat the kettle for tea, since Tobias hadn't looked into the matter "in due course" as he'd promised. But Agnes's coal was soon used, and on the afternoon of the fourth day following the unpleasant incident, Lark decided to brave the coal cellar again. This time she was armed with an empty drawer from the cupboard to collect the coal, since her scuttle was never returned.

It was early. Agnes was expected to join her for nuncheon as she had since they met, but there was still time before that, and Lark made her way down to the cellar below and faced the guard, drawer at the ready.

"And just where do ya think you're goin' with that, then?" he inquired, blocking her way to the bins. "Seems ta me I remember you havin' your ration this sennight already."

"If you remember that, then you also remember three inmates knocking my scuttle down these stairs. My coal rained down on your head right after I collected it, and 'twas you who let these below here steal it. Tobias was to speak to you. They took my scuttle as well."

"Tobias never said a word to me 'bout no scuttle, nor no coal, neither," the guard insisted, bristling. "You'll have to take that up with him. Lest I hear otherwise, you'll get no more coal till Monday week, so ya can turn yourself right 'round and march back up where ya come from."

Lark would not beg. She would go without tea and warm water to wash with until kingdom come before she would bend her knee to the likes of such as this. Squaring her shoulders, she spun on her heel and ascended the stairs with as much dignity as she could muster, tripping on her frock, which had suffered a waist-high tear during the courtyard scuffle, that had gotten worse for wear. That earned her a rowdy laugh from the guard behind, but she paid him no mind. It was still echoing after her when she reached the second-floor landing, where another annoyance lurked in wait. As she neared the door of her cubicle, Andrew Westerfield emerged from the recessed landing.

A cold shudder crawled along her spine as she pulled up short before him. He was half blocking the door, and he had one hand behind his back as he approached.

"Please, sir, let me pass," she said around a tremor. He seemed disinclined to oblige, prowling closer still. "You are blocking my doorway," she added, realizing the stupidity of the statement the minute the words were out. Of course he knew he was blocking the doorway; he was doing it deliberately. She backed away, precariously close to the landing.

"I have something for you," he said silkily, advancing on her retreat.

"You have nothing I want or need, sir," she snapped, backing still farther away.

"I wouldn't be too sure about that," he said. But as he whipped what appeared to be a wrinkled neckcloth bulging with coal from behind his back, she reacted to the sudden motion with yet another quick step backward that left her teetering on the landing. He dropped his offering, seizing her in strong, familiar arms that quickly took advantage of her vulnerability in that moment and crushed her against the taut, lean length of him.

"Let go of me, sir!" she demanded, straining against his grip to no avail.

"And let you tumble down those rickety stairs? I think not, my lady. Is this any way to treat someone who has twice come to your rescue?"

"I have not solicited your aid on either occasion, sir," she gritted out, pounding his chest and head with her fist and the empty drawer she still clutched. "Let go of me, or I'll scream!"

"And who will come to your rescue?" he chided. He snatched the drawer from her and tossed it down. "A kiss will do for recompense . . . for now. Surely you can spare just one? You'll get no better offers in the Marshalsea, my lady. I'm the closest thing to your equal in here."

Equal, indeed! Lark drew back her foot and gave his shinbone a well-executed drubbing with the toe of her Morocco leather slipper. But that only seemed to stimulate him, and he wrenched her closer and covered her lips with a cruel bruising mouth that cut off her air supply. He tasted foul, of something fermented and strong onions, and his clothes reeked of sweat and body odor. He'd obviously been drinking, and he'd gone beyond the beyond with her. There was only one thing for it, and she bit down hard on the assaulting lips—or was it his tongue? She couldn't be sure, but she drew blood. She could taste it, a strong metallic taste, and when he let her go, she grabbed fast to the banister with one hand, and with the back of the other wiped the spittle from her lips in disgust.

"Here now!" barked Tobias from below as he scrambled up the narrow stairs. "What's goin' on? His lordship ain't goin' ta pay for damaged goods. I seen ya! Get down outta there, Westie. I know what you're after."

"Our paths will cross again, my lady," Westerfield spat through clenched teeth, jerking her close as he passed. "One day you will wish you'd treated me with more respect. I know your sort. You want it right enough, and you owe me—you said so yourself. I always collect."

He bounded down the stairs then, nearly upsetting Tobias as he lumbered past, impervious to the turnkey's scathing reprimands as he stalked out into the courtyard.

"Nothin' but trouble," Tobias grumbled, reaching the landing winded. "Get yer things, yer goin'," he charged.

"Going? Going where?" she breathed, imagining all sorts of horrors—none of them rational. But then, what had been rational since her father's death? And what did it matter? Nothing could possibly be as bad as *this*. Could it?

"You've been sprung," said the jailor flatly. "Like I told him, you can't do nothin', but judgin' from what I just seen here, maybe yer just the sort o' ladybird he's after at that. I hope so, for my sake, or by the look o' ya I just lost meself a good chunk o' blunt. He wanted ya all of a piece."

"*Ladybird?*" she shrilled, incredulous.

"You heard me. Well? What are ya standin' there for? Are ya deaf? Wipe that blood off, and step lively. The Earl of Grayshire ain't goin' ta wait out there all day."

King paced just inside the gated doors in the courtyard. What was taking so long? He consulted his pocket watch. Half past twelve. What was keeping the deuced jailor? He had nearly worn a trench beside the gate when he saw Tobias leaving number six with Lark in tow, and his heart turned over in his breast. She had looked bedraggled at their first meeting, but now the tear on her dirty frock seemed wider. Her skirt was dragging through the dust on the ground. Had it been that shabby before? It certainly hadn't seemed so. Her face and hair were streaked with coal dust, and her lips were swollen and bruised. Was that blood on them—on her bodice? So this was the turnkey's idea of "all of a piece," was it? He could whistle for his bloody garnish. How was he going to present her at Kingston Townhouse looking like this? He let loose a heaving sigh. What was done was done; there was nothing for it now but to see it through to the bitter end.

"My lady," King said, bowing over her hand, "if you will follow me?"

As he took her arm and handed her through the gates to freedom, Tobias cleared his throat, attracting his attention.

"Yes?" he asked stonily, turning to face the turnkey.

"We had an agreement, if ya remember, me lord?" Tobias said, stepping in front of him.

"Indeed we did, sir," he replied. "You should have paid it stricter attention. You can count yourself fortunate that I don't charge *you*, considering the look of her. Kindly stand aside; our business is concluded."

Lark dug in her heels as he started to lead her, breaking his stride. "Wait just one moment, your lordship!" she cried. "Have I no say in this?"

"No, none," King said succinctly. Now was not the time to make his intentions plain.

"I demand to know where you're taking me," she insisted.

"Somewhere infinitely more agreeable than this," King returned.

"Lark!" cried a tear-filled voice from inside, and Lark broke away from him, ran back through the gated doors, and threw her arms around a woman, while King looked on.

"I shall miss you, my dear friend," Lark murmured. "I'd have gone mad in here but for you."

"Don't forget me," the woman begged.

"I shan't, I promise," Lark murmured, "and if there's ever any way—"

"All right—*out*," Tobias barked, interrupting. Tearing Lark away, he propelled her back through the Marshalsea gates. "Ye've been nothin' but trouble since ya come in here." He spat on the ground. "Ya better mind 'im, 'cause you'll rue the hour the sun comes up on the day ya ever get yerself chucked back inta the Marshalsea. Here—have the tart, then," he concluded to King, handing her over. "And good riddance!"

Grayshire's tiger had set the steps on the waiting coupe, and the earl helped Lark inside and followed after. Despite her anger, that strange lightning struck again when he touched her, and she nearly lost her footing. Once inside, she leaned back against the plush velvet squabs, more to distance herself from him across the way than to take advantage of the feel of the soft padding against her back. She was sore from sleeping on the unyielding bedframe and coarse, straw-filled mattress, and the cruel handling she'd suffered at the hands of Andrew Westerfield; thus a low moan escaped her at the touch of those wonderful tufted squabs.

Why was the earl staring at her like that? Had she grown two heads? Why had he paid her debt? What did he want from her—expect of her? She was almost afraid to ask. But she needed to know.

"Am I indentured, then?" she queried.

"I prefer 'redeemed,'" he replied.

"Where are you taking me?" Lark demanded. This man certainly wasn't easy to talk to, and she wanted answers. Why had he paid her bond when all England had turned a blind eye to her plight? And so much money! She shuddered to wonder what he wanted in return, this mysterious, stone-faced earl with one eye covered in black. What was that patch made of? Silk, to be sure, on a cord tied behind his head and over his queue. She had thought of him so often, reliving the fires his touch ignited, recalling the strength of his outstretched hand raising her so easily—so gallantly—to her feet in front of all. How was it that she hadn't noticed his handsome, albeit outdated, queue before?

"To my townhouse in Hanover Square," he replied, jolting her out of her reverie.

"To what purpose?" she persisted.

"That remains to be seen," he said, rapping on the coach roof with his walking stick.

Three

H anover *Square was more splendid than Lark* remembered. But then, she'd only seen it once as a child, when her father had taken her along while visiting a peer who lived in one of the rich, German-style houses built during the first George's reign. She vaguely remembered how George Street broadened as it reached High Street, giving a panoramic view of the architectural masterpieces surrounding the small, gated park in the center. She remembered it as being larger than it seemed now, but then, she had been only six at the time, after all, and it would have looked larger to her child's eye.

Her breath caught at the sight of the earl's residence, embellished with an apron of rusticated stone, rising three stories tall, the top floor all but obliterated by a cottony fog that had begun drifting inland from the river. Mullioned panes blinked in the half-light, and a courtyard to the side offered a glimpse of gardens burgeoning with late-blooming botanicals. It could well have been the very residence she and her father had visited for its likeness to the rest of the houses in the Square.

The earl whisked her quickly inside, she could only surmise for fear the neighbors would see the draggle-tailed creature he had brought home. They were met at the door by Mrs. Archway, the housekeeper, whose brow inched up a notch at the sight of her.

"Have Biddie attend her," the earl commanded, streaking past to the staircase. "Put her in the greengage suite, and see what you can do to make her presentable in time for dinner. Draw her a bath, and dress her in one of the new gowns. I shall want to interview her downstairs in the study before Lady Ann Cuthbertson and her aunt arrive. And locate Frith. I gave him time off, but I'll want a bath and putting right before dinner myself. I stink of the Marshalsea."

"Yes, my lord," the woman replied, turning to Lark. "Follow me," she directed, leading her up the stairs the earl had scaled. She turned right at the second-floor landing, however, where he had turned left, and led the way along a narrow corridor to a suite of rooms on the left side of the hall. So this was "the greengage suite." It was easy to see why. The walls were covered in a deep, rich, woodsy shade of green silk with satiny stripes. Dozens of complementary shades of the cool, soothing color abounded throughout in the décor, broken only by touches of ecru, plum, and buttercup yellow. But Lark wasn't given time to take in her surroundings; she was led to an adjoining dressing room, where a French enameled hip bath had been set before the fire that had been lit to chase the dampness.

Mrs. Archway didn't seem to approve of her. Neither did Biddie, the fair-haired, comely lass pressed into service as her abigail. That the maid was less than happy with the arrangement was obvious in her curt replies, decidedly hostile body language, and scathing use of a stiff-bristle brush that earned her more than one silent rebuke from Mrs. Archway, who supervised. The girl scrubbed Lark clean, despite the housekeeper's protests, and washed the coal dust from her hair with coconut-scented soap in water silkened with attar of roses.

Lark bit back the questions begging to be voiced. This pair seemed not to be the ones to approach, though she was anxious over her new situation, not the least of her concerns being what the earl meant to do with her. But though curiosity had her on tenterhooks, she decided to wait for the looming interview with the earl before Lady Ann Cuthbertson and her aunt arrived, whoever they were.

It took most of the afternoon, but they set her to rights—all but her bruised lips, which gave her a decidedly pouty look. But there was nothing to be done about that. They were still swollen, and the wound where Westerfield's teeth had pierced the lower lip, though no longer bleeding, was far from healed. Not even the lovely, high-waisted blue silk twill gown could divert from the otherwise acceptable image in the cheval glass. Lark couldn't help but wonder to whom the gown had belonged. The earl's sister, perhaps, or his wife, more than likely, though she'd seen no evidence of either about . . . or could it have belonged to a mistress, perhaps? Why did that thought not sit well? Mistresses amongst the *ton* were commonplace enough—almost a foregone conclusion, certainly nothing shocking as long as they were discreetly kept. Of course, that had to be it, and Lark couldn't help but wonder how the exquisite puff-sleeved, low-cut garment fit her by comparison.

Thinking those thoughts, she turned away from the glass at the first sign of a blush creeping up her cheeks from her décolleté, only to be whirled back toward it again by Biddie, who none too gently poked silk ribbon roses into Lark's short cap of satiny blond curls.

"I can't do nothing more with her," the girl said as if Lark weren't there. She stood back, arms akimbo, taking Lark's measure with cold eyes. "She'll have to do. I wash my hands of it."

"Shhh," Mrs. Archway warned, low-voiced. "You didn't think you'd be the one all got up in silks, did you?"

"I'm more qualified than *she* is," the girl snapped.

Though they were whispering off a few paces, they were hardly out of Lark's range of hearing, and she resisted the urge to blurt, *Qualified for what?* But she didn't. Though she might have if a knock at the door and a footman decked out in burgundy and gold livery on the doorstep hadn't interrupted with a summons that she descend to the study forthwith.

After a final appraisal of Lark by both servants, Biddie disappeared down the back stairs toward the servants' wing, still grousing in a low mutter. Then, since Lark had no idea where the study was and the footman had disappeared, Mrs. Archway showed her down, and left her without a backward glance in front of the tall closed door on the threshold of her long-awaited interview with the Earl of Grayshire. Now, by heaven, she'd have some answers. Lark raised her clenched fist, hesitated a moment with it suspended before the well-oiled wood panels, and then rapped forcefully. She hoped. She was too nervous to be certain, but forcefulness was her intent at any rate.

"Come!" said the earl's deep, sensuous voice from the other side. Why did the sound of it send such a nerve-wracking shudder down her spine and inflict such a rash of gooseflesh over the most private recesses of her body, hardening her nipples against her thin blue silk bodice? *Please, God, don't let them show through.* A furtive glance toward her décolleté showed the folly of that prayer. There was nothing to be done. They were too pronounced, and the fabric was far too thin. Hoping that he wouldn't notice, she squared her posture, gripped the door handle, and crossed the threshold of a vast book-lined room. It was steeped in soft auburn shadow around the periphery and smelled of expensive leather, lemon polish, and the wonderful must of old bookbindings. The earl seemed utterly at home here.

He surged to his feet as she entered, and invited her to sit, gesturing toward a Sheraton chair at the edge of the carpet. Once she'd settled herself in it—the worst spot imaginable to conceal her dilemma, since a shaft of latent sunlight breaking through the fog had thrown a stream of shimmer over that deuced chair—he resumed his place behind his ledger-laden desk. Maybe he wouldn't notice. He had only one eye, after all.

Dashing her hopes, he scrutinized her thoroughly, taking his time, meanwhile tapping his lips with his forefinger, his head cocked, and his expression maddeningly unreadable.

"Please stand and turn 'round," he charged. "*Slowly*," he amended, as she vaulted to her feet and whirled around angrily. What? Did he think he was at Tattersall's, appraising horseflesh on the auction block? Making a good impression fell by the wayside. Anger seethed under the surface—just barely: her pouty lips pursed with it.

"That will suffice. You may resume your seat," he said, nodding toward the chair.

"My lord, I think, considering the rude and rough handling I've received since I entered this house, that it is time you explain why you paid my fee and exactly what you expect of me."

There came a hitch in his gaze, and his head lifted a notch. It was only a slight reaction, but a reaction nonetheless, and Lark was exceedingly glad that she'd finally managed to focus his attention upon *her* agenda, albeit accomplished with not a little drama.

"Who has mishandled you here, my lady?" he demanded.

"The person you assigned as my abigail has practically scrubbed the skin off my body with a brush that belongs on the cobblestone sidewalks, hardly in the bath. Though slight in stature, she is possessed of impressive strength, and she spared none of it. I am aware that my . . . condition wanted repair, but scouring my body raw was excessive, and hardly necessary. I am not in the habit of carrying tales. I do so here only to inform you that I shall in future bathe myself, my lord. Just so we understand one another."

"Biddie?" he queried.

"She seemed to think she should be wearing . . . whoever's gown this is."

"It is yours, my lady."

"*Mine*? I don't follow."

"Purchased from the shops on Bond Street for you, along with the others that are being delivered to the greengage suite as we speak. Any that do not meet with your approval will be returned forthwith. Time necessitated my choosing your initial wardrobe. You could hardly go about as you were." He cleared his voice. "Now then, getting back to Biddie, where was Mrs. Archway while this scourging was taking place? Do you mean to say she did nothing to prevent it?"

"She supervised, and added water to the tub, but she made no move to interfere. She did, however, warn the gel to hold her tongue from complaining."

"I see."

"Well, I *don't*, my lord. Am I expected to be your servant . . . your slave . . . your, your . . ." She sputtered, unwilling to put the only other alternative she could think of into words.

"Calm yourself, my lady," he said, suppressing a smile. "You are not expected to be my . . . anything, actually. Forgive me. I do owe you an explanation. It is just that I had to be sure you would suit before I put my proposal before you."

"Suit *what?*" she demanded, out of patience.

"My purpose. Please, my lady, bear with me just a little longer. There are a few things I need to know about you first."

Lark made a strangled sound. Shouldn't he have asked his questions *before* paying her debt?

"That bruise on your lip . . . I do not recall it being there on the occasion of our first meeting. How did you come by it?"

"A rake in that place tried to take advantage of me, if you must know," she snapped. "He is quite similarly decorated, my lord, I promise you."

"His name?"

"It isn't important."

"I shall ask you again—his name, my lady? Come, come, I haven't time for this, and we will remain here until you answer my questions."

"Andrew Westerfield, since you insist," she said grudgingly, bristling. "A most ungallant individual."

"Stepton's second son. Ah, yes. I thought I saw him there. What made him think he had a right to your favors?"

Lark told her tale. She was unable to do so without anger bleeding into her voice, however—at Westerfield for his assault upon her, and at the earl, for forcing her to relive the unpleasantness.

"I see," he said once she'd concluded. "He made you indebted to him to serve his own lecherous ends. Ungallant, indeed."

"He thought he did. He soon learned otherwise."

"The young woman at the Marshalsea gates . . . a friend of yours?"

"Yes," Lark said, her eyes clouding. She missed Agnes already. "Her name is Agnes Garwood. She was a milliner in Shropshire until her husband died and their debts put her in that place. She's been there three years. I can't imagine anyone being in the Marshalsea three weeks, let alone three years."

"A milliner, you say?" the earl mused.

"Yes. She is trying to work off her debt making bonnets for ladies amongst the *ton* who would rather die than admit their fine chapeaux come straight out of the Marshalsea. How fickle, the aristocracy."

Her savior did laugh then. It was a deep, sensuous rumble of baritone resonance that shot Lark through with icy fire in a manner she didn't expect. If she hadn't been seated, she would have stumbled, just as her heart did, to a halt.

"I quite agree," he said. "Did you know Mrs. Garwood before your incarceration?"

"No. We met the morning after you helped me up in the courtyard. She was kind to me, my lord. After all I've been through since Father . . . died, I treasure kindnesses; they are so few now. I don't know if I could have stood it in that place without her friendship."

King heaved a sigh. "I'm sorry for your loss. It must have been dreadful for you."

"I loved my father very much, my lord," she said. "Yes, he was an inveterate gambler and a fool, but he was my father, and I loved him. His suicide was beyond bearing. They buried him in unconsecrated ground. That was the worst of it for me. I still have nightmares about it. I was so distraught I made bad judgments. That's why I was put in that dreadful place."

"Well, you're out of it now," King said, "and I should like to hear more about it if it wouldn't be too painful, but I'm afraid it must wait for another time. We are expecting dinner guests within the hour—Lady Ann Cuthbertson, of London, and her aunt, Countess Vera Arbonville Cuthbertson, or, as she prefers to be called, owing to her French lineage, 'Comtesse' Cuthbertson. We will indulge her."

"*We?*"

"Yes. I should like you to join us."

"Why?" Lark blurted, her thoughts become words. What on earth was he up to? Couldn't he see she was exhausted? After all she'd been through that day, how could he expect her to attend a formal dinner?

"Because I wish it."

"Forgive me, but I do not understand any of this," she said with restraint. "I've answered your questions, my lord; don't you think it's time you answered mine?"

"Of course. I do humbly beg your forgiveness, but as I said, I had to be sure. This concerns my mother. She resides at our country estate in Cornwall. Have you ever been out to the coast, my lady?"

"No, I'm afraid I have not."

"Ah," he breathed, seeming to want to address that, but then thinking better of it. "Mother despises Town life," he continued. "She comes here only for the regular Season. She much prefers Grayshire Manor, on the south coast of Cornwall at Downend Point. The family owns a rather sizable fishing fleet. My steward, Leander Markham, and I oversee that enterprise and for the most part I reside there—or at least I did. I'm not doing this well, am I?"

"I must admit, it is a bit confusing," Lark agreed. "I don't see how any of what you're saying concerns me."

"I must soon marry if I am to get an heir in a timely fashion," he went on, "and I haven't been able to concentrate upon that with my life in sixes and sevens. Though I haven't yet offered for her, I have been seeing Lady Ann socially on a regular basis, and I expect that I shall propose marriage to her once Mother's situation is settled."

"I still don't see—"

"Bear with me, my lady, and all will soon be made clear. Mother is a bit of a philanthropist," he continued. "When I came to Town for the Season in pursuit of a seemly bride, she asked that I visit the debtors' prisons and select a suitable companion for her at Grayshire Manor while I am honeymooning with my bride."

"But . . . from the *prison?*"

"I could have sought a companion for her elsewhere— gone against her wishes, if you will—but she would know. I said she was a bit of a philanthropist, and more than a bit of an eccentric. She is also uncannily perceptive, I'm afraid, as you shall soon see . . . if you agree to accept my offer, that is. She would certainly have demanded proof, and found me out forthwith. She wanted to help some unfortunate soul without a feather to fly with, and set me to the task of liberating one—the right one, of course. That is why I must be sure you will suit before we go forward. I haven't time to do this twice. I know of your . . . trouble, at least the essence of it. I didn't know your father personally, but I've heard the on-dits; all the *ton* has. You can hardly be taken to task for his shortcomings, nor tarred by the same brush, though, as you say, the aristocracy is fickle, and I'm sure you've suffered at their hands in recent days. While I am also *ton*, I do not number myself among those who visit the sins of the fathers upon their children, as it were. I've been looking for a suitable companion for Mother since the Season began. I wouldn't go off and leave her in the hands of just anyone, my lady. I am hoping you are she."

How was it that the man could make the most illogical situation seem perfectly normal? It was too bizarre to be a lie, and too good to be true. That, however, was neither here nor there. Lark didn't have a choice in the matter. He had paid her debt to the Crown to satisfy her father's creditors, but she owed that debt still—to him, this enigmatic earl with his mysteriously provocative eye patch. The vouchers had merely changed hands. What had she gained? She had merely exchanged one prison for another, one without gates and bars, but a prison nonetheless. Tears threatened, but she blinked them back. She was no watering pot.

"What say, are you agreeable to give it a go, my lady?" he prompted. "If after you've met Mother you feel that you are unable to accommodate me, I shan't force you."

"Have I a choice?" she blurted.

"Actually, you do," he said. "I could recommend you elsewhere . . . as a governess or companion. I'm sure I could find you a position that would suit—and will if needs must. I shan't leave you stranded, my lady. You cannot be pressed into service below stairs as a laundress or chambermaid. You are a gentlewoman. Your having put on tick does not change that."

"What? And work to pay off my debt to you?"

"You make me out a slaver. I'm hardly that."

"What would you call yourself, then?"

"Your benefactor. What I suggest would be mutually beneficial to both of us—no pressures, no hidden agendas, only the conditions I have laid out. If you accept my offer, you shall receive a generous allowance, a fine, luxurious home to live in, and everything you need for a comfortable life—all for the price of putting up with a rather . . . difficult woman. I shan't lie to you. My mother can drive a body quite beyond the pale at times. But you seem no shrinking violet. You appear the sort to be able to deal with difficult situations from what I've seen. What do you say, my lady?"

"Must I pass muster with your dinner guests as well?" Lark asked, more harshly than she'd intended.

"Not exactly. I simply wish you to meet them, because if my plans come to fruition you will see them often, and I want you to become acquainted with them, and they with you, right at the outset. It is important that you get on well with them."

"I *am* required to pass muster, then. This is some sort of entrance examination?"

"As a gentlewoman and my mother's companion, you will be treated as one of the family. What I need is assurance that our 'family' leads a harmonious existence. I realize that all this coming on so suddenly must seem . . . rather bizarre, but unfortunately that cannot be helped. I am needed on the coast. I've stayed in Town far too long as it is."

"Very well, my lord," Lark said with caution. "I will accept your offer, and I thank you kindly for it." Decidedly, it was an odd business, but there wasn't any other real choice, and nothing could be worse than the Marshalsea. Besides, her curiosity was piqued.

"Capital!" the earl said, surging to his feet. Lark followed suit, and he skirted the ornately carved desk, took her hand, and raised it to his lips, where firm pressure lingered for a longer time than she deemed proper, though she didn't withdraw her hand. His warm breath on her skin aroused strange sensations at her very core that were frighteningly enjoyable. "There," he murmured against her fingers, as he lifted his lips at last. "We have sealed the bargain. Please join me and our guests for sherry before dinner in the drawing room in half an hour so that I may introduce you properly. Mrs. Archway will direct you. Tomorrow we begin our journey to Cornwall, you and I. I will remain on the coast until you and Mother become acquainted and I am satisfied that you two will suit, and then I shall be able to get on with my life with a clear conscience."

Lark had so many more questions, but they would have to wait. The interview was over. The earl jerked the bell rope, and went back to his desk. She had been dismissed.

King was pacing before the hearth when Osbert, the butler, poked his head in, turning him toward the study door with a jerk.

"Yes, my lord?" the butler queried.

"I wish to see Biddie and Mrs. Archway, in that order, separately," King said, "and I wish to examine the, er . . . brush that was used in Lady Lark Eddington's bath earlier."

"Very good, my lord," the stone-faced servant intoned.

"Bring me that first."

"Yes, my lord. Will that be all?"

"Yes, Osbert, thank you."

"Very good, my lord," the butler replied, disappearing.

King took some notes from a tin coffer in the valuables chest, counted them, returned some to the coffer and then tucked it away inside again. Folding a parchment envelope to hold the funds, he sealed it with wax, and continued to pace, trying to concentrate upon Lark's image instead of the unpleasant task at hand. His judgment was sound after all: She was exquisite. He was proud of his selection in the blue paneled gown she wore; the minute he clapped eyes on her that periwinkle shade had come to mind. It was almost the exact color of her eyes—when she wasn't angry, that is. On those occasions, he had noticed, they deepened to a dark, fathomless shade reminiscent of cobalt violet. Yes. The periwinkle suited her admirably whatever her mood.

He frowned. That mole on her left breast alongside the cleavage . . . was it genuine, or had she painted it there to attract his eye, as so many of the ladies and ladybirds did these days—and had done for centuries, come to that?

Real or contrived, it served its purpose well enough. He hadn't been able to tear his eyes from her décolleté. That tantalizing little brown spot was like an arrow pointing toward what hidden treasures he could only wonder. And he did wonder. Fine thoughts for a gentleman about to entertain his future bride in the dining hall! He would have to be mindful of his gaze at dinner. Admittedly, it would be a challenge.

He wasn't left to pace for long before Osbert returned with the brush and left once more to collect the others. King studied the dubious tool, still damp from its chore, running his thumb along the stiff bristles. Even wet they were unbending. He raised it to his nose and inhaled the fragrance of coconut oil soap. At least they hadn't used lye. Without ceremony, he placed it on the blotter of his desk, then continued to pace, taking long, deliberate strides over the Aubusson carpet. Presently Biddie's light rap on the door froze him in his tracks, and when he bade her enter, she flitted over the threshold, offering a smart little curtsy.

"Ya sent for me, my lord," the girl purred through a fetching smile.

"Yes," King returned, frosty-voiced, dissolving it. Striding to the desk, he took up the brush and extended it toward her. "Was this the instrument you used in making my lady presentable?" he said.

All color fled from the maid's cheeks, then returned as swiftly, painting her fair skin a brilliant crimson. Her round eyes oscillated between the scrub brush and his stern-faced scowl. But it was her stuttering that damned her.

"I have asked you a question," he reminded her.

"Y-yes, my lord."

"Yes, *what*—that you acknowledge my question or that you are guilty as charged? Speak up!"

"Y-ya said to make her presentable. How else was I to scrub the dirt o' that place off her?"

"Mind your tongue," he warned. "This brush belongs in

the scullery, not the bath. I wouldn't even think to scrub the hounds with it."

"She's clean, ain't she?"

King stiffened. His fingers curled around the brush and clenched in a white-knuckled fist, which he raised, brandishing the weapon, for that was what he considered it to be. But there was more to be addressed, and after a moment he lowered it to his side with a rigid arm.

"I'm told you felt the frocks I bought for Lady Lark should have made their way to your chamber in some way. What possessed such a thing to enter your mind? What has led you to believe yourself in line for such endowments?"

"Ya said when ya hired me that I might expect to elevate my position in future, if I looked sharp and something come up. I have done, and I've been passed over."

"Well, I can see that's put a strain upon you. Therefore you shan't have to 'look sharp' any longer, since you no longer have a position to elevate."

The girl's breath caught. "Here!" she cried. "Ya ain't going to sack me? I ain't done nothing wrong. I only done what I was told ta do."

"In an unacceptably cruel and vindictive way," he returned. "There is no place for such behavior here." He strode to the desk, lifted the envelope and presented it. "Your wages. Collect your things and be off. I shan't recommend you. I couldn't in good conscience after this."

"Fine," she snapped, snatching the envelope from him, "but you mark my words, you're goin' ta be sorry. I'm far more suited to the position ya give ta that milk-and-water miss. You'll see. I can say it now to your face, since I'm no longer in your employ and ya won't recommend me anyway: The countess is a handful, none knows that better'n me since I'm the one who attended her on all o' her visits ta Town—without so much as an extra tuppence for my pains, mind ya. I'm used ta her ways, and I know just how to keep her in line. Is *she* goin' ta do that?" She made a wild hand gesture meant to indicate Lark. "The first time that old witch goes off your Lady Lark'll head straight for the hills. Then where will ya be? I'll tell ya where—in the suds for whatever ya paid for her. You wouldn't have had to pay anywhere near the sum ya give to spring her for me. Ya told me I could better myself. That's all I wanted to do. It isn't fair. I've been here slavin' in this house two years, and ya passed me right by for a . . . a . . . filthy little *convict*."

"How dare you speak so to me? You go too far. You are dismissed. You have until dinner—roughly one half hour—to collect your belongings and leave, or I shall send for a bailiff to assist you."

For a moment they stood, eyes locked, King's lack of a pair in no way weakening the meaning expressed by the one: He knew how to use it far better than most men could manage with two. That he had to have this conversation with Biddie saddened him. He prided himself on a contented household. How had he not seen the depth of this gel's discontent? Had he been that self-absorbed? Evidently. There was nothing for it now but to follow through. He turned his back on her in a gesture of dismissal, listening to her whimpers become wails echoing along the empty corridors as she fled the study, all but knocking the housekeeper down, who approached for her interview.

"*Come!*" King thundered at the hollow sound of the woman's knock on the open door the maid had left flung wide.

"You wish to speak to me, my lord?" the housekeeper asked, putting her head in.

"I do," he responded, brandishing the brush. "What is the meaning of this outrage, Mrs. Archway?"

"Th-that, my lord?" she hedged.

"Don't fence with me. You know exactly my meaning. How could you stand by and permit a scathing with such as this?"

"She wasn't harmed, my lord. The filth of that place was caked on her. She could have soaked in the bath for a sennight and not gotten shot of it. It needed a good scrubbing."

"But not with such as this," he insisted, brandishing the brush again, "and at the mercy of one whom you knew to be in a state of acute dissatisfaction."

"I took no part in it, my lord."

"No, but you allowed it. Have you issues as well? Why has my acquisition of Lady Lark Eddington as companion for my mother put you in a taking, pray?"

"Am I sacked, too, after nigh on twenty years o' service to this house?" she queried boldly.

That she had avoided his question troubled him; he'd expected more of her after "nigh on twenty years." What's more, Osbert was facing an imminent lecture on instructing the servants in regard to proper discourse with the master of the house. King was appalled. Nevertheless, he considered the housekeeper's question. If he wasn't able to trust his staff to conduct themselves with responsibility and decorum, he should let them go, regardless of who they were or their length of service. And he would have done—on the spot, just as he had Biddie—if it weren't for the fact that Mrs. Archway was an excellent housekeeper, and considering his mother's preference for the Cornish coast, they would seldom see her. Someone would have to keep the townhouse in order while the family was scattered to the four winds, as it were, and there wasn't time to seek a new housekeeper, much less break one in. No. Biddie's example should be sufficient to serve as a warning to Mrs. Archway or any of the others in future. But that was not to say he would let her off easily. Therefore, he paced, and paced before the dead hearth quite dramatically for some time before he stopped and turned to face her.

"No," he said, gravel-voiced. "But make no mistake, I shall dismiss you without hesitation if anything similar is to occur in future. I am grossly disappointed, Mrs. Archway. You are to apologize to Lady Lark for any discomfort your in-action may have caused her, and serve her personally in Biddie's place. Furthermore, you are to have no communication with Biddie whatsoever before she leaves. She is to be gone by the dinner hour. If that does not occur, you are to come and tell me directly, am I plain?"

"Y-yes, my lord," the housekeeper said, the breath leaking out of her as though he had opened a petcock.

"Very well, then. You may go," he charged. "Tell Osbert I wish to see him here directly."

The woman disappeared, and King crossed to the hearth and tossed the scrub brush in amongst the logs. He would have one of the footmen light the fire once he'd dealt with Osbert. There was a chill on the place all of a sudden. A lit fire would soon put paid to that—and to the entire episode of Lady Lark Eddington's bath. He hoped.

He'd barely taken his seat behind the desk again when Osbert knocked. *Probably eavesdropping in the hall. Cheeky lot, bigod!* He shook his head in disgust. He really had to take a firmer hand with the staff. That would begin now, even if he weren't planning to stay long in Town.

"Come," he barked.

"You sent for me, my lord?" Osbert said loftily.

"What the deuce is going on here, Osbert?" King demanded. "As butler in this house, you are in charge of the staff—particularly the male members of the staff, but since Mrs. Archway takes her orders directly from you, and obviously needs taking in hand, you are to get the brunt of this lecture."

"Y-yes, my lord."

"Hmmm," King hummed. His eyebrow peaked, causing the cord that held his eye patch to bite into his pleated frown. "The master of the house should *never* have to have discourse with the servants as I have just had to do. It was most unpleasant, and unnecessary. I needn't tell you this, Osbert; you've been butler in this house since time out of mind. You *know* communications are passed from master to staff, and vice versa, through you—the butler—and by no other means. Unfortunately, things have gotten so out of hand here that I had no choice. It will not happen again, or I'll sack you all. God knows you have little enough to do since I'm so rarely in residence. You ought to be able to get it right while I am. Do you value your position here?"

"Y-yes, my lord," the butler said.

"Then I strongly suggest that you act like it, and take matters in hand, beginning with Mrs. Archway. I've already begun that chore for you. See that she understands what is expected of her as housekeeper in this house. You needn't concern yourself with Biddie; she is leaving at once. Keep her below until she does. See that she exits by way of the servants' entrance. I won't have her upstairs again. Ever. And once she leaves, she is not to be admitted here again. Now then, take yourself off and convey my instructions to the others. I shall be leaving shortly for the coast, but I will soon return to make my marriage arrangements. When I do, if things have not improved here, you will all be seeking new situations. Is that clear?"

"Yes, my lord," the butler murmured.

"Good. Because I wouldn't think to bring a bride into this house as things are. Now then, you are dismissed. Send one of the footmen in to light the fire here. There's a draft in the place."

"Very good, my lord," Osbert replied. Sketching a bow, he fled, coattails flying.

Once the butler had vanished, King squared his posture, stalked from the study, and went in search of his guests.

Four

Lark was on her way down to the drawing room to meet the earl's company when she came upon Biddie in the hallway dressed for an outing, and what looked like a bundle of laundry tied in a knot clutched to her bosom. Lark didn't mean to stare, but curiosity being her personal demon, she couldn't help herself, and as Biddie approached, she stopped in her tracks, taken aback by the venom in the maid's flashing brown eyes.

"I hope you're happy, my lady," the servant snapped, "losing me my situation. Ya just had ta make a brouhaha outta nothin' at all and get me sacked, didn't ya?"

"I have no idea what you're talking about," Lark returned.

"You're goin' ta rue the day, I can promise ya that. Wait till ya meet her, the high and mighty countess—just wait!"

"You have no right to address me in this manner," Lark reminded her.

"Hah! The fine lady, eh—queen o' the Marshalsea. I can address ya any way I like. You're no better'n me. You're goin' ta see it, too, and he won't have none o' ya. He'll do to ya just like he done ta me. Two years, I give him. *Two years!* I won't wish ya luck. You'll have none after what ya done ta me. Ya wasn't harmed. Ya should o' kept your tongue between your teeth."

Just then Osbert trotted stiff-legged along the corridor, and took the maid's arm.

"Here!" she shrilled. "Get your hands offa me. I'm goin'. Are ya blind?"

"Not out the front," he intoned, turning her. "You know better. You're to go off by the servants' entrance. His lordship's orders."

Biddie wrenched free and pushed past, leaving Lark standing mouth agape, and disappeared into the shadows of the forked corridor that led to the servants' wing with the butler on her heels. Had Grayshire actually *dismissed* the gel? Evidently. A twinge of guilt washed over Lark, but it was brief. If he hadn't sacked her, she would have become her permanent abigail, sure as check. Heaven forefend. Biddie had forgotten her place, and she was hostile, spouting threats. Even now, she boldly thought to quit the house by the main doors in defiance of a protocol centuries old that strictly prohibited the servants' use of the house proper for their comings and goings. No, it was for the best. Without a second thought, Lark meandered along the corridor and made her way according to the housekeeper's directions to the drawing room, where the others had already gathered.

Lark faced the earl's guests with grace and ease. She was an aristocrat after all, and since she was raised without a mother—or any other female guidance, come to that—she had to subscribe to the notion that aristocratic bearing was a thing inbred. How else would she know such points of a gentle lady's behavior necessary to exist amongst the *ton*? She certainly hadn't learned it from the servants who raised her; only the bare essentials. Truth be told, this was one of the reasons she had agreed to the earl's proposal so readily. The prospect of a mother figure in her life was most appealing—even if that figure was a bit daunting. That such a risk was worth taking, considering the veiled references to the woman as being difficult, told her much about herself. She was lonely, with no love in her life, and she desperately wanted the comfort and security of a family—the family the earl had painted for her. It was a hope to cling to, because though she had left the Marshalsea, she knew she was still incarcerated. She now carried her prison with her.

While they sipped sherry in the handsomely appointed drawing room boasting fine Duncan Phyfe furniture, marble statuary supporting the mantel over the hearth, and fabrics in a wide range of soothing blues, Lark studied the earl's prospective bride. Lady Ann Cuthbertson, while not to be classed a diamond of the first water, was certainly well to pass when it came to deportment, her only shortcoming being a decidedly irritating voice, high-pitched and whiney, with a distinct lisp. Possessed of a shy and retiring nature, however, she seldom used it. This wasn't a criticism on Lark's part, merely an evaluation, and only fair, since Grayshire was evaluating her in return. All things considered, the raspy voice and insipid demeanor notwithstanding, she had to admit that Lady Ann Cuthbertson would still be an asset to any aristocratic suitor. Why did that trigger a twinge of something decidedly uncomfortable? She shrugged the feeling off, excusing it as leftover unease from her confrontation with Biddie, but found herself hoping that Lady Ann and her aunt wouldn't be accompanying Grayshire and herself on their journey to Cornwall.

She took the woman's measure in furtive glances, noting Lady Ann's smoky brown hair, very shiny, and rather long, judging from the high chignon it had been coiled into. A short fringe of bangs rested on her forehead above eyes of a very deep brown that were expressive and clear. She wore a high-waisted dinner gown of dove gray muslin. Her aunt, Lady Vera Arbonville Cuthbertson, was short and rotund, though regal in lavender voile that offset her short-cropped silvery hair. Both women wore jewels, though the comtesse was more heavily decorated, from a diamond tiara to multiple rings perched on bulbous fingers. The earl escorted her in to dinner, while Lark and Lady Ann followed.

Lark was beginning to wonder at the wisdom of accepting the earl's dinner invitation. Considering everything that had befallen her since the day began, she was far more exhausted than hungry. Her body still ached from her hard bed at the Marshalsea, her confrontation with Andrew Westerfield, and now the scathing bath, while her heart ached from losing the only friend she'd had in a very long time. She would never forget the look in Agnes's eyes as the gated doors of the Marshalsea slammed shut. Would she ever see Agnes again? It wasn't likely. Soon she would be on her way to Cornwall—the hindside of nowhere, considering its distance from Town. Having never been there, Lark couldn't even imagine it.

But she had consented to dine, and liveried footmen were already serving the soup à la Reine, which would be closely followed by stewed trout, for the first course. Next, there would be mutton cutlets, braised ham and peas, cold pheasant pie, and capon with mushroom stuffing. Then for desert, rum and apple pudding, pear compote, and Neopolitans— so said the little porcelain menu cards—and, of course, the usual assortment of sweet dessert wines. How would she ever do it all justice?

The delicious smells wafting toward her from the sideboard, however, were tantalizing. Except for a piece of stale bread that morning before her odyssey began, she hadn't eaten all day. It was not that food wasn't offered; she had just declined. She hadn't seen fare such as this since she had left Eddington Hall, and she almost moaned aloud tasting the mutton cutlet, richly sauced and delicately spiced. She savored every slow bite.

"King tells me that you hail from Yorkshire," Lady Ann said during the pause, while the earl approved the braised ham and peas one of the liveried footmen had presented to him. "I've never been."

"'King?'" Lark queried. The minute she asked, she realized, of course, wishing she hadn't shown her ignorance. They would surely think her a jinglebrain.

"'King,' the short of Kingston," Lady Ann squealed. "He so despises 'Basil,' you see—I can't think why, and he won't say." She returned to her previous point: "Since

Yorkshire is quite a distance, I should like a firsthand recommendation. Is it lovely there, my lady?"

"Quite lovely," Lark recalled with a wistful smile. Remembering was a bittersweet experience, conjuring the images of rolling moorland splotched with heather beneath the fleecy, ground-skimming clouds she so loved as a child. Of the lonely gated graveyard that had always terrified her, and of a certain soul denied its sanctity. All at once she realized she could never go home. For better or worse, her life was begun anew. So be it.

"The heather is spectacular in warm summer months," she said, as though she hadn't just plumbed the depths of her soul and reached a painful understanding. "The climate can be quite cruel with heavy snows in winter, however, and the spring storms are often wild and unpredictable. All in all, late summer is by far the best time to visit, if you are ever so inclined. It shan't disappoint." She was amazed at her composure. Maybe now the nightmares would stop.

"Better to wait until this ridiculous war is ended, and come to France," the dowager said in her delightful accent, which was almost pretty enough to soften her derision. "It is just as provincial, and far less wild."

"Aunt!" Lady Ann reproved.

"No, no," Lark interrupted. She wasn't offended by the dowager's remark, and she had no intention of being drawn into a scene over it. There had been entirely enough of that sort of thing since dawn broke. Instead, she smiled her most winsome smile, bruised lips notwithstanding. "Comtesse Cuthbertson is quite right," she said, addressing both ladies. "But do go if you get the opportunity. The heather alone is worth the trip, and Yorkshire is a good deal closer than France, after all. Besides, who knows when travel abroad will be possible again as things are."

Somewhat strained though pleasant banter followed, and a sidelong glance in Grayshire's direction proved that her strategy was sound. Approval shone in his gaze, if not as a smile on his lips. And so it went until the dishes and tablecloth were removed, and the footmen set out the sweet wines and desserts.

"Must we lose you tomorrow?" the comtesse pouted, addressing the earl.

"For a time," he replied, taking a sip from his wine glass.

"Can we not persuade you to remain in Town just a little while longer?" she coaxed.

"Once things are settled on the coast, I shall return forthwith," he said.

Relief relaxed Lark's posture. At least this pair wasn't coming with them. She hadn't missed the coquettish glances Lady Ann cast at Grayshire, or the warm smiles the invitation in them prompted from him. Now and then Lark caught him glancing in her direction as well, but not in that way. Except for that little burst of approval she had detected earlier, his gazes were decidedly prosaic.

"We shall hold you to that," the comtesse said, "and if you take too long, you just might find us on your doorstep to collect you."

"The pleasure would be mine," the earl responded, bowing toward her over his plate.

"What time will we be leaving tomorrow, your lordship?" Lark inquired. It was the only direct question she'd posed to him all evening.

"I am not yet certain," he replied. "I have several matters I must attend to first thing in the morning. If all goes well, we should be off right after nuncheon."

"*Mon Dieu!* Surely not without a chaperone—an abigail at the very least?" the dowager put in, clearly scandalized. "Did you not say you dismissed Lady Eddington's maid earlier?"

Lark froze, her fork suspended halfway to her mouth, her eyes glancing between them. *Please don't volunteer.* She almost said it aloud. Her heart was hammering in her breast. She was certain Grayshire could see it moving the low-cut bodice; that's where his gaze was focused.

"That is one of the things I must see to," he replied.

"Take ease, dear lady. I assure you all proprieties will be strictly observed."

Lark folded her serviette, and set it aside. "Well, then," she said, as steadily as she could manage with the man's gaze still focused on her décolleté. "If we are to be off early, I hope you will forgive me if I retire. It has been quite an . . . exhausting day and I must rest before the journey." She rose to her feet, and the earl rose with her. "Comtesse Cuthbertson, Lady Ann," she continued, "I am very pleased to have made your acquaintance, and hope we shall soon meet again. With your kind permission, I wish you a pleasant good night." A chorus of approving salutations followed from the women, and Lark turned to the earl and said, "My lord," awaiting his nod of approval as well.

"Can you find your way?" he asked.

"Quite so," she assured him.

"Then good night, my lady," he murmured, bowing dutifully over her hand.

He signaled one of the footmen as she moved past, and whispered something to him in an undervoice, but all that came clear as she quit the room was Mrs. Archway's name spoken in that deep, sensuous voice—so much more riveting as a whisper.

She had scarcely shut herself inside the greengage suite when a rap on the bedchamber door sent her to answer, and she opened to the housekeeper on the threshold.

"Yes?" Lark queried, observing the woman, dressed in black twill and white linen, standing ramrod rigid on her doorstep. Her gray hair, drawn back from a painfully straight center part, was all but hidden beneath a starched white cap. "Is there something you wanted, Mrs. Archway?"

"His lordship has asked that I attend you, my lady," the woman said, avoiding eye contact.

Lark stood aside and let her enter. The woman seemed amiable enough, but who could blame her for being wary?

"Begging your pardon, my lady," the housekeeper said,

low-voiced, "but I owe you an apology. Biddie was wrong to handle you so rough. I should o' stopped her."

"There is no need to reproach yourself," Lark assured her. "I'm just as guilty. I should have put up more of a protest. If I had, the girl would still have her situation."

"Why didn't ya?"

"Mrs. Archway, have you ever been inside the Marshalsea?"

"I have not," the woman said, bristling.

"Count yourself fortunate," said Lark. "I was mistreated there, then brought here with no explanation of what was to become of me. I wouldn't have let the situation go beyond the beyond, I assure you, but I thought it more prudent to hold my peace until the reason for my being brought here was made clear."

"Don't worry none about Biddie, my lady," Mrs. Archway said. "She'll manage. She's got pluck, that one. Still, the master was right to give her the sack, and you'll have nothing but a gentle hand from me in future. You can depend upon it."

"Thank you," Lark said. It was plain that the woman had been forced to apologize, threatened with heaven only knew what—dismissal, most likely. But her words were genuine, and she was laudably contrite. "I don't know how you can serve me, though. I expect I'm quite clean enough," she said, aiming for levity, "and I haven't a nightgown to change into."

The housekeeper produced one from a drawer in the dresser and held it up. Lark's breath caught. It was obviously new, and beautiful.

"Your frocks are in the armoire," said the housekeeper. "I hung them away so you can check them over . . . in case any aren't to your taste. Whatever you want to keep, I'll pack for you myself in the morning." She gestured toward the chiffonier behind. "Your unmentionables are in these drawers here."

"His lordship chose my unmentionables?" She was incredulous.

"Oh, no, my lady," the housekeeper hastened to say. "He sent a note 'round to the proprietress at one of the Bond Street establishments giving a size description, and telling her to pick out what was needed and have it sent. He never saw any o' it."

Hot blood rushed to Lark's cheeks at the thought, but she smiled, and let the woman help her undress and slip into the gown of buttery soft ecru batiste, trimmed in the palest of pale pink silk ribbon roses. They said little more. The air was cleared between them, and once the housekeeper left her, Lark climbed into bed and soon drifted off, carried by total exhaustion into a deep and dreamless sleep.

King stepped out onto his bedchamber balcony that overlooked the well-manicured lawn and sculptured gardens at the back of the townhouse. His guests had finally departed, and all was still as he stood breathing in the subtle perfumes stirred by the night breeze. The house was quiet around him; the thoughts banging around in his brain, however, were anything but. What could he be thinking? What had made him imagine he might possibly hope for some semblance of a normal life? He couldn't even manage his own house.

Much was at stake—his future for one thing, not to mention the future of his line . . . of the earldom! He was the only one to perpetuate it, after all. Damn the luck. It was a staggering responsibility, but there it was. He wasn't getting any younger, and it was expected, necessary, long overdue.

He thought of Lady Ann. Marriage to her would be a smart move. She was well-bred, presentable, bland enough not to cross swords with his mother, and dense enough not to be too curious about his affairs. *Don't analyze it, just do it.* But something wasn't . . . right.

"I've filled your tub, my lord," said a soft voice close behind that turned him around with a lurch. It belonged to his valet, Frith, a tall, slender man in his fifties, with the bearing of a bishop and the eyes of a sage, placid and penetrating, the color of mercury turned to hematite now in the moonless darkness. "I beg your pardon, my lord," he breathed. "I hadn't meant to startle you."

"That's quite all right," said King, loosening his neckcloth as he stepped back into his chamber, while the valet shut the French doors. He was halfway across the Aubusson carpet when he stopped in his tracks. "Two baths in one day, Frith? Isn't this a bit excessive? A century ago we'd probably have been burned at the stake for such a thing—me for indulging, you for preparing it."

"I thought perhaps a hot bath might . . . relax you, my lord."

King walked on to his adjoining dressing room, eyeing the steam rising from the copper tub expectantly. How the deuce did the man know such was in order? Was he so easily read? Stripping off his clothes with the valet's help, he sank into the tub, indulging in a long, delicious moan as the water rose around him, surging over his shoulders as he scrunched down beneath the surface. How his body needed that wonderful pulsating warmth. Marveling that Frith always managed to get the water temperature just right, he moaned again in ecstasy, until the valet handed him a bar of coconut-scented soap. Pop! There went the bliss. Every muscle in his corded body that submersion had relaxed snapped taut like a sprung spring, and he groaned again, this time in exasperation. No. His little world was definitely not right at all.

"Is something amiss, my lord?" Frith queried, brows knit.

King heaved a ragged sigh. "Much is amiss, I think," he said, holding the soap beneath his nose. He breathed in deeply. Why did he detect the distinct scent of attar of roses over the coconut? There wasn't a rose in sight. He worked up a ruthless lather with the soap and proceeded to assault his neck and chest with such a savage hand that the valet took it from him. "I'm in a bit of a quandary, that's all," he growled by way of explanation.

"Having . . . second thoughts, my lord?" Frith said, applying the soap to his hair with a gentler hand.

"In what respect?" said King. It was useless to evade the issue. Frith had been with him for so long, and through so much in service to him over the years, he'd become convinced the valet was possessed of the power to read his mind. He was certain of it. It wasn't any use; the man had an uncanny aptitude for extracting information in such a way that was positively hypnotic. He would have made a formidable Bow Street Runner.

"You haven't yet proposed, I notice," the valet pointed out.

"No, I have not," King snapped. That was another thing. Frith had long since put aside crossing the line. He only took bold liberties in asserting himself in private, thank Divine Providence; they were too close to stand on ceremony. But there were times . . .

"Don't you think you ought?" said the valet.

"Don't rush me!"

"Do you not find her fair?" Frith persisted.

All at once King conjured the image—not of Lady Ann, but of a certain provocative mole pointing toward a revealing expanse of cleavage belonging to another fair maid. Real or contrived, the damned thing had done its worst, and did still, he discovered to his profound dismay. A sudden tightening in his loins and hardening of his sex at the mere thought of the perfect brown spot on that creamy-white breast was testimony to that. His body clenched at the unexpected phenomenon, but his discomfort was short-lived. A bucket of suspiciously cold water dumped on his head made an end to it.

He loosed a string of oaths colorful enough to turn the steam blue, and roared, "Damn it, Frith, that water's cold!"

"To kill the soap suds in your hair, my lord," said the valet mater-of-factly. "We didn't do it justice earlier."

"Enough! Get me out of this!"

"As you wish, my lord," said Frith.

"I've traipsed one end of the *ton* to the other, searching for the perfect wife for my . . . situation," King groused, stepping out of the tub and into the towel the valet held for him. He gave his traitorous body a scathing rubdown. "I believe Lady Ann to be she . . . all things considered."

"*All* things, my lord?"

"What are you implying?"

"Are you in love with the lady, my lord?"

"One doesn't have to be in love to get an heir, Frith. Don't be absurd."

"You mean to take a mistress for your pleasures, then," said the valet, answering his own question.

"There shan't be time for that, if the Admiralty has its way, old boy. This isn't like the old days. I need to accomplish three things and three things only—settling Mother, getting an heir, and taking care of the trade. Period."

"I see," said Frith.

"Hmmm," King growled, standing for the valet to help him into his dressing gown. He cinched the sash ruthlessly. He had no doubt in his mind that the valet did "see," all too well, and his brow inched up a notch as he eyed the stoical expression Frith had fixed in place. "It's best I think, considering, that heart and loins not be joined in this instance, old boy," he said. "I need a level head and my wits about me right now."

"And . . . what of later, my lord?" the valet probed.

"The way things are at the moment, there may not be a 'later' for me, Frith," he returned. "My duty, as I see it, is to the earldom. I've sowed my wild oats. I have no regrets."

"Whatever you say, my lord . . ."

"But?" King prompted through the valet's pregnant pause.

"You don't seem to me a man with his wits about him at the moment, is all."

"No, you're right, I'm not. The point is that I *will* be once I deal with Mother, and press my suit to Lady Ann.

Accomplishing those feats will leave me free to concentrate upon the rest."

"In that order, my lord?"

"Well, of course in that order. Mother must be settled first."

"With her new . . . companion, I take it, my lord?"

"Yes, if they get on. If not, I'm faced with yet another problem. Where in all of this do you see time for 'love'?"

"Love goes where it's sent, my lord; so said my sainted mother. Few men born of women have been successful dodging Cupid's darts."

"Don't tell me you're about to wax romantic on me, Frith?" He ground out a guttural chuckle. "I hardly think you're qualified to counsel me in that regard."

"Oh, I don't know, my lord. I do well enough."

"Do you, then?" King erupted. The valet had his full attention now. "Well, well, who would have thought it? I shall have to keep a closer eye upon you in future, shan't I, old boy?"

"Yes, my lord. Begging your pardon, but what are your plans for the countess after you're wed . . . when she becomes dowager countess? Will she remain at Grayshire Manor or—"

"She will occupy the dower house," King hastened to inform him.

"Is she aware of that, my lord?"

"Not . . . yet."

"I wish you well, my lord," the valet ground out. It was one of the only times in the fifteen years Frith had served him that the valet had showed emotion. It was disconcerting that King couldn't for the life of him recall the other occasions. That did not bode well.

"I'd rather not borrow trouble from that account at the moment, if you wouldn't mind," King said. "Stubble it!"

"Yes, my lord. Will there be anything else, my lord?"

"No," said King. He heaved a mammoth sigh. At least the valet hadn't forgotten how far over the line he could stray, the way the others had. Perhaps it was that privilege, the special bond he had with Frith that was at fault. It wouldn't be the first time one privileged servant incited jealousy amongst the rest. "I want to get an early start tomorrow," he announced, shaking those thoughts free. "There are several things that I must attend to before we set out," he went on, monitoring the valet's skeptical expression. "Pack our bags while I'm at that, and see that Mrs. Archway does the same for Lady Lark. Then have them loaded on the brougham. I want to leave right after nuncheon."

"Very good, my lord."

"There can only be one 'Countess Grayshire,' Frith," he said, answering the valet's all too readable look, which hadn't altered, giving birth to consternation that he couldn't conceal as he went on. "Mother will have to yield to my wife. She knows that. It happened to her when she married Father. There can be but one mistress of the Manor."

"I wish you well, my lord," the valet responded, "but it wouldn't hurt to petition the Divine in that regard."

"Or scare up a sacrificial lamb," King said in a dark mutter, crossing the threshold into his bedchamber.

Five

King's day began with a disturbing summons from the Admiralty Office that arrived before breakfast and took him off with nothing in his stomach but half a cup of tepid coffee. From there, he made a stop at Old Bailey, followed by a trip to Borough High Street for a visit to the Marshalsea, a place he never thought he'd have occasion to visit again. After conversing with Tobias briefly beside the gated entrance and presenting his papers, he paced before the keeper's quarters, tugging at his gloves as he always did when agitated, and when the turnkey approached with Agnes Garwood in tow, he yanked the gloves off altogether and clutched them in a white-knuckled fist.

"Something's happened to her!" Agnes shrilled at sight of him.

"No, no, take ease, Mrs. Garwood," he soothed. "Lady Lark is well."

"Begging your pardon, my lord, but why did she send you, then?" she said skeptically.

"She doesn't know I'm here," he replied. "Is there a place where we might speak in private?"

"In *here?*" she blurted. "Not likely, my lord."

"We need a moment," he said to Tobias, ushering the woman past him into the keeper's office.

"Here!" the turnkey protested. "What do ya think yer doin'? Ya can't just come bargin' in through them gates without so much as a by-your-leave and take over the place. We've got rules in 'ere."

"I've just changed them," said King, pulling Tobias close to his face with a fist in the front of the startled man's wrinkled coat. "This is only the beginning. I'd advise you to collect your things. Your replacement arrives shortly." He let him go with a shove that sent him backpedaling through the open office door. "Meanwhile," he pronounced, as he shut the door in the turnkey's face, "as I said, we need a moment."

He turned to Agnes, who was standing slack-jawed. "Forgive me, but I am pressed for time," he said. "Lady Lark has consented to serve as companion for my mother, the dowager Countess Grayshire. We leave for Cornwall shortly. Lady Lark is in need of an abigail. I realize that the position is beneath what you are accustomed to as a milliner, proprietress of your own establishment, but I'm certain Lady Lark would welcome your companionship, and quite frankly, I believe that from what she has told me, I could trust you to treat her well, something I could not trust those among the candidates in my employ to manage, I'm sorry to say. Would you be willing? You shall want for nothing. Grayshire Manor is quite grand, and I shall provide you with a generous stipend."

"Y-you want me to . . . to . . . But my *fee*, it's more than a hundred pounds!"

"I've already paid your debt. I've just come from Old Bailey. You are free, whether you accept my offer or not. Of course, I hope that you will."

"I-I'm dreaming!" she breathed.

"Hardly. She misses you, Mrs. Garwood. She said you showed her kindness. I'm trying to do the same, but she doesn't trust me yet, which is understandable in view of her recent experiences. That, I hope, will come in time, but in the meanwhile, I believe your continued presence in her life would be beneficial to us all. What do you say?"

"Y-you mean . . . now?" she murmured. "I . . . I can get my things and go with you *right now*?"

"Yes, right now," he parroted, suppressing a smile. "My coach awaits."

"I won't be a minute," she said, vaulting toward the door. She turned back while going through it, her patched skirt sweeping the doorjamb. "You'll still be here when I return?" she urged.

"Don't worry, I will be here."

"I . . . I don't know how to thank you, my lord," she sobbed, sketching a bow. "I still think I'm dreaming. You'll never be sorry—*never*!"

"I hope not," he murmured aloud as she disappeared into the crowded courtyard, where more and more inmates were gathering to take advantage of the glorious morning. With September waning there wouldn't be many more like it. Soon the fogs would roll in more often, and colder. Then the snow would come. Deuced nuisance. At least that was one thing he wouldn't have to contend with in Cornwall. It rarely snowed there—once in twenty years or so, when the prevailing wind allowed it. Trust this to be that year.

His mother would be pleased that he'd rescued not one but two unfortunate inmates from low tide in the Marshalsea, but would they be pleased with her? He couldn't imagine it. He shook those thoughts free, however, and quit the keeper's office. There was another matter to be settled before he left Borough High Street, and there was no room for thoughts of anything but that as he went in search of Andrew Westerfield.

He found his quarry in much the same spot that he'd last seen him, loitering aimlessly in the shadowy doorway of number four. Striding up to him, King struck him thrice in the face with the gloves in his white-knuckled fist, then seized his neckcloth in a viselike grip with little regard for the flesh underneath, and jerked him close to his thin-lipped rage.

"You are called out, Westerfield," he gritted through clenched teeth. "You have to answer for Lady Lark Eddington."

"You can't call me out in here, Grayshire," Westerfield

jeered. "Duels aren't allowed in the Marshalsea—or anywhere else, come to that."

"You aren't always going to be in here," King pointed out, "and I don't give a bloody damn for the legalities of dueling, only the necessities. I have never permitted a lady to bear insult, much less injury, without rising to the occasion. Don't come back to Cornwall, because if you do, you can expect a call from my second within the hour of your arrival. You had best pray that they keep you in here until your dotage, because there is no place in the kingdom where you can hide that I shan't run you to ground. In the meanwhile, this will have to suffice me for satisfaction." Propelling him through the open doorway out of the others' view, he drew back his fist and planted it squarely in Westerfield's face, sending the man sprawling against the narrow stairs. He stared down at the young scoundrel—scarcely conscious, bleeding from the nose and mouth—and gave a crisp nod. "Trust me, you don't want to be set free," he snarled. Then, turning on his heel, he marched out into the sunshine where Agnes waited, mouth agape, and spirited her away to the waiting coach.

Lark and Mrs. Archway had just finished packing the portmanteaux when a rap at the door sent the housekeeper to answer. Lark could scarcely believe her eyes at the sight of Agnes Garwood and Grayshire himself standing in the doorway.

"Agnes?" she cried, rushing to the woman. In the midst of their tearful embrace, she caught sight of the earl smiling down. "My lord!" she breathed, meeting his gaze.

"I shall leave you to your reunion," he said, sketching a deep bow. Then, to Mrs. Archway, he said, with emphasis, "I will trust you to see that Mrs. Garwood is properly refreshed. She is to be my lady's abigail. I will supply her with a suitable wardrobe once we reach Grayshire Manor. Find something that will suffice her for travel, and have the footmen load these portmanteaux on the brougham with the rest of the luggage."

"Yes, my lord," the housekeeper replied.

He turned to Lark and Agnes, who were still embracing. "Nuncheon is in half an hour in the breakfast room," he said. "We shall leave immediately thereafter. Mrs. Garwood, you may join us there on this one occasion, mainly because I do not want to waste time running you to ground afterward. You understand, of course, that once we reach Grayshire Manor—"

"Oh, la, my lord," Agnes interrupted. "I understand completely. I know my place, and I'll keep to it."

"My lord, I don't know how I shall ever be able to thank you for this," Lark choked, tears streaming down her cheeks. She had never been a watering pot, but if there was ever an acceptable occasion for becoming one, this was it.

"That I have pleased you is thanks enough," he responded, bowing again. "And now I beg you, please excuse me. I, too, must make ready for our journey."

In the blink of an eye he was gone, and before Lark could learn of the events preceding her good fortune, Mrs. Archway had whisked Agnes off to affect a hasty toilette. Lark didn't see her again until nuncheon. She had just begun to fear that their meeting earlier was some cruel hallucination when Agnes entered the breakfast room dressed in a black twill traveling costume, with a matching bonnet lined with white ruching in her hand.

"You look . . . oh, Agnes, I was so afraid I'd dreamed it!" Lark cried, embracing her again.

"I can't tell you what went through my head when his lordship came this morning," Agnes replied. "At first I thought something had happened to you, and that he'd come to break the news. Then, when he told me—"

"You don't mind?" Lark interrupted. "It's beneath you, you know."

"Beneath me? I'd have signed on to rob bodies from the graveyard to get out of that place. He's a gentleman—a *real* one. He paid my fee! And he's offered me a stipend as well. He had Tobias sacked, too. You don't know the half of it."

"He did *what?*"

"You heard me well enough, and that's not all. He called Westie out—planted him a leveler!"

"H-he challenged Westerfield to a duel?" Lark was incredulous.

"That he did, because of what he did to you. From what I overheard, Westie better never go home to Cornwall if he ever gets out—or anywhere else, come to that."

"I don't know what I've gotten us into," Lark said, her eyes clouding. "It all seems quite too good to be true. But anything is better than that awful place we've just come from, and he does seem a proper gentleman. Heaven knows I've met more than a few who weren't since Father died. Still, there's . . . something . . ."

"Oh, la, I wouldn't go borrowing trouble," said Agnes. "We've been lent more than enough already the way I see it."

Lark shrugged. "You're doubtless right," she conceded. "I'm probably being unreasonably wary. And it doesn't matter in any case. We haven't got a choice."

While the trip could be made on horseback or by a fast coach in two days, King elected to do it in three, thus sparing the ladies and the horses by allowing for rest stops at posting houses and coaching inns along the way. At least that was what he'd convinced himself. Truth be told, he was in no hurry to face the countess. Though both of his choices seemed well to pass, who knew what his eccentric mother would think of them, or if he would have to absorb the cost of their liberty only to be faced with finding them suitable positions elsewhere. And then there was the Admiralty business that had stuck like an undigested morsel of something unsavory in his craw. No. Though he knew it was expedient that he do so, he was most definitely not in any hurry to reach Downend Point.

Owing to their late start, they stopped for the night at a

well-appointed coaching inn just north of Winchester. The fare was exceptional as such places went, and the rooms large, clean, and comfortable. Lark and Agnes repaired to their adjoining suite of rooms right after the meal. After several rounds of ale, King repaired to his. What he needed to discuss with Frith could not be broached in the pump room.

Shed of his neckcloth and coat of indigo superfine, he paced the Oriental carpet in his room, hands clasped behind his back, while Frith picked up his discards where he'd flung them. He had hardly been able to contain himself until they were closeted there, and two rounds of ale had done precious little to blunt the edges of his dilemma.

"Have a care, my lord! We have no flatiron," the valet complained as King's ivory brocade waistcoat sailed through the air and joined the pile via the toe of his polished black Hessian. "I'll have to unpack one of your bags," he groused, swatting stubborn tufts of fiber from the cream-colored rug off the superfine cloth. "You can't wear these togs again till I've seen to them; you'll look like a scarecrow."

"Leave them," King barked. "Lint is the least of my worries. I was out of it—*well out of it*, Frith—and they've reeled me right back in, like a sea bass! I wonder if they knew, and did it a-purpose."

"Did what, my lord?"

"They've licensed the *Cormorant*, damn it! They've awarded me a Letter of Marque."

"You can't mean—"

"That is precisely what I mean," King growled. "She's been licensed for profiteering—given leave to attack and capture enemy ships in the channel, and confiscate their cargoes for the Crown. The trade's come alive again, and I'm going to have to turn in every one of our friends and neighbors on the coast."

"The trade has always been 'alive,' my lord, and since you own two-thirds of the vessels on the coast, you should have expected this new surge as a matter of course. I told you when you wriggled out of it last time and took up your commission that this would come. You should have never left the navy."

"Yes, well, that couldn't be helped, old boy. It's a land war now, for the most part, and I was duly mustered out. The Admiralty was hardly about to turn a blind eye—no pun intended—to my . . . disability, as it were."

"Balderdash. Half of Cornwall wears an eye patch. No self-respecting pirate would be caught dead without one. You're paying now for letting them put you out to pasture when, not being in the army, you couldn't be in the thick of things any longer."

"That is neither here nor there at this juncture. The *Cormorant* is to work hand in glove with the *Hind* at sea, and with the riding officers on land to make an end to the smuggling trade on the Cornish coast. It's ludicrous. Smugglers have thrived out there since the seventeenth century. What they imagine I can bring to the issue is quite beyond me."

"Surely they don't expect *you* to man her?"

King cast his valet a poisonous look, lips pursed, eye glowering. "That is exactly what they expect."

"Oh, dear," Frith said. "You mustn't perpetuate your sainted father's legacy. He would not want you to take up his cudgel, my lord, he was quite adamant—"

"Father's 'legacy' leaves me little choice," King cut in. "I was still here fifteen years ago when Lieutenant Gabriel Bray led that raid by land and sea that netted him four local chaps—all known to us—and saw them hauled off for armed assault and obstruction. Then the next year, when the deuced *Hind* captured the *Lottery* and that damned customs officer was killed in the fray, I saw Tom Potter executed for it; I was there. Neither Tom nor any others amongst the crew ever disclosed that the *Lottery* belonged to Father, only let to her captain to safeguard Father's anonymity. Tom took that to his grave or Father would have joined him, sure as check. All that took place before Father bought me my naval commission—you were here through all of it.

"Granted, I was scarcely twenty-one at the time, green as sea grass, and chomping at the bit to join the war effort, starry-eyed with battle lust, but I remember it all as though it happened yesterday. Now I'm in between a rock and the quarry. They protected him—all of them. Every man Jack of them from Looe, to Fowey, and beyond, disavowed Father's complicity in the trade—many to the death. How can I betray their trust here now? Then again, how can I not, without bringing shame upon the name of Kingston, and upon the earldom?"

"It's a muddle, my lord, I grant you, but—"

"What with my commission," King interrupted, "and then being engaged in the marriage mart here in Town since I'm come home, I've managed thus far to stay out of that coil, but Father didn't, did he, Frith, after I went off? He was active in the trade till he died, wasn't he?"

"Yes, my lord, he was," said the valet, "but he didn't want that life for you. He bought you that commission to keep you out of it. You were leaning that way, you'd already gotten your 'feet wet,' as it were, if you recall?"

"How much does Mother know?" King said, trying to ignore the valet's reference to his checkered past involvement in piracy on the high seas during his misspent youth. It wasn't something he was proud of, though he had to admit he had a penchant for it, and the Admiralty Office had literally just licensed him to indulge himself to his heart's content, so long as the Crown profited. It was a tempting prospect.

"The countess has never taken an interest in the trade to my knowledge, my lord, but that is not to say she is in ignorance of the goings-on around her," the valet said, interrupting his thoughts. "Will you make her privy to this new turn of events?"

"Good God, I haven't thought that far ahead, old boy."

The valet cleared his voice conspicuously. "You might want to do that before we reach the coast, my lord," he said. "It won't sit well should her ladyship find out second-hand, and you know how news travels. You might want to send word on ahead."

"I wish I'd gotten out of Town before they nabbed me," King complained.

"Couldn't you have . . . declined, my lord? You have been mustered out, after all."

"*Declined?* Frith, no one refuses the Admiralty without risking being tried for treason."

"I hardly think *that*, my lord. Surely you exaggerate."

"One simply does not refuse the Crown—especially now, considering the fragile state of the government since the king's madness forced the Regency. These days, everyone's loyalties are suspect. If I had attempted it, I would have surely cast suspicion upon myself, and I can ill afford to do that now—not if I am to abet the smugglers."

"What will you ever do?" the valet murmured. "I do not envy you, my lord. And now, just when you're contemplating marriage! Should that not wait?"

"No. Marriage might be just the blind I need employ to see this through unscathed. It will get Mother out of the Manor and see her removed to the dower house forthwith—far enough away to keep her ignorant of the goings-on at Grayshire. Lady Ann is not nearly as sharp as Mother is. There is no danger there. Mother, on the other hand—"

"You have decided not to tell her ladyship, then," the valet put in, answering his earlier question.

"I have decided, Frith, to play the hand I've been dealt. All else is speculation."

Six

*T*he last lap of the journey was nearly upon them, and Lark still had no more understanding of her strange benefactor than she did the day he lifted her up from the dirt of the courtyard at the Marshalsea. He sat across from her as the brougham tooled over the highways, ramrod rigid against the plush velvet squabs in his impeccable attire, and engaged her in cordial conversation that gave no insight regarding the man himself. He asked often after her comfort, and answered generic questions regarding the Cornish weather, which held a fascination for her, never having been out to the coast. He told her of the pranks Mother Nature played in league with the prevailing winds that upset the seasons and had plants blooming out of sync with the rest of the country, and how the wind never ceased to blow. What fascinated her most were his blood-chilling tales of the dreaded flaws, as the elders called the wild, ravaging storms that plagued the coast, and she shuddered at the prospect of witnessing one firsthand, which he told her grimly was inevitable.

Agnes did not participate in these discourses. She listened intently, speaking only when spoken to, and Lark marveled at how quickly she'd adapted to her situation. But then, after three years in the Marshalsea, judging from her own short incarceration there, Lark wasn't at all surprised that the woman would do anything in her power to prove herself to her new employer.

They were approaching Ivybridge on Dartmoor at dusk,

only a few hours from Grayshire Manor, when a storm broke. Not one of the dreaded, long-winded flaws that could, the earl told her, settle in and wreak havoc for days on end, but wild enough, with limb-snapping gusts, driving rain, and snake lightning streaking down as though some irate deity straight out of myth were hurling flaming spears at their carriage. The narrow roads were soon underwater, which may have well been the reason that Grayshire's driver missed a sizable pothole that threw the brougham off-kilter just enough to bog it down in the mire. Lark cried out as the carriage listed, tipped, and jerked to a shuddering halt, throwing her into the earl's strong arms and propelling Agnes unceremoniously across the seat she had just vacated. Frith soon righted Agnes, but it was a long moment before the earl released Lark. His arms were strong and warm, and his quick action had prevented her from taking an injury, though there was no reason for him to hold onto her for *that* long.

She had landed with her face against his shoulder. His driving coat was of excellent stuff—superfine, to be sure, of the finest quality. It held his distinct, very male scent, married mysteriously with lime and leather . . . and, yes, tobacco. She had not seen him smoke, but the telltale evidence was there, trapped in the fibers of that dashing caped coat. There was another scent, too: the recently drunk wine on his warm breath puffing uncomfortably close to her cheek. Her heart nearly stopped as their faces touched briefly before he held her away and searched deep into her eyes.

"Are you hurt?" he said, still holding her.

"No . . . I . . . I don't think so," she stammered, feeling for the seat behind.

He promptly lifted her onto it, and settled her back against the squabs. "Hold fast to the strap," he said. "I must assess the damage. Frith," he said, nodding toward the door.

Only then did she realize that the carriage was tilted at

a precarious angle. Something incredibly frightening had happened to her in Grayshire's arms. It had momentarily paralyzed her senses of all but his hypnotic scent, his touch, the strange surge of icy fire that raced through the most private recesses of her body. It had ignited something that was shockingly scandalous. The touch of his cheek wearing a growth of budding stubble against hers had done it, calling a rush of hot blood to her face, which she just knew had turned scarlet. She had always been cursed with the tendency to blush at the drop of a hat from a good deal less than this hapless circumstance, and she was profoundly grateful that it was dark inside the brougham. Her cheeks were on fire.

Outside, the earl's coachman had scrambled down and quickly taken the horses in hand. Especially the nervous right leader, whose loud complaints and hooves pounding the ground as the men tried to control him contributed to the din of the thunder rolling closer overhead, and the men's strident shouts over the racket. Meanwhile, Frith busied himself unloading their bags from up top, and the back boot.

"You shall have to get out," said the earl at last, poking his head in through the open coach door. Rain glistened on his face, and dripped from the brim of his beaver hat. "No, not yet," he hastened to add as Lark shifted in her seat in compliance. "Once the rain slacks. I am just preparing you. We shall have to lift the carriage to free the wheel, and it will be easier if it's empty."

"You are getting very wet," Lark observed, taking him in totally.

He laughed outright—deeply, from the diaphragm. His whole body shook with unbridled guffaws. How white and straight his teeth were, how sparkling his eye.

"Well, you *are*," she replied to the outburst, pouting. "I see nothing humorous in that."

"I've just come from a ten-year tour of duty in His

Majesty's Royal Navy, my lady," he said through a guttural chuckle. "I assure you, I have been wet before."

"Oh," she returned, low-voiced, the heat in her cheeks scorching now despite the rain splinters stabbing in around him. "Can you not step back inside meanwhile?" she queried.

He shook his head, scattering raindrops every which way. "We're bogged down in a deep rut, and underwater besides," he explained. "I cannot assess the full extent of the damage till we're out of it, and we daren't chance adding more weight to the strain the horses are already bringing to bear."

"I shall have to unhitch the team, m'lord, if it doesn't stop soon," the coach driver called out. "I can't hold 'em much longer. Their mouths are too soft; they'll be all torn up."

"I don't mind a drenching," Lark said, "and I'm sure Mrs. Garwood doesn't either in these circumstances. You may need the horses to help pull us out. Really—hand us down."

"Mrs. Garwood?" the earl inquired, looking past Lark to the ashen-faced woman beside her.

"O-of course, my lord," Agnes stuttered.

"Very well, then, ladies, on your own heads be it— literally. I cannot set the steps for obvious reasons. My lady, place your hands on my shoulders and please forgive the familiarity. Mrs. Garwood, kindly take notice. You shall be next."

With no more said, he reached inside and grasped Lark's waist with both his hands. They were so large they nearly met in front and back, and her breath paused at the strength in them. Leaning into him, she did as she was bidden, hanging on to his saturated shoulders, her hands fisted in the soggy superfine, marveling that he lifted her as if she weighed no more than a feather. When he set her down, their bodies brushed together as he slid her the length of his lean, corded torso before setting her on her feet at the roadside. Her breath caught again, watching no such scandalous physical contact occur as he lifted Agnes down at arm's length.

"Stay where you are—out of the way," he commanded, bracing his back against the body of the coach with a grip on the derelict wheel. Then to the coachman he said, "Climb up and take your position, Smythe, and when I tell you, give the horses their head."

"Let me help you, my lord," Frith said, rising to the occasion like a man half his age. "You'll do yourself a mischief."

"No!" the earl cried over a thunderclap that shook the ground they stood on. "I need you to give Smythe a hand with that deuced right leader. Smythe, toss down your carriage robe." The coachman obeyed, and Frith caught it in flight as it sailed through the air. "Cover that horse's eyes," the earl charged. "The lightning is spooking him—and keep a firm hold on that tack, else he bolt and this thing runs me over. I've naught but ooze underneath me."

"Take care!" Lark and Agnes cried in unison, as, gritting his perfect white teeth, the earl bent his knees and heaved against the carriage with all his strength.

The brougham groaned and lifted somewhat, but the team's prancing worked against him, and he eased it back into the hole, panting for breath.

"Let me come and help, my lord," Frith shouted. "Or give us leave to unhitch this team before you break your back."

"When I tell you, remove the blind and let that leader go!" the earl responded.

Lark and Agnes stood clinging to each other in the teeming rain as the earl applied his back to the coach and wheel again. His Hessians were dug in, submerged to midcalf in the mud of the road, sinking deeper as the carriage lifted, and he rocked the wheel until it mounted the rim of the pothole and cleared it—just barely. Then, shifting position and his weight to the wheel itself with a mighty cry, he hefted it out as he pushed himself off.

"Now, Frith!" he called. To the coachman he shouted:

"Give them their head, Smythe, and tack to port, or the rear wheel is going to go in!"

The coachman obeyed, and the team danced off several yards, dragging the coach with its mud-crusted right front wheel along after it, splattering Lark and Agnes, already bedraggled from the drenching. The earl staggered. As it passed him by, undermining the ooze underfoot, he backpedaled, swayed, lost his balance, and flopped on his behind in the mud of the road.

Caught between a laugh and a gasp, Lark covered her mouth with both hands as the floundering earl cursed the air blue in a dark mutter. Judging from the expression on his face as he took Frith's extended hand, neither response would have been welcome, and she was wise enough to suppress both.

"Oh, my lord, your new driving coat!" the valet lamented, hauling him to his feet rather gracefully under the circumstances. He started to slap at the mud, but threw up his hands in defeat at the impossible and retrieved the earl's beaver from the mud instead. "This is salvageable, at least, though I daresay it will want a good steaming and blocking quite beyond my skills. You might want to have it to the hatter when we reach the coast."

"Never mind that," the earl growled. It was plain to all that his less than graceful tumble in the mud before the ladies had embarrassed him, to say the least. "Is the deuced thing drivable?" he queried of the brougham, leaning crooked on higher ground a few yards off.

"I think so, my lord," said the valet. "Looks like we've lost a spoke or two on that wheel, and the spring looks a bit worse for wear—bent to be sure—but it seems to be holding."

"What say you, Smythe?" the earl asked, striding to the brougham. "We're so damned close. Can you limp her to the Point?"

"Loaded? I dunno, m'lord," said the coachman. Lifting his cap, he scratched his head. "Maybe if I take the short-cut across the moor. Do you want to chance it? It'll be a bumpy ride, what with that spring. The road is better'n this one, though. There won't be so much water on higher ground, but you know the moor, m'lord. This time o' night, I wouldn't exactly call it the safest place in the realm."

"I can deal with that." He looked to the heavens, drawing Lark's eyes there as well. The storm was slackening. There still was no sign of the moon, nor the twinkle of stars, but the thunder and lightning had grown distant. "The storm has passed over," he observed. "That's one thing, at least. Frith, I want you up top," he charged, handing the valet a pistol from beneath his soggy coat. "Do not hesitate to use this should the occasion arise," he said softly, though Lark, who had come nearer with Agnes, heard and took a bone-gripping chill at his words. "I needn't tell you, the byways on Dartmoor are crawling with thatch-gallows."

"And ghosties," the coachman put in, hefting the last of their bags back into the rear boot now that the horses were calmed.

The earl stripped off his muddy coat and handed it to Frith. "Take this with you," he said. "I'd rather not sully the coach any more than I have to. Just look sharp up there."

"As you wish, my lord," said the valet.

"*As needs must,*" the earl corrected. Then, sketching an all-encompassing bow, he handed first Lark and then Agnes back into the carriage as though nothing untoward had occurred.

Lark adjusted her soggy bonnet. Tendrils had come loose from her coiffure underneath. They were plastered wet to her face and the back of her neck, somewhat frosted with mud. She smoothed out the skirt of her gray twill traveling dress, and tugged on the matching velvet spencer that had ridden up her back until it ceased to choke her. Her teeth were chattering. She was soaked to the skin from her head to the toes of her Morocco leather slippers that squished whenever she moved her feet in them. Looking on, the earl stripped off his indigo frock coat, which was somewhat dry, the driving coat having spared it, and wrapped it around her shoulders. It happened so quickly it took her by surprise, and she held her breath as his hands lingered, arranging it familiarly.

"You are quite fetching all mussed," he observed, flashing a lopsided smile that sent a flash of hot blood and a chill racing through her all at once. "Very like the occasion of our first meeting, as I recall." He burst into laughter.

"What you find so amusing escapes me, my lord," she snapped. "Do share the joke, so that we might laugh along with you."

"Forgive me my wont of conduct," he wheezed through a chuckle. "I was just imagining Mother's reaction to us when we arrive, and that was rude of me, because I am afraid that you cannot share the joke; you haven't met Mother. So much for favorable first impressions." He glanced toward Agnes, with a wry twinkle in his eye. "Mrs. Garwood, of the three of us, I daresay you look well enough to pass, but my lady and myself are quite another matter." He burst into laughter again. "We look like two swamp rats from the mud flats."

"Oh, la!" Agnes murmured under her breath.

Lark gasped. "I shan't have to face her like . . . like *this*?" she murmured.

"I had wanted to drive straight through," the earl said. "I have pressing business on the coast, and all this has delayed me too long already. There are no decent accommodations hereabouts. We could head south to Plymouth and stop at one of the inns there to freshen up, if you wish, but, believe me, you'd be much more comfortable at the Manor. I sent word ahead. We are expected, and your rooms are prepared. I think you will find them far superior to anything Plymouth has to offer."

"I . . . I don't want you to go out of your way," Lark said

halfheartedly. One would think he wanted her to make a poor impression on his mother, or at the very least have a good laugh at her expense.

"It isn't a matter of going out of my way," he said. "We're only a couple hours from the coast if we cut across the moor. The coach is damaged; if we can limp it home by the shortest route, it would be best all the way 'round."

For whom? Lark wondered. She curled her toes in the soggy slippers, avoiding his gaze. The squish was audible.

"Well, that's settled, then," he replied to her silence. Raising his walking stick, he aimed it at the carriage roof.

"No, don't!" she cried, arresting him with a quick hand. She'd done it without thinking; all at once she realized that her icy fingers were clamped around the bare skin of his strong, thick wrist, which responded to her touch by tightening beneath. It was like grabbing on to an electric eel for the shock physical contact with that slice of warm male flesh set loose upon her. For a moment their gazes locked before she let him go as if his wrist had combusted in flame. "Th-that's not necessary," she said. "Really."

He stared, the walking stick still suspended, that smoldering one-eyed gaze riveting. The man could see more with one eye than any other living soul could see with two; she was convinced of it. She felt naked—at least her mind did. Could he read her thoughts? Heaven forefend!

"Are you . . . certain?" he said at last. "Your hands are like ice, my lady. If you're cold—"

"I am fine, my lord," she pronounced. "P-perfectly fine."

His lips curled in a half smile. He lowered the silver-headed walking stick and snaked a linen handkerchief from his waistcoat pocket. Without taking his eyes from hers, he moistened it with his tongue and, to her surprise, reached to cup her chin in his hand. Instinctively, she pulled back. There were just too many wild, rampant, unfamiliar emotions riddling her then. Her hands may have been cold, but *oh!*—inside she was on fire.

"If you will allow me?" he said, gesturing toward his own

face to illustrate his intent. She relaxed somewhat as he began to dab at the mud spattered on her cheeks. "It's the least I can do," he murmured. "Can't have you thinking that I deliberately let you beard the lioness at your worst."

The man *could* read her mind. Oh, la, indeed—to borrow a phrase from Agnes. What else could he detect with that sensuous, all-seeing eye of his? She swallowed dryly and groaned aloud imagining.

"Have I hurt you?" he queried, frowning, the handkerchief suspended. "Some of this stuff is really stuck."

"No—no," she said. "It's just . . . worse than I thought. I must look a fright."

"Mmm," he grunted, continuing the makeshift toilette, taking longer than she deemed proper, or necessary. It was several moments before he ran his finger with a slow, light touch along the curve of her cheek in appraisal of his efforts, then tilted her head for one last inspection. His scent was on her skin now, spread by his moist tongue on the fine linen.

His eye was dilated in the darkened coach. It was like gazing into a bottomless obsidian sea. No eyes could be that black, that *mysterious*. Intrigued, she made a mental note to observe him in daylight, surreptitiously, of course. She certainly wouldn't want him to think she was staring, considering. Or worse yet, that she were being so forward as to ogle him.

They might have stayed, eyes locked indefinitely, if a pistol shot hadn't ripped through the silence, wrenching a shrill cry from Agnes. Strident shouts boomed from Smythe's hoarse throat as he tried to bring the complaining horses to a halt. The anxious commands mingled with Frith's cries, calling out to the earl for instructions from the driver's seat above.

Loosing a string of expletives under his breath, the earl jammed his handkerchief into his waistcoat pocket and peered through the coach window, leaning back against the squabs, out of the intruders' view.

"What is it?" Lark breathed.

"Nothing to trouble over," he replied. "You and Mrs. Garwood will come to no harm, you have my word. Stay where you are unless I tell you otherwise, and follow my instruction exactly."

"Stand down and deliver!" the intruder barked, reining his horse alongside the coach. "Everybody out!"

Lark sat frozen in place at the earl's silent command. Whimpering, Agnes did likewise, though her pinching fingers gripped Lark's arm severely.

"You, there, up top—toss down your weapons. Be quick, my patience ebbs low," the highwayman charged.

As Smythe's antiquated blunderbuss and Frith's pistol came crashing to the ground, the earl threw open the coach door and stepped out onto the road, shoulders squared, arms akimbo, glaring in white-lipped rage toward the mounted brigand. He was an unkempt man dressed in black, his features hidden beneath a slouch hat and silk mask, a pistol in each hand. One was still trailing smoke that hung heavy in the oppressive air steeped in the post-storm mist. Lark couldn't take her eyes off him.

For a moment there was utter stillness. Not even the horses made a noise. Then, all at once, the highwayman backed his mount up apace and uttered a strangled sound. Lark's heart was pounding—visibly moving her spencer as she stared nonplussed at the scene that would haunt her for some time to come. Her eyes were drawn to the diamond stickpin glistening irresistibly from the folds of the earl's neckcloth in the light of the coach lamps. How foolhardy of him not to have concealed it. She thanked Divine Providence that no such adornment graced her person. But that thought gave rise to a new fear. Highwaymen were notorious for taking . . . other things when there were no spoils in the offing, and she scarcely drew breath praying the stickpin would be enough to spare her God alone knew what at the freebooter's hands.

All at once, to her profound surprise, the highwayman

found his voice, and stuttered, "S-sorry, guv'nor, wrong c-carriage." With no more said, he tipped his hat, revealing a crop of mahogany hair with a sun-bleached shock in front, wheeled his sleek black mount around, dug in his heels, and rode off over the moor to disappear into the darkness without a backward glance.

Lark and Agnes stared at each other, slack-jawed. The earl snatched up the guns. He hefted up the blunderbuss to Smythe, and tossed the pistol to Frith, who caught it as though he did such things as a matter of course.

"Oh, la! What do you make of that?" Agnes whispered in wide-eyed wonder. "I thought we were done for."

"Shhh! He's coming back," Lark cautioned as the earl yanked the coach door open and climbed inside. Her jaw sagged again, watching him resume his seat and apply the silver head of his walking stick to the roof of the brougham, giving it a sharp tap with a nonchalance that bordered on the ridiculous after what had just occurred.

The coach moved on then, jouncing along on its groaning, wounded spring. Lark eased back against the squabs and pulled the earl's coat close around her. No. She would not inquire about what had just occurred. If she hadn't seen it with her own eyes, she would never have believed that the mere sight of the Earl of Grayshire, armed only with a one-eyed glare, had been enough to send a vicious, pistol-wielding highwayman on his way empty-handed. Not one word had passed between them. The thatch-gallows had simply gurgled as though his throat had been cut, made his excuses, no less, and fled. Literally. That rocked her back on her heels, and though she was resolved not to inquire about the bizarre incident, her sharp-witted intellect demanded that she let him know she knew it *was* bizarre.

"Well, my lord," she said, her voice buoyant a-purpose, "you did warn that there would be highwaymen on the moor, and I believe your coachman said something about . . . 'ghosties'? Since we've had the one, don't you think it wise, and only fair, that you prepare us for the other? And if we are unfortunate enough to encounter a ghost, let us hope that you have the same effect upon it as you did upon that gallows dancer."

Seven

Grayshire Manor stood on a bluff in the lee of Downend Point, overlooking Talland Bay, a scant mile and a half from Polperro. It was a rambling, walled keep, roughly hewn of stone rising three stories high with its back to the bay. Lark took it to be an ancient fortress, impregnable, forbidding, and yet there was something magical about it that drew her . . . until they actually reached it, and the earl got out, produced an enormous gate key, and opened the high arched gates set in the spiked iron fence attached to the wall. She almost gasped aloud. Was this the dreaded gate of her childhood? Was this the very spiked iron nightmare that had haunted her since before she could remember? The fingers of a crawling chill crept along her spine that had nothing to do with her damp, bedraggled state. No, it couldn't be the same. She was cold, and exhausted, and a gate was a gate, nothing more. What a birdwit. She was overset; that was all there was to it. Besides, her phantom gate was to a graveyard, keeping in the sainted and barring the damned. Remembering that calmed her somewhat, until the carriage tooled around a bend in the lane not fifty yards inside the compound. There, the tall, square bell tower of a little church that seemed hewn of the same stone as the mansion appeared in a shaft of moonlight that had finally broken through the clouds.

Lark did gasp then, though she disguised it under the umbrella of a cough, and stared wide-eyed at what lay beyond: *gravestones*. Dozens of them, from what she could see, inside another iron gate. Would there be no end to them—to the haunting? She blinked, but when she opened her eyes again it was all still there; the graveyard, the quaint stone church, its recessed arched windows set in diamond-shaped fretwork winking eerily in the moonlight. There was a neat, one-story cottage beside it. A faint light flickered from what appeared to be a loft in the eaves; then it was gone, shut out of view by another turn in the snakelike ribbon of lane that wound its way through a wooded stretch. Once the trees thinned other dwellings and outbuildings appeared. Lark had only fleeting glimpses of these, set back behind low stacked-stone fences interspersed with sculptured hedgerows. The narrow lane seemed to go on forever, before it widened at last, and the wounded brougham listed to a shaky halt before the entrance of Grayshire Manor in the sweeping circular drive.

Agnes, who had dozed, lurched bolt upright as the carriage rolled to a shuddering stop. She had slept for some time, and missed the distant silhouette of the house. At sight of it now, her jaw fell slack, and her eyes came open wide.

"Courage," Lark whispered, gripping her hand.

"Ohhh, *la!*" Agnes murmured.

The horses were still skittish; it was all Smythe could do to keep them in line. The earl set the steps himself and helped Lark and Agnes climb down on the crushed Welsh bluestone.

Frith, meanwhile, wasted no time unloading the bags, and emptying the boot. The earl collected his mud-caked driving coat from Smythe. With it looped over his arm, he handed Lark up the front steps to the portal, a pair of arched doors of heavy oak fitted with enormous hammered iron hinges that looked as though they belonged on a medieval dungeon. They'd scarcely reached them when they came open in the hands of a stiff-backed butler, who greeted them with stoic indifference to their state and condition as if such a sight upon the doorstep of Grayshire Manor at half past eleven in the evening was quite a normal occurrence. Flanking him were two wigged footmen decked out in full indigo and gold livery, who swarmed past him to address the luggage.

"Good evening, Smeaton," the earl responded. "Has the countess retired?"

"No, she has not," said an authoritative female voice echoing along the Great Hall. The speaker came into view, her silver-handled cane sounding against the terrazzo underfoot as she shuffled closer—a short, slender woman past sixty wearing peach-colored silk twill, whose once-dark hair was handsomely streaked with gray. Her eyes, like quicksilver, raked them all with thorough disdain. "Can it be my behindhand son tracking mud on the marble? And who are these plucked chickens?" She gave a lurch and steadied herself with the cane. "Surely not your—"

"No, no, Mother," Grayshire cut in, his words riding a deep chuckle. "This isn't Lady Ann. May I present Lady Lark Eddington, your new companion, and her abigail, Mrs. Agnes Garwood."

"Countess Grayshire," Lark responded, looking daggers at the earl, meanwhile performing a perfect curtsy in spite of her present state. Agnes followed suit.

The countess stood with her cane in front of her, both gnarled hands resting on the engraved silver handle, taking Lark's measure.

Lark glanced down at herself, her sullied gray traveling costume, hopelessly wrinkled and still damp, clinging provocatively to her curves in a manner that made her extremely uncomfortable considering that the earl's gaze was fixed there as well. Her ankles were exposed, and her thighs and belly clearly defined. She quickly tugged at her skirt, but static in the fabric abetted the dampness, and her efforts only made matters worse. She would have been mortified if she weren't so furious with Grayshire for the way he had introduced her. *"No, no, this isn't Lady Ann,"* indeed! Spoken as though any bufflehead could see it. As though he wouldn't be caught dead betrothed to the likes of her. How dared he? Why she should care eluded her at the moment, unless it was the dreadful shock those words inflicted coming so close on the heels of such an intimate experience with the man in the carriage. In spite of the rapid breath puffing from her nostrils, and eyes narrowed from the heat of her scorching cheeks, she marshaled all of her energies to the task of trying to make a good impression on Countess Grayshire under the worst possible circumstances.

"Please forgive our unfortunate disarray," she said with perfect diction, though she was beyond incensed. "His lordship"—she flashed him a scathing glance—"provided us with a most eventful journey."

"Evidently," said the countess, her lips curling in a speculative smile.

"There was a storm, Mother," the earl explained. "The brougham went into a pothole, bent a spring, and I had to lift it out. The road was a washout, and the ladies got a little muddied. Couldn't be helped."

"Don't forget the bit about the highwayman," Lark volunteered, earning herself a reproving look in return. Yes, the iris of his eye *was* black, or so dark a shade of brown that it appeared to be; the candle flames dancing in the wall sconces on either side of the hall showed it well. How irresistible might two such eyes have been? She shuddered to wonder. It had only taken one to hypnotize her.

The countess's eyebrow lifted. It was clearly a silent command for an explanation, and the earl's tight-lipped scowl was just as clearly an indication that he wasn't about to elaborate. Something was going on under the surface. From that brief first encounter, the countess impressed Lark as a sharp-witted woman who didn't mince words and usually got her way. Well, she wasn't about to get it this time. The earl was just as unbending, staring her down with what had to be practiced skill. They were well matched. Mercy! What had she gotten herself into?

"Don't you think the ladies need looking after, Mother?" Grayshire snapped.

The countess raked Lark with doubtful eyes and shook her head. That articulate, critical stare down her straight Roman nose spoke louder than any words she might have offered, and Lark expanded her posture and raised her chin defensively.

"Not to worry, Mother," the earl said, a wry smile teasing the corners of his sensuous mouth again. "Lady Lark cleans up quite nicely. I can vouch for that firsthand. On the occasion of our first meeting, she was flat on her back, covered with coal dust and Marshalsea muck—quite literally."

Both of the countess's eyebrows shot up, and Lark resisted a nagging urge to stamp her foot or award the earl's shins a sound drubbing with the toe of her slipper, and would have done—earl or no, she was that provoked—if the waterlogged leather would have been effective in either case. She cast him a poisoned-dagger glare instead. If she were only a man, what she wouldn't do. She would pin his ears back—she would plant him a facer—she would draw his cork for him. Wouldn't she just! Her hands fisted at her sides in anticipation.

The countess halted the first footman with the tip of her cane as he passed. "Have Mrs. Hildrith show the ladies to their apartments and see to their needs before they retire, Peal," she said matter-of-factly. "We shall just see how nicely they 'clean up.'" As Lark and Agnes voiced the proper amenities and moved on, the earl started to follow, but his mother's cane whacked him hard across the middle before he'd taken two steps, halting him in his tracks. "Not you, Basil," she intoned. "I shall interview Lady Lark Eddington on the morrow. You, however, will join me in the salon. *Now*."

One look at Lark and Agnes was all it took for Mrs. Hildrith to order the footmen to bring water for bathing to their apartments posthaste. The maids had already begun unpacking Lark's bags when she entered her suite, a spacious, well-appointed apartment on the third floor of the rambling Manor, consisting of a sitting room, bedchamber, and dressing room, with an adjoining chamber for Agnes. Self-conscious of her disheveled state, Lark stayed out of the way until they'd finished hanging her frocks in the armoire, arranging her unmentionables in the chifferobe, and floated out. Meanwhile, she strolled through the rooms, taking in the wonderfully matched Duncan Phyfe furniture, sumptuous carpets, and rich, opulent fabrics. Blue was the common thread running through all the décor, with subtle touches of gold and cream. The rooms were not unlike her suite had been at Eddington Hall, and her eyes clouded, remembering.

Nothing had been overlooked. Fine ivory-handled grooming tools were set out on the vanity. Frosted glass and crystal bottles, clear and cobalt blue, filled with oils and creams and attar of roses marched along the gilded mirror. There was even a dish in the shape of a shell that held a bar of coconut-scented soap like the one at the earl's townhouse. Could he have it custom-milled? She examined it, and found it hallmarked with a "G" in scrollwork on the underside: evidently so.

Once the footman had finished filling the tub and bowed out, she stripped off her bedraggled bonnet, with its wilted burgundy plume, and faced the cheval glass. The sight that met her eyes wrenched a groan from her lips. It was worse than she'd imagined—much worse. Her hair, stiffened with mud, flattened by the bonnet and sticking out every which way, was no longer recognizable as blond. For all the earl's labor cleaning her face with his handkerchief, all he'd managed to do was smear the dirt about, and it didn't hide the redness. Just as she suspected, the heat anger sparked in her cheeks downstairs had colored her crimson. And her dress! It was still wet in spots, and practically transparent, clinging stubbornly to her curves.

No wonder he hadn't taken that all-seeing eye of his off her since they arrived. Much had been hidden in the darkened coach. She groaned again, sinking down on the rosewood-trimmed tapestry lounge; this time the outburst was loud enough to bring Agnes.

"Oh, la! Isn't it grand?" the abigail babbled, bursting through the door that joined their chambers. "I was sure there'd be a camp bed set up in your dressing room for me, but instead I've a wonderful room all to myself! I can scarcely believe . . ." She skittered to a halt at the edge of the Persian rug. "Oh, la, what's happened?" she breathed. "You look about to take a fit of apoplexy."

"Look at me!" Lark cried, slapping her skirt a scathing blow. "The rain has made this deuced stuff transparent. No wonder they were staring. You can see . . . *everything*. This never would have happened if *I* had chosen my traveling costume. What do men know about ladies' clothes? I wouldn't put it past him to have done this deliberately."

"Oh, now, I don't think his lordship could have known there'd be a storm and we'd get caught out in it."

"Don't you dare defend him," Lark warned, glowering. She vaulted off the lounge, stripped off the spencer, and tossed it down at her feet. Then, wriggling out of the gown, she kicked it across the room. "It goes straight into the dustbin. I never want to see it again"—she snatched up the spencer and sent it flying also—"ever!"

"He's taken your fancy," Agnes observed with sage conviction, and a positively evil grin.

"Nothing of the sort," Lark contradicted.

"Deny it as you will, but I've got eyes in my head and from what I've seen, it wouldn't take much to kindle a fire there."

"Agnes, you're mistaken. I have met his lordship's intended, Lady Ann Cuthbertson, a very agreeable lady of quality. As soon as I am settled here amiably with his mother, he intends to return to London and press his suit. They are practically betrothed."

" 'Practically' isn't final," said Agnes. "He doesn't seem to me like a man who's smelling of April and May over this Lady Ann what's-her-name. He didn't even mention her once on the journey."

"Why would he? He doesn't discuss his personal affairs with me, Agnes. He merely made me aware of his intentions when he offered me this position, and introduced us so that we might become acquainted, since we will be seeing a good deal of each other after they are married."

"Mmmm. What's she like?"

"Lady Ann? She's quite well to pass, gracious . . . attractive, I suppose." She wanted to say: insipid, missish, scratchy-voiced, a regular milk-and-water miss. But that wouldn't be kind, and she had no right to make judgments. She just wished that the earl hadn't blurted, *"No, no, this isn't Lady Ann"* in that thoughtless, offensive, hurtful way.

"Not exactly a diamond of the first water, I take it?" Agnes observed, interrupting her thoughts.

"No, not, but who am I to judge?"

"Someone who *is*," Agnes said flatly.

"Well, I thank you for the compliment, dear friend," Lark said, "but you are mistaken. The only thing I am interested in here is a position that will hopefully give me back some measure of dignity. It doesn't appear as though I've gotten off on the right foot toward that, does it? He warned me that she could be . . . difficult."

"*Difficult?* Did you see how she handled that cane? A weapon if ever I saw one. She fairly knocked the wind out of him down there with the whack she gave him; a termagant to be sure."

Lark sighed. "I'm afraid you may have the right of it, but it isn't as though I wasn't warned. There's nothing for it in any case, but to play the cards we've been dealt." Her eyes strayed toward the inviting steam rising from the French enameled tub. It was almost identical to the one at the townhouse. She surged to her feet and snatched up the bottle of attar of roses from the vanity. "At any rate, nothing will be settled tonight," she said, sprinkling some of the fragrance into the water. "For now, I shall take advantage of this fine tub before the water grows cold, and see if I can make myself presentable for my 'interview' tomorrow. Termagant or no, I'd rather brave Countess Grayshire than the Marshalsea."

"Oh, la! I hope she doesn't want to interview *me*," Agnes cried.

"If I were you," Lark said, "I'd count upon it."

Having given his account, King rocked back on his muddy heels before the hearth in the salon, avoiding his mother's scrutiny. She had taken her seat with a flourish in an antique Glastonbury chair at the edge of the Aubusson carpet, looking, for all the world, like a queen on her throne—arm extended, spine ramrod rigid, her bulbous fingers working the silver handle on the cane at her command. His belly still smarted from the whack she'd given him; he rubbed it absently. He'd forgotten how skilled she was with that weapon. He sighed. He was soaked to the skin. Frith was preparing his bath in the second-floor suite he longed to repair to, but that was clearly not to be, at least until he'd had his reprimand.

"Basil Alistair Kingston, how could you have been so insensitive as to put that poor girl . . . those . . . women, through such an ordeal?"

"*I* put her through?" he blurted, spinning to face her. She never called him King; she usually called him Basil, and he knew he was under fire the minute she used his full name. He was incredulous. "Good God, Mother, I'm hardly responsible for the weather."

"Do you know who she is?"

"I do," he said, with a deep nod. "The daughter of the biggest card shark in the realm, who sank to stealing at the end, wound up in the quad where he killed himself and left her sailing the River Tick."

"You met that girl's mother, Basil," the countess intoned. "She was increasing with Lark at the time. You met her father, as well, come to that. We used to receive the Eddingtons, dear, before Abigail Eddington died in childbirth and that unscrupulous man's gambling reputation drove the family out of polite society."

"I couldn't have been more than ten," King pointed out. "I don't see how you can possibly expect—"

"Is she out?" his mother interrupted.

"I hardly think so. As I have it, her father's suicide put paid to her Season. They buried the poor blighter in unconsecrated ground and chucked Lady Lark into the Marshalsea instead. All London is still buzzing over it. You know how fickle the *ton* can be—they thrive upon scandal and then turn on the victims like a bitch often turns on the runt of her litter."

"Not *all* the *ton*, Basil. I have never cut anyone for the sins of their father. Nor have you."

"Well, she couldn't find any among the almighty aristocracy to keep her out of the Marshalsea."

"Now do you see the value of my philanthropic enterprise?" the countess said with smug satisfaction. "And you pooh-poohed the notion, and doubtless thought to disobey my directive, didn't you?"

His head shot toward her, and he scowled fiercely.

"Mmmm, but you were afraid that I would know," she went on in triumph. "And I would have. You acted wisely. But then, you were never a stupid boy—rash, and foolhardy certainly, but not stupid."

He had never been able to keep anything from his mother; it was as if he were made of glass and she could see right through him. Never once in his childhood had he managed to pull off a prank and dupe her. She always knew. What did she know now? He dared not meet those quicksilver eyes else she find him out—in more ways than one, he'd begun to realize.

"This abigail," the countess continued. "What do you

know of her? Quite frankly, I thought you might appoint one of the maids from the townhouse to the task, not that I'm unpleased to have liberated two unfortunate creatures from that god-awful place. Still, one cannot be too careful these days."

"I had intended to engage Biddie," he replied, "but as it turned out, I had to sack her instead."

"Oh? And why was that, pray?"

"She somehow took a notion that she should have been the one engaged as your companion, and mistreated Lady Lark because of it."

"And what, pray, gave the gel such a notion?"

"How the deuce should I know that?" he snapped.

"Something must have given her that impression."

"Just what are you suggesting, Mother?"

"Basil, you are not a child in leading strings. You know the way of things. I never thought I'd find it necessary to have this conversation with you, but perhaps it's best."

"Where is this going, Mother?" King said, his patience waning, knowing full well exactly where it was going and not liking it one iota.

"Your father had his share of mistresses over the years, as you are probably aware, but he never succumbed to bedding the servants; nor shall you while I draw breath."

"Do you actually think I *need* to succumb to such shoddy practices to get a woman underneath me?" He threw his head back in riotous laughter. "Mother, you never cease to amaze me."

"Don't be crude, dear; there's never an occasion for it."

"You brought the subject up, as I recall," he shot back. "Do give me credit—if for nothing else, at least for some measure of self-control. *Bedding the servants*. Bloody hell!"

"Who knows what sort of lewd perversions you've gotten up to with tarts in the navy?"

"Plenty!" he flashed. "But they weren't servants, and neither are any of my—never mind! I wish Nelson were alive. I'd dearly love to see you take him to task over the bedchamber politics of the British fleet!" He rocked back on his heels again, this time convulsed in laughter.

"Well, the gel had to get the notion somewhere," his mother blustered, bristling.

"Not from me," he snapped. "When I hired her two years ago, it was for low-scale wages. I told her then, since she had no references to recommend her, that if she behaved herself and took her employment seriously, there might be an opportunity for advancement along the way. It was meant as an incentive. That was all, and if this whole conversation weren't so utterly ludicrous, I'd have quit the salon at the outset of it. Enough now! And, by the way, I'm in my thirties, Mother. You have no say in whom I choose to take to bed."

"You should be thinking about marriage and getting an heir instead of bedding the wenches. I haven't heard word one about that since you marched in here tracking up my clean floors—*don't* step on that carpet! Walk around."

"I intend to be about that as soon as Lady Lark is settled," he returned, dancing awkwardly around the edge of the fringed Aubusson rug he'd almost sullied. "I can't just dump her here and have you eat her alive, like you have done all the others in the past, now, can I? If you are in so much of a hurry to dandle grandchildren on your knee, behave yourself. You have a reputation, Mother; even Biddie was onto you—called you a witch, I'll be bound. You're fast becoming a laughingstock—a joke to be bruited about in society circles. I shudder to wonder what tales the servants have spread."

"I suppose you've warned Lark?"

"Quite so. It was only fair. I could hardly have her here on false pretenses."

"And she came on anyway," his mother mused.

"She did. I do believe she'd have agreed to take a position in hell itself to get shot of that dung heap of a prison. But she doesn't impress me as the sort to stay where she is mistreated; a word to the wise. She was set upon in there, you know—Westerfield's younger son, interned for debt and vagrancy. I called the blighter out."

"Set upon? How set upon?"

"He deliberately put her in his debt for favors, then tried to collect. I shan't go into the details. Suffice it to say that she handled herself like a lady, and I put Westie in his place. If he ever gets out of there, we shall finish it."

"Speaking of that place, you haven't answered my question in regard to Lark's abigail."

"Mrs. Garwood is quite well to pass. She was a milliner in Shropshire before her husband passed on and she lost her shop three years ago. She was interned for debt. As I have it, half the *ton* is parading about Town in bonnets she has crafted in that place trying to pay off the debt, which harkens back to my earlier comment—'how fickle are the ton.' Believe me, she'd have been shut up in there forever. She showed kindness to Lady Lark during the brief time she was incarcerated, and they became friends. Taking her on seemed the obvious solution for them both."

"And this Mrs. Garwood didn't mind lowering her social standing?"

"Not a whit, she was that grateful. And I daresay she hasn't strayed out of character since."

"Mmmm," the countess mused.

"May I go now, Mother? I itch, my feet are squishing, I have mud down my neck clear to my drawers—front and back—and Frith drew my bath over an hour ago. It should be pleasantly cold by now for all this gibble-gabble. You should be abed yourself. You'll be cross as two sticks tomorrow, for not having rested properly."

"Not quite yet," she said. "Two things first . . ."

He thrust out his chin in anticipation. All things considered, he'd gotten off relatively unscathed, and he was anxious to be away.

"What is this highwayman business? You glossed over that nicely earlier. Explain."

His posture collapsed. "It was Will Bowles, Mother," he said.

"I see. Taken to the highway now, has he? Smuggling wasn't enough for him?"

"I will speak with him."

"You had better. I won't have scandal brought down upon Grayshire. Not like the old days, when your father—"

"Don't raise the dead! I said I would speak with him."

"Not 'with' him, *to* him, dear, or I shall. That one has never known his place."

"He has always known it all too well," King said in a low mutter. Whether she heard or not, his mother failed to respond, continuing to study him, her eyes like mercury, all-seeing and immutable, which was why he only studied them briefly in furtive glances. Who knew but that too much of her otherworldly stare might turn a body to stone, like Medusa, or the mine-dwelling gnomes in the fairy tales of his cradle days. "May I go now?" he entreated dramatically.

"Just one more thing, dear," she said, sweet-voiced. The tone, and the look that accompanied it were her most dangerous tactics. "Do you intend to keep your . . . whatever you choose to call them, after you wed? I shall refrain from resorting to the crude vernacular."

"My mistresses . . . Cyprians . . . ladybirds?" he served. "I've never known you to either mince words or be at a loss for them, Mother. Speak plain." Truth to be told, he hadn't started all that up again since his return from service; not on a permanent basis, at any rate. Most of his former contacts for such alliances had taken permanent lovers, or disappeared from the Town scene by now. However, there was still one . . .

"Well, do you?" she prodded, jolting him out of his reverie.

"Probably," he said, his delivery succinct. Why shouldn't he shock her?

She nodded, giving a sharp rap of her cane on the carpet.

"What—no lecture? No interrogation?"

"No," she pronounced to his amazement, with no more emotion than she would have mustered addressing a list for the greengrocer. "You have told me just exactly what I wished to know."

Eight

Lark didn't go down to breakfast, nor was she expected. The countess had ordered a tray sent to her room, with a sealed missive inviting her to the drawing room midmorning, with directions. It took that long to prepare herself, with Agnes's able help, since her hands were all thumbs of a sudden, especially when it came to dressing her hair, which, thank Providence, had turned blond again. Agnes brushed the short crop of curls up from the nape of her neck, but for the tendrils that wouldn't cooperate, and held them in place with a blue grosgrain ribbon that utterly matched the blue muslin frock she decided upon for the looming interview. It was low cut, after the fashion, but that was soon addressed by the addition of a demure organdie chemisette of pristine white gathered in loose pleats about her throat. She was thankful that the Bond Street proprietress had the good sense to include several such accessories. They wouldn't do at supper, but worn now, after the sight she'd presented upon her arrival, at least the countess would not think her ill-bred, or worse yet, more ladybird than lady.

She would not mention that unfortunate first meeting. What was done could not be undone, and Lark was wise enough to know that profuse apologies or explanations would only make matters worse. It was a new day, with new opportunities, and she was determined if not to start out on the right foot, for that opportunity was clearly lost, to effect a quick changeover without breaking stride.

"There, then," Agnes cried, standing back from her

masterpiece after just having worked the finishing touches. "There's nothing to be done with the tendrils. They insist upon having their own way, but you'll do."

"Oh, Agnes," Lark murmured, addressing the abigail's reflection in the vanity mirror. "Mercy, I look . . . I look . . ."

"I'm glad you're that pleased."

"Pleased? I've never seen one of your bonnets, but you could certainly have made your way dressing hair." She got up from the vanity and drew a deep breath. "Wish me luck," she said, squaring her posture.

"Oh, la, you don't need luck, though I wish it. Just remember who you are, and don't take any nonsense from the old peahen."

Lark laughed. "Now you've done it," she said. "Every time I look at her, I'll see a strutting peahen. Outstanding!"

They both burst into giggles at that, and it wasn't until Lark had nearly reached the drawing room that she sobered. Squaring her posture, she smoothed her frock and floated through the arch quite composed.

The countess wasn't alone; Peal was with her. She was seated at a small rosewood escritoire, affixing a missive with a glob of red sealing wax, which she handed, still warm, to the hovering first footman.

"Forgive me, my lady. I didn't know you were engaged," Lark murmured, turning to go.

"No, no, come!" said the countess, waving the footman off with a flutter of her lace-gloved hand. "That missive is to be posted at once, Peal," she charged. "No dallying. Have it taken to the village straightaway. I want it off on the evening coach."

"Very good, my lady," said the footman, set into motion.

"Take a seat, my dear," the countess offered, sweeping her arm toward a blue jacquard and rosewood lounge. While Lark did as she was bidden, the older woman rose from the escritoire, took up her cane and settled in a Chippendale chair opposite, arms outstretched, leaning her wrinkled hands on the handle of the cane in what

Lark was soon to recognize as her signature pose. "My son was absolutely correct," she observed, "you have 'cleaned up' quite nicely. Have you forgiven him?"

"I beg your pardon?"

"Come, come, I saw the look you gave him last night. Has he . . . misbehaved himself?"

"Your son has conducted himself as a perfect gentleman, your ladyship," Lark responded. Reliving the strange sensation his touch had aroused when he took bold liberties cleaning her face with that handkerchief, she just knew her cheeks were beet red; they were on fire.

"Hmmm," the countess said, clearly unconvinced.

"We had a rather difficult journey," Lark explained.

"He might have stopped off somewhere and let you freshen up," the countess opined, "rather than presenting you to me like a ragamuffin."

"No," Lark said. "He offered, of course, but I bade him drive straight through."

"Then why that look?"

Lark hesitated. There was no more speculation. The heat radiating from her cheeks had narrowed her eyes. She *had* to have blushed crimson. She couldn't very well answer the woman's question truthfully. But then, her blush would already have damned her. One glance in the countess's direction proved her theory: She was caught out. But she wasn't about to admit it.

"I was . . . overset from exhaustion," she said through an unsteady quaver of voice.

"Mmmm," said the countess, changing her position and the subject seamlessly. "We shall leave that for now, and take up the question of protocol. You shall address me as 'Lady Isobel', or 'my lady,' whichever suits the occasion. 'Your ladyship' is far too formal. I shall call you 'Lark.' You see, you might say that I have already made your acquaintance. I knew you before you were born. We met while your dear mother was increasing. A pity you never knew her, dear. You are very like her.

"You and my son will work out your own protocol between you. However you choose to address each other, I prefer that it be casual, despite the dictates of the *ton* on proper forms of address. I refuse to be manipulated thus. I have always been a trendsetter in these areas, hardly a follower. By now, it is expected of me. This is a family, after all, and I wish our arrangement to reflect that sort of intimacy. I may as well warn you, he detests 'Basil.' I use it to maintain authority. He much prefers to be called 'King.' He considers it more . . . masculine. Everyone else living seems to agree, though I believe his great-grandfather, Basil Sebastian Kingston, would take a different view were he not in his grave."

"As you wish, my lady."

"Now then, you have met my son's soon-to-be intended. What do you think of Lady Ann Cuthbertson?"

"I really haven't formed an opinion, my lady, nor do I consider myself qualified—"

"Balderdash! You are equals. You met the gel. What is your opinion? I shall give you time to consider your answer."

The countess wiggled her cane into position, and settled herself for a long-term wait. There was no way around it; the woman had a maddening penchant for putting people on the spot. This was some sort of baptism by fire, and she'd nearly passed through it unscathed . . . but not quite. Here was one question she hadn't prepared for. Why her opinion should matter, Lark couldn't fathom. She certainly couldn't say what she really thought—that the earl would likely stray if he married the woman. Lady Ann wasn't his intellectual equal, and she was rather frail-looking to make a good breeder, if getting an heir was his primary objective. But then, Lark was hardly a surgeon to make such an assessment. She was, however, on the spot to make a judgment—Providence alone knew why—and so she decided upon a diplomatic tack.

"Well?" the countess prompted. "That should be time sufficient."

"I found her quite well to pass, my lady," Lark said noncommittally.

"Yes, yes, I'm sure you did. But what did you really think? Come, come, this is hardly a difficult question. I want your personal opinion."

"With all due respect, Lady Isobel, my personal opinion . . . is personal."

"Well done!" the countess erupted, with a sharp tap of her cane on the Persian carpet that managed to resound on the floor beneath. "Without answering, you have answered me precisely. You've also drawn the line, and rightly so. Becoming my companion by no means dictates that you compromise your integrity. Your personal opinions, of course, are your own, without fear of reprimand. If, however, the time should come that you might wish to share them . . ."

Lark didn't much like being tricked, but there it was. She was decidedly no match for the countess, and yet, intimidating though the woman was, she genuinely liked her. And so, though curiosity could well prove to be her undoing—it was her most grievous fault after all—Lark couldn't resist.

"Why did you ask me, my lady? I shouldn't think my opinion would matter."

"Oh, it doesn't. I've already made my mind up," the countess replied.

"Certainly not out of hand, my lady?" Lark breathed. "You do mean to—"

"Give her a chance? Of course, but that shan't alter my opinion. All is as clear as the crystal in that cabinet." She gestured with her cane. "To me, at any rate."

"You've lost me, my lady," Lark said through a lighthearted laugh. "It seems quite the muddle to me."

"I think we shall get on nicely, you and I," the countess said, shifting the subject again with another sharp tap of her cane. "We shall ease you into your duties gradually.

Take the next few days to accustom yourself with the Manor, and settle in. You found the drawing room easily enough with my brief directions. Browse yourself, or ask the servants. Any and all will be more than happy to show you about. You will join us in the breakfast room each morning, and again for nuncheon, and in the dining hall for the evening meal, dressed appropriately. We are formal here."

"Of course, Lady Isobel. Thank you."

"I shall interview your abigail, of course, but that is just a formality. I am sure she is quite acceptable. There is one thing, however . . . While you are certainly free to explore Grayshire, I must insist that you not leave the confines of the estate unchaperoned. I do not want to alarm you, but it simply isn't safe. There are too many scoundrels about the coast these days. Mrs. Garwood alone will not suffice on such outings. You shall need a male chaperone outside the gates—my son, Leander Markham, his steward, whom you will meet tonight at dinner, or any of the footmen will suit. And now," the woman concluded abruptly with another sharp tap of her cane, not giving Lark a chance to reply, "let us have a good, old-fashioned chitchat."

King took advantage of his mother's interview with Lark to absent himself from the Manor. He set out right after breakfast astride Eclipse, his favorite thoroughbred stallion. Dismayed that the sleek black animal was in dire need of exercise, he headed—albeit by way of a detour along the strand—in the direction of the Bowles croft in the shadow of a long-abandoned tin mine on the moor just north of Polperro. Glad of the freedom, both man and horse became one with the land, with the salt-laced wind. For an all too short space of time, they moved as one being along the shore, churning up hard-packed sand beneath creaming surf, so cold in autumn. The spray pelted his buckskins and Hessians; they were soaked by the time he turned the horse onto the marshes that they both knew well enough to avoid the patches of deadly quicksand. Then finally up over firmer grasslands to the tousled moor beyond, and the neat little thatch-roofed cottage that hadn't changed in ten long years. It was as though he'd never been away.

He was almost sorry when he reached it; his freedom was too short-lived. He slowed Eclipse's pace from a gallop to a canter, to a trot, to a prancing, shying walk. The horse snorted, puffing visible breath from flared nostrils, and tossed his head, spreading his mane on the wind, making jingling music as the tack metal clacked together. King reached to stroke the animal's lathered neck, and whispered softly in his ear—low, soothing murmurs of affectionate appreciation for such a fine ride, for the rippling, muscular horseflesh beneath him that anticipated his every move and hadn't forgotten him. He reined the horse alongside the cottage gate, slid from his back, and tethered him to the fence post.

He'd scarcely addressed the door with his knuckles when it came open in the hand of a middle-aged woman with hair the color of summer wheat scarcely touched by gray. Slender, and shapely still, he might have taken her for someone much younger if he didn't know who she was. Her faded eyes, like cornflowers in the mist, trembled at first, and her breath caught with recognition.

"Mattie," he said, doffing his beaver. "Is Will about?"

"H-he's in the mine, my lord," she stammered. "I didn't know you'd returned."

"Thank you," he said, tipping his hat again as he spun on his heels. "I am just come home again," he said over his shoulder. "It's good to be back." Then, bounding over the crushed shell walk, he swung himself up on Eclipse and made his escape.

It was always awkward facing Mattie Bowles, his father's longtime mistress and the mother of Will, his father's bastard son, ten years his junior. Oddly, facing Will had never been awkward or difficult until last night in the rain on Dartmoor, staring down the barrels of Will's pistols.

The marked difference in age between Mattie and his mother had always been jarring. Mattie was nearly twenty years younger. He always stopped just short of trying to analyze his feelings over that coil. It didn't matter anymore. His father was dead—drowned, of all improbable things. He knew his mother's mind in the matter, but he'd never let her hold sway over him in regard to Will. They were, and always would be, brothers. That, however, did not mean a dressing down wasn't in order.

Dismounting at the abandoned mine, he tethered Eclipse to a clump of bracken by the dilapidated engine house and tall, tapered chimney shaft. Entering in, he followed a feeble flicker of light from a hanging lantern to the rickety ladder that led to the shaft below, two hundred and thirty fathoms into the craggy earth at the edge of the moor. Another faint glow emanated from it, and he shook his head and breathed a nasal sigh. Only Will would be daring—or stupid—enough to brave that antiquated collection of ladders that led to what had once been the core of the lode, long since depleted now, and all the more unstable from disuse.

What to do? He dared not call out, for fear the vibration of sound might cause the shaft to collapse in on itself—and on Will. And he dared not descend and surprise him into using one of the pistols he was sure to have at the ready, which would certainly collapse the deuced thing and bury them both. He paced for a moment, tugging at his gloves, then picked up a handful of pebbles from the engine house floor, and dropped them down the shaft at precise intervals—three, then a pause, then one, then a pause, then three more, the way he used to do. How could he have forgotten? Now all he had to hope for was that Will hadn't gone all the way to the bottom to hide whatever he'd robbed on the highway last night.

It was several minutes before the ladder began to

shimmy in the open shaft, and Will Bowles finally poked his head over the edge. King strode to the opening and handed him up to level ground.

"Damn it, King, I'm sorry!" Will blurted. "If I'd know it was you—"

"I ought to draw your cork!" King snapped. "If you're so determined to defy the law, you need to stick to the trade and stay off the highway; you're no good at it."

"I didn't know you were back," said Will, clapping him on the shoulder. He ground out a guttural chuckle. "I thought you were staying in London awhile. I nearly fell off old Gideon when you got out of that coach."

"Didn't you recognize Frith?"

"No, I did not, all got up in a slicker against the rain. Besides, once they tossed down their weapons up top, I was concentrating on what was going on inside the coach. Who were the birds? Are you importing them now? Hazel will be crushed."

"Is she still . . . unattached?" King probed, recalling the flame-haired Gypsy and one-time lover of his youth.

"No, but since when has that stopped you? She married Captain Jim Helston just after you left for Town six months ago, and moved into his place up at Fowey. He's off at sea most of the time. I'll wager she'd be glad of a visit. Unless you'd rather cock a leg over the birds you brought with you."

"They aren't 'birds.' The ladies you saw in my carriage were Lady Lark Eddington, my mother's new companion, and her abigail."

"Is the countess ailing, then? I haven't heard of it."

"No, I'm soon to be married, and Mother will be moving to the dower house. She'll need a companion."

"Ah! Mama will be glad of that. You'll be in charge. She has always been afraid the countess would run us off. She's threatened it often enough."

"Never while I live. You know that."

Will raked his hand through his tousled, sun-bleached

hair. "I know you never would," he said, "but the count-ess . . . well, we haven't drawn an easy breath since Fa-ther—"

"We've gotten off the track," said King, yanking Will closer with a hand fisted in his shirtfront. "You stay off the highway, do you hear? Frith recognized you last night, else we wouldn't be having this conversation. He's an excellent shot. *I* wouldn't have known you from Henry Pilson's heifer if I hadn't spent a month at the Manor before I went off to Town after they mustered me out. You were only twelve years old when I went off to war. I never would have recog-nized you if I hadn't seen you grown, and I would have picked you off like the sitting duck you were. I held the record at Manton's Gallery for two years running before I joined the navy. But that's neither here nor there—you won't have time to play thatch-gallows. The Crown has commissioned the *Cormorant*. I'm going to need your help. Is this damned mine still a viable place for storage? It doesn't look it."

"Depends. What are you planning on bringing in?"

"I don't know yet. Whatever we catch."

" 'We'?"

"We," the earl parroted.

"She'll hold whatever we can carry down on our backs," said Will.

"And still no one is the wiser? It's hard to believe that someone hasn't caught on in all this time. Father was us-ing this mine for storage long before you were born."

"Nobody comes way out here now. It's too far to haul booty. Besides, they're afraid she'll collapse. There was talk of bringing her down a while ago, but that petered out. Not enough manpower, what with so many plying the trade. Everybody uses the caves down 'round Colors Cove, Shag Rock, and Chapel Cliff now; there's a regular net-work of hiding places strung out all along the coast, and the privateers pay off the land guards."

"Good God! That won't be safe much longer. They'll

need a new hiding place—one above suspicion, and this mine is too risky, too obvious. We need to talk, Will, but not here—out on the open moor where we aren't likely to be overheard. Come."

King took a shorter route returning to the Manor. It was well past nuncheon, and he toyed with the idea of paying a visit to Hazel Helston, nee Potts. A brisk wind was blowing northward from the sea, and he licked the salt from his lips, remembering the salt-drenched days of his reckless youth, lying naked in a certain cave in Colors Cove, immersed in willing flesh. He squinted skyward, judging the hour from the position of the sun. No, there wouldn't be time. Captain Jim's house was a good league to the west, and Grayshire Manor was equidistant in the opposite direction. He'd never make it back in time for dinner. That luxury would have to wait for another time. Once things were settled. Once he was wed. Once he'd done his duty and gotten an heir to succeed him. How callous that sounded; yet there it was, his agenda, hauled out in the bright light of day. He was becoming his father, and it sickened him.

No, he would not probe the mixed emotions of that— of his feelings for Will, and his father's whore, as he always thought of Mattie Bowles to ward off jealousy, to beat back a secret wish to trade places with his half-brother and cancel the shame of disloyalty to his mother that such thoughts brought to bear. He tried instead to conjure pleasant visions of the comely Hazel Helston, of toothsome breasts and milk-white thighs, her flame-haired coloring. He tried to imagine her moving underneath him, taking him deeper and deeper, undulating to the rhythm of his thrusts, cooing contentedly, calling his name. But something kept getting in the way—another vision, of soft blond ringlets he ached to touch, of a provocative mole at the curve of an ample span of cleavage. Was that mole real or contrived? He hadn't yet discovered. He could only imagine what lay beneath, and how it would feel in his naked embrace.

There wasn't a rose in sight, yet his nostrils filled with the scent of attar of roses. Something stirred in his loins, but it wasn't just arousal that set the blood racing through his veins, it was the accompanying surge of adrenaline that all but crippled him. He shook his head to clear the images. They had no right to be there—no right to meddle with his perfect plan for an acceptable future. Maybe he should pay a visit to Hazel. He hadn't satisfied his urges in some time. Maybe that was the trouble. He was aroused now, but it wasn't Hazel's image, or any of the others from his past that had caused it. That frightened him, and he cursed the air blue in a spate of expletives he hadn't invoked since his navy days, and kneed Eclipse into a gallop toward home.

Nine

Lark wore periwinkle blue silk voile to dinner. The neckline was lower than she deemed proper, but that was her personal opinion. It was quite beyond reproach fashion-wise. She had no jewelry to detract from the provocative décolleté, and Agnes had suggested a bit of ribbon worn choker fashion, but Lark rejected the idea. It would look like just what it was; a substitute for what she lacked, and a poor one at that.

Gathered in the drawing room beforehand were Grayshire, the countess, and Leander Markham, the earl's steward, an attractive, fair-haired man in his midthirties with laughing brown eyes and a congenial manner. If it hadn't been for the earl's irascible scowl, she would have been at ease. When dinner was announced, Grayshire escorted his mother into the vast dining hall while Leander Markham handed Lark through the arch and seated her.

Footmen in indigo and gold livery began presenting the courses arranged on the buffet for the countess's inspection, commencing with julienne soup, to be followed by lobster rissoles, *canards à la rouennaise*, and mutton cutlets. Lark knew she was being scrutinized; she had expected it. But the earl's riveting one-eyed gaze fixed upon the only area of her person that made her self-conscious threatened her composure. Why did the man have to stare so? And why did that mysterious-looking eye patch make his obsidian gaze seem so seductive . . . and sensuous?

"Well, Lee, how do we stand?" he said, breaking the awful silence so abruptly that Lark gave a start in spite of her resolve. "Are we rolled up yet, thanks to Mother's philanthropic . . . enterprises, or just swimming at low tide?"

"Basil!" The countess seethed, dealing the parquetry a blow with her cane that echoed through the long, rectangular room. Lark noticed that a bracket was affixed to her chair to hold the cane, while also letting it ride freely enough to be effective as it was now. "Our financial affairs are hardly a suitable topic for dinner table discourse."

"You have no sense of humor, Mother," he retorted.

"I fail to see anything humorous in such childish behavior. You may take up estate affairs with Leander at an appropriate time in an appropriate place."

"When might that be, Mother?" Grayshire persisted. "Your itinerary for me over the next sennight hardly leaves time to visit the water closet."

"*Enough*," the countess barked, punctuating the word with another bang of her cane. "You are not too old at thirty-three to be sent from the table. What can you be thinking of, in front of Lark?"

"Do forgive me, Lady Lark, I humbly apologize," the earl responded with a flourish. "It's the wine, to be sure. I've either had too much or not enough. We shall leave that for Mother to determine."

"We'll take our brandy in the study instead of the library after dinner, and I'll fill you in," Leander offered. "My itinerary is just as formidable, I'll be bound. We shall be as two ships passing in the channel for at least a fortnight, I'm afraid."

His voice chiming in was like balm on a blistering burn, even the tone of it was soothing, and Lark was profoundly grateful. Whatever the earl's problem was, it seemed to revolve around her, and she couldn't fathom why. After a moment of deathly silence, the countess relinquished her cane to the bracket again, took up knife and fork with her beringed fingers, and commenced to address her lobster.

Lark studied the countess over her wineglass. She was

regal in mauve watered silk, dripping amethysts and diamonds. She even wore a diamond tiara perched on her flawlessly coifed head. Once or twice their eyes met over the course of the meal, and though Lark was embarrassed at having been caught staring, the look in those eyes twinkled with some secret knowledge that, while not threatening in any way, certainly put her on her guard. There was just too much smug satisfaction in it. What was the woman up to?

The conversation was less inflammatory until the footmen removed the tablecloth and began setting out the sweet wines and desserts. They included a delectable assortment consisting of cherry compote, custard and apple tarts, and an elegant trifle made of rum-soaked sponge cake, fruit, and almond custard cream.

"How do you find the coast, my lady?" Leander said, selecting an apple tart dusted with vanilla sugar. "I understand you've never been before."

"I haven't seen enough of the coast to say as yet, Mr. Markham," she replied.

"'Lee,' please," he corrected jovially. "King's father and mine were . . . shipmates, you might say, and King and I have been fast friends since we were breeched. Why, we even got sent down from school together. All that and my head for figures landed me this posh situation."

"Lee," she allowed, smiling demurely.

"Which brings us to a topic that needs addressing," the countess cut in, receiving a dish of trifle. "I prefer amenities to be casual between you and Lark, Basil. It is my wish that you address each other by your given names. Leander has taken the initiative. Kindly tell Lark how you wish to be addressed."

"She may call me however she will," he replied with a shrug, filling his crystal dessert glass with sweet wine. "I shan't be hereabouts much to be addressed in any case, and after the wedding, we shall see very little of each other."

"And how is that?" the countess said, her spoon suspended.

"Because you and Lark will be occupying the dower house," he blurted.

Even mild-mannered Leander seemed taken aback, as all eyes save the earl's converged upon the countess. Her color had heightened. She set her spoon aside, hands trembling with rage by the look of them, and gripped her serviette; for a moment Lark was certain she would toss it down in the trifle.

"You must be mad," she intoned, reaching for her spoon again.

"There can be only one Countess Grayshire," the earl reminded her. "You are fully aware of that, Mother. When I marry, my wife will become countess. You will become dowager countess, relinquish your chatelaine, and retire to the dower house. It is quite comfortable, and close enough for you to socialize on occasion without interfering with my wife's management of the estate."

"How dare you presume to put your mother out to pasture? How do you *dare*?" the countess shrilled. She surged to her feet and seized her cane, meanwhile tossing her serviette down, spattering the doomed trifle. Lark marveled that it hadn't happened sooner.

"What happened to Grandmama when you married Father, Mother?" the earl queried.

"That was different. Your grandmother was in her dotage—much older than I, and perfectly content to relinquish her chatelaine and bow out gracefully."

"No, Mother, you forced her out—a sick, old woman—protocol be damned! Now it is your turn. Why on earth do you think I engaged you a companion? As you say, you are hardly in your dotage. You have no plans to travel. It's hardly possible now at any rate, what with things as they are these days, and any servant in the house could have catered to your whims under this roof. Surely you knew this was coming."

Lark didn't know which way to direct her eyes. The gentlemen were on their feet now also. She was the only one seated, and the earl's bone-chilling narrow-eyed glance and inclined head warned her to remain that way. But when the countess spun on her heel, scarcely relying upon her cane as she marched stiff-backed from the dining hall, Lark rose as well, and followed her.

"You've got a death wish, I'll be bound," Leander said to King, handing him a poured brandy snifter.

They had repaired to the study, as the steward had suggested, but King wasn't in the mood for tackling the accounts. Nonetheless, he flopped in the horsehair wing chair beside the hearth that had been lit to chase the dampness, stretched out his long legs, and braced one of his Hessians on the andiron.

"Were you deliberately trying to embarrass the girl? That's what it seemed like. You didn't succeed if you were. She's a diamond of the first water, if ever I met one. Rarer still, she's a woman who knows when to speak and when to keep silent. I'm impressed. Where did you ever find her?"

"In the Marshalsea," King replied, and before he could stop himself, the whole tale came pouring out in an unbroken spate that left him breathless.

"Well, she's out of my league," Leander observed. "A pity she's titled, eh? There'd be no hardship on you, practically at the altar as it were."

"Be serious, Lee."

"I am!" the steward erupted.

King scowled. "If we're to do this, let's get on with it, eh?" He tossed back the brandy. "I'm not in the best of humors at present."

"Whatever possessed you to bring up the dower house? You should have known there'd be a brouhaha over it."

"Actually, I hoped to avoid that by addressing the issue in company. I didn't think Mother would make a scene before you and Lark."

Leander rocked back in laughter. "I'm about as visible to your mother as a dust mote. She doesn't 'see' the servants, King. All due respect, but she can't—she's too far above them."

"You're not a servant, Lee."

"Neither is Lady Lark Eddington, but you know what I mean."

"I'm well aware that Mother is a termagant. I know she drove Father into Mattie Bowles's arms years ago—drove him to his death, come down to it—but she is still my mother."

"She isn't going to sit still and let you evict her, King. I don't envy you. You're in for a fight. What sort is your betrothed? Will they suit?"

"Oh, they'll suit. Mother will love Ann; she'll not be competition. She's quite innocuous."

"You don't love her, do you?"

"What has that got to do with anything?"

"Have you proposed as yet?"

"No."

"Why not?"

"I want this settled here. Once I see that Mother and her new companion are getting on—"

"No. You need to rethink this marriage, King. If you are not in love with Lady Ann, and haven't proposed, you're under no obligation. Don't make your father's mistake. He was a man tormented. You weren't here at the last. You've no idea."

"You can lecture me another time," King said, rising to refill his snifter. "I wasn't just being flippant earlier; my agenda is staggering. We need to get down to the stuffy estate business at hand, and then perhaps you might advise me as to how to break the news to Mother that the Crown has licensed the *Cormorant* for privateering, with me at the helm."

The steward's jaw fell slack.

"That's right, my friend," King said to Leander's helpless stuttering. "We're right back in the trade."

* * *

Andrew Westerfield turned up his collar and braced himself against the blustery September wind whistling through the Marshalsea, which was stirring up the dust and lifting dead leaves in little whirlwinds off the courtyard floor. He could go inside, of course, but then he might miss the message he was expecting and have to pay garnish to the new turnkey to get it. Things weren't the same since Tobias was sacked. That was just one more thing he had against the Earl of Grayshire.

The post was due. It usually pulled up at about the time the new arrivals came on in the prison equipage from Old Bailey. It was a fortnight since he had the jailor post a missive to his father, begging him to satisfy the debt—*begging* him. Andrew Westerfield never begged—never—but he wasn't about to suffer another winter in the Marshalsea. Not while his illustrious father, the Earl of Stepton, had more money than Croesus.

The plan was to charm his father into buying him free, take whatever blunt the old reprobate would spare him, and disappear. He'd winter in Ireland, perhaps, "the urinal of the planets," as it had been dubbed, owing to the deuced rainfall there. No. Too wet, too dreary. The Channel Islands possibly, where the gambling hells were more civilized, and the women more provincial . . . more willing. Yes. That would suit very well, indeed.

He wasn't running from Grayshire. That threat held no sway over his plans save revenge. The truth was, he'd fleeced all his gambling chums on the coast. None among the old crowd would welcome him with open arms, which was why he'd moved his operation to Town in the first place—to find a new gudgeon willing to stake him. He'd set his sights on the most notorious amongst them, Malcolm Eddington, a baronet of some renown with a reputation in the hells as a formidable gamester, who might have kept him out of the Marshalsea if they'd teamed up as he'd planned, and the coward hadn't done for himself.

Andrew tugged his threadbare frock coat closer against the wind. The gusts were stronger, trapped in the confines of the Marshalsea walls, whistling between the dull stone buildings like trapped beings screaming to be set free. He couldn't blame them. Dust flew up in his face; his eyes smarted from it. Tending to that, he nearly missed the gates creaking open, but it wasn't the post. That had come and gone empty. It was the prison coach from Old Bailey. A girl climbed down, fending off the bailiff's helping hand with a vicious wrench, a buxom little fair-haired spitfire, to be sure.

Andrew Westerfield brightened at once. Here was a ripe little dalliance to pass the time while he waited for his father's missive. The blood was racing through his veins in anticipation, warming him. He turned down his collar, brushed off his coat, and straightened his posture. Hanging back in the doorway, he watched the turnkey herd her into the building next door. Was that a furtive glance? Sure as check. He doffed his dented beaver and bowed from the waist.

His hands were numb from the cold, and he rubbed them together, then cupped them around his mouth, and blew on them while he waited. After a time, the turnkey went about his business. Still he waited. It wouldn't do to appear too anxious—it wasn't as if there were any his equal among the interned who might threaten him with competition.

It wasn't long before his patience bore fruit. The girl entered the courtyard, her black twill skirts sweeping the arch of number three next door. He pushed himself off from the recessed doorway, straightened his posture, and sauntered nearer.

"Andrew Westerfield, at your service, miss," he said, doffing his beaver and bowing again, this time with a flourish. "Welcome to the Marshalsea."

"Hah!" she sneered, tossing her wheat-colored curls. "Some welcome! Did ya see? The bailiff fairly broke my arm, and the turnkey pinched my bottom!" She rubbed it, causing his hooded eyes to wander there, lingering expectantly.

"The devil you say?" he sympathized, prowling nearer.

"I'm no doxy, I'm a highly respectable lady's maid," she said, holding her head high, and preening.

"Of course you are, dear thing—anyone can see it. But I am at a disadvantage. You have my name, while I have yet to learn yours . . ."

"Bedelia Mead," she snapped. "'Biddie' ta you. All my friends call me Biddie."

"Biddie it is, then," he agreed, silky voiced. "And how have you come to this dreadful place, dear Biddie?"

"I pinched a bauble from my lady's vanity case. Only a small one. She had so many, I didn't think she'd miss a tiny little brooch like that."

"They put you in here for *that*? Couldn't you just have returned it?"

"I sold it, sir. It brought a pretty price, too, but I spent it all, and couldn't pay my way free. I'll be in here for the rest o' my life now and it's all *his* fault."

"Whose fault?" Andrew's mind was racing. A thief might be useful. He would, of course, have to teach her how to steal without getting caught.

"His lordship, the almighty Earl o' Grayshire, that's whose fault!"

"*Kingston?* How on earth does he fit into this?"

"Oh, he fits, all right. I worked for him for two years in that grand townhouse o' his—scrubbin' pots and floors and cobblestone steps, caterin' to his every demand, bowin' and scrapin' to that mother o' his whenever she was in Town. Then all at once he sacks me, without so much as a by-your-leave, for *nothing*. He says I was a mite too rough cleanin' up the little bird he fetched outta here to be his mama's companion. I was in line for that situation—*me!*" she snapped, tapping her chest with a scathing finger. "But no, he had to have his fine lady, queen o' the Marshalsea."

"I still don't see—"

"He wouldn't give me no reference, and I had ta take a position for less wages," she explained. "'Twas hardly enough ta get by on, so I stole the brooch, figurin' I could do that from time to time with nobody the wiser to make up the difference."

Andrew Westerfield licked his lips in anticipation of the sweet revenge he was plotting over the broken nose Grayshire had given him; it had spoiled his handsome face. Then, there was the matter of Lady Lark Eddington. He'd seen her first, and would have turned her head if Grayshire hadn't snatched her away.

He let Biddie ramble on for a time, scarcely aware of the content of her diatribe. What was she to him, after all, but the means to an end that offered a bit of bed sport along the way? But he needed to know more.

". . . and if the earl had been a decent sort and kept his word, none of it would have happened," she concluded, tugging her shawl close about her.

"Are you cold, dear thing?" he said, stripping off his jacket. He didn't wait for an answer but wrapped it about her shoulders. A bitter blast of air hit him and he shuddered, but he was proud of the move. It was a nice touch, and he smiled as she snuggled into the smelly, threadbare wool fouled with ripened summer sweat. How strange that he hadn't noticed the odor while he was wearing it. "Tell me, is the earl still in London?" he probed.

"No. He's gone back to the coast with his precious Lady Lark Eddington, so he can settle her all in with that dragon o' a mother o' his before he comes back and asks the Lady Ann Cuthbertson to marry him."

"Mmm," Westerfield hummed. "And the Lady Ann . . . she is staying on in Town, I take it, patiently awaiting his return?"

"Aye, she is that, and they can all go straight to Jericho— the lot o' them."

He slipped his arm around her shoulder. "Now, now, let's

not be too hasty, dear thing," he crooned, walking her along the narrow courtyard. "Stroll awhile with me—tell me all the on-dits you have to share about Lord Grayshire. I have a grudge against him as well, as it happens, and a score to settle that is long past due. If we were to join forces, as it were, and put our heads together over this, it might just be quite . . . profitable for us both."

She needed precious little coaxing and, the cold forgotten as he strolled with her in the most unlikely of places, he lent her his most sympathetic ear.

Ten

*T*he countess was well pleased with Lark's behavior during her first dinner at the Manor and wasted no time telling her so. Had Lark stayed behind in obedience to the earl's silent command, it would have put the kiss of death upon any relationship with the inimitable Lady Isobel, and Lark thanked Divine Providence that she'd had the good sense to make the right decision. Would it be that way every night in the dining hall, a battle of wits against Grayshire and his mother? If so, she was resigned to cry off in favor of a tray in her apartments whenever the earl was in residence.

What had she done to invoke his wrath? Why had he gone out of his way to embarrass her? It hadn't always been that way. He had been most gracious at the Marshalsea, and at the townhouse as well—the perfect gentleman. This new, offensive facet of his persona had surfaced on the journey to the coast, and blossomed when he introduced her to his mother soggy, disheveled, and plastered with mud. It was almost as if he derived some fiendish satisfaction from her debasement, and though she wracked her brain for a reason why, she could find none.

Breakfast passed without incident, and shortly after, they set out in the Grayshire barouche—Lark, Agnes, Lady Isobel, and the earl—on a jaunt to Plymouth to expand Lark's wardrobe and outfit Agnes.

The barouche was a slightly smaller, lower-perch conveyance than the brougham they had arrived in, which had been sent to the livery for the wheelwright to repair; therefore, the four sat in rather cramped quarters. To Lark's dismay, the countess engineered the seating arrangements, insisting that they sit opposite, so they could converse face-to-face during the day trip. Citing the earl's size, she complained that he would cramp her and ruin her frock, what with her cane and the leather satchel she always carried on trips that housed her medicines and toiletries. Lark suspected it was often used to take up space a-purpose, especially on a public coach, should an undesirable think to take a seat too close. The upshot was the countess dragged Agnes in beside her, and shooed the earl to the vacant seat on Lark's side. Though Lark scrunched so close to the coach wall that the hand strap banged her bonnet, she and Grayshire were still too close for comfort.

Lark tried to brace herself against the padded leather squabs in the corner, wishing they were plush velvet instead, like the ones in the brougham that might have held her more firmly. As it was, the smooth leather wouldn't let her get a grip, and each time the coach listed, she slid closer against the earl's firm, well-muscled thigh. As it was, on level ground, they were touching. She could feel his body heat through the folds of her white muslin frock, wishing she hadn't been so hasty in tossing her traveling dress into the dustbin. It might have been refurbished by now, the fabric was heavier, and there was no threat of another downpour today. There wasn't a cloud in the sky.

"Are you comfy, dear?" the countess inquired.

"Oh, quite," Lark assured her. Did her voice really crack? Judging from the earl's inquisitive expression, she didn't have to wonder.

"You seemed miles away just now," the countess purred. "Whatever were you air dreaming about?"

"The weather," Lark said. "I was thinking that in London now, I might be wearing twill and a pelerine to ward off the chill, instead of muslin and a spencer. The weather is phenomenal here on the coast."

"You'll get used to it," said the earl in his deep baritone. Coming from so close beside her, the sound resonated between them. Like ripples radiating from a pebble dropped in a stream of still water, the sound floated over her, causing the most amazing sensation—warm and cold, fire and ice. It raced along her spine, rushing through her loins in a most debilitating chill. Their thighs were still touching, and she stiffened against him. To her horror, his corded leg muscles responded. Hot blood rushed to her cheeks. Was he looking in her direction? She dared not venture a glance. She prayed not. She was blushing again. She always knew when she was blushing; her face was on fire. It was her most exasperating fault.

"It's an odd business, the Cornish climate," the countess drawled. "Compared to Town, it's like a mild February gone into a soft June out here. Strange mists often drift in off the sea year-round. They will miss one valley completely, and settle into the next as if they had the intelligence to choose. Basil has told you about the flaws, but I doubt he's mentioned the perverse drizzles that often set in for weeks on end, and Cornish fogs are strong enough to defy the wind. They simply drift and shift and blow about."

"Hush, Mother, you'll frighten them," the earl said through a chuckle.

"Be still, Basil," the countess admonished. "As I was saying, the fruits that are harvested in the east country won't ripen here till near Michaelmas. Why, you can pick primroses in January, and daffodils will bloom at the onset of February right along with the rhododendron. We are so diverse here that some fools refuse to acknowledge us as even being part of England at all."

"It sounds like a place enchanted," Lark mused, imagining fairy folk cavorting in ash groves and sleeping under fugitive mists on the moors—anything to take her mind off that long, lean leg pressed up against her no matter what she did to shrink from it. It was as though he had become glued to her side.

She stared through the eisenglass window toward the scenery zipping by: stacked-stone fences, pleasant groves of rowan and ash. Soft swaying meadows still wet with the morning dew gleamed gold beneath the rising sun. Then as the road sidled nearer the sea, came the flatlands, where the marshes and moors were carpeted with coarse bracken, furze, and black heather. Now and then trees appeared, their backs bent so low by the wind that the skeletal fingers of their twisted, leafless branches sometimes combed the ground. Ghosts seemed the only fit inhabitants for such tracts as these. The trouble was, they seemed more the rule than the exception, recalling graveyards, and spiked iron fences to mind. The sight soon drove her eyes away.

The pressure of the countess's cane against the toe of her Morrocco leather slipper caused her to jump, which triggered a reaction from the earl's muscular thigh pressed up against her. Meaning to grab the seat, Lark grabbed his leg instead, and jerked her hand away as though she'd lowered it on live coals, meanwhile muttering a breathless apology. It earned her nothing but a grunt in reply from Grayshire, and a much more articulate response from that deuced athletically muscled, black pantaloon-clad, perfectly turned thigh.

"Are you cold, dear?" the countess inquired. "You shuddered just a bit ago."

"Not in the least," Lark replied, aiming for composure, having visions of the earl stripping off his gray coat of superfine and wrapping it gallantly around her shoulders as he had in the wounded brougham. She was grappling with more physical contact with the man than she could handle as it was. Would the butterflies never vacate her stomach? "The view was a little . . . depressing," she explained. "I half expected one of Smythe's 'ghosties' to make an appearance."

"Are you afraid of ghosts, my lady?" the earl queried.

Why did the man have to talk? That deep, sensuous voice turned her bones to jelly.

"I cannot say, my lord," she replied. "I've never met one."

"We have several at the Manor," he told her. "Legend has it that Great-grandfather Basil's spirit roams the halls for one, though I have never had the pleasure of his acquaintance. It's just as well. I doubt he would approve of me forsaking his name. And then, the servants swear they've seen a ghost or two in the churchyard at St. Kevern's on occasion. We passed it leaving the estate just now, just inside the gate, did you notice?"

"I noticed it when we first arrived," she informed him.

"Ummm, in the dark? Astute of you," he mused. "Well, I must remember to inquire of the good Vicar Faulkner, and see if he has noticed anything untoward . . . or any headless horses, come to that, though I think the ghostly steeds are confined to Dartmoor."

"You're twigging me now, my lord," Lark said, braving a sidelong glance in his direction. The eye without the mysterious-looking patch was toward her, dilated black, and hooded seductively, the long dark lashes sweeping low in that scandalous provocative attitude. His barely parted lips had formed an irresistible lopsided smile that thrilled her to the core.

"Oh, no, my lady," he said. "It is all quite true, but don't take my word—ask anyone."

"Enough!" the countess trumpeted, banging her cane on the floorboards, causing Agnes to jump, and Lark to draw her feet back out of harm's way. "Basil, I *told* you it is my wish that you two address each other informally. I would prefer that you do so on all occasions, but if not then, at least in my presence. I hope I am making myself plain—to both of you—because I do not intend to repeat myself."

"Perfectly," the earl pronounced. " 'Lark' it shall be, then," he said, nodding toward her with a flourish. The sound of her name delivered in that throaty baritone took her breath away. But she wasn't about to yield to it.

"Basil," she responded deliberately, nodding in return.

" 'King,' " he corrected, wincing. "We mustn't take away Great-grandfather's reason for stalking the halls of Grayshire Manor." He delivered the last through a spooky shudder, bending too close for comfort, which caused Agnes's dark, round eyes to bulge, though the countess seemed satisfied. And the rest of the trip was passed, if not comfortably, more quietly, since Lark was in no great hurry to use his chosen name and he didn't seem anxious to address her in like manner, either.

The countess insisted that Lark's wardrobe take precedence, and they went at once to Royal Parade, a street rife with tearooms and establishments such as the linen draper, milliners, and the countess's favorite mantua maker, Madame Gerard. Agnes got Lark's ear, begging her not to buy bonnets from the milliner, but to purchase what was needed for Agnes to make them herself. Though the countess took a dim view of the suggestion, she finally agreed, as long as Lark could be persuaded to take her advice and agree to a beautiful bonnet of plum-colored velvet that she insisted would be striking against Lark's sun-painted ringlets. Once that standoff was resolved, King left the ladies in order to attend what he termed "Crown business" at the docks, much to Lark's relief. Though chaperones in such disreputable cities were mandatory, the last thing she wanted was King looking over her shoulder while she purchased her unmentionables. She would take her chances with cutpurses and brigands. Besides, she couldn't picture anyone attempting to accost the countess armed with her deadly cane, and almost laughed aloud imagining it.

They regrouped for a late nuncheon at the White Rose Coffee House, where Lark enjoyed delicate little hot rolls and slices of ham curled around soft cheddar. There were assorted breads, all freshly baked, savory chutneys, and French nougat cake for dessert. Afterward, the countess announced her agenda for outfitting Agnes "according to the dictates of her position," and again King cried off, requesting that Lark accompany him to the jeweler's establishment down the street, explaining that he would value her opinion on some pieces he was planning to buy for his intended, and possibly model a few to help him make up his mind. Lark opened her mouth to protest—helping him pick out his bride-to-be's jewelry was the last thing she wanted to do—but the countess chimed in and insisted, and there was nothing for it but to concede.

Lark thought that Lady Ann's wedding ring was to be among the earl's purchases, but it was not. Instead, he pored over cases of blue stones—zircon, sapphire, and several others that she wasn't familiar with. He discarded the zircon out of hand, studied the sapphire, and then took up a pair of earbobs in one of the stones unfamiliar to her. They were drops, a rather large blue stone in the center surrounded by diamonds set in filigree that seemed like burnished spun gold.

"What do you think?" he inquired, handing her one while he held the other up to her face.

"They are quite beautiful, my lord," she murmured, turning the stone this way and that to catch the light.

" 'King,' " he murmured.

"When your mother is present, my lord," she said, "and then only because I have no wish to suffer a drubbing with that dreadful cane of hers."

His brow pleated in a frown, he heaved a great sigh. "As you wish, my lady," he replied. "What do you think of the color?"

"I have never seen such a stone," she murmured. "What is it?"

"Iolite," he said. "Quite rare actually. It has been mined for centuries. As a matter of fact, the Vikings used to carry it on board their dragon ships as protection from drowning. Iolite amulets are said to protect sailors, even today."

"I suppose you should know," she said, handing it back to him, "being a naval officer, with such deep-rooted ties to the sea. It's quite lovely."

The shopkeeper cleared his voice. "If I may say, my lord, the color is an exact match to my lady's eyes—quite striking."

"Oh, they are not for me," Lark hastened to inform him, backing away from the counter as though it had suddenly burst into flame.

"O-oh, I see," said the little man, dropping his monocle. He was clearly embarrassed, fussing with his neckcloth. "Forgive me, I thought—"

"Have you a necklace to match these?" King inquired, handing the earbobs back to the man.

"Indeed I do, my lord," the shopkeeper gushed, passing a wrinkled handkerchief over his brow. It was plain he was relieved that he hadn't inadvertently scotched the sale. "Actually I have two, one rather more elaborate than the other." He snaked them both out of the case for King to view, and a bracelet as well. One of the necklaces was an exact match to the earbobs, having a number of identical drops falling from a filigree and diamond choker. The other was a larger, pear-shaped stone surrounded by diamonds, which King held up to Lark's throat to view.

She felt the heat radiating from his white-gloved hands, and instinctively backed away apace.

"I shan't strangle you with it, my lady," he said wryly. "I am only attempting to assess where the deuced thing will fall once it's on the neck. Open the spencer, and kindly hold still."

Lark did as he bade her and stood for him to fasten it around her neck. Her frock was cut rather low in front, and hot blood rushed to her cheeks as his eyes traveled to her décolleté. The moment seemed to go on forever before he unfastened the necklace and handed it back to the shopkeeper.

"I shall take both," he said to the man. "The earbobs and bracelet as well."

Lark resisted the urge to gasp, but when Grayshire asked the man to show him some pearls and some exquisite cameo jewelry, and elected to take those as well, her breath did catch. He'd spent a fortune.

She stole to a settee beside the wainscoting on the streetward wall, and took a seat there, waiting. Her heart sank inside, and she couldn't imagine why. She had never been a clotheshorse, nor had she been one to covet jewels. She'd sold ten times the jewelry he'd just purchased while trying to settle her father's debts—let it go gladly, without regret. No, it wasn't the jewels that had sparked jealousy. *Jealousy?* There it was; she'd admitted it. But she wasn't covetous of his purchases. The emotion was rooted in the way he'd introduced her to his mother, as though she were a common scullion—even if she had looked like one—unfit to wipe the feet of Lady Ann Cuthbertson. He had hurt her deeply making use of her as he did just now, showing her who she wasn't any longer and never could be again: a lady of social standing. She evidently still carried the stigma of the Marshalsea in his eyes, and always would. Why that should matter to her was becoming harder and harder to ignore . . . or deny.

After jotting down initials to be engraved on the center of a gold brooch he'd selected at the last, and passing the snippet of folded paper to the shopkeeper, King collected his purchases, instructed the man to have the brooch sent, and escorted Lark back along Royal Parade to rejoin Agnes and the countess. Then, after a sumptuous meal at the Royal Arms, a fine-dining establishment in the square, they set out again for Grayshire Manor.

The seating arrangements remained the same in the barouche, much to Lark's dismay, and so did her scandalous reaction to the King's closeness. *King.* She wouldn't give him the satisfaction of saying it; why couldn't she stop *thinking* it? Hot blood rushed to her temples. She was grateful that the light failed early in Cornwall. The darkness hid her burning cheeks from his obsidian stare. He hardly took his eyes from her the whole distance, and the few furtive glances she dared showed her a smug, satisfied countenance. No one else seemed to notice. Lady Isobel dozed after a time, and Agnes, who could barely contain herself in her ecstasy over the countess's generosity, finally quieted as well.

When the cane slipped in the countess's hand, King quickly and gently retrieved it without waking her, and handed it to Lark. She gave a violent lurch as it touched her, having given her full attention to the moonlit landscape flying past as the coach tooled along the highway.

"The 'dreadful' cane," he said, inclining his head toward her. "You may relax now that you have custody of it."

"I am quite relaxed, my lord," she said.

"I beg to differ," he opined. "You are strung as tightly as a fiddle bow. Have I offended you in some way? We seem to have lost . . . something."

"We never had anything to lose," she returned. "I believe you are imagining things, my lord."

"Lark . . ."

She opened her mouth to protest his use of her name, but the sound of it rolling off his tongue with such seductive resonance washed over her in mesmerizing waves that paralyzed her for a moment. It was the first time he had spoken it to her directly, and *how* he had spoken it. It was a caress, an embrace—no, a seduction.

"We agreed to be informal in Mother's presence," he reminded her, nodding toward the sleeping countess across the way. "No mention was made of her being in a conscious state."

"Oh!" she seethed. "You are . . . you are . . . insufferable!"

"So I have been told on numerous occasions," he said. "And you *are* angry with me. Am I to know why I have fallen from grace?"

"I'm sure I do not know what you mean," she replied.

He leaned closer. His heady masculine scent teased her nostrils: leather, pipe tobacco—which puzzled her, for she had yet to see him smoke a pipe—and the wine he'd drunk at dinner, married with his own tantalizing essence. All were heightened by the heat radiating from his body in the close confines of the coach. It was dizzying. In spite of herself, she inhaled deeply.

"You do," he contradicted, "and I cannot correct it if I do not know how it is that I've erred."

"There is nothing to correct, my lord," she intoned. She wanted to say, *I bent to your will and let you drive through, knowing how wretched I looked, to be presented to your mother, and instead of coming to my defense, you humiliated me in a cruel and insensitive way. You embarrassed me with crude, inexcusable discourse at the dinner table, of all places. And today, you used me as you would a servant, putting me in my place, having me help you choose jewelry for the woman whom "no, no, I am certainly not," knowing that all such finery I once owned is now, through no fault of my own, lost to me.* "I am quite tired," she murmured instead. "You misread fatigue for anger, my lord. Everything has happened so quickly. I'm afraid I am quite overwhelmed."

"Will you not say it . . . just once?" he coaxed.

"Say what, my lord?"

"My name."

"No, I will not!" she snapped, taking firm hold of the cane and resisting the urge to bang it on the floorboards. What had she sunk to?

"One day you will," he murmured, his words like molten lava, hot and steamy, burning toward her, and then mercifully he said no more.

Eleven

K*ing kept his distance for nearly a fortnight after the trip to* Plymouth. Taking advantage of Lady Isobel's occupation accustoming Lark to her duties, he gathered his crew and put the *Cormorant* into service. It felt good to be at the helm again.

He hadn't told his mother that the Crown had licensed the fully armed cutter, a fast, single-masted, fore-and-aft rigged vessel that lived up to the reputation of its voracious namesake. There was no need for her to know; the fewer who did, the better his chances of success. Secrecy was tantamount to that, and the countess was not known for her discretion.

How much she actually knew about the trade, he wasn't certain, but he did know that she knew more than Frith gave her credit for. She certainly wouldn't approve of her son following in his father's footsteps and becoming heir to his benighted legacy of privateer—notorious captain of smugglers—albeit perfectly legal this time . . . as legal as privateering could be.

After rendezvousing with the *Hind* and presenting his Letter of Marque, he set out cruising the channel, and during that fortnight the *Cormorant* captured two French merchantmen. This was not achieved without cost, however, and the cutter was forced to put into port for repairs.

King had secretly hoped Lark would miss him during his absence. The two-week separation had made one thing painfully clear to him, though he'd known since Plymouth: He wanted her more than he had ever wanted any other woman in his life. Try though he did to exorcise her exquisite image from his mind, he could not. Nor could he forget the petal softness of her cheek beneath his roughened fingers, the mud spatter notwithstanding, or the searing jolt the touch of her hand on his bare wrist inflicted. Not to mention the brief blink of time when their cheeks touched as the listing brougham threw her into his arms. More recent and acute, there was the gentle pressure of her warm thigh leaning against his in the cramped barouche, and the riveting shock that had gripped his loins when she grabbed his leg, albeit by mistake. More than once at the oddest times—in the dead of night, in the thick of battle—the scent of attar of roses ghosted past his nostrils, when the smell of salt spray, tar, and sodden timbers should have done. Now, having reached Grayshire Manor, his heart was hammering in his breast, and his breath quickened like a schoolboy's in anticipation of seeing her again.

Did she harbor any such feelings toward him? Judging by the coldness that had come over her since they left London, he sincerely doubted it. That, of course, he recognized as his fault. He had punished her for his feelings—feelings for her that were not part of his plan. In fact, they threatened it. The insipid Lady Ann Cuthbertson was the ideal candidate for the life he had in store. Nevertheless, he was profoundly relieved that he hadn't yet proposed to her.

Lark's coldness was the very reason he hadn't given her the jewelry he'd purchased for her in Plymouth under the pretext of selecting pieces for his intended. He knew she wouldn't have gone with him if she'd known what he was planning. He had studied her at dinner that first night, seated beside his bejeweled mother, looking like the plucked chicken the countess had accused of in her lovely gown with not so much as a paste bauble to recommend her as nobility. It simply would not do. Besides, he needed to provide something to divert his eyes from the provocative mole on her breast. Since she had no jewelry of her own, he took it upon himself to remedy the situation, and he had his mother's full approval, since, of course, they would be entertaining, and dressing the part was positively de rigueur. All that remained was to persuade Lark to accept the jewels. Judging from her behavior of late, things did not bode well.

He went at once to the parlor, expecting to find her there with the countess at midafternoon. To his surprise, he found his mother alone, working on her needlepoint, and pulled up short in the doorway.

"Well!" Lady Isobel gushed, laying the needlework aside. "How nice of you to grace us with your presence, Basil. Where have you been these past weeks, might I inquire?"

"Taking care of business, Mother," he returned, strolling into the room.

"That is what we have Leander for, dear."

"Yes, well, there are some aspects of the family business that require my personal touch."

"Like that shameless Hazel Helston person, I presume? Really, Basil, you defile your own body, whoring about with the likes of that one on the eve of your betrothal. You might at least practice restraint until after the wedding. You are just like your father—no more finesse than a ram in rut."

"Stubble it, Mother," he said in an undervoice, glancing about, half-expecting Lark to materialize out of thin air and overhear. If truth were told, he had given a visit to Hazel's passing thought. Her husband was at sea, after all. He knew she would welcome him with open arms, only too willing to slake his lusts, and his libido had been charged for some time—since he'd met Lark Eddington, come down to it. No. He wouldn't settle for less—not this time, and that lightning strike awakened him to the plain and simple fact that he was falling in love, frightening though that prospect was. Frightening because, while he was well skilled in the art of making love, he had yet to find himself *in* love . . . until now. "I have not been to see

Hazel, not that it's any of your affair. But if you drive me out of the house with your incessant nonsense—"

"Are you threatening me, Basil?" she shrilled.

"Nothing threatens you, Mother," he served, "but I am warning you that unless you want to drive me away, you might want to reconsider alienating me with the first word that passes between us at each encounter. Where is Lark? Or have you driven her from the house as well?"

"Lark is out riding."

"Riding?" he erupted. "Where? How, riding? Surely not alone?"

"She is riding Toffee. I have made the mare available to her. She quite enjoys riding about the estate during her free time."

"Alone? Mother, have you gone senile?"

"Calm down, Basil. The girl has an excellent seat. It isn't as though she is a novice. Her father did keep stables, you know. Why, the man owned more horses than we do. She sat her first horse when she was five, and that sorrel mare is as gentle as a lamb."

"But to let her go out alone! Suppose she—"

"We are gated, Basil. Where is she going to go?"

"I don't want her going off unescorted. It's just asking for trouble."

"Then stay home and accompany her. How dare you question my authority in this matter—or any matter? I am still chatelaine here. Once you've wed Lady Ann, and packed me off to the dower house, then you can lay down your own rules. Until that time comes, however, you will follow mine."

"I'm going to go and find her," he announced. Spinning on his heel, he stalked toward the door only to pull up just short of colliding with the first footman, Peal. "Good God, what is it, man?" he snapped, steadying him.

"The Lady Ann Cuthbertson and Comtesse Vera Arbonville Cuthbertson have arrived, my lord," said the footman.

"Good!" the countess called from behind. "Show them in, Peal, that I may greet them, and have their bags brought up to the yellow suite."

"Very good, my lady," the footman replied, bowing out.

"You are *expecting* them?" King murmured, incredulous. His jaw fell slack. "No! You've *invited* them? Mother! What have you done?"

"I have extended an invitation to your future bride, and her aunt, to come for a visit," she intoned. "What on earth could possibly be wrong with that?"

Lark hadn't known such freedom of body and spirit since the tragedy that impoverished her. The last thing she would have expected from the countess, given her reputation, was access to such a fine mount, much less time to ride her. There was no mistaking the woman's severity. She was a hard taskmistress, and, yes, a termagant, a trier of saints without a doubt, but Lark searched out the unhappy woman buried beneath the armor presented to the world, who seemed to want a daughter to dote on just as much as Lark wanted a mother figure in her life. Could she dare hope that such an arrangement might work? She did hope, but then there was King. There was no mistaking her feelings for him, either, which wasn't even logical considering the way she had been ill used by the insufferable clod. Like it or not, however, he had paid her fee. He had made her beholden to him. He had put her in his debt not unlike the way Andrew Westerfield had done. And while that left a bitter taste, she had no choice but to play with the cards she'd been dealt. Besides, an hour hadn't passed in the two long weeks of King's absence that she hadn't conjured his image from the very air, and relived the frightening sensations his closeness brought to bear.

Each day she rode a little farther on her outings, exploring the ash and rowan groves, the exquisite gardens and rolling manicured lawns. A maze of shaded lanes snaked their way through the estate, winding past stacked-stone fences, sculptured hedgerows, even a shallow beck that rambled through the forest, icy cold and singing musically as it flowed over beds of genuflecting cress, and moss-covered pebbles.

She visited the gardener's cottage, and introduced herself to Ben Higgins, and his wife, Abby, who, with the aid of their three grown sons, kept the estate raked and trimmed and scythed and planted to perfection. She shared her love of herb gardening with the Higginses, and convinced Ben to let her have a small patch in the kitchen garden and her very own plants to tend.

She visited the gamekeeper's cottage, where she met old Ned Wilkins, the gamekeeper. He was wary at first, but she soon charmed him as well, and she haunted the stables, soon forming a fond regard for the stabler, George Wellen, a bearded, white-haired man past sixty, with a mischievous twinkle in his clear blue eyes, who knew more about horses than anyone she had ever met.

She even found the dower house, flanked by a grove of trees and literally backed up against a high stone wall that marked the westernmost boundaries of the estate. It was a rambling three-story building, with an impressive court-yard and gardens that looked exactly like a smaller version of the Manor itself, albeit blatantly in exile.

The one place Lark avoided on her outings, however, was the little church just inside the east gate, with its shaded crop of crooked tombstones inside their spiked iron fence.

She was always conscious of the time when she was away from the house. It wouldn't do to abuse her privilege. Today, a stiff wind thick with the taste of salt turned her back early, and the first flurry of stinging raindrops began pelting down just as she reached the Manor. Anxious to let the countess know she had returned before going up to bathe and change for the evening meal, Lark walked at a brisk pace in the direction of the parlor, only to pull up short at the sound of raised voices audible from behind the closed doors, which had been open when she left. One could hardly call it eavesdropping; she was halted in the middle of the corridor, and one of those voices sent a crippling thrill through her body that rooted her to the spot. King had returned.

"Who gave you leave to invite them here without consulting me?" he thundered.

"Lower your voice, Basil! Do you want them to hear you?"

"I don't give a bloody damn if they do. You had no right to bring them all the way from Town for . . . for—"

"You are planning to ask for her hand, are you not?"

"Well . . . yes, but I haven't done as yet, and now you've forced the issue."

"What 'issue,' Basil? Either you are planning to ask Lady Ann to marry you, or you aren't. I have merely made it easier for you to press your suit. But, of course, if you want to trek back and forth to London . . ."

There was a deafening moment of silence, broken only by the hammering of Lark's heart, as she stood stock still, afraid to move and be heard, or stay and be caught out.

"I am not ready to press my suit here now," King growled at last. "There are . . . things afoot that you know nothing of, Mother, things that make such a commitment . . . impractical at this time. Bloody hell! How could you do this? Whatever possessed you?"

"What 'things,' dear? Do you imagine that I do not know what you have been about this past fortnight—what you've gotten up to? I lived with your father for thirty-five years, Basil. Do you imagine that I cannot smell the trade on you?"

"Mother, stay out of my life!" he roared.

"I thought you were anxious to marry and pack me off to the dower house," the countess retorted. "You can't have it all, Basil. I have every right to get to know your intended. I need to be certain that what I'm giving up is worth the price."

GET UP TO 4 FREE BOOKS!

You can have the best romance delivered to your door for less than what you'd pay in a bookstore or online. Sign up for one of our book clubs today, and we'll send you **FREE* BOOKS** just for trying it out...**with no obligation to buy, ever!**

HISTORICAL ROMANCE BOOK CLUB

Travel from the Scottish Highlands to the American West, the decadent ballrooms of Regency England to Viking ships. Your shipments will include authors such as CONNIE MASON, CASSIE EDWARDS, LYNSAY SANDS, LEIGH GREENWOOD, and many, many more.

LOVE SPELL BOOK CLUB

Bring a little magic into your life with the romances of Love Spell—fun contemporaries, paranormals, time-travels, futuristics, and more. Your shipments will include authors such as KATIE MACALISTER, SUSAN GRANT, NINA BANGS, SANDRA HILL, and more.

As a book club member you also receive the following special benefits:

- **30% OFF all orders through our website & telecenter!**
  (Plus, you still get 1 book FREE for every 5 books you buy!)
- **Exclusive access to special discounts!**
- **Convenient home delivery and 10 days to return any books you don't want to keep.**

There is no minimum number of books to buy, and you may cancel membership at any time. See back to sign up!

*Please include $2.00 for shipping and handling.

YES! ☐

Sign me up for the **Historical Romance Book Club** and send my TWO FREE BOOKS! If I choose to stay in the club, I will pay only $8.50* each month, a savings of $5.48!

YES! ☐

Sign me up for the **Love Spell Book Club** and send my TWO FREE BOOKS! If I choose to stay in the club, I will pay only $8.50* each month, a savings of $5.48!

NAME: _____

ADDRESS: _____

_____

TELEPHONE: _____

E-MAIL: _____

☐ **I WANT TO PAY BY CREDIT CARD.**

☐   ☐   ☐

ACCOUNT #: _____

EXPIRATION DATE: _____

SIGNATURE: _____

Send this card along with $2.00 shipping & handling for each club you wish to join, to:

Romance Book Clubs
1 Mechanic Street
Norwalk, CT 06850-3431

Or fax (must include credit card information!) to: 610.995.9274. You can also sign up online at www.dorchesterpub.com.

"And what say you, then? Does she pass muster?" he demanded, his anger palpable through the tall, gilded doors.

"How can you expect me to answer that with nothing but a five-minute greeting to make a judgment? Hah! You will propose in any case, no matter what my opinion."

"Then why the bloody hell did you invite them to Grayshire Manor?"

"For several reasons," she replied. "Firstly, there is an heir to be gotten here, or has that slipped your mind with all your 'things afoot'? That should be first and foremost on your agenda now, Basil. Since it obviously is not, then it has to be on mine. I want to go to my grave secure in the knowledge that my duty has been done. Secondly, I *will* make my assessment of the girl, and would of any girl you decided to wed. You know better than to oppose me in this."

"Are you threatening me, Mother?"

"Let us just say that it would behoove you to proceed with extreme caution."

"I am hardly a child in leading strings, to be slapped on the wrist with a measure."

"Then why are you acting like one? What about Lark? How could you go haring off and leave that unfinished? You should have settled the matter before you left, and given it time to mellow in your absence."

"You know why I didn't."

"Yes, but you've let too much time lapse. I am in agreement, but I shan't do it for you, if that's what you're waiting for, and it wants to be done *at once*."

"No one has asked you to," he growled. "But . . . now that you mention it, that may be the only way she'll—"

"Ohhhh, no!" the countess erupted. "You are many things, Basil Kingston—reckless, cavalier, imprudent . . . a rogue of your father's proportions without a doubt—but what you are not is a coward. I think you've finally met your match."

King's heavy footfalls, evidently pacing the floor inside,

reached Lark where she stood, and set her in motion. It would not do to be discovered witness to this conversation, and she fled to her third-floor suite on feet that scarcely touched the floor, while their raised voices still echoed through the halls. What could he possibly have to "settle" with her? She wished she could have stayed and learned more.

She burst in through her sitting room door, threw the bolt, and sagged against it. She had scarcely caught her breath when Agnes came rushing to meet her.

"Oh, la! I thought you'd never return," the woman gushed. "You won't believe the goings-on. The earl's bride-to-be and her aunt have come from London for a fortnight's stay, and the earl is livid. Why, you can hear him all over the Manor, except up here, of course, and in the west wing, where they've been given apartments. They've brought their servants—lady's maids, seamstress, and all. You can't imagine the brouhaha."

"How long has his lordship been back?"

"'Twas just an hour ago he arrived, and they came on right after. The servants' hall is buzzing, and Leander . . . I mean, Mr. Markham says we'd better batten down."

Lark ignored the "Leander," flagging it for future query; there was too much to be done with just three hours until the evening meal to get entangled in a new coil. Besides, her mind was occupied with the last part of the conversation she'd just overheard . . . the part pertaining to her. What could it all mean?

"I'll want a bath," she said, stripping off her bonnet, "and we shall have to find me something appropriate to wear down to dinner. I should let Lady Isobel know that I've returned, but they were arguing so fiercely down there . . ."

"Don't you worry," Agnes said, "Smeaton or one of the footmen will surely tell her. Let's get you ready."

Lark chose an ivory-colored twilled silk gown, with panels embroidered in silk ribbon forget-me-nots draped over the skirt to wear down to dinner. The décolleté was rather low, but that was the case with almost everything she'd bought, considering the fashion. The dainty puffed sleeves it sported redeemed it somewhat.

Agnes dressed Lark's hair with blue ribbons threaded through her upswept ringlets. Consulting the cheval glass, Lark's eyes filled with tears of gratitude over the countess's generosity in providing her with such an extensive wardrobe.

She shook off the emotion, and was just about to go down to the drawing room to join the others before dinner when a knock at her sitting room door pulled her up short, and she opened it to find King on the threshold, carrying a carved teakwood chest.

"My lady," he said, offering a shallow bow, the chest being in the way. "Might I have a word with you?"

"Yes?" she replied, making no move to stand aside and let him enter, though she was well aware that was exactly what he was suggesting. Her heart was literally leaping in her breast at the thought of him in her rooms.

"Might I step inside?" he queried. "It is quite proper, I assure you. I know Mrs. Garwood is close by."

"In my bedr—in the other room, yes, she is," Lark said, still not yielding ground.

"Then, there is no impropriety here. Please?" he entreated her, gesturing with a nod.

Lark considered. She didn't want this vision in her mind. There was something much too intimate about what would be, when she lay in her four-poster trying to exorcise his energy from her space, his shockingly male scent from her nostrils, that seductive obsidian stare from her mind. But it was already too late, and she breathed what she hoped was her most annoyed nasal sigh, and stepped aside for him to enter.

"I know this should have been attended to long ago, but I have just returned." He nodded toward the gateleg table as a likely spot to set his burden down. "May I?"

"What is this about, my lord?" she said, folding her arms and offering a reluctant nod toward the table.

He set the chest down, and rearranged the objects there to accommodate it.

"I was just preparing to go downstairs to dinner," she continued. "I do wish you'd get on with this. We have guests, I'm told, and I shouldn't want to keep the countess waiting."

"Yes, guests," he mumbled. "I know we have guests. Please bear with me, Lar"—she cast him a scathing glance—"my lady," he amended, opening the chest. "That's why I've come. You will need these before you go down."

Lark peered into the chest, and looked up, puzzled. "Lady Ann's jewels?" she said. "I don't understand. Why have you brought them here?"

"They aren't Lady Ann's . . . they are yours," he said flatly.

"*Mine?* How mine? I was with you when you purchased these. You made use of me rather boldly as I recall. I modeled them for you. You said—"

"I know what I said," he interrupted. "I knew if I told you the truth you would protest—"

"Protest?" She uttered a strangled sound. "I cannot accept these. Are you mad? Am I not deep enough in your debt already? What could you have been thinking?"

"Mother is in complete accord with—"

"Oh, no!" she cut in, wagging her head until tendrils crept out around her face. She swatted them back. "I think you'd best explain yourself, my lord."

"Very well," he said. Pulling himself up to his full height, he squared his posture and cleared his voice. How tall he was. How he towered over her—so close—*too* close. His body heat and evocative scent backed her up a pace, and still she had to bend her head back to meet his gaze. "That first night at dinner, I observed you next to Mother in all her glory, and I realized that you had no . . . adornments—not that you need them, you understand," he hastened to add. "Eh . . . what I mean to say . . . that is . . . oh, the devil take it! Mother called you a 'plucked chicken,' and that's just exactly what you looked like next to her without . . . without . . ."

"Oh!" she cried. "I never! *You* were responsible for the way I looked."

"Oh, no, not entirely," he defended. "You insisted upon vacating the coach in that downpour, and it was you who also insisted that I drive through. I offered to detour south to Plymouth to give you a chance to refresh yourself, if you recall."

"Halfheartedly, yes," she retorted, "and don't you dare to deny it."

"No, I shan't. I will admit that I wanted to drive through, but I did offer—"

"None of this has any bearing on what's in that case," she interrupted, her finger wagging toward it. "I cannot accept those jewels."

"You accepted your wardrobe," he reminded her.

"Yes, I had no choice. The clothes were a necessity, and I thanked your mother for her generosity, but this . . ."

"This is no different."

"Then why didn't you say that at the outset? Why was it done in secrecy, and why has it taken you until now to deliver . . . these, if it is 'no different'?" She waved her hand toward the chest again.

King's posture collapsed. "I had good intentions of dealing with this properly," he said, "but . . . after we arrived, your attitude toward me changed, and—"

"Indeed it did," she interrupted.

"—and I was afraid you would misconstrue my intentions and do exactly what you're doing now," he concluded with raised voice. "And you still won't say why?"

"If you don't know why, then you are a bigger clod than I give you credit for."

He threw his hands into the air. "All right," he said in

defeat, "you win! I'm a clod and a clunch and a rogue—
Mother would certainly agree with you on that last
point—but my intentions were nothing but honorable in
this. With your help, I selected jewels to complement *you*,
and your deuced wardrobe, that would see you through
your situation here in style. Mother entertains. You need
to look the part. Surely you know that."

"Oh, this was for your mother now?" Lark said, affecting
a deep nod. "How you do amaze me. Let me tell you what
I think, my lord. I think that if these were intended for
me, you would have given them to me then, without all
this subterfuge. You bought them for your betrothed-to-be.
You made that quite clear, and, yes, I would not have accompanied you if what you said earlier were so. Lady Ann,
for whatever reason, doesn't want them, and you cannot
return them; I saw the shopkeeper's sign. So you think to
foist them off upon me, which is a highly inappropriate
gesture to say the least."

"I have already told you, I had my mother's complete
approval in this."

"If that is so, then why has she never mentioned it—
offered them herself?"

"Because . . . because she thinks that it is my responsibility. You must have gathered that Mother and I tend to
clash at times. She can be very . . . stubborn."

"She loves you very much," Lark observed, her voice
softer.

It was purely a reflective observation. She hadn't meant
to shame him, though he did look painfully ashamed at
her words. He took a step closer. She could not escape his
advance without rearranging the furniture. He had backed
her up against the lounge. His gaze was riveting, roaming
over her hair, her face, her décolleté. His hands were fisted
at his sides, but not in anger; the way he worked them, it
almost seemed as though he had balled them into fists to
keep from touching her. Her heart leapt as he inched
closer still, stooping over her until his hot breath puffed

against her face. She was foxed by his closeness, too paralyzed to look away from that smoldering obsidian gaze,
much less flee from it. Was he going to kiss her? Mercy,
yes! She ducked under his arms as he raised them to embrace her. How could the man be making such an amorous
overture toward her with his intended right down the hall
in the opposite wing—not to mention Agnes in the bedchamber within hearing distance, since the adjoining door
was open between? Rogue, indeed! Jackanapes!

"Whether your mother approves of this or she doesn't
matters not," she said, reestablishing herself with the gateleg
table between them. "I would not have accepted these then,
and I do not accept them now." She crossed to the door,
which hadn't been closed all the way, and threw it wider still.
"If you will excuse me?" she said. "You have guests awaiting
you, and I am behindhand."

He strolled toward the door and stopped abreast of her.
"I want you to keep those jewels, and wear them. I want
you to wear them tonight."

"Well, we cannot always have what we want, now, can
we? I think we've had this conversation before, my lord. I
cannot accept the jewels. I will not wear the jewels tonight or any other night, no matter what you want. They
were not intended for me, and I believe you should follow
your original agenda, and give them to your intended."

The door closing on his body literally pushed the earl
into the hall. Lark locked and leaned against it, her posture collapsed against the polished, gilded wood.

That was it. He had gone beyond the beyond. Was he in
his altitudes? No, there had been no telltale odor of alco-
hol about him, only his distinctive male essence and the
ghost of a pleasant-smelling shaving paste. She glanced at
the open jewel chest he'd left behind, fingered the exquisite iolite necklaces, cameos, and pearls, and slammed the
lid shut. She would have Smeaton return them to
Grayshire at once.

With that decided, her way was clear. She would have

to abandon all hope of a home at Grayshire Manor, and a mother figure in her life that she had hoped for and felt she was achieving, for a genuine bond was indeed forming between herself and the countess; King had just put paid to that. It was suddenly all as clear as glass to her; he did have ulterior motives. Of course he meant to propose to Lady Ann, but Lark knew that the outlandish offering he'd just laid before her, and the shocking amorous advance that went with it, could mean only one thing: He actually had intentions of grooming her to become his Cyprian after he'd wed the innocuous socialite. It was unthinkable!

No, she could not stay. But there was dinner to be gotten through. She would not embarrass the countess before her guests. She saw that as her last obligation, however. She would speak with Lady Isobel in the morning and make some satisfactory arrangement to pay off her debt—even if it meant returning to the Marshalsea. With that decided and head held high, Lark straightened her disarray, squared her posture, and went down to dinner.

Twelve

Deuced female. Damn and blast! King had all he could do to keep from seizing Lark then and there and putting her over his knee. Instead, he dutifully threaded the Comtesse Vera Arbonville Cuthbertson's flabby arm through his own, taut—as his whole body was, with rage—and offered a closed-mouth smile over gritted teeth, and handed her through the dining hall arch. Leander Markham followed suit with the countess on his arm, while Lark and Lady Ann followed after.

They would be dining *à la russe*, each served individually by footmen from entrées arranged on the sideboard. Several of the leaves had been removed from the table to shorten it for a more intimate gathering. While the countess occupied the head of the table, the little silver wagon on wheels that contained decanters of claret, port, and Madeira, was passed by King from his left at the opposite end of the table. His mother's odd seating arrangement left much to be desired. He was flanked on the right by Lark and on the left by Lady Ann, while Lady Vera sat at the countess's right and Leander Markham on her left. The last thing he wanted then was to be sandwiched in between the two women who were causing all his woes.

The meal began with prawn bisque.

"It's so nice to see you again, Lady Lark," Lady Ann lisped cordially. "Are you enjoying it here on the coast?"

King wheeled the wine cart toward Lady Ann, who indicated a preference for claret, not taking his eyes from

Lark's flushed face as he poured. No. It wasn't his imagination; Lark was avoiding his gaze, which had strayed once again toward the provocative mole at the edge of her cleavage. Damned thing *was* real. Divine Providence was cruel indeed, painting that there where a man couldn't miss it. He shifted in his chair as his loins responded to that natural beauty spot, and the scent of attar of roses drifted toward him from her flushed skin. Had he caused that blush, or was anger responsible?

"It's quite . . . different from Town," Lark responded, "different from anything I've ever known."

Well done, my lady. You won't even give my land absolution. He saluted her with his wine glass and took a swallow, earning himself a stern look from his mother, which he ignored. He would have rather been at the helm of a sinking ship in that moment, knee-deep in bilge water—anywhere but at that table.

"That, I will agree with," the comtesse observed. "*Mon Dieu*, is it always so damp? And the *wind*."

"We are glad of the wind, and the damp, in exchange for a gentler climate," Lady Isobel said smoothly, though King didn't miss the grating delivery, or the clenched posture that accompanied it. "In Town now you would have need of twill, and woolen frocks, and your fur-trimmed pelisse."

"It is milder, I suppose," the comtesse conceded, "but the damp goes right through my bones." She shuddered in punctuation.

"That delightful accent," Leander Markham said, "is it from the south of France?"

"Bordeaux," Lady Vera replied, sipping her port. "This is not from our vineyards—too grainy, too sour."

"That, my lady, is Spanish contraband," said King for effect.

Collectively, his mother stared and fingered her cane propped against the table; an obvious warning. Leander Markham's jaw sagged open, Lady Vera bristled, and Lady

Ann gasped. Everyone's eyes were trained on him except Lark's. Hers were on her soup, and she finished it unmoved.

"Oh, I assure you it is all quite proper," King told them, "presented to me by the Admiralty after Trafalgar. You are drinking to a great victory and a great leader. I give you Lord Nelson, God rest him." Glimpsing the comtesse's pursed mouth and rigid posture jogged his addled brain into remembering whom Lord Nelson had defeated on that auspicious occasion. Oh well, too late now. He wasn't even mildly repentant.

"Hear, hear!" Leander Markham cheered, saluting with his glass. The wine wagon had reached him, and after re-filling his own glass, he moved it on and poured claret in Lark's.

That got a rise from her. Her hand shot out to cover the goblet, but returned to her lap just as quickly. It would have been rude to refuse.

"To Lord Nelson—all!" King invited, holding his glass high that there be no mistake. She would drink from hers now, by God, if he had any say. She may want to insult him, but unless he missed his guess—and when it came to women he rarely did—she would not allow Lord Nelson to bear insult. The only one at the table set on that was the comtesse.

Lark lifted her glass and moistened her lips with the stingiest sip he had ever witnessed. It was all he could do to keep from bursting into laughter. Instead, he choked on his port.

"Are you feeling poorly, my lady?" Lady Ann queried of Lark, her straight brows knit in such a manner that there appeared no space between them. "You look awfully flushed of a sudden."

"Transplanting hothouse flowers to the wild is always dangerous," the comtesse opined. "They don't take to it—especially servants. Ann's new abigail is proof of what I say. The gel's been ailing since we set foot out of that coach today. *Mon Dieu*, we cannot get a lick of work out of her."

"Our Lark is hardly a servant, Lady Vera," the countess put in, "but her color is a bit suspect." She craned her neck toward Lark. "I noticed it when you first came down. Are you feeling feverish, dear? One can't be too careful with the days soon drawing in."

"A bit of windburn . . . from my ride this afternoon," Lark explained. "Nothing to trouble over."

King monitored his mother's scrutinizing stare. The footmen had just finished distributing the larded pheasant course, and she sat with her fork suspended, her sharp eyes narrowed. He couldn't help but notice how her jewels sparkled in the candlelight, as did the comtesse's and Lady Ann's. No such sparkle emanated from Lark, so close on his right, and yet she glowed. How beautiful she was with her cheeks aflame. How exquisitely her golden ringlets shimmered in the candle glow, like a halo of spun gold. He longed to run his fingers through those short-cropped curls, to feel their texture, to inhale their fragrance at close range.

He'd begun to perspire. The blinding white neckcloth Frith had tied so expertly had suddenly begun to chafe his neck. He resisted the urge to slip his finger underneath his modest shirt points and relieve the pressure of their starched perfection. What stopped him was that, in Lark's close proximity, he couldn't keep his hand from shaking.

All at once a barely audible strangled sound on his left brought his eyes around to Lady Ann, the picture of despair, desperately trying to hide behind her serviette as she avoided his gaze. Her cheeks, too, had flushed all of a sudden, and her eyes seemed glazed beneath their knit brows and sparse lashes not nearly dense enough to hide the moisture welling there.

Now he'd done it. He wasn't adept at wearing masks. His thoughts were evidently written all over his face, and Lady Ann had read them; so had his mother, judging from her scrutiny. What was that odd expression? He couldn't recognize it. Hah! When was the last time he couldn't read that needle-sharp gaze? He couldn't remember.

"Getting back to France," Leander Markham said, breaking the awkward silence. "What wines do you produce in your vineyards, Comtesse Cuthbertson?"

Thank God for Lee's powers of observation. Trust the man to save the day. But did it really want saving?

"You are unfamiliar with the wines of Château Arbonville, Monsieur Markham?" she replied, incredulous. "Our port is far superior to any other, and our champagne is the finest in the world. Harumph! *Stupide anglais paysan*," she added, low-voiced.

King had no difficulty reading his mother's expression, and he almost winced. He couldn't imagine her allowing anyone at her table to call one a "stupid English peasant" and live to tell the tale. Had she finally met her match? He almost laughed at the prospect of these two termagants pitted against each other, larded pheasant flying. That fantasy was almost as delicious as the food, and blood sport was just what he needed to cool the fire in his loins that made him exceedingly glad he was sitting down in his skin-tight oyster-white inexpressibles.

Instead, the countess smiled her sweetest smile and said in perfect French, "*Un tel ennuyeux langue, francais, mais bien la valeur que e'ennui pour apprendre.*"

King did laugh at that, in spite of himself. "*Touché!*" he said, saluting her with his wineglass.

He glanced at Lady Ann, who had paled in obvious embarrassment. It was plain that she had understood what the countess said that had silenced her aunt. Now that Lady Vera knew insults delivered in French would be clearly understood, "tiresome" as the language was but "worth the bother to learn," the line was drawn. The viper had stung with a sugarcoated spurt of venom that made the wounding crueler. Oh, yes. King always bet his blunt on a sure thing—in this case, his mother.

Lark understood as well. Was that a smile? The countess saw, too, and acknowledged it with a slow blink.

Lady Vera waved off the oysters au gratin with a ring-encumbered hand. "No, no. Too rich," she said. "The fish will do instead." She gestured toward the sideboard. "My stomach is too delicate for your English sauces—too much white flour. You English have not mastered the art of a decent roux."

While the footman obliged her, Leander offered Lark more wine, which this time she did refuse, since she had scarcely touched what she had, and King almost felt sorry for her as she wheeled the cart toward him. It was clear that she didn't want to be at that table. He could well appreciate her discomfort. He didn't want to be there, either. The difference was *he* could do something about it.

"Lady Ann," he said, his voice like silk, as he leaned in her direction. "I wish I had known in advance of your coming. Had Mother informed me, I might have arranged my schedule to better entertain you . . . and the comtesse, of course. As it is, I fear I shall be absent from Grayshire Manor during most of your visit. I do hope you enjoy your stay, and that you will allow me to make it up to you at some time in the future convenient to all of us."

"Y-you didn't . . . ?" she stammered, shaking her head. "B-but I thought . . ."

King almost winced. Of course she thought that he was behind the invitation to the Manor. Her disappointment was palpable. Be that as it may, he would not deceive her. He may be the rogue his mother accused, but above all he was a gentleman.

"It was Mother's idea to have you down for a visit," he said. "I knew nothing about it. I believe she meant to surprise me, but unfortunately she was not privy to my schedule. I've been away for a fortnight, at sea, on Crown business. I've only put in to port for repairs, and must put right out again. Mother heard me speak of you . . . and Lady Vera, and she does so love to entertain."

"O-oh," Lady Ann murmured in the meekest voice he had ever heard, and gave her full attention to her oysters.

He flashed his mother a scathing look that said: *On your own head be it, old girl. You've wound the coil. Now you can unwind it.*

Lady Ann's eyes were brimming with tears. She took two nibbling swallows, and cleared her voice. "I have the most dreadful headache," she mewed, laying her serviette aside. "I'm quite exhausted after the journey. I should like to take a sachet and retire . . . if you will all excuse me. . . ."

King and Leander rose as she did, and resumed their seats once she cleared the arch, only to pop up again as Lark also rose from the table, her serviette neatly set beside her plate.

"I think I shall retire also," she said, nodding toward the countess. "With your kind permission, of course, Lady Isobel?"

"Certainly, dear," the countess purred. "I've planned some activities for our . . . guests tomorrow, and you'll want to be rested for that."

King tried to read Lark's eyes, but they met his only briefly, before she bowed and floated out with all the aplomb of royalty.

Lark strode toward the staircase, her hollow footfalls echoing over the terrazzo. She wasn't about to sit at that table and dodge insults. There was a certain fiendish satisfaction at the thought of King being shackled with both the dowager comtesse Lady Vera Arbonville Cuthbertson and his mother for life. It seemed a justifiable purgatory.

None of that mattered anymore, however. In the morning she would have turned her back on Grayshire Manor, never to be troubled over what went on under its roof again.

Climbing the stairs, she slowed her pace and slumped against the banister. There was no satisfaction in gloating.

The thought of leaving the countess saddened her. Lady Isobel was just as love-starved as she was. She might have had her dream come true but for what she knew was behind King's advances. He wanted her for his mistress. There was no question. Why else would he lavish her with jewels worth hundreds of pounds when he was planning to wed another? And why did that hurt her heart so?

She started to climb again. One of the housemaids was moving along the hall above. For a moment, she thought it might be Agnes, but no, she looked like . . . but that couldn't be. There was something familiar about the girl nonetheless, but she melted into the shadows before Lark could get close enough to find out. Lark dismissed the notion, and struggled up the rest of the stairs to the landing above that divided the second floor of the Manor in two. She'd scarcely set foot on it when strong hands grabbed her from behind and spun her into stronger arms.

It was King.

Teetering on the edge, Lark lost her balance and nearly cost them both their footing on the carpeted staircase. She fell into him and, stumbling himself, he swept her up and set her down firmly on the landing, but he didn't let her go.

It was her wildest dream—her most delicious fantasy—being clasped fast in his scorching embrace. He smelled clean, of the mysterious tobacco she'd never seen him indulge in, and the port he'd just drunk. The warmth of him riveted her as he molded her trembling frame to every inch of his long, lean, well-muscled body.

She should pull away. She should beat his chest with her fists. Granted, they wouldn't inflict much damage, but that wasn't the point. What would he think of her? What *did* he think of her—the ragged, dirty little chit he'd raised up from the dust of the Marshalsea? The "plucked chicken" that he had assured his mother was definitely not Lady Ann Cuthbertson. She knew the answer to that all too well. It was painfully obvious. He thought her quite well to pass, all right, for a convenient mistress once he'd married. What did she expect?

She needed to resist. Propriety demanded it. But, oh what her body demanded! His hooded gaze burned toward her. He bent his head lower, and hot breath puffed against her face from his nostrils in labored spurts. Was that due to the dance he'd just done trying to prevent them both from tumbling down that steep staircase, or was that rapid breathing something more, something connected to the cords strung as hard as steel in his thighs pressed against her? When his mouth covered hers, there was no more doubt. He lightly tasted her lips with his warm, searching tongue, before probing deeper, deftly sliding it between her teeth as they parted to let a startled gasp escape. Her bones seemed to melt. She had been kissed before, but never like *this*, that shot waves of achy heat to parts of her quivering body far removed from her mouth.

He buried one hand in her hair. He seemed to be feeling the texture. He slid the hand lower, along the curve of her arched throat, bent back beneath his kiss. For a moment she thought that warm, steady hand was going to inch lower—shockingly lower. The heel of his broad palm grazed her décolleté. The roughness of his skin against the delicacy of her exposed flesh riddled her loins with a thick, throbbing sensation unknown to her. It flagged danger. Her breast heaved against his hand. She should push him away. She should give his shins a healthy drubbing with the toe of her slipper, but her bones had melted, hadn't they? Just when she thought she could stand no more, he drew away his lips, but only barely. They were still so close that they were lightly touching hers when he spoke.

"Are you all right?" he murmured. "I didn't mean to frighten you. I—"

The sound of his voice sobered her, and she drew back her hand and lowered her open palm hard against his face with all the strength she could muster.

King stiffened. His arms fell away rigid at his sides, and

he took a step back from her, his eye narrowed and tearing from the blow. Lark covered her mouth with her hand. Her bones hadn't melted after all. Her handprint was plainly visible blooming on his cheek in the form of a puffy red welt, and she had nearly dislodged his eye patch. She gasped. How dreadful that would have been if she had. She was mortified, but she was angry as well. It was the anger that spoke.

"How dare you take such liberties with me, my lord?" she seethed. "Your intended is right down that hall there"—she wagged a scathing finger—"in tears, I have no doubt, due to your boorish behavior downstairs. Let me pass!"

"Lark—"

"I will *not* be your mistress! What? Do you think because you found me in *that place* you can make free with me, sir? Westerfield thought as much, and soon learned the folly of such a notion. I know what you think of me. You made that quite plain on that first night, when you assured your mother that I was most certainly not your intended—"

King's groan interrupted her. His posture collapsed, and he awarded his brow as scathing a blow as she had done his cheek, and spun away from her, raking his hair ruthlessly.

"—and that she only need endure the likes of me as her companion," Lark went on, her voice raised over another groan leaking from him. "That went without saying, Lord Grayshire. Believe me, I know my place. I was resigned to it when I came here, and I did so with all good intentions and a cheerful heart. Your introduction was hurtful, and cruel. But I rose above it with as much dignity as I could muster, and then . . . those jewels! I knew you meant to take liberties when you presented them to me. Your explanation was preposterous. You meant to buy my favors with that offering. Well, I am not for sale. That's why I put you out of my apartments. And now this!"

"Lark, I don't need a mistress. I never meant—"

"*Lady* Lark," she flashed. "The jewel case is still right where you left it on the table in my sitting room. I shall unlock *that* door in my suite, and it will remain unlocked until Smeaton or Peal collects it. Please have the decency to send one of them up at once. I am too embarrassed to summon either myself, and enough of a lady to allow you to save face. Judging from the tale you told me, I'm sure you'll be creative. Good night, Lord Grayshire."

Thirteen

Damn and blast! So that's what had overset her. No wonder she thought he wanted her for his mistress. King stroked her swollen handprint on his cheek and heaved a ragged sigh. How could he have said something so insensitive? He knew better. He certainly wasn't perfect, but then, who was? He was properly schooled in the art of gentlemanly behavior in all facets of life—even in the guise that had earned him the reputation of a rogue; it was a point of honor with him. How could he have not realized his error?

There was just too much on his mind: the trade, for one thing, and his forced reinvolvement in it—now, of all times, when he was under pressure to marry and produce an heir. And then there was the damage to the *Cormorant*. Would she still float after repairs? Would she sink in the midst of his next foray alongside the *Hind*? He almost hoped for that, but dismissed the thought. He had more ships. The Admiralty would only choose another. He was trapped, either facing a charge of treason against the Crown for refusing the appointment, or betraying every friend and neighbor he had on the coast to avoid it. Small wonder he was addled.

He began to pace the hall carpet. Will Bowles was on his mind, and Mattie, his father's mistress, fearful of being evicted from their croft—their future was hanging by the tenuous thread of his mother's fickle and oftentimes ruthless mood swings where they were concerned. And not to be overlooked was the most current debacle, of course, brought about by who else but his mother *again*—houseguests and their entourage that he hadn't invited settling in. But surely they wouldn't stay now, not after what had just occurred in the dining room. That was one consolation at least.

His mother. The woman was diabolical. She hadn't invited just any houseguests. No, she had lured the woman he had been considering to be his bride and her insufferable aunt into her web, for that was how he saw his mother: a giant spider, spinning her threads of entrapment, casting them out upon her unsuspecting victims. He was the one she'd really trapped. She had done this to embarrass him. What other reason could there be? He wasn't moving fast enough for her in the marriage department, so she'd taken the matter into her own hands.

Last but not the least of his burdens was this . . . whatever it was that gave him no peace concerning a certain little spitfire with eyes the color of iolite, and hair like spun silk painted by the sun. He had much too much on his mind, indeed. Granted he was making excuses for himself, but one important thing had come out of his reiteration: He had referred to Lady Ann Cuthbertson in the past tense. His subconscious had finally caught up with his conscious mind. What would his mother say about *that*, he wondered—especially since she was directly responsible?

He had stopped pacing now, and was standing alone in the shadowy corridor, Lark's energy all around him. The honey-sweet taste of her was still with him. Like an addict, he craved more. Her hair was soft as eiderdown between his fingers just as he thought it would be—dreamed it would be—and the haunting fragrance of roses drifting from her skin was still with him. The tightness that embrace had inflicted upon his loins revisited him suddenly. There was no question that he wanted her. He had wanted many women, but never like this, with such a crashing disregard for all else around him, and he'd ruined it. He'd been so keyed up anticipating his mother's impression of Lark, and acceptance of her, that the first words out of his mouth had damned him. But he wasn't the only one to blame for that. The countess had much to answer for, and he streaked down the stairs and stalked off in search of her.

Lady Ann Cuthbertson sat on the edge of her bed, her eyes red and swollen, her nose buried in a delicate lace-edged handkerchief. She honked into it unattractively, wrenching an exasperated sigh from her aunt.

"Mon Dieu!" Lady Vera admonished her. "Stop that sniveling. You are weak as water, Ann. *Weak as water.* Tears will serve nothing."

"What could she have possibly meant, inviting us here without his knowledge?" Lady Ann wailed. "I have never been so embarrassed . . . so humiliated!"

Lady Vera shrugged. *"Qui peut dire?* It doesn't matter. The woman is a barracuda."

"Speak English, Aunt," Lady Ann snapped. "You've only been twice to France since you married Uncle Simon thirty years ago. The affectation doesn't suit—especially now, when we are at war. It's a wonder we are invited anywhere, the way you do go on!"

"Ahhh, but my soul is still French, *ma petite.*"

"We shall pack and leave at once, of course," Lady Ann decreed. "Where is that lazy abigail? I knew you never should have hired her without references. You simply cannot take in every stray you find on our doorstep. It's a wonder we haven't all been murdered in our beds."

"The desperate come cheap."

"That remains to be seen, Aunt Vera. I don't like her."

"It doesn't matter," her aunt intoned. "Perhaps the servants in this house will teach her proper behavior for a lady's maid. There will be ample time for that, because we are not going anywhere, *ma petite.* We are going to stay right here, and you are going to stand your ground and fight for your man."

"He doesn't want me, Aunt Vera. Any fool could see he is in love with Lady Lark." She wiped her eyes and blew into the handkerchief again.

"Nonsense. She is disgraced—a nobody. She has no money, no land, nothing to bring to such a union. Why, if she were not under his lordship's sponsorship, she would be right back in that dreadful place she came from, or cast upon the parish somewhere. She may as well be indentured. There can be no match there. She cannot compete with you—with your settlement. He wants her for his mistress." She shrugged. "For that, she is as good as any, quite well to pass—far superior to the 'birds of paradise' in Town, and far less likely to get you poxed."

"That is obscene. I cannot be expected to sit at table with my husband's mistress, no matter how well to pass. I won't bear it."

"That is the way of it, *ma petite*, you know that, and you will be glad of it once he beds you. You will not want his hot, sweaty flesh upon you every night, believe me. Besides, you will be spared sitting at table with her once the countess relinquishes her chatelaine to you and takes up residence in the dower house."

Lady Ann gave it thought. She did not entirely agree. Conjuring King's image, she thought the prospect of being in bed with him quite appealing. Was she in love with him? She was attracted certainly; who wouldn't be to such a dashing, eligible catch? Love could be cultivated. More relevant to the situation, her time was running out. This was her third season with no takers. It would be too embarrassing to suffer a fourth. She would have to put on her caps. Imagining herself in biggins and drab clothes terrified her.

Tears welled in her eyes again. She had always been a watering pot—a lisping, self-conscious, thin-skinned watering pot. Aunt Vera was right. She should dig in her heels and fight for her man. She'd come so close—closer than she'd ever come before—too close to let a down-at-the-heels interloper usurp her. But did she have the stamina, and was it worth the effort even if she did? The thought of bearing a child—of the pain of it, of what it would do to her body—frightened her more than she dared let on.

"Come, come, *ma petite*, what is there to think about?" the comtesse said, jarring her back to the issue. "It works both ways, you know. Once you have given him his heir, you, too, can take a lover, as long as you do so with discretion. That is all he expects of you, after all—that you give him a son. Such arrangements are perfectly acceptable these days. Why, we've had such in France for ages. You are such a romantic, Ann. Love! Balderdash! Love is for *paysans*."

Lady Ann was about to defend herself when the behindhand abigail arrived, a soft knock preceding her entrance, and she sketched a curtsy, her eyes cast downward.

"Where have you been, Biddie?" Lady Ann demanded. "The dinner hour is long past. Why is your face so red? Well? Answer me!"

"The stairs, my lady," Biddie replied, "there are so many—more than in Town."

"Hah!" Lady Vera erupted. "Here but a few hours, and she has spread her legs for some hall boy or footman below stairs. Look at that face. *Mon Dieu!*"

"Yes, well, and now she will go back down those 'many stairs' again and help bring the water up for my bath. So, Aunt, do you finally see how expensive 'cheap' can be?"

Biddie trudged down the back stairs wearily—only the third time she'd trod them since their arrival. There wasn't much chance of running into Grayshire below stairs, but she first had to get there, and she spanned the distance fleet-footed with furtive glances over her shoulder the whole distance. He was abroad somewhere in the house, and in a taking. He had almost caught her out in the hallway earlier, and would have done but for the queen of the

Marshalsea, who had spied her, too, of all the luck. That would have been an awkward business if the earl hadn't come on when he had and distracted Miss High-and-Mighty. Then they embraced, and she was trapped, a captive audience in the shadowy recesses of the third-floor landing, holding her breath for fear of being discovered there. She'd heard every word before their raised voices gave her the opportunity to slip away. Well, almost every word, until the silly chit told his lordship where she'd left the jewels. There was no reason to remain there after that. But she hadn't returned to the servants' quarters. She'd hidden in the shadows farther down the hall, until Lark unlocked the sitting room door for Smeaton or Peal, and then nicked the jewels the minute the coast was clear.

Having nearly reached the bottom landing, Biddie glanced back over her shoulder again. She could ill afford to be found out now. Eavesdropping outside Lady Ann's sitting room door earlier, while she caught her breath, she had been greatly relieved to hear the silly chit whining about returning to Town. It was madness to stay at Grayshire Manor now, with the jewels in her possession. She needed to be away before they were discovered missing. But then in a blink, her hopes had been dashed, when that old harpy persuaded Lady Ann to stay on.

Yes, her face was flushed crimson, and running with sweat, but not from bedding one of the staff. It was from racing to get hold of those jewels before Lark's maid came back up from supper, and then hiding them, all of which involved racing up and down those steep, winding, narrow stairs. Bed sport was the furthest thing from Biddie's mind then. She had Westerfield for that. How pleased he would be when he learned what she'd accomplished so quickly. But there was still more to do, and she could only hope, so little time to do it.

"Whatever possessed you to invite the Cuthbertsons here without my permission?" King shouted at his mother. He had tracked her down in the sitting room of her apartments. His pacing had displaced the fringe on the Aubusson carpet, drawing her eyes. "How could you, Mother?"

"Don't shout, dear, you know how your voice carries. They'll hear you. Have you forgotten that their rooms are just down the hall? And don't muss the fringe on that rug. You know how I detest untidy fringe. It spoils the look of the whole room."

"This time you've gone too far," he raved, kicking the rug in defiance. "I won't help you unwind this coil. I made that plain downstairs in the dining room right in front of everyone, so there would be no question. Stop meddling in my life!"

"I thought you'd be pleased with my little surprise," she purred. "I knew how it must have pained you, parting from Lady Ann's company to come way out here on my account. I thought I was doing you a kindness."

"Codswallop! You're trying to manipulate me again. Well, this time it won't work. You're going to apologize to the Cuthbertsons for bringing them out here on false pretenses. I'm going to thoroughly enjoy watching you wriggle your way out of this one. You've finally overreached yourself."

The countess banged her cane on the floor. "Mind your tongue, Basil. Remember yourself. I needn't remind you again that you're not too old at thirty-three for a proper hiding." She cocked her head, studying him. "What's that there on your cheek—that red patch?"

"It's nothing," he snapped. "Don't shift the subject."

"Mmm, by the look of things, someone has saved me the trouble of chastising you. You haven't disgraced yourself, have you, Basil—not here? You have the townhouse for that sort of thing. That's why I so seldom go there."

"No, I have not 'disgraced myself,' here or at the townhouse for that matter. You have a suspicious nature."

"I don't take that from the wind," she shot back, bristling. "Your father—"

"I'd hoped we could have this conversation without dragging Father into it," he interrupted, "but I see now how naïve I was to imagine it. You expect me to follow in your footsteps—yours and Father's. You know I don't love Lady Ann. She doesn't love me, either. She *wants* me—to save her from spinsterhood. You weren't in love with Father when you married him, either. It was a prestigious match for you. Spare me that look, Mother. Don't dare deny it. I know who he was, and where you came from. Once you had me, you locked him out of your heart and your bedroom—"

"*Basil!* How dare you speak to me thus? I will not stand for it—such crudity—from you, my son, of all people."

"You force me to it, Mother, with your infernal meddling. This discourse is long overdue. Father was a virile, healthy man, and a loving one. Small wonder he turned to Mattie Bowles. You drove him into her arms, and while he lived, though he couldn't acknowledge Will, he treated him properly, and he loved him, just as he loved me. Father never pressed the Bowleses in hard times—"

"Hah!" his mother blurted. "I should say not, or he'd have been evicted from another bed, wouldn't he?"

"—and he never threatened them with eviction, either," King carried on with raised voice. "You're a hypocrite, Mother. You didn't want him, but you didn't want anyone else to have him, either. I don't think you even wanted *me*. At any rate, if you did you've never showed it." Should he go on? Probably not, but too much had rankled him for too long to stop now, and at the risk of going beyond the pale with her, he squared his posture and continued. "What you did want was to play the long-suffering martyr. You do it so well you could have had a future in Drury Lane. What I wanted was a whole family. That was not to be had in this house, so I sought it elsewhere. Do you know that I've always wished that I were Mattie Bowles's child? Did you never wonder why, when I was growing up, I so often stole away to the Bowles's croft? You caned me often enough for it. No, I can see not by your expression.

"I love you, Mother, but I cannot honestly say that I like you much—now least of all. What you've done is cruel—not only to me, but to Lady Ann, who is an innocent victim in this. Now, I have to make it plain to her that I do not seek her hand. I can only thank God above that I had not yet offered for her, or I'd be facing a breach of promise suit—then *pop!* would have gone the family fortune. You were playing a dangerous game. Please God, you've learned your lesson."

The countess's lower lip had begun to tremble, and her hand worked the handle of her cane relentlessly. All at once, she vaulted to her feet, and for a moment King expected the deadly thing to come crashing down upon his head.

"All this had to be said," he went on, putting distance between them, "because things must change. You will undo what you've done with the Cuthbertsons, and you will never threaten Will or Mattie Bowles again, or you will answer to me. Don't dare put me to the test; you won't like the outcome."

"Have you finished?" his mother intoned.

"Not quite," he said. "You should have done as I asked, and offered the jewels to Lark yourself. Had you done so, she would not have been so offended. Now, you're going to put that to rights as well. She has refused them. She thinks I was soliciting her to be my mistress. Small wonder, what with Lady Ann come to visit at your invitation expecting a proposal of marriage at the end of it." Though he was just as guilty in that regard, he deftly omitted his insensitive blunder. Now was not the time to give quarter—not while he had the upper hand. It was so rare an occurrence.

"Where are the jewels now?" his mother said.

"In her rooms. She asked that I send Smeaton or Peal to retrieve them. She's too mortified to summon either one of them herself, for fear they might take her for a Cyprian, which I have no doubt would be the case. My reputation would have damned her. I shall have Smeaton collect them, and return them to the safe myself, until you put things right."

"Just what do you expect me to do?" the countess asked.

King raked his hair back ruthlessly, until the shorter, wavy shock in front fell in mussed waves across his brow. "Explain to Lark that we were in accord about the jewels—that I had no such intentions."

"Just what *are* your intentions, Basil, aside from breaking my heart?"

He almost felt sorry for her. She was clearly on the verge of tears. He couldn't help but wonder how long it had been since those steely eyes had shed a one. Not in his lifetime that he could recall.

"I don't think you have a heart, Mother," he said. "The *ton* evidently doesn't think so, either. They have labeled you a termagant. Don't ever lecture me about disgrace. As to my intentions, they are simply this: Thus far, I've had a loveless life. I will never settle for a loveless marriage, much less bring a child into one. I know that isn't a fashionable attitude these days, or a popular one. 'One to wed, and one to bed,' is much more convenient for the masses, but not for me. Despite your underhanded manipulations, I will not marry Lady Ann. I'd made up my mind to that before I left London."

"Who, then?" the countess persisted.

"That, unfortunately, depends upon you."

"Upon *me*? How, upon me?"

"Until you interfered, I had intended to press my suit to Lark. As things stand now, I doubt I'll get the chance."

Fourteen

*L*ark didn't join the others for breakfast; she abstained. Bearding the lioness in her den was something that needed to be done on an empty stomach. Besides, it would hardly do to sit at table pretending, when all the while she planned to be gone from Grayshire Manor by nuncheon. She was no hypocrite. All that remained was to come to some amiable agreement with the countess. The thought of being sent back to the Marshalsea all but stopped her heart, but better that than to stay under the roof of a man she was falling in love with, a man who only wanted her for his mistress. Her heart was breaking.

She found the countess in the morning room, where it was their custom to meet after breakfast to go over the itinerary for the day. Bright light shining in through the windows showed her a different face than that which usually greeted her. Could the countess have been crying? Lark couldn't imagine it.

"You were missed at breakfast," the countess said. "I was left to fend on my own with our guests, since Basil and Leander seem to have gone missing this morning also."

"I can explain—"

"To be sure," the countess interrupted. "You might also explain why you refused the tray that was brought to your apartments. Are you unwell, my dear?"

Lark couldn't meet the countess's eyes. She sank into a Duncan Phyfe chair across the carpet even though she hadn't been invited to sit; her legs would no longer support her. She'd expected this to be difficult, and she'd thought she'd steeled herself. Not so. She folded her hands in her lap to keep them from trembling, or worse yet, fidgeting, and stared at the dainty blue forget-me-nots on her sprigged muslin morning dress.

"I am not unwell," she said, as steadily as she could manage. "I didn't come down to breakfast because it would have been dishonest of me to pretend. I cannot remain here, Countess Grayshire. Not in these circumstances. I've come to ask . . . to *beg* you to allow me to make some other arrangements to repay what your son spent buying me free."

"'Countess Grayshire'?" the woman intoned. "Why so formal of a sudden? I know that 'Lady Isobel' is not the best of form, but I permitted it because I wanted you to feel at home here. You know that I prefer you and Basil be less formal with each other . . . and with me."

"That is no longer possible, my lady."

"Oh, I see."

"I beg your pardon, but you do not see, and I am too much of a lady to elaborate. Suffice it to say that I cannot remain here. I will gladly go back to the Marshalsea, if needs must. I am hoping, however, that some other arrangement might be made. His lordship did give me that option at the outset . . . should things not . . . work out here."

"Should you not be able to countenance *me*, you mean?" the countess amended. "Well, my dear, we have gotten on well, and your leaving Grayshire Manor is entirely out of the question."

"But his lordship said—"

"Basil has no say in this," the countess put in, banging her cane. The shock waves rippled through the parquetry beneath the rug and penetrated the soles of Lark's Morocco leather slippers. "My son paid a staggering sum to see you and your abigail released from that odious place. Do you imagine that you can just wipe out such a debt so easily? Suppose you tell me just what is at the root of this bizarre request."

Lark hesitated. On the one hand, she had no wish to cause a deeper rift between mother and son; on the other, though she did acknowledge the debt, nothing was going to keep her under the same roof with the Earl of Grayshire.

"I'm waiting," the countess prompted, working her cane's silver handle.

"I'm afraid your son has brought me here under false pretenses," Lark began. "He is under the mistaken notion that I would be receptive to becoming his . . . mistress."

The countess's left eyebrow lifted. It was the only change in her stoical expression, though it spoke volumes. If only Lark could read them.

"So, you see why I cannot remain here," she concluded, avoiding the countess's all-seeing eyes, so like her son's. Suddenly Lark realized what she had so often wondered about under King's penetrating gaze—what it would have been like gazing into two such enigmatic eyes. They were nothing alike in size, shape, or color, but, oh, the expression.

"He actually asked you to—"

"Not in so many words, no," Lark hastened to add, "but he didn't have to. His actions were quite eloquent. He . . . he plied me with a fortune in jewels, and took liberties—with his betrothed-to-be right down the hall!" She shook her head, scattering her curls, and vaulted to her feet. "No. There is no question as to his intent. He said he bought me free to be your companion, not to . . . to . . . ! I am no Cyprian, Lady Grayshire."

The countess winced. "I will *not* have you call me 'Lady Grayshire'!" she said. "I detest it, especially coming from you. Sit back down there. Sit!" she commanded, banging her cane again. "I am largely to blame for this unfortunate to-do."

"You, my lady?"

She nodded. "You've caught me out, so you must let me try and explain. For one thing, my dear, I can assure you Basil does not want you for his mistress. He already has one, it pains me to say. . . ."

Lark gasped in spite of herself. Hot blood rushed to her cheeks and seemed to drain her heart dry; there was no other explanation for the pain left behind in the wake of those words. Why should this surprise her? More to the point, why should it bother her so? Because she'd come so soon from his steamy embrace, and couldn't bear to think of another woman in those strong arms, feeling what she'd felt under his spell—that's why.

"Oh," was all she could get out. The low-voiced delivery sounded back in her ears. Did her tone really seem as pathetic to the countess as it sounded to her? She prayed not but feared so.

A cold smile creased the countess's lips. "More than one, if you count the Gypsy wench he favors when he's here on the coast," she continued. "So, you see, there is no need for him to—"

"I beg you, please excuse me," Lark murmured, surging to her feet again.

"I have asked you to sit," the countess shrilled. "I do not intend to ask you again."

Lark sank back down. How so slight a woman could command such volume of voice was beyond her. It rang from the vaulted ceiling and echoed, surely audible to the far reaches of the rambling house. Lark's lips trembled, but neither fright nor imminent tears moved them; they trembled in prayer that King would not return, overhear, and confront them. She would die of mortification.

"That was crude of me, I know, but I meant only to reassure you that there is no necessity, you see."

"Then why didn't he give the jewels to one of his mistresses, since he has so many? Why did he try to buy *my* . . . favors with them?"

"He didn't, my dear. They were not a bribe—"

"Not at first, no," Lark interrupted. "He bought them for Lady Ann. I modeled them for him at the jeweler's, if you remember. You were along on that junket. That makes it worse."

"They were never meant for anyone but you, Lark," the countess said, her voice grown soft. "We were in complete accord in regard to their purchase, Basil and I. It was decided that jewels be bought for you before we ever made the trip that day. You simply cannot sit at table—much less attend social functions—with no adornment, like a poor relation. The *ton* has enough ammunition for on-dits at my expense. I won't have them labeling me a cheeseparing miser or you a castoff at my mercy.

"I see you are still skeptical. Well, that will soon be put to rights. There is one piece purchased that day that has yet to come—a gold brooch engraved with your initials. That is what has detained it. It had to be sent to an engraver in London. The craftsmen here are not as skilled. It should be here any day now."

"That proves nothing except that one piece was selected for me."

"I shall remind you of those words once it arrives," the countess replied through a cold smile.

"It doesn't explain his making advances toward me, after inviting his bride to be here to visit," Lark persisted.

"You heard him at dinner, my dear. He told you the truth. He didn't invite the Cuthbertsons to Grayshire Manor. I did. She isn't right for him, dear. I wanted to wake him up to that. He was furious with me for it. He still is. I doubt he will ever forgive me, and he hasn't heard the worst of it. They aren't leaving, I'm afraid."

Lark's jaw dropped, and her posture clenched.

"What?" the countess erupted. "You can't imagine that I would sanction such a union? Surely you know that Basil is in love with *you*?"

"I know nothing of the sort!"

"Neither does he . . . yet," the countess triumphed, "but he will."

Lark was on her feet again, for good. This time the countess didn't stop her.

"You're no use to me on the high seas, Will," said King. "I need you on shore, keeping watch for the land guards— taking charge of the plunder. Besides, there's no need for the both of us risking life and limb. Now let that be the end to it."

They were seated around a scarred oak table at the Six Bells Inn, on the outskirts of Colors Cove—King, Leander Markham, and Will Bowles—as far as King could range himself from Grayshire Manor, and the chaos he'd left behind. They had picked Will up on the way, and King was already regretting it.

"I'm not a child, you know, King, I'm twenty-three," Will groused. "Here on the Cornish coast, that's practically middle age, the way the land wastes a body. Look at my hands—" He extended them over the scarred wooden table. "—just like leather. They can swab decks, haul ropes, man tillers, and trim sails with the best of them. I want a turn at sea. It's in my blood, too, you know."

King shook his head. "There's too much at stake for me to be distracted keeping an eye out for you," he said. "Besides, your mother would kill me."

"She wouldn't have to know."

"*I'd* know," King served. "I shan't deceive your mother— never that. It's enough that I'm deceiving everyone else. If you really want to help me, Will, keep to your post in the cove. I'm straddling both sides of a very slippery fence here, and I'd like to come to the end of it all of a piece, with my neck intact."

"How long are you going to be walking that fence?" Leander queried, through a swallow of ale from his tankard. "You've been lucky thus far, but that can't last. It's getting harder and harder to bribe the land guards—the new ones especially."

"Until the Admiralty lets me off the bloody hook," King snapped, "which isn't likely any time soon."

"Surely after you've wed . . . ?"

"I'm not going to wed, Lee," King said wearily.

"Not Lady Ann, surely, but the countess will never give you a moment's peace until you produce the almighty heir."

"No, not Lady Ann," agreed King, "that's why we're here—to let the dust of the Cuthbertsons' departure settle. They'll be long gone by time we return, thank God, and I have no other prospects at the moment."

Leander's eyebrow lifted. He opened his mouth to speak, but closed it again when a buxom serving wench appeared laden down with three pewter plates overflowing with stew. King was glad of the interruption. While the change of subject had steered the conversation away from Will's request, it was leading down a more dangerous path. His cheek still smarted from Lark's assault. Though the imprint had long since faded, he often caught himself rubbing the spot absently—even now, in a crowded pub, packed wall to dingy wall with boisterous, red-faced, drunken sailors.

No one spoke during the meal. The stew was good, and hot—hardly competition for Cook's fare at the Manor, but just as satisfying after a long purging ride. Though for the life of him, King couldn't think what had been purged. Certainly not one little soft-bodied, heart-stealing creature that had come between him and his sleep last night, and would, he had no doubt, for some nights to come.

He set his serviette aside and drew a small clay pipe and a pouch of tobacco from his waistcoat pocket. Filling and lighting it was a ritualistic indulgence more satisfying than actually smoking the stuff, because it relaxed him, and he only did it when he needed relaxing. Badly. Like now, with Lark's image framed in every perfect smoke ring climbing toward the exposed-beam ceiling.

But another image materialized through the aromatic veil of drifting smoke. An image that brought the feet he'd propped up on the vacant bench alongside crashing to the floor—Hazel Helston, in all her flame-haired, full-breasted glory.

He surged to his feet. "H-Hazel," he said, nodding in greeting as the others got up awkwardly and followed suit.

She waved them off. "Sit down, you lot," she said, through a wry chuckle. "I work here, don't I?"

Leander and Will sat back down, but King remained standing. He flashed a sidelong glance toward his two companions. Leander looked innocent enough. Will, on the other hand, was easily read. His face was blotched crimson, and he didn't seem to know where to direct his eyes. King narrowed his. So that was how it was. He'd been set up.

"It's been a long time, King," Hazel purred, strolling closer. "Will tells me you've been back for weeks. You might have come to see a body."

"I hear you've married," King said. "Please accept my felicitations. Captain Jim Helston is a fine man; I wish you well."

She shrugged. "Jim's married, all right—to the sea," she said, pouting. "He put out months ago. I've lost count."

"So you've become a serving wen . . . maid, meanwhile?" said King, deftly recovering.

"Out of boredom, aye," she responded.

"I'm about to take the plunge myself." He looked daggers at the red-faced youth burying his nose in his empty plate across the table. "Didn't Will tell you?"

She shrugged. "I believe he made mention of it, yes," she said.

King stared into eyes the color of an angry sea. They devoured him. How well he remembered them hooded with passion, dilated with desire as she lay in his arms. She wore a starched white cap that didn't diminish the flame-colored hair beneath; it set it off, like a fiery halo. But this was no saint. And she had an uncanny way of seducing him without a word spoken.

Her costume exposed more than was decent of her pendulous breasts. They challenged the fabric of her bodice. Their pointed tips were clearly visible through it, and now and then, as she sauntered nearer, he glimpsed the tawny dimpled curve of an areola. They were far too close to his chest for comfort. What shocked him most, however, was that for all her undulating seduction, it wasn't working. Even though he recalled the feel of those milky-white breasts in his hands, nestled in the hair on his naked chest; the shape of those incredible nipples defined against his tongue; the silky warmth that he knew awaited him between her thighs—he wanted none of it. Hazel Helston, nee Potts, belonged to another time, when he was young—younger than poor embarrassed Will across the way. All the lust and fire and sweaty conquests of those days lived only in distant memory, as if they'd happened to someone else. Now, it was sun-painted ringlets, like eiderdown, and lips that tasted of honey that he wanted. It was the soft, yielding, perfection of innocent flesh that he craved. Flesh that molded so exactly to his own despite the difference in their heights. That was never so clear to him as now, staring down at what was being offered him in plain sight of every leering patron in the Six Bells Inn.

"Here! Where've ya got to, Hazel?" an anonymous voice barked from the direction of the ale barrels. "I don't pay ya ta loll about with the customers. There's thirsty men waitin'!"

Hazel flashed a venomous look over her shoulder. "Comin'!" she shot back. The look dissolved, and she turned back to King. "I'm home most nights after the supper hour here's done," she purred. "In case you'd like to come by . . . ?"

"Hazel!" the voice boomed again, sparing King a reply.

"All right, all right, I'm comin'!" she returned, her breasts jiggling as she spun toward the sound. "It's good to see you again, King," she said over her shoulder. "Don't be a stranger." Then, raking him from head to toe with her gaze one last time, she disappeared in the crowd, swatting the familiar hands that groped her breasts and pinched her bottom as she went.

King didn't resume his seat. He snatched up his caped coat, beaver hat, and riding gloves, and narrowed his dark stare upon Will Bowles.

"Don't ever put me on the spot like that again," he gritted through clenched teeth, as he shrugged the coat on.

"You've been tight as a drum since you came back, King," the youth defended. "I thought maybe—"

"Well, you thought wrong," King interrupted. "Just so we understand each other, I have never needed anyone to do my procuring for me. I'm a rogue, remember? Leastwise, that's what everyone accuses, and I certainly wouldn't want to disappoint my critics. Besides, you heard her: Helston's been gone for months. The last thing I'd need is for him to put in now, and find us coupled together in his bed. He knows we once were lovers.

"Now then, the *Cormorant* will be ready to sail again in a sennight, but unless we have a miracle, I will not be, though I must nonetheless. She'll rendezvous with the *Hind* next Friday week, and I've got too many coils to untangle right here on land to worry about intercepting French merchantmen for contraband in the name of the Crown. That's why I'm 'as tight as a drum,' as you so aptly put it."

"I'm sorry, King," Will said. "I meant no harm."

"And no harm's been done. Now, let us take our leave while we can all still say that, shall we?"

Fifteen

"What do you mean, they aren't leaving?" King roared, pacing the carpet in the drawing room like a caged lion.

"Lower your voice," his mother commanded. "You'll have the lot of them down here, Basil."

"Perhaps that's best," he flashed, stopping in front of her, arms akimbo. "Mother, what have you wrought here?"

"Certainly not this—intentionally, at any rate," she responded, the words riding a sigh. "But now that it is wrought, don't you think the better course would be to work together for the common good, dear? Running mad won't solve this, Basil."

King's posture collapsed. "Mother, you have put me in the impossible position of having to tell Lady Ann Cuthbertson that I do not intend to offer for her, since you haven't corrected your mistake as I asked you to."

"I've made no mistake. If you will hear me out, you'll see that."

King loosed a bestial howl.

"What are your intentions in regard to Lark?" the countess asked as the guttural sound died to a low moan. "She thinks you want her for your mistress."

"I never—"

"She said that also, when she begged me to find some alternative means by which she could honor her debt that didn't include the Marshalsea. However, in view of the situation *you* have wrought, she was willing to return to that odious place if needs must, rather than remain under the same roof with you. How have you managed that?"

"So, you two have been picking me apart, have you?" he snapped. "I should have guessed."

"Do you love her, Basil?" his mother asked. She had a maddening way of answering a question with a question, and completely ignoring almost everything put to her directly. That had driven him to distraction since he could stand without his knees buckling. But this was different. She'd spoken in a soft tone that he'd last heard in the nursery. Taken aback, he stared as she went on speaking in that same manner. "Is it love that you feel for this girl," she said, "or infatuation or simply lust? No! Do not be so quick to answer. Search yourself, dear. I'm not passing judgment. It's important."

"I've been infatuated a number of times. No one knows that better than you, Mother; you've pointed it out to me often enough. I want her, yes. When I held her in my arms last night, it was all I could do to let her go. If she hadn't . . . put me in my place, I don't know what might have happened. But it wasn't just lust. This is . . . different. I don't presume to understand it. I definitely don't like it; it's too painful, like something with sharp teeth gnawing at my bones from the inside out, but there it is. Make what you will of it, though I sincerely doubt that you, of all people, are qualified to counsel anyone on the complexities of love. Not even the sages of old have been able to manage it."

"I never hated your father, Basil. I hated the society that found it acceptable to join two people for the sole purpose of continuing the line, with no more emotion than one might summon breeding horses or hunting hounds."

"Isn't that exactly what you're trying to do to me? You contradict yourself."

"Let me finish," she pleaded. "This needs to be said finally, and it's difficult for me, dear. I was young and idealistic, full of romantic notions and desperately in love when I married your father. He was . . . doing his duty, nothing more. He was a product of the times. I lost my illusions and soured quickly."

"That explains much," King conceded. "Under such circumstances, why did you never take a lover . . . or did you?"

"No. I refused to become a part of the society I hated."

"Why, after all these years, do you tell me this now?"

"Because I do not want to see you tread the same path that your father did—that *I* did, trapping myself with him in a loveless marriage. One cannot live without love, Basil. Living such a life withers the spirit and makes one bitter . . . and old before one's time.

"I was insanely jealous of Mattie Bowles and her love child," she went on. "Jealous—to this day if you can imagine it—of a poor crofter's daughter with nothing to recommend her except the one power I lacked, a power neither wealth nor nobility could buy—the power to make a man love her. Oh, how I envied it!

"I see you struggling with the same demon—your father's demon . . . and mine. I couldn't bear to see some love-starved young thing destroyed after bearing your successor, while you flit from bed to bed seeking something you've had all along and were too blind to see. I'm speaking of Lark, Basil. She is in love with you, and unless I miss my guess you are in love with her also."

King sank down on the lounge and stared. That his mother was even having this conversation with him boggled his mind and left him speechless.

"Who better than myself, having hungered for love all my life, could counsel you in this? I'll admit that I resorted to drastic measures to bring out the truth. But don't you see it had to be brought out whatever the cost? I invited the Cuthbertsons here to that purpose. You cannot deny that it worked. I will admit that this is unfortunate for Lady Ann, but she is not for you, Basil. Such a union would send you into the arms of another before the ink on the marriage lines had dried."

King was beginning to see his mother in a whole new light. How could he have been so blind to her pain? He heaved a ragged sigh and dropped his head in his hands. Though he didn't agree with her method, she was right, of course. Marriage to Lady Ann Cuthbertson would have been a disaster.

"That very first night, when you paraded Lark before me in the Great Hall, all bedraggled and caked with mud, I saw in her eyes what lived in her heart. She was radiant. I saw myself forty years ago, and then I saw her change toward you—just as I changed toward your father—in the space of a blink. I relived the hurt, the terrible heartache in that one fleeting moment. The reverie was crueler coming that way, at your hands. What did you do to that girl to put that look in her eyes?"

"Something I doubt she will ever forgive," he lamented. "I assured you that she wasn't Lady Ann Cuthbertson."

The countess nodded. "And from that, she took it that you intended her for your mistress, nothing more," she said, answering her own question.

"Evidently."

"Absolutely," she corrected. "You seem to have inherited your father's barbaric lack of finesse. Please God, you haven't inherited his penchant for mistakes."

"Your talk with Lark," King said. "How did you settle it?"

"We didn't," she blurted. She took a small velvet jewelry box from the card table beside her chair and opened it. "This came just a while ago, at last," she said. Handing it to him, she held her peace while he stared at the brooch inside, and fingered it with a light touch. "This may . . . settle it," she said, drawing his eyes. "Do you want to give it to her, or shall I?"

Two pressing issues. Which to tackle first? There really wasn't a choice. Dinner was a disaster. Lark was absent,

and Lady Ann's fawning, gushing attempt at blatant seduction was more than King could bear—more than he
would bear again.

He couldn't help but pity her. This wasn't a lovesick
young thing's coy flirtation; it was a desperate woman's
crashing attempt to beat back inevitable spinsterhood. It
was pitiful to see, and he couldn't in good conscience let it
go on any longer. How it had gotten this far out of hand,
he couldn't imagine. He had never even kissed the
woman, at least not anywhere but her daintily gloved
hand. Yes, he had danced with her at balls and socialized
with her at fetes—even invited her and that harpy of an
aunt to the townhouse for dinner. And yes, he had been
considering her as a wife for the self-same reason his
mother accused: to breed the heir to the earldom.

He had never offered for her formally. He would have
done, however, but for Lark. There was no point in lying
to himself; that was something he made it a point never to
do. His actions had given Lady Ann hope, and his
mother's invitation had clearly given her expectations of
an imminent proposal. Never was that more obvious than
now, as he sat with the starry-eyed woman in the salon,
where he'd invited her to join him after the meal. Making
matters worse, the comtesse insisted upon accompanying
them "to see that all proprieties are observed," as she had
so dourly put it. If she only knew how ridiculous that was.
Lady Ann would have been as safe alone with him as she
would have been in a sacrosanct cloister.

Basil Kingston, Earl of Grayshire, had battled the
French on the high seas under Nelson. He had been under
fire, under siege, and under the knife. He had lost his eye
in service to the Crown, and stared death in the face on
more than one sinking ship in his career, but never had he
known such heart-stopping trepidation as he did now in
his drawing room, seated across the Persian carpet from
these two women.

Lady Ann's face was flushed—*blotched* more accurately described the odd red patches that spotted her cheeks, King decided. His mother should not have been spared this confrontation. She'd wound this coil, after all. If it hadn't been for her invitation that brought them to the Manor, the budding relationship between himself and Lady Ann could have simply died out, since the Season was over. By the end of the little Season, it would in all probability have been forgotten. These were intelligent aristocrats after all. They would have gotten the message without having to have it spelled out as painfully as it must be now. Be that as it may, King exempted his mother, and took the blame squarely upon his shoulders. Above all he was a gentleman, and as such he would take responsibility.

"I will be leaving forthwith on official business for the Admiralty," he began, "and since it isn't likely that I will be returning to the coast before your departure for London, I wanted to bid you farewell, and express again my regrets that I was unaware Mother had arranged your visit, and thus have been inaccessible for most of it."

It was a half-truth, but a kind half-truth. Unfortunately, judging from their expressions, he wasn't to be let off the hook so easily. Lady Ann's lower lip had begun to tremble, and her eyes were glazed with unshed tears. Her aunt, sitting ramrod rigid on the lounge, had pulled a face that might have clabbered cream, and narrowed eyes on him that looked like two withered prunes.

"Do you mean to say that we have misunderstood your intentions, my lord?" the comtesse breathed, her pearl choker riding up and down on her wrinkled neck as anger deepened her breathing.

"No, my lady," he said. "My mother has done that, I'm afraid."

The comtesse gasped. "Explain yourself, my lord!" she demanded. "Your mother was not in Town this Season.

She did not ply us with invitations to fetes, with jaunts to Almack's and Drury Lane, with intimate dinners at your townhouse in the Square."

"They were hardly intimate, my lady," King said. "I invite many guests to my townhouse—to dinners, and fetes, and to the theatre. I see that you have read more into my friendship than I intended, and for that I am heartily sorry—"

"Balderdash!" the comtesse shrilled, surging to her feet. "You and Ann were as good as betrothed!"

What had happened to her French accent?

"Aunt, *please*," Lady Ann wailed. "Don't make this any worse than it is. It's clear that he . . . he doesn't want me. . . ."

"Be still, you little fool! He's made you a laughingstock," the woman seethed, as though King weren't there. "I *told* you to take the initiative. Men are such buffleheads. They think *they* do the choosing. It's too late now. You've lost your chance—your last chance. No one will offer for you now. I could just thrash you!"

"Lady Ann," King said softly, "you are a very lovely young woman. Your aunt is wrong. You will find a suitable mate in spite of her. She has done you more harm than good, and a great disservice trying to persuade you otherwise." He ignored the comtesse's gasp. Those tear-filled eyes of Ann's were hard to bear, but bear them he would. "I will admit that I had once hoped our relationship might eventually come to something . . . more, but I respect you far too much to deceive you. After much soul-searching I have come to the conclusion that it cannot be. If I were to offer for you, it would be for the purpose of getting an heir, nothing more. It would be a loveless marriage. I am the product of such a marriage. I want more for us both than the shallow existence I could offer you."

"But what of me . . . of what I want?" Ann whined. "It would be enough . . . to bear you a son . . . to . . . to—"

"For God's sake don't beg," the comtesse shrilled. "Remember yourself! Hold your head high and spit on him, this cad, this rogue, this—"

"Madam, be still!" King thundered. "Forgive me, but you are the reason your niece is unwed after three Seasons. No man will offer for her with you in the bargain." He turned to Lady Ann. "Search yourself," he said. "You do not love me. You are desperate to wed—driven to it, just as I am driven to produce an heir. I could not do that to you. Could you honestly do it to me?"

Lady Ann lowered her eyes.

"I thought not," he murmured. "You are too fine for that. Let us salvage what we can of this unfortunate business, and part friends—"

"Hah!" the comtesse erupted. "'Friends'! When I have done, Grayshire, you will never hold your head up in Town again."

"As a friend," King went on, his voice raised so Lady Ann could hear over her aunt's bluster, "I advise that you follow the one bit of sound advice your aunt has given you: take the initiative—but with *her*, while you still can."

"Come, Ann. Stop that sniveling! We leave at once," the comtesse charged.

"That isn't necessary," said King. "It's late, and travel in these parts is unsafe for two women alone at night. My groom will accommodate you in the morning, if you wish to leave. No one is sorrier than I for this unfortunate situation. My mother should have consulted me before putting any of us in this awkward position. She is most distressed over her error in this misunderstanding, and I humbly apologize on her behalf." He turned to the comtesse. "Lady Vera," he said, "in regard to your threat earlier, I might remind you that any aspersions you cast upon me—in Town or otherwise—will only reflect upon Lady Ann and upon yourself. And now, there are pressing matters that I must attend to before I retire, and I must ask that you excuse me. I bid you good night."

* * *

Lark had a tray in her room for dinner. Agnes Garwood had gone missing. Lark presumed she was having another assignation with Leander Markham. That had been happening more often after dinner of late, and rather than wait for her abigail and friend to return, she packed what was left of the clothes she'd worn in prison into her old portmanteau herself. She would take none of the fine dresses and spencers and wrappers and gowns that King had provided for her to wear as his mistress. Besides, such finery would only be stolen in the Marshalsea: Since the countess hadn't offered her an alternative, that was where she intended to go. Perhaps then an arrangement could be worked out to refund what King had given, if such a thing were possible. It was the only way she could think to ever repay the debt. All that could be worked out later. What mattered now was that she leave Grayshire Manor without seeing King again.

Lark was more than a little chagrined about leaving Agnes behind. She certainly wouldn't need an abigail in debtors' prison, however, and no matter what King and his mother's issues were with her, she couldn't imagine either one turning Agnes out because of their grievances.

She fingered her old pelisse as she folded it. It had once been fine. Now it was threadbare, and ripped from the tug-of-war it had suffered on her first day of incarceration in that awful place. It wouldn't be warm enough with winter coming on. She shuddered, imagining the cold wind off the Thames whistling through the Marshalsea chasing snowflakes and whipping up little cyclones in the dust. No. She wouldn't think of that. There was nothing for it but to go, and go quickly.

All at once it struck her: _Grayshire Manor is a walled, gated compound with its back to the bay. I shall need help escaping, and neither King nor his mother will lend a hand to that._ She sank down on the edge of the bed, pelisse in hand. There was someone else who might. She hated to interrupt Agnes and Leander Markham; they had so little time together. But she convinced herself that they would have plenty of time for assignations and trysts and stolen moments under the wisteria bower once she'd left the Manor.

Would the steward help her, or would he betray her to King? There was only one way to find out. She propped the note she'd written explaining her decision on the dressing chest. Then, snatching her portmanteau, she threw the pelisse over her shoulders and stepped out into the hall, only to pull up just short of colliding with someone she never thought she would see again.

"Biddie?" she cried. "Biddie, it *is* you. What are you doing here? Has his lordship rehired you?"

The girl stood, arms akimbo, raking her with contemptuous eyes. They settled on Lark's portmanteau, and she gave a nod and a scornful grunt, then disappeared through an all but invisible door on the landing that led to the back stairs and the servants' quarters below. Lark started after her, only to come face-to-face with King, mounting the stairs two at a stride.

"Where do you think you're going?" he thundered, relieving her of the portmanteau.

"Please let me pass," Lark said with resolve, though her legs were atremble and undermining her balance. "I am not running away from my responsibility . . . from what I owe you, but I cannot remain here, my lord. I mean to return voluntarily to the Marshalsea. I will work off my debt to you there—"

"How? How will you work off your 'debt'?" he interrupted. He had hold of her upper arms, and he'd bent close, that all-seeing eye burning toward her. "Well?"

"I . . . I don't know how yet, only that I will, I swear it, but I beg you, please don't send Agnes back there. She would die shut up in that place again after . . . after this."

Her head was reeling. King's scent overwhelmed her. His body heat scorched her. His nostrils were flared, and his hot breath puffed on her face smelling of the sweet dessert wine he'd had after dinner. She was foxed by his closeness, hopelessly caught in the sexual stream flowing between them on that cold, drafty landing.

"You aren't going anywhere," he seethed through clenched teeth. Slinging her over his shoulder with one strong arm, he snatched the portmanteau with his free hand, and bounded down the stairs with her.

Lark kicked her feet and pummeled his rigid back with her tiny fists until they were numb, but he didn't break his stride until he marched through the drawing room door, where the countess was waiting. She vaulted to her feet, her cane banging furiously.

"Basil Kingston, what is the meaning of this outrage? Put that girl down at once!"

"She was on her way back to the Marshalsea, if you can imagine it," he replied, dropping the portmanteau. "Sit down, Mother. I've just spent the most embarrassing hour of my life explaining to Lady Ann Cuthbertson and that harridan aunt of hers that you brought them here under false pretenses, and now this. Do you have any idea of the havoc you've wrought? Never mind. Don't bother to answer. I took your medicine with the Cuthbertsons, but I will not do so in this. You're going to help me here!"

Lark was hoarse from pleading with him to return her to earth, but he seemed not to notice. When her voice finally broke, her fists pummeled all the harder. She'd lost one of her slippers from kicking, and her bonnet had gone awry. It wasn't until she called him by name that he seemed to remember she was slung over his broad shoulder like a sack of flour.

"King . . . please put me down," she moaned.

He set her on her feet then, and searched her face, but he didn't let her go. She was grateful for that. Her cheeks were on fire and she was dizzy from the hot blood that had rushed there as she dangled upside down in such an indecorous position for so long. If he had let her go, she would have fallen in a heap at his feet.

"What did you say?" he breathed.

"I . . . asked you to . . . put me down," she murmured.

"No, before that . . . You called me 'King'! You *did*."

Lark's head was still reeling, but she heard the countess's cane thump the floor again. This time, it was a triumphant sound.

King reached inside his waistcoat and produced a black velvet case. "Do you remember when I gave you your jewels, I told you that one piece was yet to be delivered—a brooch with your initials engraved upon it?"

"And I told you it would prove nothing," she shot back. "I want nothing from you. You can't keep me prisoner here. You have to let me go!"

He opened the case, and thrust it toward her. "It was delivered this afternoon," he said. "Look at it, Lark. *Look*."

She took the case and stared down at the brooch inside. It gleamed at her from the satin lining, swimming in the unshed tears that flooded her eyes. She blinked them back, and the image came clearer. It was an exquisite gold oval on a horizontal bar framed in filigree. To the left, an elaborate "L" was engraved in scrollwork, to the right, an "E," for Eddington, and in the center, twice as tall as the other letters, was a flowing scrollwork "K." A "K" for "Kingston."

Sixteen

D<small>O</small> you still believe I wanted you for my mistress?" King murmured, folding her in his arms.

"I don't know what to believe," she replied, her face pressed against his indigo superfine jacket. It smelled faintly of tobacco, and his provocative male essence. In spite of herself, she ran her hand over the soft woolen cloth of his lapel.

"Lark," he murmured, tilting her face up until their eyes met. "I think I fell in love with you when I lifted you out of the Marshalsea dust that first day. Oh, I didn't know it then. That realization was quite recent. Mother here engineered much of it"—he cast the countess a scathing glance—"and while I certainly don't approve of her methods, I'm glad she intervened. I'm not doing this well, I know, but I want you to be my wife."

"You no longer need detain me," the countess said, rising. She leaned heavily on her cane, and Lark was certain she actually needed its support then. "It has been a grueling day, and I wish to retire."

"You make it sound as though I've been holding you hostage, Mother," King said. "She's hardly going to consent to marriage with a brute."

"If this is a serious proposal, it is passing bizarre," Lark observed, speaking to no one in particular.

King burst into hearty laughter. "My poor Lark," he chortled, sinking down with a dramatic flourish on one knee. "Will you marry me? Say yes, or I shall die and haunt you evermore."

"Now you're making mock of me," Lark said, suppressing a smile. She couldn't help it. No one would subject himself to such a ridiculous display in front of a witness—his mother, no less—unless he was serious, indeed. But talk of death and haunting sobered her. "You mustn't talk of dying," she said.

"Does that mean you would care?"

"Of course I would care. Don't even jest about death . . . ever." She was thinking of her father and gated churchyards and lost souls seeking sacred ground denied them. A cold chill crawled along her spine. She shuddered visibly, and King surged to his feet and pulled her into his arms.

"Marry me?" he murmured.

Lark looked into the depths of that all-seeing eye, into the moisture that had welled there glistening in the candlelight as he searched her own, and she melted. Never in her wildest dreams had she hoped . . .

"Yes, King," she murmured. "I will be your wife."

Lady Isobel's cane punctuated that with a rapid-fire response that resounded from the ceiling, as King took Lark in his arms and covered her lips with his warm, searching mouth. When their lips parted, the countess had poured them each a glass of sherry to mark the occasion, and resumed her seat, while King led Lark to the lounge and sat beside her.

"Now will you take the jewels I bought for you?" he asked. "I chose the iolites because they are the exact color of your eyes. I told you so when you modeled them if you recall. How could you not have known they were for you?"

"What's become of them, Basil?" the countess asked, before Lark had a chance to answer. "Have you put them in the valuables chest?"

For a moment, King stared into space, as though he were trying to conjure the answer from the shadows that had gathered around the periphery of the room now that darkness had fallen over the coast.

"They're no longer in my sitting room," Lark put in. "They were gone that very night. I asked you to have Smeaton or Peal collect them. One of them must have done."

"You did send Smeaton, didn't you, Basil?" the countess said. "You said you were going to, dear."

"No . . . no, I didn't," King responded, his voice hollow. "I completely forgot about those jewels until now."

"Check the chest, dear," the countess suggested. "You've been so overset of late. Perhaps you've forgotten you told Smeaton to retrieve them."

"I've a lot on my mind, it's true, but I'm hardly that absentminded, Mother."

"You were in a taking here that night. We argued, if you recall. You were beside yourself over the Cuthbertsons—ranting and raving, stomping about. Go and see, Basil."

The valuables chest was a large wooden locker fitted with a heavy padlock, bolted to the floor in the study. He was only gone for a brief time, but it seemed an eternity to Lark before he reentered the drawing room. His body language told all too well the futility of his search.

"Did you inquire of Smeaton?" the countess questioned.

"Yes. He thinks I'm quite mad to be sure. Lark, are you certain that you haven't misplaced them?"

"Positive," she replied. "They were on the gateleg table beside the door in my sitting room right where you left them. When I went back to my apartments, I unlocked that door so one of the servants could collect them, then I entered my bedchamber and locked the door between."

"When did you notice them missing?"

"Before I retired. I wasn't comfortable going to sleep until all my doors were latched. Considering what happened, I . . . didn't trust you. Shortly after, I heard my sitting room door close. I looked in, and the jewel case was gone. I assumed Smeaton or Peal had . . ." All at once she gasped.

Her mind reeled back to the figure of the maid she'd seen in the third-floor hallway before King had spun her into his arms. Then a more recent image took shape. She gasped again. "Biddie!" she cried. "I'd nearly forgotten!"

"Biddie?" King blurted. "What the devil has Biddie to do with this?"

"She's here—in the house. Did you rehire her, King?"

"Certainly not. You must be mistaken."

"No, I am not," Lark persisted. "She was up in the third-floor hallway just before you stopped me on the stairs. I thought I recognized her then, but I convinced myself that it couldn't be . . . until just now, that is, when I was leaving." King stared, clearly nonplussed, and the countess's jaw sagged open. "She was outside my door," Lark went on, "I nearly fell over her when I stepped into the hall. We spoke! I asked her if you had rehired her, but she didn't answer; she pulled a face, and ran through the service door on the landing. I was just about to follow her when you grabbed me and brought me down here. What with all that's happened since, it quite slipped my mind. Oh, King!"

"Bloody hell!" he trumpeted. Surging to his feet, he streaked from the room.

King crashed through the green baize door off the Great Hall that led to the servants' quarters below and bounded down the stairs. Most of the servants had retired, but Smeaton, Mrs. Hildrith, and Peal were still seated in the servants' hall when he burst into the room. A collective gasp greeted him. All three stared, mouths agape, their coffee cups suspended at sight of him. It was highly unusual for the master or mistress of the house to venture below stairs. Traditionally separate in aristocratic houses, the butler was master here, then the housekeeper, followed by the number-one footman. All others fell in the pecking order according to their importance in the household, with the hall boys and scullery maids at the end of the roster by seniority in accordance with their hire. All three below-stairs hierarchs were staring at him, their paste-gray faces testimony to the unlikelihood of his visit. If the cause weren't so critical, King would have laughed at the absurdity of the situation. Instead, he motioned them to stay, since they'd begun bobbing up and down out of rhythm, as though they didn't know what to do with themselves.

"Forgive the intrusion," he said. "Is there a person below stairs in this house who answers to the name of 'Biddie'? Bedelia Mead is her full name, and until recently she was employed at the townhouse."

"There is a lady's maid called Biddie here, my lord," said Smeaton. "She is in the employ of the Cuthbertsons."

"The Cuthbertsons?" he blurted. "I'd like to know the whys and wherefores of that, by God! Where is she reposed?"

"She is not below stairs," said the butler. "She is housed in the Cuthbertsons' suite, my lord, in the maid's quarters, adjoining."

King turned to the housekeeper. "Will you please go up and fetch her down, Mrs. Hildrith."

"*Now*, my lord?" the housekeeper responded. "Beggin' your pardon, my lord, but they'll likely all be asleep up there at this hour."

"Now," he insisted. "I know it's late. Wake them if needs must."

"Shall I have her come here, my lord?"

"Yes," he replied. "Don't mention me. I don't want her to know she's been caught out until the last. Just tell her she's wanted in the servants' hall. And don't leave it to her to come on her own. You are to accompany her. Is that clear?"

"Y-yes, my lord," she replied, set in motion.

"W-would you care to join us?" the butler queried, clearly at a loss as to the proper protocol for such an event.

"Thank you, no, Smeaton," said King. "Please carry on with your refreshments. I shan't inconvenience you long here. In future, however, you will inform me of the names and positions of all servants accompanying guests in this house."

"Yes, my lord."

"Bedelia Mead was sacked for good reason," King explained. "Since on-dits are inevitable, you may as well have the straight of it, so that at the very least the gossip will be accurate. The girl was physically abusive to Lady Eddington, and insubordinate upon reprimand for it. Had I been aware that she had gained admittance here she would have been evicted forthwith, and one of our staff would have been appointed to accommodate the Cuthbertsons in her place."

"Yes, my lord."

"As it is now, we'll likely have to have Bow Street in. There appears to have been a theft, and since the rest of the staff is above reproach, and Miss Mead is disgruntled, and has I have no doubt gained entrance for vengeance, she is suspect."

Both men's faces turned whiter still. They said no more while they waited, and King was grateful for that. He was just as uncomfortable being there as they obviously were having him pacing their domain. Mercifully, it wasn't long before Mrs. Hildrith skittered into the room, her skirts sweeping the door frame.

"She's not up there," she panted, out of breath, "and they're all in a tither for bein' woke up, and wonderin' where the girl has got to."

"Bloody hell!" King trumpeted. He spun to leave, only to pull up short as Leander Markham entered, hauling Biddie along by the arm. He was the only one besides his mother and Frith who knew Biddie on sight from visits to the townhouse.

"Are you looking for this?" Leander said to King, shoving Biddie ahead of him. "Lady Lark told Mrs. Garwood what was afoot, and she sent for me straightaway. Biddie here was leaving with this." He handed the girl's travel bag over. "You'll find what you're looking for inside. When

Ag . . . Mrs. Garwood and myself were strolling in the garden earlier, we saw the gel making for the main gate. We didn't think much of it until Lady Lark explained. I went after her at once, of course."

"Thank you, Lee."

"The whole house is in an uproar above stairs. The Cuthbertsons are beside themselves. You can't imagine the brouhaha."

"Oh yes, I can," said King. "Will you do me one more service tonight, old man?"

"Anything, unless you want me to go back up into that!" he replied, gesturing toward the upper regions.

King laughed in spite of himself, ignoring Biddie's whimpering protests. "Will you ride into the village and bring one of the land guards? You know where to find them. The grooms will take all night. I'll deal with the rest."

The following morning dawned dreary and gray, threatening rain. Breakfast was had late, owing to the ungodly hour that the inmates finally retired once the land guards took Biddie into custody, to be held over for the magistrate. The Cuthbertsons left at the break of dawn in a hired coach that they insisted be sent from the village, and the whole house seemed to sigh in relief. At least that's how it seemed to Lark, waking betrothed and scarcely able to part fantasy from reality.

After serving themselves a leisurely breakfast of creamed eggs, sausages, bacon, and grilled tomatoes from chafing dishes set out on the sideboard in the breakfast room, King had the landau brought around. Whisking Lark out of the house, he helped her climb into the four-wheeled, two-seater vehicle. The folding top was down, and Lark looked dubiously at the rolling slate-gray clouds bearing down on the coast.

"We'll likely need to put the top up if we don't hurry," King said, as they started down the drive.

"Where are we going?" she queried.

"Not far," he said. "There is someone I want you to meet."

Lark didn't press him for an explanation. There was a handsome wry smile on his lips that told her whatever his plan she had nothing to fear. Instead, she steered the conversation in another direction.

"What will happen to Biddie now?" she said.

"That will depend upon the court. Such a theft is a hanging offense."

"Oh," Lark murmured, swallowing hard.

"I see that the prospect disturbs you. Were she an aristocrat, transportation to either America or Botany Bay might have been an option, but since she's of the service class, such as that is hardly likely."

"And . . . if the charges were dropped, or someone were to speak up for her?" Lark said, avoiding his quizzical stare suddenly trained on her.

"By 'someone,' I presume you mean me?"

"I doubt there's anyone else who would speak on her behalf."

"You would wish it . . . after the way she's treated you?"

"It's just that . . . hanging seems so harsh for one so young. She might turn herself 'round if given the chance."

"You're serious."

"I shouldn't want to start our marriage with a . . . a *hanging*, is all."

"Ah! There it is. How insensitive of me not to remember. Forgive me? I'm not usually this muddled. There is much on my mind of late. It's no excuse, but it's the reason that I'm not myself, and botching this so badly—that, and the utter shambles love makes of a man's faculties." He took her lace-gloved hand in his and drew it to his lips. "I can deny you nothing," he murmured. "I doubt the charges can be retracted—'tis serious, this—but for you, my lovely Lark, I will speak for the gel. I doubt my word will hold much sway with the magistrates, however. You know the value of those jewels; you were with me when I bought them. Nevertheless, I shall do my bit—for you, not for her. She's gone beyond the pale."

Lark threw her arms around his neck in sheer appreciation. Her dire circumstances had begun with her father's suicide by hanging. She couldn't bear to taint their union with another, no matter how deserved. He was right, of course. His word might not be heeded, but in that moment her joy was immeasurable, until they rounded the bend and she realized where he was taking her.

The tall, square church tower appeared against the dreary sky. It had grown so dark that the flickers of candlelight winked from the recessed cottage windows in their diamond-shaped fretwork though it was scarcely midday. Only then did she realize that the glass in both buildings was mottled and tinted a rich shade of amber. There was the dreaded iron fence—even more disturbing in the jaundiced daylight—and the gravestones inside it, set awry by time and the weather. *Why is it that all old graveyards have crooked stones?* Where had she heard that such listing headstones hovered over restless souls? She shuddered, and her arms fell away from King's neck. How many were barred from the sanctity of that neat, consecrated park? How many were turned under the sod outside that eerie fence? Some of the graves were new—more than seemed natural somehow, and she gasped in spite of herself as the landau pulled to a halt before the cottage walk.

King handed her down, raised the two-part folding hood on the carriage against the threatening rain, then hurried her up the walk and banged the knocker. The door came open almost at once in the hand of a plump, rosy-cheeked woman who appeared to be in her sixties. She sketched a flawless curtsy for a woman of her size, and ushered them into a warm, book-lined study to wait for the vicar.

"I realize that this is hardly the sort of betrothal a woman dreams of," King began, drawing her into his arms, "but if we are to be wed when I return from London—"

"You're leaving again?" she cried. It was a hoarse, throaty supplication.

"To obtain the special license," he explained, "and to have that word with the magistrates." He slipped a small velvet pouch from his waistcoat pocket, and opened the drawstring. Reaching inside, he produced an opal ring surrounded by sapphires, removed her glove, and slipped it on her finger. "This is a family heirloom, handed down from generation to generation of Kingstons for four hundred years," he said, raising her hand to his lips.

"It's exquisite," Lark murmured.

"One day you will relinquish it to our eldest son, as Mother has relinquished it to you. But until then, my Lark, wear it always." All of a sudden, he frowned and drew her closer still. "I may have spoken too quickly just now," he said. "I know a grand society wedding in Town is every young lady's dream . . . but could you be happy with a quiet affair here, at Grayshire Manor? I am committed to perform a service for the Admiralty, and—"

"You've been recommissioned?" She panicked.

"No, no, it's nothing like that, but it is demanding, and it necessitates my keeping to the coast. I should be tending to it now, and would be, but for the repairs being made on the *Cormorant*. You needn't trouble your head with the particulars. Suffice it to say that by time I've returned from Town, the *Cormorant* will be ready to sail and I must man her. I shan't be about that longer than I was this last time—a sennight at best, a fortnight at the worst. These . . . absences must occur now and again until the Admiralty gives me leave to discontinue them. If we have the wedding here, we only need wait until I return with the license, next Tuesday week at the latest. If we go through the whole social brouhaha in Town, it could take months, even a year. It is, of course, totally up to you. I shall abide by whatever you decide."

"Well, well," said a white-haired figure shuffling over

the threshold. "Your lordship! Mrs. Wiggs tells me you've brought along a lovely young lady to brighten this dreary morning." The man extended his wrinkled hand to Lark. It was warm and smooth, his grip stronger than she would have supposed by the fragile look of him. His sparkling eyes were the bluest she had ever seen.

"Lark, allow me to present Reverend Timothy Faulkner, vicar of St. Kevern's Church," King announced. "Tim, this is my betrothed, Lady Lark Eddington."

"Ahhh," the vicar exhaled, giving a slow nod. There was recognition in the sound, and in the gesture. Had her scandal spread as far as this distant coast? If it had, he mercifully made no mention of it. She liked him at once, though there was something surreptitious in his glances toward King, and in King's toward him, for that matter.

"Well, my dear," King murmured, breaking her concentration. "Have you decided?" He turned to the vicar. "I asked Lark to make a rather difficult decision before you joined us," he explained.

"Not difficult at all," Lark spoke up. "Of course we shall have the wedding here. The last thing I want is a showy society wedding . . . under the circumstances. I need not prove anything to the *ton*. They abandoned me when I needed support. All that is past now."

"Then, Tim, will you do the honors?" King said. Though he addressed the vicar, he hadn't taken his hooded gaze from her face. Hot blood surged to her cheeks from that contact alone, but she couldn't look away. The riveting seduction in his eye held her relentlessly, and before the vicar, no less.

"Of course," the vicar replied. "Would you want the banns posted?"

"No," said King. "There shan't be time for that. We shall waive the banns in favor of a special license. I shall fetch it at once then, and we shall have the wedding, say . . . within a fortnight?"

"Splendid!" the vicar said. "And now you shall join me

for a cup of my housekeeper's excellent coffee to celebrate. Mrs. Wiggs is preparing it as we speak, and she has just made a batch of her legendary almond cream scones. I don't know how I should ever fare without her. She is a rare find as housekeepers go."

They engaged in casual conversation then, touching upon Lark's religious affiliation, how many would be attending, carefully chosen topics that deftly avoided all reference to her predicament. Whatever the vicar knew or didn't know of her circumstance, he was sensitive, and perceptive enough to avoid that which might make her uncomfortable.

"Vicar Faulkner, might I ask a question?" she inquired during an awkward lull in the conversation.

"Of course, my dear," he replied.

"I noticed that there are a number of new graves in the churchyard," she began, catching the look that passed between the two men as the words left her lips. There was that surreptitious exchange again. This time, the vicar's wrinkled cheeks lost color, and seemed to cave in before her very eyes. "Is there an epidemic of some kind?" she queried. By the strained look of him then, she was almost sorry that she'd brought it up.

"No," the vicar chortled—too quickly, she thought. "It's a hard life here for those who labor on land, and struggle with the sea. Folk age quicker on this coast than anywhere else in England, and the days are drawing in now that September is all but gone. The old-timers say that when the leaves fall, so do . . . well, I don't know if I agree with what they say." He clapped his hands, shifting his posture and the subject along with it. "Look here!" he said. "We've let this dreary day take us with such talk. A word of advice, my dear: If you plan to stand up to this coast, you need to leave the dead to their maker, and court the company of the living."

Seventeen

King left for London the following morning, leaving Lark and Lady Isobel to work out the details of the wedding. This was no mean task, since time was of the essence, and it called for another trip to Plymouth to choose Lark's gown. Agnes and Leander accompanied them—Agnes to choose a new wardrobe, since Lady Isobel had decided that she would take Lark's place as her companion, and Leander to serve as their escort, much to Agnes's delight.

It was a bittersweet time for Lark. Everything was changing. She would miss Agnes, but Lady Isobel pointed out that the position of abigail was simply too far beneath her, and promised to hire a suitable lady's maid to replace her. Lark couldn't argue with that, but when she lamented that she would miss her friend, the dowager, who never missed a beat, responded that she might voice that complaint to King, to the purpose of allowing her to remain at Grayshire Manor instead of putting her out to pasture at the dower house once they were married. She also pointed out that it would be more convenient for Agnes, since she and Leander were courting.

Lady Isobel made it plain that she had no objection to relinquishing her chatelaine, but she was set to dig her heels in if King stuck to his decision about moving her out of the Manor. It was worth a try to stay in close proximity to her friend, but though Lark agreed with the practicality of such an arrangement all the way around, she didn't hold out much hope of convincing King.

Agnes's wardrobe was secured, and Lark was fortunate enough to find a ready-made gown that fit her perfectly, though Lady Isobel was scandalized that it had come from Plymouth and not one of the exclusive dressmaker's establishments on Bond Street in London. Lark, on the other hand, was delighted with it, a soft, flowing, high-waisted gown of cream-colored silk twill, with an overskirt of embroidered panels and delicate puffed sleeves. Tulle and silk ribbon were purchased for her veil, since Agnes insisted upon making it herself, another facet of the trip that courted the dowager's disapproval. In the days that followed, that, at least, would change, as Agnes's skilled fingers wove their magic. It was the first opportunity Lark had to see her friend ply her skills at the trade she loved. The results were stunning. Even Lady Isobel had to admit, when the last hand-crafted silk ribbon rosebud had been sewn to the crowning wreath, that it by far surpassed any of the veils they had seen in the Plymouth shops. But the debacle over the gown was no more than a tempest in a teapot compared to the crisis that followed when King returned on Tuesday as promised, and called for an informal meeting with Lark and his mother in the drawing room.

He arrived on the brink of a storm. Festering, wind-driven clouds scudded low over the horizon hugging a sea more black than blue. It robbed the daylight early, and the footmen lit the candle branches just after nuncheon. By the time Lark and the dowager joined King in the drawing room, every pair of hands below stairs was at work fastening shutters and battening down for the flaw. Despite their efforts, drafts snaked their way across the floors, teasing the draperies and tapestries, and blatant gusts rattled the window glass, wailing like lost souls begging admittance. Lark shuddered, catching a glimpse of bilious yellow-gray sky before Peale fastened the last shutter in the room and hurried on to the next. So this was one of the dreaded flaws she'd heard so much about. It seemed to be bearing down on Grayshire Manor with a vengeance, and though the house was shut up tight, she could taste the wind-driven salt in the air.

"Are you cold?" King murmured, slipping his arm around her as he led her to the lounge.

Lark wasn't even aware that she'd shuddered. "N-no," she murmured. "It's just . . . the storm . . . it's frightening . . ."

"Don't say I didn't warn you," he chided. "Flaws are common occurrences on this coast. You're quite safe. The Manor has weathered more flaws than I can count in my lifetime alone, and it's still standing. There's nothing to fear."

There was much to fear, if she were to give rise to all of the superstitions about rain on one's wedding day. They were to be wed in the morning, and by the looks of things, in the midst of a tempest. Was it an omen? She shuddered again, so violently that King stripped off his coat of indigo superfine and draped it around her trembling shoulders. How that brought back memories. His body heat still warmed it, spreading his scent, and she leaned her face into the fabric and inhaled deeply.

"You are cold," he observed, frowning. Two strides took him to the bellpull. "I'll have one of the footmen start the fire. Can't have you coming down with a chill on the eve of our wedding."

"What is this all about, Basil?" the dowager intoned, with a tap of her cane. "Now we've lost the light, and there is much to be done before morning."

"Indeed," he replied, "which is precisely why we're meeting here."

"Explain," Lady Isobel demanded.

"I trust your trip to Plymouth went well?" he queried.

"Yes, yes, it went well. Your bride will not disgrace you in her ready-made gown, though I simply cannot see the reason for such haste to the altar. People will surely talk, and you know what they will imply."

"But we know that there is nothing to imply, don't we, Mother?" he said. "And I don't give a tinker's damn what people think. If not now, the way things are stacking up, we probably shan't get another chance to wed for months."

"Does that mean . . . ?" Lark breathed, not daring to finish the thought.

"It means, I'm sorry to say, that I've been unsuccessful in getting the Admiralty to relieve me of my current responsibilities. As soon as this flaw lets up, I shall have to put out to sea, provided the *Cormorant* is still seaworthy after the storm. I'm sorry, my love, there shan't be time for a wedding trip just now, but I promise I shall take you wherever you wish once my obligations are met. Wherever it's safe to travel in wartime, that is, and the Grand Tour once Napoleon is defeated, which hopefully shan't take much longer. Whatever your heart desires."

"I don't need the Grand Tour, King," she said, "I only need to be with you."

"And you shall. We have the rest of our lives. If all goes well, it shan't be long before I lift this millstone from 'round my neck. Until I do, I need you to trust me."

Lark nodded. "And Biddie?" she queried. "Were you able to retract the charges . . . to speak for her?"

King's posture deflated. "She's to be transported to Botany Bay," he said. "That was the best I could do. She's escaped the noose, and she'll have a chance for a decent life there if she amends her ways. This wasn't her first theft, I'm sorry to say. Her employer previous to the Cuthbertsons had her incarcerated in the Marshalsea for theft. In view of that, the magistrates were adamant."

He turned his gaze toward the dowager then, and Lark shuddered afresh at the look in his all-seeing eye bearing down upon his mother. What was this now? He was steeled for battle.

"I trust that all the arrangements have been made for the ceremony?" he asked.

"The vicar is prepared, and Agnes will stand up with Lark," the countess said.

"Is the dower house in readiness for your occupancy, Mother?"

The dowager cast a sidelong glance in Lark's direction. Lark wasn't prepared to broach that issue then, and her heart leapt. Something guarded in King's expression flagged caution, but she was trapped, and there was nothing for it but to speak.

"Must her ladyship go to the dower house?" she said. "Is Grayshire Manor not large enough for two women to occupy who are in accord?"

King's eye flashed toward the dowager. "You put her up to this, I gather?" he snapped. "Another of your manipulations, eh?"

"I shan't interfere, Basil—"

"Hah!" he blurted. "You've done that already."

"—and I shall relinquish the chatelaine gladly," she went on.

"I shall miss Agnes dreadfully, King," Lark pleaded. "It's true, I have a new abigail, Cora Baines, one of the housemaids from below stairs, who is most acceptable, but Agnes and I are friends, and I will be dreadfully lonely without her, especially with you away. . . ."

King threw his arms up in a gesture of defeat. "All right, I cannot fight the both of you," he said. "But only on a trial basis, and I shall claim a favor in kind." He turned to the dowager. "Lark has Agnes to bear witness for her, and that is as it should be. I reserve the right to have whom I will stand for me."

"And who might that be, Basil?" the dowager said guardedly.

"Will Bowles," he returned, "my brother. And high time you acknowledged it."

Lady Isobel vaulted out of her chair as though she'd been launched from a catapult, her cane tattooing a *rat-a-tat-tat* on the parquetry at the edge of the rug that mussed the fringe and left marks on the polished wood.

"Sit down, Mother!" he commanded, before she could

turn her sputtering into words. "This is my wedding, and I will have whom I will for my bridegroom's man. You may engineer the rest to your heart's content, but you have no say in this. It is my right."

"You expect me to sit under the same roof—in that holy place—with your father's bastard son?" she shrilled. She was incredulous. "I suppose you mean to have him to the wedding breakfast, as well?" She was shaking with rage. Her face had turned paste gray, except for the thin blue line her lips had become. They were pursed and trembling. Was she about to swoon? On her feet now as well, and ready to spring to the dowager's aid, Lark feared necessary action to be imminent.

"I do," said King, "and what's more, I expect you to receive him into my home graciously."

"Are you presuming to give me an ultimatum, Basil?" the countess breathed.

"If you expect me to consent to your petition to remain at the Manor instead of taking up residence in the dower house, you might say that I am, Mother. I intend to receive Will in my home. If you cannot accept that, I don't see how I can consent to your request to stay on here, which is why I conceded to it only on a trial basis. We shall see what we shall see, hmm?"

"King—"

"No, my love," he said, raising his hand in a gesture to stay Lark's protest. "Will Bowles is hardly responsible for the circumstances of his birth. Such as this is exactly why the dower house tradition was implemented since time out of mind; when the chatelaine is passed things are subject to change. Now, Mother, if you can accept this, you may remain, because Lark wishes it. If not, you will retire to the dower house, like my grandmother and great-grandmother before you. What shall it be?"

"You must really despise me, Basil," the dowager observed, gripping her cane in a white-knuckled fist.

"That is absurd," said King. "I was hoping you wouldn't

make this difficult, but I see now the folly of that. I hardly set out to air your dirty linen before Lark, but since you force the issue, I might remind you that Will would never have been born if you hadn't driven Father into Mattie Bowles's arms. You don't dislike Will. How could you? You don't even know him. I do, and we've been fast friends since we were in breeches. I know you don't like that. You don't like what he represents—Father's infidelity—because it reflects back upon you, and because you love to play the long-suffering betrayed wife. But martyrdom doesn't become you, Mother. I'm not asking you to welcome Will into our society with open arms after grinding him under your heel, so to speak, all these years. That would be absurd, but I am insisting that you receive him with the courteous good grace expected of the Dowager Countess Grayshire, just as you would any guest I invite to the Manor. If such a thing is too difficult for you, keep in mind that you would not have to suffer it were you removed to the dower house."

Lark held her breath. Was he in his cups? No, hardly castaway. His narrow-eyed stare was trained upon his mother. Her spine ramrod rigid, she stood her ground, and gave as good as she got in that duel of immutable eyes. How alike they were! That was part of the problem, Lark decided, looking on. They were too much alike. Neither was about to give quarter, and they both had a valid argument.

Lark tried to put herself in the dowager's place. How would she feel if King fathered an illegitimate child, and she was forced to tolerate its presence for thirty years? It would break her heart. On the other hand, what would it have been like if she were King, growing up an only child in a loveless house, with an absentee father and an embittered mother, seeking out his half-brother's company in secret out of sheer loneliness? She couldn't imagine it. One thing was certain. A sore that had been festering for thirty years wasn't going to be healed then and there in that drawing room, but she secretly vowed to bring such a healing about, for she loved them both.

"Tomorrow is my wedding day," she said with conviction, drawing both their eyes. "Must we spoil it with all this?"

King strode to her side and took her in his arms. "Nothing is going to spoil it, my love," he murmured. "Not this, not anything." He looked daggers at Lady Isobel. "Isn't that right, Mother?" he gritted through stiff lips. "We shall all have what we want. You shall remain at the Manor—at least for now—I shall have Will Bowles for my bridegroom's man, and Lark shall have the perfect wedding— you and this wretched storm notwithstanding. Now then, before the tempest brewing out there gets any worse, I shall see that the dower house is prepared straightaway."

"But, King, you just said your mother could remain here. . . ." Lark murmured.

"And indeed she may—on my terms," he responded. "I'm not having the dower house made ready for Mother, I'm doing it for *us*." His hooded gaze, so full of passionate promise, devoured her then. She saw nothing but her enigmatic bridegroom, heard nothing but the soft resonance of his sensuous voice.

"For us? I don't understand."

"I cannot give you a wedding trip," he said. "All we have until I put paid to Crown business is one night, and I intend it to be the most perfect night of your life. That cannot be had in this house, with its ghosts and its sorrows, and negative energy." Planting a soft kiss on her forehead he let her go, meanwhile smiling his irresistible lopsided smile. "Think of it as our own little hideaway," he said. "And now, I must away. I am behindhand, and the storm is gaining on me. I shan't be joining you for dinner."

"You aren't going out in all this?" Lark cried.

"I shall be dining at the Bowles's tonight," he replied. "You won't see me again, my Lark, until we stand together at the altar."

Eighteen

*L*ark *arrived at St. Kevern's in King's repaired* brougham, with Leander Markham decked out in his best dress coat of gray superfine over black pantaloons and an oyster-white brocade waistcoat, Agnes gowned in pale blue watered silk, and Lady Isobel wearing embroidered lavender-gray faille.

The storm spared them none of its fury. The lane was awash with puddles, and the wheels left a wake while plowing through muddy water up to their axles. Lark was fearful that the new mend wouldn't hold for the jouncing the coach was taking.

They reached the church nonetheless, and she noticed that all the fresh graves she had questioned the vicar about not a sennight ago were leveled, and neatly covered with sod, as though the ground had never been broken. She blinked her eyes, and looked again. No, they hadn't deceived her. It was passing strange. Had she dreamed those open graves and mounds of earth—so many of them? Was her mind playing tricks on her, and her eyes now as well? She wasn't given long to ponder. They had reached the church, and the driver had already climbed down and set the steps.

The sexton waddled down the church steps with slickers to spare the ladies' gowns. Umbrellas would have been useless; the wind-driven rain was sluicing down in horizontal sheets that would have turned them inside out.

Mercifully it was only a few steps to the church doors, and none of the finery suffered except for the ladies' slippers.

To Lark's surprise, the church was nearly filled with people. Lady Isobel had extended invitations to the wedding breakfast only to some of King's closest friends on the coast, but the ceremony was open to all, and many of King's crofters had come to wish him well despite the flaw. That was a phenomenal testimony to the man Lark was marrying, and she was so awestruck by it that she nearly lost her footing in her soggy slippers.

All eyes were trained upon her as she took her place beside Leander Markham, who would give her away in the absence of her father. Lady Isobel had already been seated, and Agnes was fidgeting with her veil, where the slicker the sexton had placed over her head had dislodged it.

Lark blinked toward the sea of faces—all smiling save one. There was a tall, buxom woman seated on the aisle near the altar, who was scrutinizing her in a manner that bordered on rude, even for a wedding, where scrutiny reigned. Aside from the odd expression she wore, the woman's flame-colored hair stood out in the dimly lit church.

"Who is she?" Lark whispered to Leander, without taking her eyes from the woman. "The one with the red hair."

Leander cleared his voice and inclined his head toward Lark, but it was a moment before he spoke. "That is Hazel Helston," he murmured. "Her husband is at sea some long months now."

"Is she one of King's crofters?" Lark wondered.

"No," said Leander. He hesitated, clearly struggling with his answer. "She is an old . . . friend of King's—of us all," he hastened to add. "From our childhood days."

"Oh, I see," Lark responded, reading between the lines. It wasn't hard to do. Lady Isobel was bristling, casting glances like poisoned daggers at the woman.

"Yes," said Leander.

Lark would have said more if King and a man who appeared to be a few years younger hadn't stepped from the vestry and approached the altar. When they turned toward her she almost gasped. So this was Will Bowles. The resemblance to King was striking, though he wore his hair shorter and it was sun-bleached in front. This was their first meeting, and yet . . . there was something about him that seemed familiar, though she couldn't quite put her finger on it. Something beyond his likeness to King. Was it his stance, a mannerism, an expression? There wasn't time to analyze it then; the procession had begun, and her eyes shifted to the tall, lean silhouette of the man who was about to make her his wife. All else paled before him—even the flame-haired Hazel Helston, whose misty gaze had shifted toward King also. Lark paid her no more notice then, and when she looked for her again after the ceremony, the red-haired beauty had disappeared.

Lark didn't draw an easy breath until after the wedding breakfast. The guests were very gracious, and the food, prepared by the Grayshire Manor staff, was a delectable feast from the endless array of viands, to the magnificent wedding fruitcake glazed with apricot preserves and frosted with fondant, to the delicate marzipan fruits and flowers.

Lady Isobel retired early. Being in company with Will Bowles was clearly more than she could bear, though she didn't fly into alt and disgrace herself as Lark feared she might, judging from her deportment in the church. Will Bowles soon followed, but the others were still enjoying the fare when King whisked her away to a waiting coupe, and drove her through the blustery gale to the dower house.

It loomed larger than she remembered, with its stone façade blackened and slick with rain. No lights shone from within. The shutters had been latched against the gale. King carried her up the broad steps and in through the double doors, where the warmth of blazing hearths and the glow of polished candle branches welcomed them. In spite of the short distance from the coupe to the doors, Lark's gown was plastered wet to her body. Agnes's exquisite veil hung limp down her back, dripping water on the parquetry, and the wayward tendrils that always framed her face were plastered to it now, obscuring her vision.

"You're soaked through," King murmured. "What you need is a nice hot bath; can't have you taking a chill."

"But . . . how can I? There's no one to prepare it."

"I have already prepared it," he said.

Streaking through the Great Hall, he entered through an all but invisible door cut in the wainscoting under the servants' hall stairs, and carried her down a long narrow stairway lit by candle sconces. Carved in the stone, it wound in a circular fashion below stairs, parallel to the servants' quarters and separated from it by a thick wall. A pleasantly scented warm draft wafted toward her from below, where cold, musty dampness should have permeated the air, considering how far down into the earth the stairwell had been dug. Looking down, she saw a soft mist rising.

"Where are we going?" she said. "Are we still in the house? We've come so far down. . . ."

King laughed. "You'll see," he said. "Do you trust me, Lark?"

"Y-yes," she said, wishing the minute the word left her lips that it was said with more conviction. But he laughed again, putting her at ease. That sensuous baritone rumble resonated through her to the very core, and she tightened her grip on his broad shoulders, giving a playful little squeeze. She did trust him. She had married him, hadn't she? But there was still so much she didn't know about this mysterious man she'd just pledged herself to for life. So much. His business with the Crown, for one thing, and then there was the beautiful red-haired Hazel Helston for another. She had never felt jealousy where Lady Ann Cuthbertson was concerned. King wasn't in love with her, and there was nothing of a physical nature between them. There was something between King and the Helston woman, however—something that went way back in their history—something sexual. It hardly took a scholar to deduce that, considering Leander Markham's halting explanation and the dowager's poisonous glowers at the woman across the aisle. Lark had felt more than a twinge of jealousy right then and there, but a few steps from the altar, despite the fact that she'd made herself a solemn promise that nothing from King's past would hold sway over their future. She was no bird-witted goose. Of course King had been with women—many women. It was only that this woman was the first she'd had to face.

"We're nearly there," he said, his breath coming short.

Where? she wondered. And then, as if in answer, he set her on her feet upon a mist-draped landing, but he didn't let her go.

"Your bath awaits, madame," he said. Taking her hand, he bowed from the waist and led her into a little alcove with a domed ceiling. A blazing chandelier was hung from it, and below, almost hidden by the fragrant mist, was a rather large, tile-lined bath sunken in the floor. Lark gasped. It butted up against the wall beneath a round-faced lion's head with closed eyes, and an open mouth that was carved of the stone, a bath spacious enough to hold at least four comfortably.

"What is this?" she breathed.

"This, my love, is the Kingston equivalent of a Roman bath," he said. I left orders that it be cleaned out and made ready before I left for London. Then, last night before I went off to the Bowleses', I instructed the staff to see to the last-minute preparations. It hasn't been used in ages."

"But . . . in the dower house? Does your mother know that this is down here?"

"I doubt she does. This wasn't built for the dowager residents. Aging, infirm women would hardly be inclined or able to negotiate that staircase, and the house wasn't always occupied. It was often vacant years at a time, just as it is now. The Kingston men were quite scandalous rapscallions, I'm afraid, and Great-grandfather Basil was the worst of the lot. It was he who built this bath—for his pleasure, of course."

"Oh," Lark murmured, around an audible gulp. Had King ever brought Hazel Helston down here? He must have done. There went that pang of jealousy again. "But where did all this come from? I've never seen the like," she said, attempting to beat back the jealous thoughts.

"I'm certainly glad of that," he chided, offering her one of his irresistible lopsided smiles. "Well, since you've caught me out, you may as well know that for generations, up until my father's death, the Kingston men were . . . privateers—pliers of the 'trade,' as it is known hereabouts." He swept his arm wide. "All that you see, the marble, tiles—even the plans, and the ancient Roman formula for watertight concrete—all is plunder, contraband brought ashore from ships wrecked off the Point."

"But . . . is that legal?" Lark asked, wide-eyed.

"No," he said through a throaty chuckle, which erupted into hearty laughter that echoed through the bath. "Hardly that. My God, your naïvete delights me." He pulled her close in his arms. "Don't ever change, my wonderful, beautiful Lark. You are a gift to the senses."

"But . . . how does it work? Where does the water come from?"

"Rainwater flows down through pipes from a catch basin on the roof and is stored in cisterns, where it's heated over hearths"—he pointed toward the stone lion's head with the gaping mouth—"then fed to the baths through these fellows," he explained. "Afterward, it empties through petcock drains in the floor of the tubs."

"'Tubs'?"

"Yes, there are three. You progress from one to the other. This is the first." He bent down and tested the temperature of the water with his hand. "Ahh, yes, it's perfect. This is the warm tub. The Romans called it the *tepidarium*. Through that arch, you'll find another, called the *caldar-*

ium. The water is hotter there. Beyond that is the *frigidarium*, filled with cold water, to close the pores after bathing in the others."

"And you made all this ready before you left for London? How did you know there would be a flaw to provide the water?"

"I didn't. I'd planned to use the water reserved from the last rain. It pours down often enough. It doesn't take much. These tubs are only about three feet deep. I'd have carried it here on my back if we were in drought. You see, my love, I mean to seduce you here."

"O-oh," she stammered. Had that become her mantra? Did her voice crack this time, too? If it did, he didn't seem to notice. All at once she was in his arms, melting under the soft, searching pressure of his kiss. The mist swirling about them had warmed the wet twilled silk of her gown, though it still clung to her contours, inviting his roaming hand to find her breast and fondle the nipple grown hard beneath his fingers. He slid them lower, caressing her thigh, and inched up the fabric along her side until he found the bare flesh beneath.

The close-fitting gown was made to be worn with only a slip underneath it, just as so many gowns were that season, since the fabrics were so sleek and revealing that the bulk and seams of undergarments would show through. When he touched her naked belly and fondled the hair curling beneath, she lurched as though she'd been shot, unprepared for the riveting volley of achy-hot sensations ignited by those skilled fingers.

"We'd best get you into that bath," he murmured against her lips.

"But . . . I have no maid," she said. "The gown fastens in back, and I can't undo it on my own."

"That shan't be a problem," he said.

Turning her around, he deftly undid the silk laces that gave the bodice such a graceful, high-waisted shape, and slipped it down over her shoulders. It slid the length of her and puddled like a cloud about her feet. The underskirt soon followed, and she stood naked before him. It was quite proper—he was her husband, of course—but this was all so new to her, and happening so quickly, her first instinct was to cover her nakedness with her hands and arms; they flew every which way. But he turned her toward him in a slow, gentle embrace, took both her hands in his and drew them to his lips, before placing them gently at her sides.

"You are exquisite," he murmured, sliding his familiar, one-eyed gaze the length of her. "But you're trembling. You can't still be cold in all this steamy heat."

"N-no," she stammered. "It's just . . . just . . ."

"You have nothing to fear," he said. Taking her hand, he led her to the steps at the edge of the bath. "Walk down. It's quite safe. I shan't let go of your hand."

Lark did as he bade her, if for no other reason than to hide her nakedness under the misty water. It was lukewarm, scented with rosemary and flower petals, and she groaned in delight in spite of herself, and closed her eyes to the sight of him smiling down at her. When she opened them again, he was stripping off his clothes, and she vaulted erect in the water that barely covered her nipples.

"What are you doing?" she cried.

"I'm getting ready to join you," he said.

"No!" she shrilled. "I mean . . . you can't. There isn't room."

"There's plenty of room."

"But . . ."

"I'm just as chilled as you are, my love, and just as soaked through."

"Th-there are other tubs, my lord," she reminded him.

"I am your 'lord' no longer, Lark, I am your husband," he said, peeling off the Egyptian cotton shirt plastered to his torso. "Besides, how can I seduce you properly from another tub? You overestimate my capabilities, my dear."

Hot blood raced to Lark's cheeks. Her ears were on fire.

He had stepped out of his inexpressibles and drawers, and stood naked before her. He was aroused, and the gasp left her lips before she could smother it politely with a cough. She couldn't take her eyes from the long, corded length of him towering above her in the candle glow.

He made no attempt to hide his nakedness as she had done. He descended the steps and sank into the water with a low, guttural moan. There was something in his hand—a porcelain jar. He set it on the edge of the bath and took her in his arms.

Lark's breath caught in her throat as their bodies touched with nothing but water between them. His groan upon contact drew her closer. It was a long moment before he loosened his hold and leaned back, looking her in the eyes. Their bodies were still touching. The bruising ecstasy of his member, pressed heavily against her belly then sliding lower and nestling in the hair between her thighs, extracted another gasp from her dry throat.

He leaned back then, and reached for the jar. There was oil inside. It was scented with something mysterious and exciting. Lark inhaled deeply.

"Patchouli and sandalwood," he explained, smoothing some over her shoulders and breasts. "Precious oils from the Orient . . . and other ingredients to give you pleasure."

Lark found her voice, albeit scratchy and thin. "Contraband also?"

"Of course," he replied.

Before she could answer, he hoisted her out of the water by the waist, and sat her down on the towels laid out on the edge of the bath.

"Lie back," he said, easing her down on them.

He moved his skilled hands over her body in slow, tantalizing strokes, slathering the oil over her belly and thighs. Her heart took a tumble. His fingers flitting down, up, between—over that secret place—made her shudder with pleasure as they played lightly over her sex, massaging in the oil ever so gently until the tender flesh tingled.

Pulling her back into the water, he leaned into her until the oil coated him also, and lavished a long deep kiss upon her, before lifting her out of the tub and drawing himself up beside her.

"Come," he said. Wrapping her in one of the towels at his feet, he led her through another arch, to where the hot bath waited.

Lark stepped into it gingerly. The heat was pleasantly invigorating. Her whole body throbbed like a pulse beat from the steamy hot water, from his closeness, from the dizzying scents wafting toward her from the heated oil he'd lavished upon her. The combined sensations had a mellowing effect on her senses, and a startling effect on her sex. It felt swollen, engorged, as though it were about to explode.

King began sponging the oil from her shoulders with a gentle, circular motion that wrenched a moan from deep down inside her. She recalled, in a stark flash by comparison, the scathing bath Biddie had inflicted upon her at the townhouse, and she shuddered, remembering. But the memory was short-lived. King's concentric circles slid lower, to her breasts. He was circling slowly, coming closer and closer to their puckered tips, but not close enough to the tall, hardened nipples to relieve the ache. How could she bear it? It was torture; but, oh, what divine torture, and she moved into his motion, eager for more.

"In ancient Rome," he panted, "the bathers would coat their bodies with oil to loosen the dirt, then scrape the stuff off with wicked-looking metal tools. I shall stop short of that, my love." He set the sponge aside and rubbed the oil into her nipples with his thumbs and forefingers until she arched herself against him, her breath suspended. It was almost beyond bearing. "Put your arms around me, Lark," he said in a throaty murmur.

She clasped him to her, hypnotized by the ebb and flow of the water that buoyed them, by the heady scents of the oil and his raw maleness threading through her nostrils, by the hooded all-seeing eye that devoured her, and his hot breath puffing on her wet skin. Every nerve ending, every pore was open to him, captive of his energy. She was as foxed by his ardor as a lord in his cups.

"Lower," he murmured.

Lark slid her hands over his torso, over the silky, dark chest hair that narrowed to a thin line below his narrow waist.

"Take it in your hands," he whispered, his deep voice husky with desire.

Lark did as he bade her, and she gasped as his sex responded to her touch.

"No, forgive me . . . *don't*," King groaned, throwing back his head. He lifted her hand away and raised it to his lips. "It's too soon if I am to pleasure you the way I want," he murmured. "You have a touch that wreaks havoc on a man's member, my love. Another minute, and . . ."

His mouth closed over hers then, and he encircled her waist with one arm while he spread her legs with the fingers of his other hand and probed the hair curling between her thighs. He moved slowly, lightly at first against the surface, then pressed deeper, the mysterious oil he'd slathered there heated by the friction of his skilled fingers causing waves of throbbing sensation rippling through her loins. Lark stiffened, and he drew her closer.

"I'm sorry, it may hurt . . . just a little this first time," he murmured against her lips. "There's no other way, my love. The water and oil will help ease the pain."

She drew him closer then, as though in a stupor, and found his lips as he inched his fingers deeper still, then eased them inside her, gliding on the silky dew of her first penetration. All at once, he withdrew them, and filled her with his member. The sudden motion nearly stopped her heart, and she shuddered, giving herself in rapt abandon to the icy-hot contractions convulsing her sex. Groaning, he lifted her hips and guided her legs around his waist as they moved together in a crazed frenzy of total release.

There was no pain now, only the pulsating heat generated by his member filling her—swelling inside until it seemed to burst, filling her with the warm, pulsing rush of his seed.

Lark clung to him. Her breath was coming in short gasps in concert with his pleasured moans. He dropped his head down on her shoulder, and it was some time before he spoke. When the words finally came, they were choked with tears, though none spilled down.

"Are you all right, my Lark?" he murmured through a tremor.

"Yes," she said. "Oh, King . . . I never dreamed . . . !"

"Neither did I," he gritted through a humorless laugh. "Neither did I."

After a moment, he stood and lifted her in his arms. Snatching a towel, he wrapped it around her and carried her to the third bath. No steam rose from this one. The water was cold, and she squirmed in his arms.

"Must we?" she said. "I'm so warm now, and it looks so . . . awfully cold."

"We must," he said. "The cold will help the soreness. Don't worry, my love, I'll soon warm you up again. This is only the beginning of our one most perfect night."

Nineteen

Submersion in the cold tub was brief. Afterward, King rubbed Lark briskly with towels to get the blood flowing, and carried her to a sleeping chamber off the bath. It was a small, sparsely furnished room, though well-appointed, with a sumptuous fur rug on the floor and a mahogany sleigh bed, made with thick, turned-down counterpanes, creamy sheets, and mounds of feather down pillows. A blazing hearth warmed it, providing the only light. It cast a warm, amber glow over the chamber, softening the shadows that seemed to dance in the corners like living things.

King set her down in the center of the bed, and tucked the counterpanes around her. He was still naked. The sheen on his skin from the scented oil glistened over his corded body. He was golden in the firelight, and Lark couldn't tear her eyes away from the tall, well-muscled length of him, from his broad chest and shoulders, to his sleek, flat stomach and well-turned thighs. He was the most magnificent creature she had ever imagined, and he was hers till death did they part. It was almost too good to be true.

"Are you hungry?" he murmured. "There is some fruit, some cheese, and wine."

"Not really," she replied, burrowing deeper beneath the covers. The blood had begun to circulate in her again, and the silky sheets felt cool against her skin.

"Well, you must have some wine," he said, producing a bottle from a silver salver resting on a small table in the shadows that she hadn't noticed before. There were grapes, plums, and apples heaped on it as well, and a generous wedge of creamy, fragrant cheese. "Keep the bed warm for me," he murmured, striding toward the door.

"Where are you going?" she called out. She couldn't imagine how she would find her way out of that labyrinth if he were to leave her there.

"To fetch our things," he called over his shoulder. "They'll dry nicely beside the fire."

He seemed to have thought of everything. Yes, he'd done this before, but he wouldn't do it again, unless it was with her. She would make certain of that. Hot blood rushed to her temples as she lay there reliving the intimacies they'd shared. He'd awakened her to pleasures she'd never dreamed existed. *"This is only the beginning of our one most perfect night,"* he'd said. What else lay in store? She was still digesting all that had happened in the bath, and marveling that she'd surrendered herself so completely to this mysterious descendant of pirates and rogues that she hardly knew. Husband or no, her behavior was quite shocking. Whatever must he think of her? She shuddered to wonder.

She wasn't given long to worry. Minutes later, King padded back over the threshold bearing their soggy clothes—he was still naked—and proceeded to drape them over the fire screen, where the heat from the hearth would dry them. "Well! I see you've got your color back," he observed, straightening from his chore.

She wished he wouldn't do that—stand so unabashedly naked before her. She could just imagine the color he was viewing in her cheeks, which were positively on fire. Even in a flaccid state, his manhood was a daunting presence, drawing her eyes. Her sex pinged with recognition as though an invisible cord joined them. That magnificence had been inside her, moving to the rhythm of her blood— the same blood that throbbed for him now.

His wry smile told her all too well that he noticed her

ogling him. That's what it was, too—*ogling*. She was on the verge of disgracing herself, and he was making no attempt to spare her—strutting about, pouring the wine, and picking over the fruit on the silver salver.

"A-aren't you cold?" she asked, burrowing deeper under the covers.

"If I am, I shan't be for long," he said, popping a juicy grape into his mouth from the bunch he was balancing between two wine glasses. Strolling to the bed, he offered one of the goblets. "Drink up," he said. "This is the finest wine in our cellars."

"Contraband, of course," she said playfully, taking the offered goblet.

"Of course," he agreed. Easing himself down beside her, he arranged the grapes on the pillow. "So are these," he said of the grapes. "We don't grow any nearly as fine here in Cornwall." He slid one between her teeth as she opened her mouth to reply. "What do you think?"

Lark bit into the succulent fruit. The piquant sweetness reacted on her tongue like pins and needles as the juice trickled down her throat. Her mind reeled back to what he'd said of the trade earlier. Was he trying to tell her something?

"But you said all that ended with your father," she replied, ignoring his question. There was no need to respond to his question; of course the grape was delicious. He knew it was delicious. He would hardly have fed her something sour.

"In the general sense, it did," he returned. "That is to say, I did not personally wade out into the briny deep and haul these fine specimens ashore. The trade still flourishes on the Cornish coast, however, and will for some time to come, I have no doubt, and I do have many friends in these parts who would rather see such delicacies in my mouth than upon the compost heap."

"I see," she murmured.

"No, you really don't," he said on a sigh. "This isn't the ideal time to make matters clear, either, but I suppose I ought to, considering."

"Considering what?"

"Considering the nature of my business with the Crown . . . the business that is about to take me from you for a spell."

"I don't understand."

"I know you don't. I'm not even sure I should tell you."

"Tell me what, King?"

"First, I must swear you to secrecy. You cannot tell a soul—not Agnes Garwood, not Lee, not Mother—especially not Mother. Not *anyone*. You must promise me."

"Yes, but not to confide in your mother . . . She is no fool, King. Surely she knows what's going on right under her nose. I should think taking her into your confidence would go a long way toward mending fences between you. That you haven't only fuels the estrangement. She loves you so—she *does*, but she doesn't know how to express it, and it saddens me to see the gap between you widening."

"The gap between Mother and myself is not my doing, Lark," King defended. "It was formed over thirty years ago in this loveless house. I remind her of her unhappy marriage. Oh, I know she 'loves' me in some obligatory way, but she cannot bring herself to admit even that, much less say it. If only I could hear those words from her lips just once . . . but I shan't, so it's best left as it is."

"Forgive me, but you are two stubborn souls," Lark said. "One of you must give way, and since it isn't likely that your mother will take the initiative, couldn't you?"

His gentle touch and misty gaze as he tilted her face toward him melted her heart. "Anything for you, my love," he said, "but this is not the time. Too much is at stake to open that Pandora's box here now. I need your promise not to break my confidence in this."

"I . . . I promise, of course, but—"

"And you must keep the promise, Lark, no matter what occurs. My life could well depend upon it."

"You're frightening me now!"

King took her in his arms. "I don't mean to frighten you," he said, soothing her with gentle hands. "Believe me, if you were any other woman, we wouldn't even be having this conversation. The fact is, the *Cormorant* has been commissioned by the Admiralty, and I have been charged to man her to the purpose of privateering for the Crown."

There was silence—the kind that tasted like death. His words hung in the warm, still air like living things, and Lark stiffened against him at the sound of them.

"W-what do you mean?" she breathed.

"The *Cormorant* is commanded to intercept French merchantmen in the channel, capture them, and relieve them of their cargoes, which will revert to the Crown. We are at war with France, Lark, as you well know, yet her merchant ships still use our waters—sometimes under other flags or under no flags at all—and sometimes, the cheeky bounders brazenly fly their colors. It cannot be allowed."

"But that's dangerous," she cried. "You could be killed!"

"It's not as dangerous as it sounds," he soothed. "I shan't be attempting it single-handed. The *Cormorant* will be working right alongside the *Hind*—"

"The *Hind*? I've heard of the *Hind*, and her captain. Why, he's little more than a bloodthirsty pirate. His exploits were recorded in the tabloids even in Yorkshire!"

"Captain Harry is a plier of the trade, it's true, but hardly a bloodthirsty pirate," King ground out through a throaty chuckle, "but if you're going to label him so, you may as well tar me with the same brush, as it were." He pulled her closer. "Would you rather that I hadn't told you?"

"No . . . yes . . . I don't know! Why did you tell me?"

"Because I love you, and I owe you honesty. Because if it has to be told, it needs must come from my lips, and rightly—not biased and stretched all out of proportion by vicious on-dits out of the mouths of the magpies on this coast that would thrive on such gossip, if something were to . . . to . . ."

"To what, King? If something were to go wrong? Is that what you're trying to say?" She gasped. "Y-you think something *will*," she realized. "You do! Oh, my God, I shall die if anything happens to you! I will!"

"Nothing is going to happen to me, my love," he murmured against her hair. "Divine Providence isn't that cruel. Don't let this spoil our one perfect night."

Lark blinked back the tears that threatened to do just that. No. She was no watering pot—not even in this. Nothing was going to spoil their precious time together, but she needed reassurance.

"Promise me that you'll be careful?" she urged, looking him in the eyes.

"That's one promise that I shall make gladly, my beautiful Lark, and one that I shall keep."

No. Nothing was going to spoil the magic of these moments together, but a shadow had fallen over them, like a pall, nonetheless; his promise wasn't enough to dispel it. Yet, she would not give in to it. She consoled herself with the fact that he'd confided in her, probably something he wouldn't have done if he'd married Lady Ann Cuthbertson, because he didn't love her. That's what he had implied, without actually saying it in so many words. It was, however, a small consolation, what with the weight of the dangers he would be facing burdening her now.

He had slipped under the counterpane and leaned above her, searching her face with that dangerous all-seeing gaze of his that had the power to hypnotize. His eye—dilated with the passion evidenced in his arousal—was hooded with desire.

"Now, my love," he murmured, "I'm going to love you till dawn." He smiled his roguish, lopsided smile. "Fair warning—it isn't for the faint of heart, what I'm about to do to you. Expect nothing less than excruciating ecstasy. Are you game?"

"I'm game," she mewed. She really was. Her pulse had jumped to life at the mere tone of his voice. But was it scandalous to admit it? He didn't give her time to decide.

"Good," he said, lifting the grapes from the pillow, "I'm glad, because I'm about to show you several other ways to derive great satisfaction and unexpected pleasure from the noble grape."

There was no window in the bedchamber, but Lark viewed the dawn just the same from the balustrade that crowned the seaward vista of the dower house. Cocooned naked in the counterpane and wrapped in King's strong arms, she watched the crimson sun rise over the Point above the treetops in a strange pink sky. Sated at last, the wind had died to a breathless murmur, and though all seemed as it should be, the waterfowl still circled the turrets and the tang of salt still rode the breeze.

"I hate the dawn," she announced, hugging him closer.

"Why?" he queried through a soft chuckle.

"Because it will take you from me," she said.

"And it will take me quickly," he observed, squinting toward the fiery horizon. "The flaw is done, but her sisters threaten. Do you see that glorious sky, all pink and saffron? It tells of aftersqualls. They're common enough on the heels of such fierce storms, following like grumbling complaints. Deuced nuisance, I'll be bound, but not enough of one to keep me from my rendezvous with the *Hind*. I'm sorry, my love, but you mustn't hate the dawn. Once my mission is fulfilled, I shall return to you on the morning tide. You'll view the dawn much differently then, because that is when I shall give you my wedding gift."

"What wedding gift?" she asked, searching his face. His lopsided smile betrayed nothing. "More contraband, I suppose?" she added playfully.

He threw back his head in a burst of hearty laughter. "Not this time," he said. "Although there is a certain element of piracy about it. No questions! You will just have to wait. For now it must remain my secret . . . a very special surprise that I think will please you."

"You'll be at sea for weeks," she pouted.

"No longer than a fortnight, if things go well. But first I must away. We'd best go down. I'll see you to the Manor. I need a word with Lee about my little secret before I go, and if we linger here much longer, I shall miss the tide."

"It is a strange, enchanted place, your Cornwall," Lark observed, letting him lead her. "Deceiving pink skies that forewarn of dirty weather, plants that grow out of season, fresh graves that level themselves and grow new sod in a sennight."

King's posture clenched against her. "What do you mean . . . about the graves?" he said, his voice guarded.

"Surely you remember? When we first visited the vicar before you went off to London for the license, I questioned him about the graves. There were so many fresh ones in the churchyard. I thought it . . . odd. Yesterday, when we arrived for the wedding, it was as though the earth was never opened. How is that possible, King?"

"I wouldn't trouble yourself about it," he responded. "Like you say, this is a strange, enchanted place." He stopped on the landing that led below, and turned her toward him. "I want you to stay close to the Manor while I'm gone," he said. "Don't venture beyond the gates. The moors aren't safe, and the marshes west of here are undermined with quicksand pockets that are virtually invisible to the untrained eye. I don't want you rambling about unescorted on the Manor grounds, either—especially down 'round the churchyard. The gates are often open to the locals for services, and we tend to get unsavory individuals prowling about from time to time. I need you to give me your word, Lark."

A cold chill passed through her at that. There was

something cryptic in the sound of it—especially the bit about the churchyard. It brought back her dreams of spiked iron fences and lost souls barred from the sanctity of consecrated ground. Was there a premonition in it all somewhere? She'd always been open to such things, and this was just too recurrent to be anything else.

"Lark . . . ?" he prompted.

"You make it sound as though I'm being held prisoner here," she said lightly—or at least so she thought.

"Nothing of the sort," he said, his voice almost stern. "It's just that I want my mind at ease while I'm gone. This is a rough stretch of coast, my love, and rough men prowl it to no good purpose; that's why we're gated here. But be that as it may, not even the gates can hold out the determined. I simply don't want you subjected to any . . . unpleasantness."

Hazel Helston's flame-haired image popped into Lark's mind at that. *She* had gotten through the gates, hadn't she? It was doubtful that she had been invited, considering the dowager's disdainful glances her way across the church aisle, and King certainly wouldn't have invited her. She ached to know more about the mysterious woman of King's past, and dreaded the knowledge at the same time. It triggered all sorts of unwelcome images in her head— especially now, after sharing such intimacies with him that she wanted to believe were theirs alone.

"You asked me to be careful," he went on. "I'll be able to spend my energies a whole lot easier on that if I know you're safe from harm."

"I . . . I promise," she said, but she wished he hadn't piqued her curiosity.

Twenty

One storm after another rolled up the coast, battering the headlands and flooding the coves. Even when the rain ceased between squalls, thick, dark clouds heavy with more hovered over the Point, adding to the pervasive drear indigenous to Grayshire Manor in flaw season. As much of a hindrance as the dirty weather was to King and his mission, keeping pace with the *Hind* in the channel, it eased his mind that Lark would be safe confined to the house. This was no weather for exploring.

Maybe he should have told her about the graveyard. Why hadn't he done that? Because it would have appealed to her curious nature, and if she were to act upon that curiosity and put herself in harm's way because of it, he wouldn't be nearby to protect her.

She was a quick study, his beautiful bride. No insipid milk-and-water miss, she, by God. Who would have thought she'd notice filled-in graves in the churchyard, what with all the excitement on her wedding day—and in a raging flaw besides? No. He'd made the right decision. What she didn't know, she couldn't tell, deliberately or inadvertently; the fewer who knew, the safer for all. There was just too much at stake, and too many lives would be put in danger—the vicar's amongst them—by his headstrong, moonstruck longing to tell this woman everything.

It couldn't go on forever. Even old Zephaniah Job, who kept accounts for the *Cormorant*, and many of the other privately owned ships licensed by the Admiralty for profiteering, was easing off of late. Job had always been there for the privateers charged to attack and capture enemy ships, even to the point of hiring legal counsel through his London representative, Alderman Christopher Smith, for Polperro smugglers, both legitimate and free agents, should they be hauled into court. Will Bowles fell into the latter category; he wasn't working for the Crown. It was men like Will, skimming the cream off the gleanings and selling the Crown short, who were drawing the time-honored, ages-old trade on the coast to a close. The Admiralty weren't fools. There had been rumors. Soon enough now they would be posting water guard vessels in the harbors to police what came ashore, and to see that the Crown got its fair share. Until then it was on King's shoulders to walk the tightrope between the Admiralty-licensed privateers and the local traders, who bribed the land guards to look the other way while they lined their pockets with Crown spoils. It was a balancing act that was becoming more dangerous daily—especially now, when there was finally hope for the kind of life he'd denied himself, with a woman he'd never let himself dream could be his—a woman who loved him, and whom he loved with a passion heretofore unknown to him.

The *Cormorant* had been at sea for nearly a fortnight after his wedding, and the cargo hold was only half full of salvage—not enough to put in to port. There'd been no sign of a French merchantman—or any other, for that matter—since the one they'd captured and sunk on their third day out, though King had it on good authority that several more were due by, and so they waited. He stood— feet apart for balance—on the foredeck, squinting through the rain-spattered ship's telescope toward the slice of slanted horizon off the starboard bow. It was moon-dark, and all that came into focus were the lacy whitecaps riding the swells. He'd long since lost sight of the *Hind*. That had been happening a lot of late. Could it be deliberate? Could Captain Harry be unloading some of the *Hind*'s contraband closer to his own stamping ground near Prussia Cove, with no one the wiser? Probably. It didn't matter. What did matter was fulfilling his obligation to the Admiralty, and getting back to Lark. That meant squinting through that blurry telescope with salt spray and spindrift in his face for another fortnight if needs must, until he sighted a vessel, and put her under the gun.

He had never seen a night so black, and it was only an hour or so past sunset—if there had been a sun in the scowling sky earlier to prove it. Making matters worse, no lanterns had been lit, and the running lights were out as they always were when searching for foreign vessels. The waves were swelling so high he couldn't make out the coastline. Navigation by the stars was impossible: There weren't any. Every man aboard—skilled at his task—was at his post in silence, for voices carried on the water. It was up to King to decide whether to ride out the storm or make for land until it passed over.

There really wasn't any choice—at least not until first light, when he could locate the coastline. As it was, he couldn't tell if they were running abreast of Downend Point, or Chapel Cliff, or Brent. Or were they opposite Polperro, or Shag Rock three miles west? For all he knew, the *Cormorant* could be as far as eight miles southwest, by Gribbin Head Point, or all the way to Looe, three-and-a-half miles east of Polperro the way the wind was tossing the ship like a broom straw. There would be lights on shore the length of the coast to guide him. He knew them all on sight. If only he could see them in the inky blackness. It didn't bode well.

He wasn't left long to worry over it. Just as the ship was swamped by a following sea, cannon fire ripped across her amidships and she heeled to port, plunging stern downward to the mizzenmast. King never saw who fired the shot. A slurry of ropes and spars and barrels and bodies slid down the deck, riding the backwash. The screams of men fighting for their lives rang in his ears. Then the mainmast snapped. The sound ran King through to the core as he tried to claw his way toward the bow, dragging one of the injured crewmen with him, but his legs had become tangled in the fallen sails and sheets and lines pulling him along the sinking stern into the water. It was over that quickly. The last thing he saw was the mast hurtling toward him as his wounded cutter, driven by the gale, spiraled down into the vortex and disappeared beneath the waves.

Lark had been roaming through the Manor, pacing the carpets like a caged lion for days. A fortnight was over, but still no sign of King. If only the rain would cease. Then she could ride down to the Point. What good that would do, she didn't know, but she had to do something. She'd heard tales of ships lost at sea in milder storms than these had been, and she was terrified.

Lady Isobel's insistence that King had certainly weathered worse in his daring naval career fell upon deaf ears. It was too easy to read between the lines of the dowager's well-meaning words; Lady Isobel was just as worried as she was. Not even Agnes's soothing commentary put Lark's mind at ease. She'd seen her friend's eyes seek reassurance from Leander Markham's too often to put stock in that, judging from the feeble response he mustered. He'd evidently told her something. They were all worried, and they all knew more than she did—even Lady Isobel, who pretended to know nothing of King's Admiralty affairs at all.

She was overreacting, of course. Any moment now, King would surge through those doors down the hall and take her in his arms. This time. But what about next time—and the time after that? How would she ever learn to live with a privateer?

She had been through so much since the scandal. She'd weathered her father's suicide and burial in unconsecrated ground, endured the shame of being ostracized from society, and suffered incarceration in the Marshalsea. She'd fought against the unwelcome advances of Andrew Westerfield, battled with slovens for her belongings in the filthy Marshalsea courtyard, and then there was Biddie. She'd steeled herself against all manner of indignities, and found herself equal to it all . . . all except this. This, she couldn't bear—wouldn't bear, ever again.

Midweek the squalls ceased and the sun made a feeble attempt to break through the clouds. Late in the afternoon, while Agnes was closeted with Lady Isobel during her rest period, Lark slipped out. Despite her promise to King that she'd keep to the house, she went to the stables, where she had George Wellen saddle Toffee, and rode to the estuary at Downend Point. She had to do something, or go mad.

There was no sign of the *Cormorant* in the little harbor, and she shielded her eyes and looked out across the dark, choppy waters of Talland Bay and beyond. There was nothing, nothing but angry-looking breakers racing the waterfowl toward shore. Were they just frolicking, or did that mean another storm was on the way? She shuddered at the thought, and turned back toward the Manor.

Though it was still early, the light was fading fast. Lark still wasn't used to twilight coming early in Cornwall at this time of the year, especially in stormy weather. Her mood was as glum as the scowling sky. Perhaps a visit with Vicar Faulkner would lift her spirits. She wouldn't be missed at the Manor for a while. It was hours yet until the evening meal.

Slowing her mount's pace to a walk, she picked her way through the lush wooded acreage that hemmed the south side of the drive. It was darker there among the trees, an eerie sort of velvety green darkness, fragrant with the heady aroma of pine, mulch, and sodden earth stirred by the horse's hooves. Lark breathed it in, taking deep, lingering breaths, reminded of the wooded lanes of Yorkshire.

She'd nearly reached the church when she heard it—a

sound that stopped her dead in her tracks—the rasp of a spade plunging in the wet ground, then another, and another. Her breath caught as she listened. It came again. More than one shovel was breaking ground. The churchyard was nearly in sight. Swallowing her rapid heartbeat, she slid off the horse's back without a sound, tethered Toffee in a clump of bracken, and crept through the maze of rain-blackened trunks until she had a clear view. Men were digging in the graveyard—two, no, three of them—behind the spiked wrought-iron fence.

Lark clung to the wet trunk of a twisted pine and gulped in the rain-washed air. There were coffins lined up against the fence, but there were no bodies in them. While the three men with spades dug the graves, others were unloading cargo from a mule-drawn wagon and filling the coffins with what had to be contraband: brandy, rum, what looked like firearms. She couldn't make out the rest; a fine drifting mist rising from the ground prevented her.

Lark sagged against the tree trunk. So, this was what King withheld from her when she'd questioned him about the graves. These men were smugglers, local pliers of the trade, and they were burying the spoils they'd stolen from the Crown. Of course! It was the perfect hiding place. The good vicar was beyond reproach. No one was about to disturb the dead. Who but herself—a stranger to the coast—would have thought to question? The locals all *knew*. It was evidently a multilayered operation, and the vicar was part of it! So, this was what they did when a ship was captured or wrecked on the shoals, these local pirates—cheat the Crown and bury the plunder. Then, later, when all chance of discovery was past, they could dig up their treasures with no one the wiser.

When a ship was captured or wrecked on the shoals! Cold chills gripped her as the thought sank in, and a surge of adrenaline drained the blood from her temples, starring her vision. Some ship had been ravaged. She'd been to the harbor. If one had been captured, where was it? And where was the *Cormorant*?

Inching closer, from tree to tree, Lark tried to make out the conversation of the men. Nothing came clear, and she dared venture no nearer. Who knew but that these brigands might slit her throat if they were to catch her spying on them? All at once another figure sprinted down the vicarage steps and joined the band. Lark's heart took a tumble. It was Leander Markham.

"Here, you lot, is that the last of it?" he barked.

"Aye, gov'nor," one of them replied. "The last of this trip."

"Well, hurry up with it, then. Get that cart unloaded and out of here, so we can close the main gates before we get company! You'll have to take the rest to the mine."

Lark swallowed dry. It wasn't likely that Leander Markham would slit her throat, but he was only one, and they were many. She gripped the prickly tree bark, sap, slime, and all. A horseman was approaching at a gallop, lashing his mount with the reins. There was no mistaking the urgency he exuded, this formidable presence, dressed all in black, from slouch hat to polished boots, a silk mask hiding his face. There was something vaguely familiar about him. Of course! That first night on the moors, on the way to Grayshire Manor in the wounded coach—this was the highwayman, she realized. He slipped his mask down and doffed the slouch hat, exposing a shock of sun-bleached hair to the twilight. Her heart nearly stopped, and she almost cried aloud when recognition struck.

It was Will Bowles.

No wonder he hadn't robbed them that night. He was King's brother, and King had never let on. How many more secrets was he keeping from her? Who was this man that she'd married?

"It's bad, Lee . . . I'm not going to lie to you," Will panted. Wiping the sweat from his brow, he donned his hat again. "There's another load yet—brandy mostly.

We're short two men, and I had to leave that jug-bit old sod Tim Bud standing guard over it. I've got to get back or there won't be a drop left to haul. I've only come to tell you, you'd best get out there pretty quick."

"He's at your mother's?" Leander urged.

"No. He's at Hazel's. There wasn't any choice. It would have taken too long."

"There wasn't any . . . problem?"

"With Hazel? Hah!" Will blurted huskily. "You'd have thought I'd dropped Golden Ball Hughes's fortune on the doorstep instead of—"

"I get the drift," Leander interrupted. "What about the land guards, have they been paid?"

"Aye, but they're not happy. They want full tribute for a scant load. What the devil could have happened out there?"

"King is the only one who can answer that, unless it be someone aboard the *Hind*. Any word from her?"

Will shook his head. "No sign of her," he said. "Lee, about King . . . we may never know, he—"

"Don't say it. Don't even think it. Did you report to Zephaniah?"

Will uttered a strangled sound. "There hasn't been time!" he cried. "I came here straightaway after the set-to with the land guards. The worthless layabouts have got their hackles up, I tell you." He made a wild hand gesture. "If you don't want those damned coffins raided, you'd best sink them quick, and get those gates closed. I'll go back out there by way of the strand."

"They're almost done," said Leander. "I'll stop by Zephaniah's on my way. He'll deal with the guards. Have you been to the house? Do they know?"

Will gave a start. "Christ, no!" he blurted. "I'm no Bedlamite. I'll not be the bearer of this news. I'll leave that to you, old boy."

They said more, but Lark couldn't hear; they had moved out of earshot. She was numb. She had gripped the tree trunk so tightly her hands came away sticky with sap and stained with the moldy green moss growing on it. They were talking about King; she knew it! Nothing had sunk in after the words, *"He's at Hazel's."* Why at Hazel's, when she had been pacing trenches in the carpets with worry for days? Her heart was thudding inside at the connotations those words brought to bear.

Will was in motion again, and Lark staggered back through the trees to Toffee, still tethered as she'd left her, and followed at a discreet distance.

Twenty-one

Kelement ing opened his eyes to the sight of flowing red hair and pendulous, half-bared breasts leaning over him. He groaned. His head was throbbing. Vertigo blurred his vision. Everything seemed to be moving in slow motion—the woman, the steam rising lazily from a kettle on the hearth, and the auburn shadows pulsing on the walls, thrown there by the flickering candles. It must be dark out.

He groaned again, and licked parched lips. Tasting salt, he swallowed dry around a swollen tongue and tried to rise, but a firm hand held him down.

"Here now, none of that," said the woman behind it. "Neptune's just spit you out of the briny deep right on my doorsill, love . . . well, near enough. You're in no shape to be goin' anywhere."

"H-Hazel . . . ?"

"Aye, it's Hazel, right enough," she purred. "Will brought what's left of you up from the cove below where you washed ashore for me to tend."

Her voice sounded back in his ears as though it was coming from an echo chamber. He tried to move again, but a sharp pain in his left bicep prevented him. He glanced over, saw it tightly bound in bloodstained linen bandages. His damp hair had been unbound from its queue, and lay loose about him on the pillow. Hazel's hands were cool as she tucked the counterpane around him. He gave a lurch despite the pain. He was naked underneath the covers.

"You couldn't stay in wet clothes, love," she said, responding to his reaction as part of the conversation. "It isn't like I've never seen what's under there," she went on, sliding her hand the length of him atop the coverlet until her fingers found his member. "It's been a long while, King—too long."

"Don't," he gritted, shoving her hand away. "That's over, Hazel."

"Tell *him* it's over, love," she crooned, fondling him again. "By the look of this fine fellow here, he doesn't know it."

"Don't, I said!" he snapped, attempting to rise. "All that was in another lifetime . . . when we were very young . . . and I was very reckless. I've a wife now, girl."

Hazel shrugged. "And I've a husband," she returned. "What has that to do with anything? Who's to know? Will's not coming back tonight, and God knows if husband Jim *ever* will, he's been at sea so long I scarce expect him anymore. What happens here is just between us— you . . . and me."

"I-I've got to go," King groaned, raising himself on his right elbow, his left arm being useless. "I shouldn't be here . . . they shouldn't have brought me here."

"They had no choice, King. You'd lost too much blood. That there on your arm, 'tis serious, not to mention the knock you took on the head. Whatever hit you may well have cracked your skull. We won't even know till the surgeon's come tomorrow. He's gone up to Looe. What happened out there?"

King's dazed mind reeled back to the last clear thing he remembered: the cannon fire that sank the *Cormorant*. He saw again the splintered timbers—spars, yard, and boom snapping like broom straws and raining over the wounded deck—saw the towering white-capped swells trailing spindrift that drove the cutter into the vortex. He saw the crew scrambling against the vertical hull being sucked down into dark water. He heard their cries as the men slipped beneath the waves out of his reach. He heard the terrible crack as the mainsail snapped, saw it plummeting toward him, felt the impact as it struck him a glancing blow to the head, despite his attempt to avoid it. He winced again, reliving the jagged wood slicing through his bicep like a saber, costing him his fresh grip on the first mate's arm as the man careened past, then costing him consciousness.

"M-my crew . . . ?" he urged. "There were eight men on that ship."

Hazel shook her head dismally.

"O-oh, Christ," he moaned. "Let me up. I've got to go . . ."

"Look at you!" Hazel shrilled, restraining him. "You can't even sit upright. How far do you think you'd get?"

"Hah!" he erupted. "Make up your mind, you little hypocrite. A moment ago you seemed to find me fit enough to cock a leg over you."

"It may be the only chance I'll ever get," she snapped, "now that you've got your fine lady. Oh, I heard about the trash you collected out of the Marshalsea; I seen her. I was there in that church. She cleaned up nice enough, but that don't make her lily white. At least *I've* never been jailed."

"Get out of my way," he seethed, struggling against her grip on his good arm. "I never deceived you, Hazel, and I wasn't your first. You knew from the start that nothing could come of . . . us. You have no right to expect . . . anything from me now, after all these years."

Her hands were like ice against his skin. They riddled him with teeth-chattering chills, and he began to shudder uncontrollably as he fell back down again.

She gasped. "King, you're burning up!" she cried. "You're shaking like a leaf!"

Vertigo blurred her image. The shadows were closing in around him. She was speaking, but he could barely make out her speech.

"Lay still, love," she crooned. "I'll keep you warm . . . shhhh . . . you're on fire with fever . . . shhhh, now . . ."

Was she stripping off her clothes?

Yes.

The last thing he saw before consciousness evaporated was her naked body descending; the last thing he felt was that voluptuous body snuggling up against him beneath the counterpane.

Lark crouched in the lee of the stacked-stone fence beside the Helston cottage, uncertain of what to do. She glanced behind toward the stand of dwarf pines where she'd tethered Toffee. The mare was content enough, not in the least uneasy grazing there. Lark almost envied her.

She'd followed Will Bowles with no difficulty, but now she was beginning to wonder if she could find her way back. The night was black as coal tar pitch, and cloud cover hid whatever light the heavens might have offered. The wind had picked up substantially since she started out as well, and she wasn't dressed warmly enough for the blustery Cornish night.

She shuddered. Watching unseen as Will came and went, she was well aware of whose cottage this was. She'd seen Hazel Helston's buxom figure in the doorway, the sheen of her flaming hair backlit by candle shine from within, like a fiery halo crowning those Gypsy curls. She'd glimpsed something else, too—King's tasseled Hessians in the woman's hands, pressed tight to her breast. That they could be someone else's boots never crossed her mind. It wasn't the boots but the way Hazel was holding them, caressing them, cleaving to them as if he were still in them. Lark would have done the same.

Her heart was breaking. So many emotions were running rampant through her then, not the least of which was jealousy. The seeds of that had begun to germinate the moment she set eyes on the voluptuous beauty ogling her bridegroom in that chapel. Perhaps she should have questioned King about her. Perhaps airing her feelings, slaking her curiosity, might have stunted the growth of the green-eyed monster that was gnawing at her heart so ravenously now. Was King no better than his forebears, who lived by the code of "one to wed and one to bed"? Had she put too much stock in his brilliant seduction—in the blazing promise in his enigmatic one-eyed stare? She would have sworn not. Nevertheless, he had come to his Gypsy whore when he returned, not to her, his wife, and all the while she had been frantic over his safe return. Did his vows mean nothing, then? What had she done to displease him? Had she not yielded to every nuance of his desire? What could this doxy give him that she could not, would not? The answer to that was: nothing. It must be an affair of the heart.

It would have been easy to feel sorry for herself, but she was no milk-and-water miss. She would not wring her hands and wail at her nonexistent inadequacy. If there was a failing, it was in him, not her. She could do one of two things, she decided, standing there buffeted by the wind. She could let history repeat itself—go back to the Manor as though she hadn't discovered his infidelity, keep silent, and play the dutiful wife and breeder, just as Lady Isobel had done in her turn—or she could confront him and force him to choose. Hurt gave birth to the latter, and anger set her feet in motion.

Of course she was overreacting again. There was a perfectly good explanation. There had to be. She would find them drinking coffee at the table she'd glimpsed through the open doorway, his boots drying by the fire. She'd almost convinced herself of that when she reached the threshold, but a shaft of fire glow showing at one of the windows drew her to the side of the cottage and she peered through it into Hazel Helston's bedroom. The light was coming from a dwindling fire in the hearth, a golden shimmer that reached like pointing fingers toward the two figures entwined together in the bed. King lay on his back, his hair loose on the pillow. Hazel lay beside him, her arms around him, her heavy breasts resting on his chest. They were naked.

Lark backpedaled from the window, her heart pounding in her ears. Tears stung behind her eyes. She refused to let them fall. He didn't deserve her tears. He didn't deserve her love. How she could still love him escaped her, but she did. Why else was her heart breaking, as though an unseen hand had fisted inside her, squeezing the life out of it—out of her.

Her worst fears were realized, and she could scarcely breathe, but her mind was clear enough. Why should she humiliate herself confronting him? There was no need. The scene played out before her was proof that nothing she could do or say would matter. No. She was wrong. She didn't have two options; there was only one. She would be no slave to martyrdom. She would not follow in Lady Isobel's footsteps: perform her duties, endure in silence, wither and die, sour and bitter and old before her time. She would not give King a chance to put her in her place and confirm the obvious by giving it substance with words, either. She would run, and keep on running—put as much distance between herself and the Cornish coast as possible, even though she would carry it with her for the rest of her days in that place where her heart used to be.

She wasn't brave enough to look again. Turning on her heel, she fled down the path, through the gate, and over the lush ground cover on the far side of the stacked-stone fence where her mare waited in the grove. Ignoring the animal's welcoming whinny, Lark mounted and turned her back along the path the way she'd come.

It wasn't long before she lost her bearings in the blustery darkness. Blurred by her tears, the monotonous moorland carpeted with bracken and furze and wind-twisted trees seemed the same until she'd traveled quite a distance. It sloped down to spongy marshes now, where glimmering lights beckoned, and Toffee's complaints rang in her ears as the horse shied and pranced, unwilling to carry her over the unstable stuff. Lark would brook no insubordination from a horse, however, and she dug in her heel and spurred Toffee on, lashing her with the reins when she resisted until the animal reared and pitched her . . . right into the quicksand at the edge of the bog.

The horse didn't run off, as Lark feared; she shuddered and pranced, traveling the safe ground she stood upon, bobbing her head and puffing white visible breath from flared nostrils in the darkness. Her bulging eyes shone, catching glints of reflected light from the bog itself. Lark glanced toward the source she'd taken for distant dwellings as she clawed at the receding ground—but they were marsh lights, ethereal, incandescent flashes drifting over the surface of the quicksand. Could these be old Smythe the coachman's "ghosties": Will-o'-the-wisps come to lure her over the edge and take her under as they were reputed to do? She clawed for purchase all the harder.

The skirt of Lark's traveling costume was billowed about her on the surface like a balloon, while her legs were sinking beneath her. She worked them frantically, but that only made her sink deeper. She mustn't panic. Her eyes oscillated back and forth, searching for something to grab on to—a fallen branch, a root, anything that she could use to pull herself out of the mire. Nothing. There was nothing but the mare pacing the edge of the bog just out of her reach, as though the animal read her mind.

Lark clicked her tongue and called to the horse, coaxing Toffee closer. It was clear that Toffee had more sense than she did, but there was no time to credit that. She was sinking deeper, and the more she struggled, the faster she sank. If it weren't for her ballooning skirt buoying her somewhat, she would have disappeared beneath the surface by now. She had no idea how deep the quicksand was, but her feet weren't touching bottom.

The mare was so close, the trailing reins just inches from her fingers. With all her might, Lark lunged in a desperate attempt to grab fast, but the motion failed. Her billowing skirt, having lost its air pocket, sank like a limp rag beneath the surface, the weight of it sucking her under breast deep.

All at once Toffee began answering the calls of other horses. The mire beneath her trembled with the vibration of hoofbeats. Someone was coming, and though Lark called out at the top of her lungs, the sound that came from her hoarse throat was breathless and weak, siphoned off by the wind, and by the cold muck rising higher around her.

Voices rode the wind. Someone shouted for a lantern. Lark couldn't see anything until the light of one narrowed her eyes. She shrank from the glare, and the stench of smoking lamp oil.

"It's a *bird*," said one.

"A pretty bird," said another.

"All alone out here," yet another chimed in, "and she don't know the lay o' the land enough to keep outta the bogs? She's a spy, more'n likely. Let her be. Let the marsh take her."

"Will wouldn't like that, Jeremy," said the first speaker. "He doesn't hold with doin' for women."

"No names, you clunch!" the third man trumpeted. "Will ain't here now, is he? I say let her sink."

"P-please help me," Lark murmured feebly. Only one of her arms was above the quicksand now. She was submerged to the chin. "I lost my way . . . in th-the d-dark," she stuttered through teeth chattering from cold and fright. "P-please . . ."

The first man snatched the mare's reins and leaned toward her.

"Grab on to this," he said, tossing the reins toward her outstretched fingers. The first try failed, and the second. Finally, on the third try she managed to grab fast, and he mounted the horse. "Get your other hand out," he commanded. "You'll need two hands for this. That's it! Wind the reins around your fists and hold tight while I pull you out."

Slowly, the man began backing the skittish horse up. Lark did as he bade her until the bracken and furze that had deceived her were firmly underneath her before she let go. The reins had scarcely left her fingers when the two men on the ground hauled her to her feet without ceremony, and thrust the lantern full in her face. She shrank from the light, and from the stink of the oil and the unwashed men, their strong breath foul with a sickening meld of whiskey, strong cheese, and onions.

"Now what do we do with her?" Jeremy said. "We can't let her go. There's too much at stake. She could go straight to the land guards. I told ya we should have let her sink."

"We could have a little fun with 'er first," said the man with the lantern, grinning through rotting teeth.

"We'll let Will decide," said the first man, climbing down off the mare. "He's at the mine. Truss her up and put her in the cart."

Lark stared at the smugglers who had saved her. She almost wished they'd left her in the mire, from the promise in those leering eyes raking her and the hands groping her familiarly as they marched her along toward a waiting cart at the edge of the marsh.

Twenty-two

Halfway to the mine, the heavens opened and the wind-driven rain sluiced down in horizontal sheets. Lark was beyond caring. Plastered thick with ooze from the bog and drenched from the storm, she was still recognizable. Will Bowles would set her free. All she needed to do was keep the brigands at bay until they reached him.

Toffee was tied to the back of the cart. She would need the mare for escaping. Meanwhile, she studied the terrain they traveled, lit now in the lightning's glare, and it wasn't long before she got her bearings; the land was familiar again. She'd passed a mine following Will earlier. If that was the one they were taking her to, and she strongly suspected it was, she could easily find her way back to Grayshire Manor from there.

She began again planning her future. She couldn't very well travel as she was; she would need clothes, and if not a bath at least a makeshift toilette to cleanse away what the rain did not before departing for God alone knew where. She need not think so far ahead, though. The only thing that mattered was leaving the Manor before King returned. There was no telling what would happen if she had to face him again after what she'd just seen. Ideally she could collect her things and be on her way without encountering Lady Isobel or Agnes, either. It would be better that way. Separation from Agnes would pain her, but she knew that regardless of King's differences with her, he would honor his commitment to her friend.

Lady Isobel was another matter entirely. If anyone had the power to turn her head, the dowager did; Lark had grown that fond of her. She couldn't bring herself to make the comparison between them were she forced to plead her case, and knowing the dowager as she did, such as that would be inevitable. No. There had to be a clean break. That would be less painful for all. First, however, she had to unwind her present coil. The cart had come to a shuddering halt before the opening to the mine, and Will Bowles was nowhere in sight.

Jeremy stalked off into the mine, while the other two tethered the horses and brought the cart under what appeared to be a dilapidated overhang sheltering the entrance. Lark strained her ears listening to their speech. Though they whispered, she was able to piece together bits of their conversation—enough to learn that the one who had pulled her from the quicksand was called Simm, and the other, Lige. They were part of the motley band that had been in the graveyard earlier. They were on their way to Colors Cove for another load slated for this abandoned tin mine when they came upon her in the marsh. Lark had thought their cart looked familiar. These were the gravediggers of the lot. Her heart leapt. Suppose the others were to come! How could she hope to defend herself against so many?

She strained against her tethers. They didn't know who she was. Should she tell them? Would the knowledge count in her favor, or were these who were so afraid of the land guards at odds with King, when it came to stealing from the Crown's contraband? If they were, they might hold her for ransom or kill her. She dared not chance it, not unless . . .

"He ain't in there," Jeremy hollered, stomping out of the mine. "I told ya, ya fools. We should have let her sink."

"Well, we didn't," snapped Simm. "We'll just have to wait on him, unless you want to take the blame. I'll have no hand in it."

"He's probably down 'round the cove wonderin' what's become of us and the cart," Lige put in. "I say one of us had best go down and fetch him back here."

"You mean Jeremy or me," Simm said. "You sure ain't speakin' for yerself. I know what's in your head. You want to cock a leg over the bird."

"Well, I ain't volunteerin'," Jeremy spoke up. "I sure ain't getting' my ears pinned back for somethin' I was against from the beginnin'."

"Shhhh, somebody's comin'," Simm cut in.

Until then, Lark had been silent, but the minute she heard horse's hoofbeats approaching, she began screaming at the top of her voice and didn't stop—not even when the rider swung himself down from the saddle.

"What the deuce is going on here? Who's that wom . . . bloody hell! Get those ropes off her at once! Do you know who that is? That's King's bride you've got trussed up in there, you nodcocks—Countess Grayshire! What have you done to her? Answer me, or by God you'll answer to him!"

Lark's hysterics died to hoarse whimpers. It was Leander Markham.

All three of the other men ran to untie her. The minute the ropes were off, she scrambled out of the cart and ran to Toffee, tethered in the rain. Leander was right on her heels, and he spun her around before she could mount the horse.

"What are you doing here?" he demanded in an undervoice. "Do you know the whole house is frantic looking for you?"

"Take your hands off me!" she shrilled, wrenching free of his hold. "Don't you *touch* me, you're no better than the rest." She made a wild gesture toward the others. "I saw you in the churchyard. *I saw you*, Leander Markham, with these . . . these . . . animals! That one"—she pointed at Simm—"pulled me out of the bog after this horse threw me only because he's afraid of Will Bowles." She aimed her finger at Lige. "That one wanted to rape me"—she swung her arm toward Jeremy—"and that one wanted to leave me to sink in the quicksand!"

"I'll deal with them, Lark," Leander soothed. "You don't understand any of this, I know, but you must trust me—"

"Trust? Hah! I trusted my husband, and he lies naked abed with Hazel Helston as we speak. Oh, yes, don't look so shocked. I've just come from her cottage. I followed Will Bowles there. I saw it myself! How could you possibly *imagine* that I would trust the likes of you or anyone ever again in this nest of brigands and pirates and . . . and murdering thieves?" She climbed up on Toffee's back. "Get out of my way, Lee, or I'll run you down!" she warned him.

A rumble of salacious murmurs came from the others.

"Belay it, you lot!" Leander gritted. "I'll deal with you presently." He grabbed the horse's bridle. "Lark, you don't understand. It's not what you think. He—"

The ends of the reins flung hard in his face cut him short. He let go of the bridle and staggered back, soothing the welts the leather had left behind. Lark saw her chance, and she took it. Spurring the horse and shouting a command that set the mare in motion, with little regard for Leander in her path, she rode off at a gallop into the storm.

The gale was at its full fury when Leander Markham reached Hazel Helston's cottage with Simm in tow. Of the lot, Simm was the best man to handle what he had in mind. Lark didn't know it, but it was her recommendation that won him the chore when she'd said he was afraid of Will Bowles. Trust a woman's instincts. That strategy never failed him in the past, and he prayed it would hold true now. Too much depended upon it.

What could Will have been thinking, bringing King here of all places? Or was it King's idea? He didn't want to believe it. Jerking Simm to a standstill on the path, he followed the shaft of light spilling from Hazel's bedroom window, and peeked through the gap in the curtains.

"Bloody hell!" he seethed under his breath. Lark hadn't

exaggerated. They lay like two lovers sated after sex, and he motioned Simm to stay where he was, plowed through the unkempt ground cover, and burst through the door that wasn't even locked. Was the doxy hoping for discovery? He wouldn't put it past her.

Bursting into the bedroom, he stood staring down, arms akimbo. Despite what it must have looked like to Lark—to him as well from the outside vantage—he could tell in an instant now what had actually occurred. King was unconscious, burning with fever, his breathing tremulous and labored, his flushed skin hot and dry. He was in no condition for bed sport.

He turned a cold eye upon Hazel, who had begun to stir beside King, undulating against him. Her scheme was obvious. She'd taken advantage of King in a vulnerable state, and he stomped to the bedside, threw back the counterpane and wrenched her out of the bed.

"Get up out of there! What the devil do you think you're about?" he demanded, shaking her.

"What do you mean barging in here without so much as a by-your-leave, Leander Markham?" she shrilled. "Let go of me!"

"If you don't want folks 'barging in,' you might lock your door," he snapped. "What if it was your husband come home? You really are a trollop. I don't know what King ever saw in you." Shoving her aside, he snatched her clothes up from the floor, and thrust them toward her. "Put these on," he charged, "you're disgusting. His wife saw you through the window. You've a lot to answer for, Hazel."

A smile bloomed on the woman's lips. "Saw us, did she? Good!" she triumphed.

He made a quick move toward her. "You won't think it's so good when he comes 'round. After I'm done, you won't think it's so good *at all*," he gritted through lips tight with rage.

"Don't you lay a hand on me, Leander Markham, or I'll have the bailiffs on you—aye, and the land guards. You can't afford to threaten me. The cost's too dear."

"Capt'n Jim's a friend of mine, Hazel," Leander said levelly, though his fisted hands itched to throttle her. "I warned him not to marry you—we all did. You won't voice one word against me, because the minute you do, he'll know what you've tried to do here and I won't have to lay a hand on you. As I recall, Jim's got a fearsome temper."

She jerked her bodice closed. "I didn't do anything," she grumbled, slapping her skirts into shape. "He was burnin' with fever and shakin' somethin' fierce with chills. All I did was climb into bed to keep him warm."

"*Naked*," Leander pronounced.

"Aye, naked. What of it? What's the harm? It isn't like we've never lain naked together before. Besides, he didn't even know it, he's that far gone." Tears welled in her eyes. "I love him, Lee," she murmured. "He'll never come to me now that he has his fine lady. I was hoping . . ."

"I get the drift," Leander said on a sigh. "What you and King do under the sheets is your business. My business is getting him fit again. That can't happen here. I'm taking him." He strode to the window, threw it open and bellowed, "Simm, haul your arse in here!"

"You can't move him like he is!" Hazel protested. "He's lost more blood than the average man has in him. That there on his arm needs sewin' shut. The surgeon's up to Looe, he won't be 'round till tomorrow."

"I'm taking him," Leander said. "The surgeon can come 'round to Mattie Bowles's place and tend him. That's where I told Will to take him in the first place."

"He couldn't! It's too far. King had lost too much blood."

"Or so you convinced Will, eh? I don't trust you. Stand aside."

"Don't *trust* me? Do you think for one moment I'd harm one hair on his head, Lee?"

"You just might fix it so nobody could have him if you couldn't—that or take unfair advantage of him again. At least Mattie Bowles won't try to seduce him. Hah! You should be glad to see the back of him. You'll want as much distance between you as possible once I tell him what his wife saw through that window tonight. Don't give me that look. That'll be the first thing out of my mouth the minute he comes 'round. It's on your head, this."

Simm inched over the threshold into the room, slouch hat in hand, smoothing his disheveled brown hair, his owlish blue eyes oscillating between them.

"I need Will and the cart," Leander told him. "Will's down at the cove. Lige and Jeremy will have reached there by now. Are you going after him, or shall I?"

"Ohhhh, no, I ain't goin' down there with this news!" Simm blurted, wagging his head. "You're on your own there, gov'nor."

"So be it," said Leander. Grabbing Hazel's arm, he steered her out of the room and closed the door behind her, throwing the bolt with a heavy hand despite her fists pummeling the wood from the other side. Then, deaf ears turned to her protests and ravings and threats of Gypsy curses, he turned to Simm. "Get his clothes on him and get him fit for travel—bundle him good, and mind that arm," he charged the smuggler. "After I've gone, lock that door after me. Don't let her back into this room no matter how she bawls."

"You heard her just now, she'll curse me!"

"I don't care how many curses she lays on you. Trust me, I'll do worse! Don't open that door for anything till Will and I knock on it. Is that clear?"

"Aye, but—"

"No buts, Simm. So help me God, I'll skin you if I come back and that bitch has gotten anywhere near him again. Am I making myself clear?"

"It's her house, ain't it? Suppose—"

"Don't 'suppose.' You haven't got the equipment. Look here, would you rather go after Will? I can just as easily—"

"Ohhh, no!"

"Good. Then I shall trust you to do as I've said. You

haven't a choice in any case. After what you, Lige, and Jeremy did to the countess tonight, you need to earn all the merit points you can. Oh, and Simms, if you think Will Bowles is a man to be feared, you don't ever want to come up against King or me. Especially me."

Twenty-three

*I*t was past midnight when Lark reached Grayshire Manor, and the house was still ablaze with light. There went her hopes of collecting her things and slipping out again with no one the wiser. She was exhausted, bone weary, and soaked to the skin. The teeming rain had washed most of the ooze away, but it wasn't until she climbed stiffly down from the gelding's back that she realized she'd forfeited her Morocco leather ankle boots to the bog. Her feet were bare.

She knew more now than she needed or wanted to know—about the trade, about the graveyard, and about the man she'd married—more than enough; enough to break her heart. She wished she hadn't lost her temper with Leander Markham. He would surely tell King. Of course King would come after her; he wanted his heir. Well, he could get it on Hazel Helston now, if he hadn't done already.

Smeaton, Peal, and Mrs. Hildrith were her welcoming committee, voicing in unison both their relief and dismay over the bedraggled state of her. Lark marched right by them. Racing up the stairs, she ignored their barked orders over filling her hipbath, fetching her maid, and building up the fire in her chamber. She wasn't planning on being there long enough for any of that.

She'd scarcely entered the room when Agnes burst in, wringing her hands at sight of her.

"Oh, la!" she cried. "What's happened to you? You look like a drowned rat! We thought . . . we were afraid . . .

h-have you heard about the *Cormorant?* Sh-she's been sunk off Fowey, and—"

"So I've gathered," Lark snapped, dragging down her portmanteau from the armoire.

"We don't know what's happened to his lordship. Lee's gone out there, but he hasn't returned, and then when *you* didn't come back from your ride and it started to storm again . . . ! We've been half-mad here. Lady Isobel is in such a taking that she hardly touched her supper, and retired right after."

"His lordship is in fine fettle," Lark snapped. "No worries there."

"You've *seen* him?" Agnes cried. "Where—how? Does Lee know?"

"Oh, Lee knows all right," Lark said. "His lordship lies abed with Hazel Helston at this very moment."

"*What?* I can scarce believe it," Agnes breathed.

"Believe what you will. I saw him myself, lying naked in that . . . that woman's arms. In her *bed*."

"Did you . . . talk to him?" Agnes probed.

"I wasn't about to give him the satisfaction of my humiliation," Lark returned. "I wasn't about to expose my naïvete, to be held up to ridicule for not realizing that my function in his life is endured for the sole purpose of begetting an heir to the Grayshire earldom, while Hazel Helston's place is . . . is to . . . ."

She sank down on the edge of the bed and took her head in her hands. She would not cry. In fact, she almost laughed. Not so very long ago she'd been incensed believing King wanted her for his mistress instead of his wife, and now that she was his wife, she was wishing just the opposite. How cruel was Divine Providence. Her heart was broken—crushed. It was as though he'd reached inside and ripped it out of her. How could something so empty inside hurt like this?

"You can't think of leaving," Agnes said, sinking down beside her. "Where will you go? What will you do?"

"I don't know, and I wouldn't tell you if I did, Agnes. You have a fine life here, and a good man who loves you, even if he is a . . . a pirate! None of this changes that."

"If you leave, I'm going with you," Agnes insisted.

"No, you are not," Lark flashed. "I mean it, Agnes. I don't want to argue with you. I don't want to leave you that way, but if you oppose me, I shall."

"This is madness!" Agnes shrilled.

"Shhhh! Keep your voice down. The last thing I want or need right now is a confrontation with Lady Isobel."

"That's unfortunate," came a voice like a whip from the doorway. "Because that is just exactly what you've got."

Lark dropped her head back into her hands as the dowager approached, banging her cane with every step.

"Now, daughter, suppose you explain yourself," the dowager said.

The word "daughter" was more than Lark could bear. It opened the floodgates, and her tears streamed down. She could face King dry-eyed, and Agnes, but not this woman—this surrogate mother so recently acquired, so desperately needed, so totally unexpected, so thoroughly enjoyed. How could she bear to leave her?

Lady Isobel made no move to comfort her. She stood, both hands supporting her on the infamous cane. Waiting. When Lark looked up through eyes almost swollen shut, she saw a woman she scarcely recognized. The dowager's complexion was gray, and deeply lined. Her lips were tinged with blue. She looked weary, and for the second time in recent days Lark truly believed she actually needed the cane to support her. Her jutting chin was her only prompt. She never repeated a command.

"I cannot stay here, my lady," Lark murmured. "I am a different entity." She would have liked to leave it at that, but the dowager's expression demanded that she elaborate—even though it pained them both. But how to put it delicately? "I have not the strength to mirror your life. . . ." She faltered. "I have not the fortitude to . . . to honor my duty to produce an heir while my husband . . . while he takes his pleasures elsewhere, my lady."

The dowager stiffened. "I see," she said, working the silver head of her cane in white-knuckled fists, one atop the other. "Suppose you have honored it already?" she observed.

"That isn't possible, my lady."

"Oh? You've had your courses since you wed my son?"

"Well, no, but—"

"Then it *is* possible, isn't it, dear?"

"Well, possible, yes," said Lark, "but hardly probable. We only had that one . . . night." That one *perfect* night, she'd nearly said. The word was choked off, drowned in her tears.

"While there is the slightest chance that it might be so, you are obliged to remain here," Lady Isobel intoned. "There is no argument, no negotiation—you know that, Lark. It is your duty."

"And what is King's duty?" she flashed.

"To produce the offspring you might be carrying."

"You expect me to turn blind eyes to his infidelity?"

"I expect you to honor your commitment to the marriage," she replied. "If there has been infidelity—"

"I *saw* him in that woman's bed myself tonight," Lark erupted. "They were naked together, in each other's arms. There is no *if*."

A strangled gasp from Agnes turned the dowager toward her. "Please leave us, dear," she said. "I shall join you in my apartments presently. I shall need you to ready me for bed."

"I would like her to stay," said Lark, stopping Agnes with a hand motion. "Agnes is my one true friend; she has been since before I ever met your son. There is nothing I would keep from her."

The dowager cocked her head. "You threaten to leave yet you still expect the privileges of countess here? Declare yourself!" She banged her cane in punctuation. "I shall be glad to yield to your authority, if you intend to honor that authority. Which is it? You cannot have it both ways."

There was no use engaging in battle with this woman; Lark knew she would never win. Time was passing. She needed to have the interview over and be away before King returned. That meant placating the dowager. Defeat ruled her posture. She seemed to shrink. When she nodded toward Agnes, her head felt too heavy for her neck to support.

"It's all right, Agnes," she murmured. "Do as her ladyship says."

Agnes floated out, reluctance in her bearing, but the dowager didn't speak until she had closed the door behind her.

"I don't know what is at the root of this," Lady Isobel said, "but I intend to find out, the minute King returns. I wish you to remain until then. He loves you, Lark. I know you're overset—"

"Overset?" Lark cried. "My heart is broken, my lady. I was led to believe I could expect a different sort of marriage with your son. Had I been made aware that this was the case, I never would have consented to the betrothal. I have lost all that I love. I never knew my mother. She died giving birth to me, and you know my father's tragedy." Tears welled in her eyes again, but she was determined to say it all. "My lady, I have come to look upon you as the mother I never had. I've grown to love and respect you. You have no inkling of the pain I'm in at the thought of separation, but if I were to stay, and a child were to come of this union . . . I am not made of the stuff that you are . . . and I love King so, I would go mad. It isn't only the infidelity . . . there are other issues as well."

"The trade?" said the dowager. "Don't look so shocked, my dear. My son's a fool if he believes he's hoodwinked me in that regard. I know. I've *always* known. One cannot live amongst pirates and infidels all one's life and not know. He has a Letter of Marque. He's profiteering for the Crown—

all perfectly legitimate. He could have told me that, but he chose not to in order to spare me worry. Where it becomes illegitimate is in his allowing Will Bowles and his ilk to skim the spoils, to take a share and cheat the Crown. *They* are the pirates, and he becomes one also when he accommodates them. You met them tonight, didn't you? What happened, Lark?"

"It all started out innocently enough," she replied. "I was so overset about King's return that I rode to the quay. There was no sign of the *Cormorant*. No cutters were in the harbor, only a few small fishing crafts. It was early, and I decided to pay a call on the vicar before I returned. Suffice it to say, I saw what your pirates do with their spoils, and overheard Will Bowles say that King was at Hazel Helston's. I followed him there, and I saw . . . what I saw. Returning, I lost my way in the dark, and the storm . . . and my horse threw me into the quicksand down in the marshes. Three of the pirates came to my rescue. Hah! One wanted to rape me, another wanted to leave me there to sink and have done, and the third pulled me out because he feared a reprisal from Will Bowles. They bound me, and threw me in a cart, and God alone knows what else they would have done if Lee hadn't come by and rescued me. . . ."

"You told him what you saw?"

"I did."

"Where is Leander now?"

"I've no idea, nor do I care. I cannot remain here, my lady. You cannot keep me against my will. I want no truck with pirates, and infidels, with . . . creatures like those who laid hands on me tonight. I've been mishandled for months. You know I have. I thought I'd found paradise here . . . a home. Instead, I've come into the worst kind of hell. You have to let me go."

"You are not a prisoner here, Lark," the dowager said wearily, "but the fact remains that you could be carrying my son's seed. Until we are sure that you are not with child, you will remain here. Once it is determined that you are not, if you are still of the same mind, arrangements will be made for you. This is what must be. Your bath has been drawn. I suggest you go and take it before you come down with pneumonia, and then get some sleep. Things will all look differently in the morning . . . when you've rested . . . when you've had time to quiet down and remember who you are, and where your duties lie."

Lark dragged herself to her dressing room next door, where her bath did indeed await. She hadn't prolonged the argument; it would have been pointless. Instead, she decided to let the dowager think she'd won, and later, when the household was asleep, she would slip away with no one the wiser.

The bath did look inviting. She dismissed the maid with instructions that she not be disturbed until morning, locked the door, and took advantage of the steaming tub. The water had been strewn with rose petals and herbs. The scented steam rising from it was delicious. She reclined in the water only briefly before preparing for her departure. Fearful that King would come banging on the door at any moment, she wasted no time dressing, and began cramming a few frocks and necessities into a traveling bag small enough for her to carry.

She'd scarcely begun when she let a white linen frock slip from her fingers and sank down on the edge of the bed. What if she was indeed carrying King's child? She passed her hand across her middle, deep in that thought. It could well be. They had made love through that whole perfect night. That was what she couldn't forgive: He had introduced her to passions she never dreamed existed—awakened her to pleasures she would never know again in those strong muscled arms she longed to hold her forever. If a child had been conceived, it would be a love child, for regardless of what came after, on that one night, Basil Kingston, Earl of Grayshire, had loved her. She was certain of it.

If she was pregnant, she had a duty to fulfill; there was no mistaking that. And it was possible, after all the times they'd made love. Yet she wasn't willing to stay at the Manor until the truth was known, where he could seduce her again, where he could chip away at her resolve until she yielded to the power of his passion. She knew herself well enough to realize that was a definite possibility, given her love for this man, who sadly didn't love her in return. He couldn't—not and at the same time climb between the sheets with another come so soon from her embrace. Not after the intimacies they'd shared. He'd scarcely been left wanting.

No, she couldn't remain at the Manor and she couldn't leave it. There was only one place that she could go to accomplish both—at least until she had time to think: the dower house.

With that decided, she quickly finished packing, slipped one of the dower house servants' entrance keys from her chatelaine, and left the jewel-encrusted clasp on the dresser in plain view, along with the opal and sapphire ring, where they would be found. The extra servants' entrance key would hopefully not be missed. Then, throwing her pelerine about her shoulders, she took up the traveling bag and tiptoed toward the door.

She'd almost reached it when a light tap came, and she froze where she stood, listening. It was too light a tap for King's massive hand, especially in these circumstances. She held her breath. It came again.

"Lark," Agnes whispered from the other side. "Let me in!"

Lark's posture deflated, and she opened the door, a finger pressed to her lips flagging caution, and she pulled Agnes over the threshold.

"Shhh," she whispered. "You shouldn't be here. You'll be missed! Lady Isobel will know you've come here, and—"

"She's gone to bed," Agnes interrupted. "Oh, la, you can't be leaving! It will break her heart if you do. I've never seen her in such a taking. She's positively fuddlepated. I wouldn't give two sticks for his lordship's hide when he comes home, if she doesn't take a fit and die beforehand. She's that addled."

"His lordship's hide is his own affair," said Lark. "I hope she crowns him with that cane. My one regret is that I shan't be here to see it."

"She said she'd convinced you to stay."

"I only agreed to put her off her guard so I could slip away. You know I cannot stay, Agnes. It pains me more than I can say to leave you . . . to leave her. I treasure your friendship more than I can say, and I did so want to belong to a family, but there's nothing for it. I've made a dreadful mistake."

Agnes looked so forlorn. Lark wanted to comfort her, but she would come to pieces if she did. The glow she'd noticed in her friend's eyes since her alliance with Leander Markham had fled. Sorrow glazed them now with unshed tears.

"Where will you go—*how*, in this storm?"

Lark hesitated. Should she say? Should she confide her plan? Could she trust Agnes not to tell? It was against her better judgment. Still, there would be comfort in the knowledge that someone knew her whereabouts—if that someone could be trusted. There was no question that she could use an ally. Agnes had certainly always been that. It would be at least a sennight before her courses were due . . . and if she were late . . .

"If I were to tell you, you would have to swear to keep my confidence," she said. "I mean it, Agnes, because if you betray me, you will never see me again—ever. I will run so far and fast that *no one* will ever find me, which is what I should be doing anyway."

"Betray you? How could you even think it? I owe you my life, Lark. Your secrets are safe with me, I swear gladly!"

"Very well then," said Lark. "Lady Isobel is right. I am obliged to remain until there is no question of my carrying King's heir, but I cannot remain under the same roof with him. *I cannot.* I'm going to the dower house. I've taken the key. You must tell no one. No one, Agnes, not even Lady Isobel—especially not Lady Isobel—and certainly not King, or Leander, either; they are like two halves of a whole, those two. What one knows, the other will also. You must promise me, and you must keep the promise."

"Of course I promise. Oh, la, you don't know how relieved I am," Agnes gushed, "but there is no staff there. What will you eat? How will you manage out there all alone?"

"I've learned to fend for myself, Agnes. I've been alone a good long while now. There are some things in the larder, nonperishable items King had stored there for his mother before we decided that she would remain at the Manor—staples he portioned out from the last marketing. I'll manage."

"You can't light a fire. The smoke will be visible day and night! I'll bring what you need—"

"You cannot!" Lark cried, then lowered her voice. "You'll be seen, followed. You mustn't!"

"I shall come after dark. Lee showed me the way on one of our walks. No one will follow me, Lark. When you've lived in a place like the Marshalsea as long as I did, you learn how to move with the stealth of a rat. I'll come to the servants' entrance in back tomorrow night, then every three nights, with what I can glean from the kitchens. Light no candles after dark. This place is swarming with all sorts of undesirables, if you take my meaning."

Lark embraced her. "I honestly don't know what I would do without you, my dear friend," she said.

"You shan't ever have to," said Agnes. "And you were trying to manage all this on your own!"

"I must go, before the storm gets any worse," Lark said, moving toward the door. "Remember . . . you mustn't tell a soul. I have your word?"

"You do."

"Good," Lark murmured. Then she slipped into the hall without making a sound.

Twenty-four

Screams of the dying echoed all around King in the hot, steamy air. Crashing waves washed over him, the cold water making him shudder and taking his breath away, the spindrift like icy needles stabbing at his face, his eye narrowed and stinging from the salt. He tried to force it open and failed, again and again. It was as though it had been nailed shut, and the pain—all over—every muscle ached beyond bearing. Then there was the throbbing in his head and the searing pain in his left arm when he thrashed about, but he had to thrash about. He had to keep his head above the water. He had to scrabble and wriggle and claw his way over the wounded deck, up along the vertical mass of splintered wood—against the flow—away from the vortex—away from the watery death that awaited him below that churning, swirling surface. He had to grab fast to the piece of the mainmast that had glanced off his head and speared his arm. It had bested him twice, that snapped-off mast, and now, by God, it would save him, buoy him to the shore he could see. It was close.

Why did the air feel so hot and the water so cold? What was that smell . . . that wonderful smell? He licked his parched, crusted lips expectantly. His tongue, swollen and dry, came away tasting only salt.

"For God's sake, hold him still!" someone was barking. "How can I dose him?"

Whose voice was that? He knew it, or at least he

thought he should. Why couldn't he remember? Who were they dosing?

"I'm trying," said another familiar voice he couldn't place—a younger voice, edged like a knife. "Why don't you try it awhile? It's like wrestling a water buffalo!"

"Out of the way, both of you," yet another voice said—a woman's voice. "You're doing more harm than good. I think I'm more qualified than either of you to pick up the pieces of your reckless folly. God knows I've had enough practice. You should have brought him here in the first place. If he dies, it's on your heads, taking him to that . . . that *doxy*. What would she know about tending the likes of this?"

"Stubble it, Mama."

"I will not 'stubble it,'" she bleated. "Don't you ever let me catch you 'round that whore. She's no better than a Penzance roundheels. Just look at him! From the setback he's taken in that cart all the way from Fowey, you'd have done better bringing him straight on, and then there wouldn't have been an issue, would there? If he hadn't been at that woman's—"

"Stow it, I said!" Will snapped, low-voiced. "He's going to hear you."

"L-Lark . . . ?" said a feeble voice he scarcely recognized. "Lark," it mumbled again.

King groaned awake to the blurry sight of Mattie Bowles stooping over him, a brimming spoon in her hand.

"Open," she charged.

He obeyed automatically. Something thick and bitter-tasting trickled down his throat. It chased the dreams and he slept.

It was pleasant wandering through that soft, safe oblivion on the edge of consciousness, pleasant and still, but there was something gnawing at the edges of King's peace, something that wouldn't let the laudanum Mattie had dosed him with do its job completely. If he only knew what that something was. It seemed so urgent.

Neither awake nor asleep, he floated, trying to force his eye open, but he sensed the light. It would hurt to look at the light, so he didn't. He didn't need to see it. He felt its warmth, smelled that wonderful smell that filled the room around him. It brought back memories, and when he stirred, someone groaned.

"I think he's coming 'round," said the familiarly edged voice he'd heard before.

The swirling auburn darkness behind his closed eye pulsated with movement. It grew brighter, then darker, as someone thrust something glaring and hot close to his face. King shrank from it. That something in his mind that refused to let him rest gnawed at him harder now.

It had a face. *Lark!* He stiffened, and that groan came again. It was coming from his own parched throat. His eye snapped open, squinting for the brightness of the candle in Will Bowles's hand so close to his face. Were those tears in Will's eyes? He couldn't be sure. If only everything would stop spinning and stand still.

"The fever's breaking," Mattie said, on a sigh of relief. "I'll get the broth." She paused halfway to the kettle hanging in the open hearth. To King's eye, everything was in motion. "Are you going to tell him?" she inquired, her voice no more than a whisper.

"What, *me?*" Will blurted, setting the candle down. "Not me. Lee can have that pleasure. I like my skin right where it is!"

"T-tell me . . . what?" King stammered.

They both ran to him.

"Damn it, King!" Will cried. "You gave us one hell of a scare."

"I've got to go," King gritted, trying to raise himself. "L-Lark . . . she probably thinks I'm . . . dead. . . ." The motion failed, and he fell back against the pillows with a groan.

"Believe me, she knows you're not dead," Will said dismally.

There was an odd inflection in his voice, and King stared toward him, trying to sharpen an image that wouldn't come clear.

"Get back from there, Will," Mattie scolded. "Let me give him some of this broth."

So that's what it was—Mattie's broth. How he used to love to visit here. There was always something warm and inviting in the air, and Will or Mattie to chase the loneliness.

All at once she sat beside the bed, feeding him with a spoon. He moaned as the salty, meaty liquid trickled down his throat. It tasted of leek and onion and . . . oh, it was good, just like he remembered.

"How does she know?" he questioned Will between spoonfuls. "Have you told her? And Mother . . . what about Mother?"

"Lee's gone to the Manor. You've got to rest, King, we nearly lost you here. Do you know what happened out there?"

"The *Cormorant*," King murmured. "Somebody sank her . . ."

"A French merchantman—the *Benicoeur*. She flew no colors. The *Hind* blew her out of the water off the Point up to Fowey; her cargo's still coming in—and yours. Nice haul. Wine mostly. Her log washed ashore just south of the cove."

"The storm . . . we couldn't see two feet ahead . . . no running lights," King reflected. "All at once we took a broadside hit amidships, and we split in two. The mainmast snapped. I think it hit me in the head—something did. I know it speared my arm. I grabbed fast to it, and swam, or was thrown clear . . . I don't know . . . it all happened so fast. I was so close to shore, I could see it. That's all I remember . . . till I woke up at Hazel's. *Hazel's!* What the deuce was I doing there?"

"You came ashore practically on her doorstep," said

Will. "You'd lost so much blood . . . Lee and I thought better there than trying to get you here in that storm in the cart. Then, after you'd . . . settled some, we did bring you here. The surgeon's been and gone. He left laudanum for the pain and sewed your arm up. Another half inch and that mast would have hit an artery. You'd have bled to death."

"All right, Will, that's enough chitchat," Mattie said, setting the bowl aside. "His lordship needs his rest."

"No . . . I have to go," King insisted. "Lark must be worried sick. She didn't want me to go . . . she—"

"You're not going anywhere until the surgeon allows it," Mattie spoke up unequivocally, tucking the quilts around him. "You're going to lie right here in this bed and mind. Hand me that bottle and spoon," she said to Will, setting him in motion.

"No, no more," King protested, turning his head aside. "I'm still dizzy from the last dose."

"You're dizzy because you've a concussion of the brain," said Mattie, filling the spoon. "Now, you take this and go back to sleep. I've got my orders. I'm to wake you at intervals . . . till we're sure you're on the mend proper, like the surgeon said. Open!"

Lark walked to the dower house. It was quite a distance in the hail-ridden rain, but she dared not call attention to her escape—for that is how she viewed it—by taking one of the horses. Despite that she'd gone by way of the woods, where the heavy foliage offered some protection from the rain, by the time she reached the servants' entrance, her fine wool pelerine was soaked through. Her bonnet had lost its sizing; it clung limp, plastered to her head, dripping water in her eyes. One pair of Morocco leather ankle boots had been lost in the bog; the pair she'd put on for the trek to the dower house was oozing mud from slogging through the maze of narrow woodland paths—her feet were squishing inside. Now she would have to rely on the thin

dress slippers she'd brought along. The rest were at the Manor. The boots would never dry out without a fire, and she dared not light one.

Finally, the wind blew her around the corner at the back of the house. Hail had joined the mix, pelting down cruelly. Fallen limbs lay everywhere, and two windows had been broken—one on the side, and one in the rear door. She wouldn't have needed her key, though she used it anyway. Lightning lit her way. She had no idea where she was going. She almost laughed. The only part of the house she knew was the Roman bath, and she certainly wanted no truck with that. She would find a bedchamber at the rear of the house, facing the wood and the tall stone wall that bordered the compound, hopefully with heavy draperies that she could draw so she could light a candle now and again. Not tonight. The lightning would suffice. Grateful for it, she made her way to the staircase and began to climb.

Prowling through the empty old house with rampant flashes of ghostly glare to light her way was an eerie experience at best. Everywhere she turned, odd pieces of furniture lurking beneath dusty Holland covers loomed like specters. They put her in mind of the tales of Great-grandfather Basil Kingston's ghost. But he was reputed to haunt the Manor, wasn't he? She shuddered. There were no such things as ghosts, and she was glad of it. If there were, Great-grandfather Basil Kingston would certainly take a dim view of her running out on her obligation to his descendant the way she had. But she hadn't really; she had come here instead. That should placate the spirits somewhat. Shouldn't it?

Lark shook free of those thoughts, and continued traveling the hallways in search of a room. Outside, the wind wailed like a woman. Fierce gusts buffeted the house, which seemed to groan under the assault. Boards creaked. Noises from below funneled up the staircase. Lark shuddered again, not entirely from the cold wet clothes clinging to her frame. Could it be rats? Some creature had evidently taken refuge from the storm and was scratching about downstairs. She would have to find something to board up the broken windows, if she didn't want every animal in the wood for company. That would have to wait until morning. She was beyond exhausted. The bath had revived her somewhat, but nothing was going to put her in shape but a good lie-down, and she finally found the room to have it in.

It was part of a suite of rooms at the back of the house, facing the wood as she wanted, with heavy burgundy portieres at the window, and if she placed a lit candle in the fireplace . . . but not tonight. She set her portmanteau down, stripped off her soaked pelerine, bonnet, and the muddy boots and stockings. She'd worn a winter traveling dress of Merino wool, and a sturdy shawl beneath the pelerine as protection against the storm. Except for the hem the dress was dry enough to sleep in. Glad of that, because she was too cold and tired to undress, much less unpack, she pulled the dust cover off the bed, delighted to find a downy counterpane and crisp white sheets beneath. Burrowing down in the bedding that smelled faintly of lavender, she pulled the counterpane up to her neck, and drew a deep, tremulous breath.

Across the way the draperies were parted just enough to let the lightning in. Heavy as they were, the drafts moved them. The sky would be lightening soon; then she would make a proper exploration of her new domain and see to those broken windows. For now she was content to close her eyes and drift off to sleep listening to the thunder, the groaning timbers, and the occasional scratching sounds made by whatever woodland creature had taken refuge there from the storm.

She had nearly fallen asleep when a particularly surly thunderclap echoed through the old house. The sound reverberated along the corridors, ricocheted off the ceiling, and vibrated through the very air, forcing her eyes to open wide. For a split second—just as they focused—she could have sworn she saw a figure lurking in the shadows of a recessed door to the adjoining chamber across the room, lit by the white flash of lightning that stabbed through the window. Her breath rushed back into her lungs, and she blinked to chase the sleep from her eyes. When they focused again, the image was gone.

Lark stared at the place where it had appeared. Gooseflesh crept over her skin, and her heart was hammering against her ribs. She was wide awake now, waiting for every random lightning flash to show her the periphery, and she didn't close her eyes again until the first bleak rays of a cheerless dawn crept in and chased all the shadows.

Twenty-five

Leander Markham didn't like the hand he'd been dealt one bit. He didn't relish what was to come, either—any of it— since it fell to him not only to tell King what Lark had seen, but that now she was gone, vanished in the night. Making matters worse, he found himself seated beside the dowager countess in the coupe as it tooled along the lanes awash with mud and standing water on its way to Mattie Bowles's cottage. Of all unlikely places. That was the part he liked the least: Never in her life had the dowager countess crossed the threshold of her dead husband's mistress's abode . . . until today. The two had never met face-to-face. They'd glimpsed each other only at a distance, and judging from the dowager's grip on her cane and the tight-lipped fury evidenced in her demeanor, he didn't want to speculate upon the outcome of that bleak morning's outing.

He dared not offer advice, warn her that upsetment in King's condition could do irreparable harm—not while those wrinkled, white-knuckled hands worked that cane handle so relentlessly across the way. Not while his kneecaps were within reach, or worse yet, his skull. He'd felt the sting of that cane more than once, just as King had, when they were younger. It wasn't something one was likely to forget. He could do nothing but hold his peace and sink back against the plush velvet squabs that couldn't cushion his rigid spine now. Nothing could have.

All too soon, Smythe, the coachman, drew the coupe to

a halt before the Bowles's cottage gate, climbed down, and set the steps. Leander exited first, then offered his hand to the dowager, who descended like a queen—back straight, head held high, her cane tapping a steady rhythm along the crushed shell walk. *If only there had been some way to warn Mattie*, Leander regretted. It was too late now. They were on their own—all of them.

The dowager's cane addressed the door like cannon fire. Leander winced as it came open in Mattie's hand. He tried to transmit his apologies by way of facial expression, but the gesture was wasted. Mattie's pale cornflower eyes, wide-flung and articulate, never left the dowager's, hooded and cold, like two raisins catching reflected light from the dismal morning glare.

Despite her surprise, Mattie offered a demure curtsy, and stood aside to allow the dowager to enter. It was a small cottage in dire need of repair, boasting the little parlor they were standing in, a kitchen, and two sleeping quarters: Mattie's bedchamber, which she had relinquished to King, and a loft where Will slept when he wasn't camping at the abandoned mine.

"Where is my son?" the dowager said.

"Abed, my lady," Mattie replied. "The surgeon's with him."

"We should wait until he's finished, my lady," Leander whispered in the dowager's ear. He hadn't even noticed the surgeon's surrey outside, he'd been that apprehensive about these two meeting. How was it that such a tiny impaired woman could strike terror in the hearts of all who came in contact with her?

"Thank you for instructing me in the proper etiquette for such a circumstance, Leander," the dowager intoned. "You overreach yourself as usual."

"Yes, my lady," he mumbled.

No fur was flying yet, but Leander Markham took no comfort in that. He'd known Countess Grayshire too long. This was clearly not going to be an easy morning. He was helpless looking on while the dowager, staring down her sharp aristocratic nose, raked Mattie from her neatly coifed wheat-colored hair to the toes of her worn leather slippers. He watched her gaze linger upon Mattie's shapely, youthful figure. It was hard to believe that Mattie was the mother of a son in his midtwenties. Only when one really looked closely were the fine lines visible— around the eyes, threaded across the high, smooth brow, punctuating the softly bowed lips. What struck Leander most, now that he saw them standing side-by-side, was the vast difference in their years. Mattie Bowles was half Lady Grayshire's age, and judging from the dowager's expression, that was the very thing that had struck her also— shaken her to the core.

"Would you care to sit while we wait, my lady?" Mattie said, offering a chair.

The dowager stiffened as though she'd been struck, and bristled, though she made no reply other than a stiff negative shake of her head.

"Has the surgeon just come, Mattie?" Leander inquired, anxious to have the interview ended before catastrophe struck.

"No," she replied, "he's been here since sunup."

"How serious is the nature of my son's injury?" the dowager asked Mattie, her voice edged with steel.

"He has a brain concussion, my lady," Mattie returned. "'Twas a blow to the head, and a wound on his arm that required stitching. There was fever, but that has passed, and the surgeon says—"

"Spare me your diagnosis," the dowager snapped. "I shall have it from the surgeon direct, if you please."

"As you wish, my lady," Mattie conceded.

Well, well! Mattie wasn't easily shaken. Leander would have bet against it. *He* was shaken, but then, the formidable Lady Grayshire had always had that effect upon him.

Silence prevailed, while they all stood at attention like a ragtag misbegotten regiment, for what seemed an endless time before the surgeon joined them. A short, balding, mustached man of middle age, he hesitated a moment before closing the bedchamber door behind him, and scrutinized what must have seemed a strange gathering.

"Dr. Snoad, this is his lordship's mother, the Dowager Countess Grayshire," Leander introduced.

"Mmm," the surgeon grunted. "Your ladyship, it is my pleasure to report that his lordship is improving nicely. The fever has broken, and his arm is mending satisfactorily, though it still needs careful attention if we are to avoid infection. The vertigo is subsiding somewhat, also—all good signs for a complete recovery."

"I've come to take him home . . . to Grayshire Manor," the dowager said. It seemed to Leander, looking on, that tension had flowed out of her like water from a spigot.

The surgeon stiffened. "It will be days before he can be moved, my lady," he said. "Why, to move him now—"

"Surely he cannot remain *here*?" she shrilled. "He needs proper care and tending. I have a house full of competent servants—his own personal valet among them, who has seen him through worse, I assure you. How can he hope to get such quality treatment here in this . . . this hovel, with this untrained person to nurse him?"

"Countess Grayshire," the surgeon chortled. "But for the skill and quick thinking of this lady here, his lordship would be dead. By time he arrived here, he'd lost much blood—too much—and he'd been too long in the water. Aside from that, he'd had a nasty knock on the head. Any one of these circumstances could easily have killed him in the wrong hands, the shock and exposure notwithstanding." He turned to Mattie. "Have you slept yet, madam?" he inquired.

"I could not while his lordship was so grave," she replied.

"I thought as much," Snoad observed. "We'll have you down next." He turned back to the dowager. "By time I arrived, this lady had already dosed his lordship with an herbal draught to help him sleep, applied a poultice that in truth has prevented infection, and sponged him down with spirits to lower the fever. *I* did very little, your ladyship, except to stitch him back together and offer laudanum for the pain. You have this fine nurse here to thank that he shall recover. If she hadn't laid the groundwork for me we would be having quite a different conversation."

"May I see him?" the dowager murmured.

The surgeon nodded. "Only briefly," he said. "He's just been dosed. But bring no bad tidings into that room, I beg you—nothing to excite him. He has been a . . . difficult patient, your ladyship. He fights the opiate. He's on the mend, but hardly out of the woods."

Leander attempted to follow her into the bedchamber, but the surgeon's quick hand arrested him. "One at a time, sir, if you please," he said.

Leander leaned close to the man. "Believe me, sir, there will be much less chance of 'upsetment' if you allow me also," he whispered. "In this one instance, I know the situation far better than you do." He couldn't take the chance that the dowager might not know how to handle mention of Lark, since he was certain that would be the first thing out of King's mouth.

Snoad thought on it for a moment, but Leander's eyes were immutable, and the surgeon's hand fell away.

"Very well," he said, with a nod, "but please be brief."

Mattie sank quietly into the chair she'd offered the dowager earlier, as Leander and the dowager approached the bedchamber. He did arrest the countess then, despite his resolve to hold his peace. She wouldn't attack him with that weapon in this company . . . he hoped.

"My lady, if you please, make no mention of Lark," he said. "I will break that news myself . . . when he's stronger."

Though she made no reply, he trusted her thoughtful expression, and handed her over the threshold.

Inside, King lay pale and unshaven on the edge of consciousness, until he saw the dowager. Leander almost laughed. If ever a man was dumbstruck, utterly stupid with astonishment, King was that man.

"M-*Mother?*" he breathed, slack-jawed. "Good God, what the devil are you doing . . . *here?*"

The dowager was clearly shaken at the sight of him—so shaken Leander took her arm. To his surprise, she didn't object. She actually leaned upon it.

"I hope, Basil, that this has made an end to your romance with the trade," she said, the sharpness of her tone contradicting the misty softness in her eyes looking down in dismay. "I came to take you home, where Frith and the staff can look after you properly. The man's beside himself—we all are. The surgeon tells me you must . . . remain here until you're stronger. I do not agree, but I will abide by his decision."

"Lark . . . is she here . . . does she know?" King pleaded. He was clearly fighting the laudanum.

Leander stepped forward. "Her ladyship wanted to come alone . . . considering where you are," he said. "Why, the surgeon didn't even want to admit *us*. You need your rest, King. Lark knows you've survived the shipwreck. There'll be time for all that later . . . when you're stronger."

"Did you do as I asked . . . did you go to Yorkshire . . . my wedding present to Lark?"

Leander had nearly forgotten. "Yes," he said. "It's done."

"Ahhhh," King groaned. "D-don't tell her . . . let me . . . my gift . . ."

Leander turned to the dowager. "My lady, please, the laudanum will do no good if he continues to fight it. We must away and let him rest."

The dowager cast a furtive glance around the warm, welcoming room. It was plain to Leander looking on that she was envisioning her husband there, in the arms of the woman who waited on the other side of the door. After a moment her posture clenched, as though she'd woken from a dream, and she stared down at King with a reverence in her faded eyes that Leander had never seen in them before.

"Rest, son," she murmured. "I shall send Frith to attend you . . . until we can bring you home."

King didn't reply. The laudanum had taken him under. Whether he'd even heard the last was unclear as they joined Mattie and the surgeon in the parlor.

Mattie rose to her feet with all the poise and grace of a courtier as they approached. The surgeon, meanwhile, stole back into the bedchamber to look after King. Come abreast of Mattie, the dowager paused, and Leander held his breath as she let go of his arm and relied on her cane once more, standing spine rigid before the woman she had hated for more than thirty years.

"Thank you for attending to my son," she said steadily, though her lips were pursed as if she'd been sucking on lemons. "I should like to send his valet to attend him until he's fit for travel. Frith has served Basil for years. He knows how to keep him in line . . . and he can . . . spell you."

"As you wish, my lady," said Mattie, sketching a curtsy.

"Very well, then," the dowager replied, punctuating her words with a rap of her cane.

Mattie didn't flinch. "My lady," she said, turning the dowager around from the doorway. "You are welcome to . . . return," she said. "That is, if you wish to check on his lordship's progress."

Lady Grayshire hesitated, and again Leander held his breath.

"My son once said to me that he preferred your company to mine," the dowager confided.

Mattie gasped. "For shame!" she said. "That was a hurtful thing to say!"

"Let me finish," the dowager insisted, raising her hand. "He asked me if I ever wondered why he wanted to come here so often as a child. I wondered, of course, and I resented it, but I never really understood . . . until now."

With no more said, she turned and let Leander lead her out into the dreary morning mist to the waiting coupe. He almost lost his footing. If he hadn't heard those words come from the dowager's lips himself, he never would have believed she'd spoken them.

Twenty-six

Lark was able to push a cupboard in front of the broken side window beside the servants' entrance to keep curious creatures out, but there was nothing she could do about the door. That couldn't be blocked, since it was to be Agnes's means of entry with her provisions after dark, but the hole was small—scarcely larger than a man's fist—and a wadded-up towel shoved in place sufficed to keep out the wind and rain, and hopefully any unwanted guests. Once that was done, Lark devoted the rest of the day to exploring her new lodgings.

How differently it all looked in the light of day, bleak though that light was. There were no shadows now, no creaking boards, strange noises, or specters, and the eerie incident of the night before was soon forgotten as she strolled from room to room admiring the artifacts and trappings.

She'd slept away most of the morning, and by mid-afternoon she was ravenous. The larder had been partially stocked with staples, it was true, but not much was edible amongst them without access to a fire, which she dared not light. She did find a string of what looked like withered, cured sausages hung up to age, and a canister of dried apricots and pears, which she nibbled just to silence her complaining stomach. The anonymous meat was heavily spiced and salty, and the fruit was like leather. She soon found herself wishing for nightfall, when Agnes would hopefully bring her something more appetizing, the shadows that darkness would bring notwithstanding.

The hour was late when Agnes finally arrived—so late that Lark didn't think she was coming. She had just made her way to the larder to attempt another meal of dried meat and fruit, when she heard the servants' entrance door she'd left unlocked creak open, and Agnes's voice, mouselike and hesitant, calling her name.

The moon, full and bright, had broken through the cloud cover, shedding enough light for them to make their way to the servants' hall, where Lark removed the dusty sheet from the long oak table, and Agnes set her basket down and began emptying it.

"I'm sorry for the hour," she said. "The whole house is in an uproar. I didn't dare leave till now."

"I thought you might not come. I shouldn't be putting you at risk like this."

"Oh, la, what risk? You've got to eat. It's difficult, I'll own, but not impossible. I've brought enough to keep you for three days, till I return." She gestured toward the basket. "There's fresh bread, and butter; it should keep in this cold. Some fresh fruit—apples, plums, and pears—meat pasties, and a wedge of hard cheese. Oh! And there's a bit of Cook's apple cake for your breakfasts, and a crock of water to wash it all down. There's half a chicken, too. You'd best eat that tonight, though. It won't keep like the rest; it's been sauced."

Lark took the offering. "Will you join me?"

"Oh, la, no; I've eaten," said Agnes, sinking into the chair beside her. "I daren't stay long, either. Her ladyship's quite done in from the goings-on today, and I left her sleeping soundly, but if she should wake and find me missing . . ."

"What 'goings-on'?" Lark asked, meanwhile nibbling at the savory chicken. She froze, a wing suspended. "It isn't King. He hasn't . . . he isn't . . . ?" She couldn't bring herself to give her fears substance with words.

"No, no, he's recovering well enough . . . at Mattie Bowles's cottage." She hesitated. "Lark, Lee took him there straightaway after . . . what you saw. He swears there's nothing to it, and—"

"Trust one brigand to stand up for another," Lark interrupted, slapping the chicken wing down. "Honor among thieves! I saw what I saw, and so did Lee if he went out there as you say. King and Lee are joined at the hip, Agnes—they have been since boyhood. Believe me, you can trust one to lie, and the other to swear to it."

Agnes sighed. "I'm not going to get into a set-to with you over it," she said. "I saw your face just now. You still love him—I know it. You need to give him a chance to explain."

"Give him a chance to charm me out of this, you mean. I can't do that—I *won't*."

"Why, because you don't think you can trust him anymore?"

"Because I know I cannot trust *myself*."

"Oh, la," Agnes groaned.

"You haven't told me the nature of the uproar at the Manor," Lark reminded her, in an attempt to change the subject. "If not King, what?"

"You'd never guess," Agnes said, wriggling in her chair. "Her ladyship went round to Mattie Bowles's place—armed with that cane—the minute Lee told her King was recovering there. She was set to bring him home. Lee went with her. Smythe drove them 'round in the coupe."

Lark stared slack-jawed.

"That's not the half of it," Agnes went on. "Before she left the place, she made some sort of peace with Mattie. It was a queer business, as Lee tells it, like some sort of bizarre awakening, but it happened nonetheless. Her ladyship was that grateful for Mattie's care of King, after she had an earful from the surgeon on Mattie's behalf, and got a good, long look at the woman and how she keeps her home, despite that it's all but falling down around her for lack of repair. Lee still can't believe it, and he was *there*. Her ladyship actually agreed to leave King at Mattie's, and she even sent Frith out to the cottage to give her a hand with his tending."

"I can scarcely believe it myself," Lark murmured.

"Her ladyship hasn't been the same since she discovered you missing this morning," said Agnes. "It's as though all of the life's gone right out of her. Won't you reconsider? Staying out here with no fire and only what scraps I can bring to you . . .'tis madness."

"It shan't be for long," said Lark. "No more than a sennight if—"

"*If*, la!" Agnes interrupted. "And what if nothing happens in a sennight?"

"I shall worry about that if it occurs."

"Well, 'if it occurs' you can't stay on here like this with winter coming on. Cornish winters are milder, I'll own, but not *that* mild, and what if you *are* with child? What then? You'll need proper nourishment, not just the gleanings I bring."

"Oh, Agnes, don't torment me!" Lark cried, holding her ears. "Do you think I like this any more than you do?"

"You've got to tell someone where you are. You cannot hide out here in the dark! Get a staff out here. You are entitled. You've made a decision on valid grounds; you set the conditions."

"You actually think that would keep King from marching out here the minute he knew?"

"He's in no condition to 'march' anywhere right now," Agnes retorted.

"Does he know I've left the Manor?"

"No. Lee's going to tell him when he's stronger."

"Hmmm . . . he doesn't know I saw him at that woman's either, does he?"

"Well, no, but—"

"The minute he does, he's going to move heaven and earth to find me for the very reason I decided to remain close until . . . until I'm sure. His *heir*. That's all he wants or needs of me, Agnes. I wanted and needed so much more."

Agnes hesitated. "What will you do if you are with child?" she asked.

"I will do the honorable thing . . . return to the Manor, raise my child—not as Lady Isobel raised King, at a distance, but with all the love I can possibly bestow—and die inside doing it. I will, Agnes. That process has already begun. I wish I never set eyes on Basil Kingston, Earl of Grayshire. I wish I never left the Marshalsea, where all I had to deal with was that dreadful mawworm, Westerfield. I wish—"

"Shhhh! What's that?" Agnes whispered.

"What?"

"That noise—listen . . ."

It came again: a creaking sound, as if someone were treading the floorboards somewhere close by.

Lark wiped tears from her eyes, and shrugged. "It's nothing," she said. "The house is full of strange noises, scratching, creaking. I think it's rats or some woodland creature that got in during the storm. I found two windows broken, you know, and limbs all over the grounds. They were flying about like javelins in that wind when I arrived."

"It gives me the creeps," Agnes said with a shudder. "Listen! There it goes again. . . ."

"I only noticed it at night," said Lark, "when the house cooled after sundown. It must be settling or something."

"Or haunted! How many centuries has this house stood here? I should think it would have settled itself by now."

"You know, last night I thought I saw a ghost in the sleeping chamber I've chosen, I was that worn to a reveling."

"Oh, la! I'd have died on the spot!" Agnes blurted.

Lark smiled in spite of herself. "You'd best get back before you're missed," she said. "You're such a dear friend to me, Agnes. I shan't ever forget it."

"Please promise me you'll think on what I've said," Agnes returned. "I'll stand behind you no matter what, you know that. Your heart's ruling your head here now. You've got to see reason."

"You're wrong," said Lark dourly. "My heart is no longer capable of ruling *anything*. It's broken."

It was three days before King was allowed out of bed for brief intervals. No one except Frith had come from the Manor since the morning his mother marched on the place. Why hadn't Lark come? Something was wrong. He didn't need their conspicuous absence to tell him that. He could see it in Frith's face. The man never was any good at hiding his feelings, but he *was* good at keeping secrets. Very good. *Too* good. Mattie wasn't talking, either, and Will hadn't been home since the shipwreck. He had to go home, and he spent all his energy during the next two days trying to prove he was ready.

When Leander arrived early on the second day of his efforts, and Frith left them alone without protest before he was even asked, King's worst fears were realized. Something very grave was afoot, indeed.

"Where the devil have you been?" King demanded. "And where is Lark? Why hasn't she come?"

"All right, King, settle down," Leander said, "and stop that infernal pacing. It can't be good for you, all that stomping about so soon out of that bed. *Sit!*"

King sank into the bedside chair with a flourish. "All right, I'm sitting. Now, what the bloody hell is going on?"

Leander cleared his voice, and began to pace himself. "Do you remember Will and a few of the men hauling you up on shore after the *Cormorant* went down?"

"Vaguely, why?"

"You were in shock, King, semiconscious and bleeding badly. Since Hazel's was so close, they decided to take you there for tending, rather than chance bringing you all the way here to Mattie's as you were in that storm."

"So?"

"You remember being at Hazel's, do you?"

"I remember. The bitch tried to seduce me, and I passed out. The next thing I knew, I was here. Why?" He posed the question guardedly, his voice grainy and sharp.

"Were you . . . did you . . . damn it, King, did you diddle her?"

"What?" King gave a low chuckle. "Of course not! That was over fifteen years ago. She tried her damnedest; I'll say that. *Zeus*, she stripped me naked in that bed while I was unconscious. Then I came 'round and the last thing I remember was her climbing in beside me. Lee, even if I'd wanted to I was too far gone. That knock on the head—I couldn't stay awake."

"That's what I told her," Leander mused, as though to himself.

"Told . . . who?" King asked.

"Lark was worried about you. You were behindhand, and she rode down to the Point, hoping the *Cormorant* had come in. When it hadn't, she went 'round to the vicarage, I expect for a little spiritual reassurance, and she happened upon the men burying the cargo that came ashore after the wreck. . . ."

"Go on," King said through clenched teeth.

"I was with them. Will rode in and told us he'd taken you to Hazel's. Evidently, Lark overheard, followed him there, and saw . . ."

"Saw *what?*" King prompted, vaulting to his feet.

"She saw you and Hazel naked together in that bed—I did, too. Hazel was all over you. It looked like—"

"Bloody hell!" King thundered. "And you're just telling me *now?*" He began foraging through the clothes Frith had hung in the chifferobe, and grabbed his greatcoat. "I've got to go," he said, his voice dangerously calm. "No wonder she hasn't come. I've got to see her—talk to her! Christ, Lee, you're damned lucky I've got a lame wing here, or I'd plant you a leveler!"

"You may as well stay right here," Leander returned, his head bowed. "She's gone, King."

"Gone? What do you mean, *gone?*"

"She left the Manor that night . . . nobody saw her go."

"You and Mother knew this when you came out here? You knew, and you didn't tell me. Frith knows as well, I suppose—and Mattie? Bloody hell!"

"King, look at yourself. The mist on the moor has more color. You're staggering, shaking. If we'd told you then, you'd have killed yourself for naught."

"I'm shaking, all right—with rage—at the lot of you. Suppose she goes up to Yorkshire now—what then? Did none of you think of that? You *did* do what I asked you to there?"

"Yes, I did. I told you that when I came out here with her ladyship. It's done—just as you wanted."

"Hah! My wedding gift! And God alone knows where my wife is. I've got to find her! You'd all best pray I get to Yorkshire before she does. Is there anything else you're keeping from me?"

"Well, actually, there is one more thing," Leander hedged.

King's jutting chin and white-lipped grimace was his only reply. His whole world had just come crashing down around him. What more could there be?

"After Lark left Mattie's, she lost her way on the marsh and her horse pitched her into the bog—"

"In the *quicksand pits?*"

Leander nodded. "Jeremy, Simm, and Lige pulled her out . . . after a fashion."

"Explain. Damn it, Lee, I'll pitch you in the bog myself before this is done!"

"They didn't know who she was, King," Leander defended. "Jeremy wanted to let her sink, Lige had . . . other ideas, and it was Simm who finally pulled her out. He was too afraid of Will to let her go under."

"Was she harmed?" King gritted out.

"Her dignity, a little. I came along before there was serious harm done, and the men have been properly chastised, I promise you."

"They have, have they? I'll be the judge of that. No wonder she's run off!" He struggled into the greatcoat, draping it casually over his injured arm. "I love her, Lee. You'd best pray I can find her! Well? What are you standing there like a bufflehead for? Did you come on horseback, or by carriage?"

"I brought the coupe. I figured you'd be fool enough to do something like this. You're certainly in no condition to ride."

"Good! Get Frith in here to pack my things. We're leaving!"

Twenty-seven

"Don't badger the poor girl, Basil," his mother shrilled. "Agnes is just as concerned as the rest of us. I'm sure, if she knew anything—"

"Someone has to know *something*!" King raged.

They were gathered in the drawing room for his inquisition—the dowager, Leander Markham, and Agnes, who was clearly on the verge of tears, despite Leander's comforting arm around her.

"A house full of servants, and you three—diligent to a fault—yet she slipped right through your fingers."

"Fled your imprudence, to put it delicately," the dowager corrected, "and the cruel mishandling of your . . . minions. Basil, how could you?"

"How could I what, Mother—nearly lose my life in service to king and country? And what am I to do now, eh? I've lost the *Cormorant*, but that doesn't matter, does it? The Admiralty will only commission one of the others— the *Falmouth*, the *Charger* . . . or . . ."

Dawn broke over his addled brain.

"Or maybe, just maybe, they won't," he said, thinking out loud. "I need to see Will and Zephaniah Job at once . . . but not till this is settled. Now then, I shall ask you all again, one at a time: When was the last time you saw Lark? Mother?"

"We had a talk when she returned from her . . . outing. She begged to leave, and I thought I'd convinced her to remain, at least until . . ."

"Until what, Mother?" King prompted.

"This isn't the forum for that discussion dear."

"I beg to differ. Forum be damned! Until *what*?"

"Very well, since you insist upon indelicacies in company, until it's known if she is carrying your heir."

King's posture clenched. That had never occurred to him.

"Are you satisfied?"

"We only had that one night," King murmured, his mind racing backward in time. *But, oh, what a night!*

"My worldly son," his mother admonished. "Offspring have been conceived in far less time than that, I assure you. However, albeit highly unlikely, I used the argument to appeal to her sense of duty. Evidently I failed. The minute I retired, she fled."

"How could she have—alone? She would have had to have help." King's eyes oscillated between Leander and Agnes, clinging to the steward now as though for dear life.

"Don't look at me!" Leander blurted. "I was too busy transporting you to Mattie's, and dealing with Simm and his crew. I didn't get back till dawn."

King turned his cold-eyed stare on Agnes.

"I . . . I, too, tried to persuade her to stay," she whined. "Oh! I don't know how I shall bear it without her!"

King stared long and hard at the maid. "You were the last one to see her, weren't you?"

"I . . . believe so, yes," said Agnes. "Unless one of the servants . . ."

"Did she give you any clue as to where she was going?"

"Sh-she was very overset," said Agnes. "Not only because of . . . you know, but because of falling into the bog . . . and what those dreadful men did—tried to do."

"So, you just went off to bed and left her in that state? Don't insult my intelligence. It doesn't ring true. You wouldn't do that. I know you too well. You're too good a friend to Lark to dismiss such a situation that lightly. Here it is: I submit that you either know where she's gone or helped her on her way—or both. Which is it?"

"I . . . she . . . we . . ." Agnes stammered, and burst into a flood of tears.

"There's nothing for it," King growled. "I can't abide this. We're wasting precious time. I'm off to Yorkshire. If that's where she's gone, I'm probably too late already."

Leander found his voice. "King!" he bellowed, turning him around on the threshold. "You can't travel all that distance as you are. You're scarcely out of bed. Are you trying to kill yourself?"

"I love her, you fool! What use is my life without her? I'd rather be dead than lose her."

"Wait!" Agnes wailed. "Your lordship . . . wait . . ."

For a moment King froze in place, then reached her in two strides and took firm hold of her upper arms, ignoring her strangled gasp.

"You know where she is, don't you, Agnes? *Don't you?* Answer me!"

"Don't, King! You're frightening her," Leander cut in, taking hold of his arm.

"Stay out of this, Lee!" King warned, shaking Agnes gently, but with just enough force to show he meant business. "Where is she? Tell me, or by God, I'll—"

"Agnes? Do you know where her ladyship is?" Leander queried.

"She's not up to Yorkshire," Agnes wailed. She turned to King. "I . . . I can't see you go all that way as you are. My conscience won't stand it, sir."

"Where, then?" King insisted. "For God's sake, woman, she's in no danger from me. I want to find her . . . to explain . . . to have her back. If you know where she is, you must tell me!"

"I gave my word," Agnes sobbed. "I promised I wouldn't tell—especially you, after . . . But lately . . . something's not right, leastwise it doesn't seem right to me. Oh, la, I don't know what to do!"

King whipped out his handkerchief and presented it. "Dry your eyes," he said, as kindly as his rage would allow.

He led her to the chaise, and sat her down on it. "Now, Agnes, I know you've made a promise to Lark, but if there's even the slightest chance that she could be in some danger, that promise is forfeit. Better you suffer her wrath than mine. I'm half-mad here!"

"Sh-she's at the dower house," Agnes sobbed, defeated.

He pulled her to her feet again. "The dower house, without a staff? How is she managing? How is she eating?"

"I . . . I've been taking her food."

"Bloody hell!"

"Oh, my God!" his mother groaned, banging her cane in punctuation. "And all this while I've been worried sick. Agnes, I could throttle you!"

"She wanted to stay close because . . . till . . . she wanted to be sure she wasn't . . . with child before she goes for good." She turned to the dowager. "You put that bee in her bonnet, my lady," she said, "or we would have lost her for fair. I played up to it, too, but it's scary out there. There were some windows broken in the storm, and the place is full of strange noises in the night—ghost noises. I heard them myself. She laughs about the possibility of ghosts— even says she saw one. But what if it wasn't a ghost that she saw? She won't light a fire or a candle for fear somebody might see and come out there. She wants to be alone. She's that determined. But suppose she isn't? Suppose somebody's gotten in there . . . some brigand fixing to steal or one of the local ne'er-do-wells is camped out in there? That's what's been worrying me. . . ."

"Bloody hell!" King thundered. Nearly throwing her down, he shoved her aside and bolted from the room.

Lark was beginning to dread the night. Everything looked and seemed different then, what with darkness coming early to Cornwall on the cusp of winter. Though the moon had accommodated her for the past few days, there was just no telling how long it was going to be cooperative. In anticipation of that, she made it a practice to finish her evening meal and settle herself in her chamber before sunset on nights like this, when Agnes wasn't expected. That's when the strange noises seemed to begin—when the house cooled down without the sun to warm it.

She hadn't seen the ethereal shape in her chamber again. Still, each night she paid special attention to the shadows, half expecting Great-grandfather Basil's ghost to jump out at her. Whenever she thought on it, which was often, she admonished herself. There were no such things as ghosts. There were times when she almost wished that there were. How she would relish the sight of her father—welcome his ghostly presence—if for no other reason than to reassure herself that being buried in unconsecrated ground hadn't damned him. It had damned her in a way. There would always be a sorrowful place in what was left of her heart that grieved for him cast out on the heath, in sight of but denied the sanctity of the churchyard. Whatever he had been, whatever he had done, whatever pitiful madness had overcome him at the last and convinced him to take his own life, he was still her father. He had loved her, and she him. She always would, though the world—the only world she knew—shunned and despised her for it.

Cloud cover swallowed the sun early, and she'd scarcely reached her chamber when the shadows cast long, dark fingers across her path. She hurried along, and she'd nearly reached her chamber door when one of the shadows moved alongside her. For a moment she couldn't believe what her eyes were seeing. This was no ghost. Someone was there—a man! She screamed when he grabbed her, and his hand quickly clamped her mouth shut.

"Mawworm, eh?" he snarled in her ear. "That's what you think of me?" It was barely more than a whisper, but there was no mistaking the odor of him—the sour stench of vintage perspiration on an unwashed body in unwashed clothes.

It was Westerfield.

Distasteful as the prospect was, Lark bit into his fingers until she drew blood, and he flung her away with a savage hand. Caught off balance, she fell to the floor and slid up against the hearthstone. When she tried to rise, he held her there with a foot firmly planted on the hem of her frock.

"I've been trying to decide what to do with you," he said. "You are an unexpected pleasure, you see—a windfall, as it were. I've come to settle an old score with your husband . . . and a new one. He has to answer for Biddie."

"What have you to do with Biddie?"

"We met in the Marshalsea, of all unlikely places. She wasn't as hostile as you, *my lady*. We got on quite admirably until Grayshire had her jailed."

"But for my husband, Biddie would be stretching a rope," Lark snapped, struggling to free her gown without success. She heard the fabric rip as the skirt partially separated from the bodice. "He tried to retract the charges," she went on, "but she'd stolen before, and the magistrates were unmoved, so he did what he could. He spoke for her. Surely you know that. Would you rather see her dead than transported? It was not my husband's fault that the gel took to thievery. If she hadn't stolen his property in the first place, she would still be free. I suppose you put her up to it?"

"Clever girl," he said. When Lark gasped in spite of herself, Westerfield laughed. "You do have a certain charm," he said. "An alluring naïvete. A pity you weren't more . . . receptive in the Marshalsea. We might have made a spectacular twosome—you, the fine lady without a feather to fly with, and me, the second son, the spare, likewise at low tide . . . for the moment. Misery does love company, after all. We might have bonded. Who knows where our mutual resourcefulness might have taken us? As it is now, I shall simply have to take you down and have you to revenge myself on Grayshire. Oh, yes, a far better plan. That picture in his head will last a lifetime."

Terror gripped her heart. The shadows had deepened

around her, except for a wan shaft of moon glow seeping through the clouds. Dust motes danced inside it like living things as it filtered through the mullioned windowpane, attracting her attention. Eerily, it illuminated the fireplace tools rattling in their stand at her elbow. Was it the noise, or the light, pointing like a finger, that drew her eye? Almost without thinking, she seized the poker and delivered a blow to Westerfield's shins that raised his foot from her frock, and she scrambled to her feet and ran from the room.

Hopping and cursing, he followed. Her chamber was too far from either entrance to hope to escape him that way. Her mind was racing as she fled through the corridors. She had an advantage there, having done little else but explore the vast house during her stay. Westerfield had had just as much time to do the very same thing—more, come to that. Who knew how long he'd been camped there? All at once she realized that he must have broken the windows, not fallen limbs. He'd been here all the while! He was the ghostly shadow shape in her chamber. He had watched her while she slept, eavesdropped on her conversations with Agnes, feasted on dried meat and apricots from the larder, and God only knew what else he'd devoured before she came, or what he had stashed away. The house wasn't settling; his feet treading the old floorboards had made the creaking sound while he'd skulked about, deciding her fate. What he'd finally elected to do made her blood run cold, and forced her legs to move a little faster. She prayed that his lazy nature had prevented him from finding the place she was leading him to: the place where she would have the advantage—the Roman bath.

She heard him stumble and fall when she reached the first-floor landing, and slowed her pace to be sure he'd see where she went, before entering the hidden door in the wainscoting beside the servants' quarters. Leaving the door flung wide to let in the little funnel of light from the oriel across the way, she careened inside and flattened herself in the shadows beside the open stairwell King had carried her down. Her head was spinning. Pinpoints of white light starred her vision. Her heart was hammering in her breast, her breath coming short. She dared not let him hear it, and she nearly swooned trying to hold it in.

It was a moment before Westerfield staggered through the stairwell door. He was out of shape. That, too, was in her favor. Were he fit, she would never have been a match for him. His tall frame would have made him tower over her. Instead it was hunched, his posture noticeably round-shouldered, and his muscles had turned to flab from lazing bone-idle in the Marshalsea.

Lark still held the poker in her hand, and she gripped it fiercely. As he stumbled by her unaware and began to climb down, she lunged, knocking him off balance with a blow to the back that sent him tumbling down the narrowly hewn stone stairwell. Then, turning on her heel, she fled to the echo of his scream.

Back through the hidden door she raced—into the servants' quarters, past the kitchen, the scullery, the larder, and the game room, and out through the wounded rear door right into the arms of another man. She let out a scream that woke the birds in the grove and sent them skyward.

It was King.

Twenty-eight

King wrestled the poker out of his wife's grip, threw it down, and shook her none too gently with his good hand. She was still screaming at the top of her voice, and he shook her again.

"Stop that!" he thundered. "It's *me*. Don't tell me I'm the one you meant to savage with that there?" He jerked his head toward the poker at his feet.

Lark stared up at him, and her screams dissolved in a flood of tears. It took him a moment to realize how he must look to her in his altered state, his wounded arm dangling at his side. He hadn't taken the time to put on a jacket or coat in his haste to reach her. In his shirtsleeves, the bulky bandages were visible. Somewhere along the way since he'd left Mattie's, he'd put undue strain on the arm, and fresh blood had begun to seep through the Egyptian cotton.

"W-W-Westerfield!" she stammered. "The Roman bath. I knocked him down the stairs. . . ."

Leander Markham had reached them, and King turned as he swung himself down from the horse he'd ridden bareback in pursuit.

"You might have waited for me," Lee grumbled. "When I followed you out of the Manor and the coupe was gone—"

"Never mind that now," King snapped. His arm was throbbing with pain, and he dared not let go of Lark for fear she'd bolt and run like the frightened doe she looked. He wasn't about to take that chance, even though Smythe waited nearby with the coupe, should there be need to run her to ground. He cursed his weakness in an undervoice, and flexed the aching arm. "In the Roman bath . . . Westerfield," he gritted through a grimace. "Go, damn it, Lee. There are candles and tinder in the kitchen. Haul him out of there, and pray he's dead." He turned his all-seeing eye upon Lark. "Did he . . . harm you?" he said, sliding his frantic gaze over the disheveled state of her—the mussed cap of golden curls, the dirty tear tracks on her flaming cheeks, and the skirt of her frock dragging on the ground, all but separated from the bodice.

"N-no," she stuttered, her breath coming in spasms. "He was hiding in there. He had broken in . . . to settle the score with you, so he said."

"What's this then?" he demanded, swatting at her skirt, an action he regretted the minute he set his injured arm to the task.

"He grabbed me from behind. When I bit his hand, he knocked me down and stood on my frock to tether me. I tore it . . . trying to get away."

"And?" he prodded.

"And I grabbed that poker and whacked him in the shins with it," she returned. "When he jumped off my frock, I ran and led him to the Roman bath stairwell. He followed after me, and I whacked him again and knocked him down the stairs. What does it matter? Let go of me! I don't owe you any explanations, not after . . . after . . ."

King tightened his grip. "Ohhhh, no," he said. "I don't know what you thought you saw, but nothing happened between Hazel Helston and me, Lark—"

"I don't need to hear this!" she snapped. "It doesn't matter anymore."

"Yes, you do, and it does matter. You have to hear me out, Lark. You owe me that much, at least."

"I don't owe—"

"Oh yes, you do, and you *will* listen," he interrupted. "Look at me! *Look.* I nearly died in that shipwreck. The

Cormorant and all hands on her went down when the *Benicoeur* blew her out of the water. I still don't know how I managed to stay afloat with this arm as it is until Will and the men pulled me out of the backwash down 'round the Point at Fowey. I never would have made it to the Manor. I'd lost so much blood they didn't even want to chance taking me to Mattie's, so they took me to Hazel's instead, since her cottage is right on the Point."

"I don't care. Don't you understand that?"

"You do care, and so do I. I'll not have you thinking . . . what you're thinking. Oh, I'll not deny that she tried to seduce me. She even climbed naked into bed with me. Lark, I was scarcely conscious, in shock, with a raging fever. Even if I'd wanted to, which I didn't—not after you, never again after you—I couldn't have! If you don't believe me, ask Lee. He went out there all out straight and packed me off to Mattie's the minute you told him what you . . . saw. He had the truth of it from her, and if needs must, so will you."

"It isn't that important," Lark returned. "Besides, I told you, that isn't the only reason I left you, King."

"What then? What else?" he demanded. "I'm in a great deal of pain right now, not that I expect your sympathy, but I shan't let you go. We shall stand here till our feet take root if that's what it takes till you tell me, so you may as well have done."

Lark drew a ragged breath, but made no reply.

"I'm waiting," he reminded her.

"You had a right to explain your . . . involvement in the trade to me, King," she said, with downcast eyes. "Those men who laid hands on me—"

"They've been dealt with," he cut in. "They didn't know who you were."

"Oh, so that makes it all right, does it? Is that how you smugglers treat your women hereabout? Well, I want no part of it—any of it."

"No, that doesn't make it all right—of course it doesn't," King defended. "And I'm not a smuggler—not of my father's ilk, at least. I'm a privateer for the Crown, with a perfectly legitimate Letter of Marque . . . or at least I used to be. I'll come back to that. The Admiralty commissioned the *Cormorant*, Lark, to intercept and capture French merchant vessels that stray into our waters, whether deliberately or by accident in wartime. The Crown then takes the spoils of such vessels subsequent to a proper investigation. The 'smugglers,' as you call them on this coast, for centuries have been engaged in the trade. It is their living to take for profit what the sea gives up. In olden days, such men would light fires in cairns on the beach in order to lure vessels aground. Yes, my father was caught up in it, and I almost was as well, before he bought me a commission in the Royal Navy to keep me out of it—and I stayed out of it till I was mustered out, but the Admiralty wasn't through with me."

"I don't see what—"

"Let me finish!" King insisted. "Do you remember at the townhouse . . . when I left for a time to answer a summons from the Admiralty, just before I paid Agnes's debt and we made our departure for the coast?"

"I . . . I believe so. Why?"

"It was during that appointment that they awarded me the Letter of Marque. I own four of the finest cutters on the coast, as well as two fully outfitted merchantmen, and a whole fleet of fishing vessels. I couldn't refuse. One just doesn't say 'no' to the Crown—especially now that the king is so poorly and the Regent so given to . . . decadence." He delivered the last through a humorless chuckle.

"I still don't see—"

"When my father was caught years back—shot and nearly killed—these 'smugglers' hereabouts hid him, covered for him, nursed him back to health, and saved his life—one of them at the expense of his own life. The Admiralty doesn't only want me to cruise the coast looking for foreign vessels; they want me to capture and turn these loyal friends of my father in to face the hangman. My own half-brother numbers amongst them, Lark. This I cannot, *will not* do. I've been wracking my brain trying to find a way out of it without being brought up on charges myself. It's like balancing on the edge of a sword. Not a very pleasant experience, because it cuts no matter which way you step, but I've finally figured out a way that I might be able to get out from under without betraying my friends or stretching a rope. Would that make a difference?"

Lark hesitated. "King," she began, "the trade is in your blood, just as gambling was in my father's blood. I stood by helpless and watched it kill him, but not before it had driven him to the brink of madness. That's all I've ever known. You are just as obsessed with your demons, and I could not go through it again. I deserve more than that. I thought I finally *had* more than that, with you. It wouldn't have mattered one whit if you were in Dun territory, so long as I didn't have to sit by and watch you struggle with your demons till they killed you."

He laughed. "Dun territory, eh?" he said. "Well, if what I've in mind to do works, we might have a few pockets to let for awhile. I'm glad it shan't matter." He pulled her closer, looking deep into her moist eyes. "I know you love me, Lark," he murmured. "Do you trust me enough to give me a chance to prove myself?"

Lark opened her mouth to answer, but the advent of Leander Markham prodding Westerfield around the corner of the house at the end of a rope left her speechless but for a gasp.

"Well, well," King chortled. "I'd no idea you'd be so anxious to make good on my challenge. The choice of weapons is yours, and the place. Dawn tomorrow? I want you over with."

"King," Leander gritted, nodding toward his arm.

King ignored him. "You cannot win," he said to Wester-field. "If I don't kill you, Lee here will see the bailiffs take you in for trespass, breaking into this house and assaulting my wife."

"Not if I kill him, too," Westerfield snarled, earning him a sharp jerk on the rope in Leander's hand.

"Hardly likely," King drawled. "Come, come, choose your weapons, I've pressing matters elsewhere."

"Pistols," Westerfield hissed.

"And the place?"

"The strand at Colors Cove."

"Fair enough," said King. He turned to Leander. "Will's at the mine. Take him 'round there and get him a second. Keep the coward tied." Turning Lark toward the waiting coupe, he steered her to it and helped her inside.

"Where are you taking me?" she demanded. "I'm not go-ing anywhere with you, Basil Kingston!"

"Oh, yes, you are," he said, climbing in beside her. "I'm going to give you your wedding present."

"I don't want it!" she cried. "Keep it yourself . . . or re-turn it."

He burst into laughter. "It's of no use to me," he said, tongue-in-cheek, "and I'm afraid returning it isn't an op-tion." He leaned his head out the open coach window and called out to Smythe: "Drive us 'round to St. Kevern's."

Lark scrunched herself against the squabs in the corner, her arms folded across her middle, hiding the torn frock. What was this now? All she wanted was to be as far away from Basil Kingston, Earl of Grayshire, as was humanly possible, before he could mesmerize her with his silky words, before he could turn her head with his seductive voice and the lightning that struck when he touched her. Before she yielded to the temptation to throw herself into his arms and beg *his* forgiveness—for what, she couldn't imagine.

Why was he taking her to the church? It was the last

place she wanted to go. She needed no reminders of the night that seemed a lifetime ago for all that had happened since—the night she solved the mystery of the graves, and found her husband in the arms of another woman.

When the coupe tooled past the churchyard into the circular drive, and Smythe pulled it to a halt before the vicarage steps, King climbed down.

"Wait here," he said. "I shan't be a moment."

Lark didn't protest. It wouldn't have done any good. She sank back against the squabs, and did as he bade her, only marginally curious as he indulged in a brief conversation with the vicar in the doorway before returning to the coupe.

"We shan't be long," he charged Smythe, meanwhile handing Lark down. But he didn't take her to the vicarage. He took her arm, and walked her through the graveyard gate instead.

Lark dug her heels in, her fingers biting into his rock-hard arm.

"Steady, my lady," King said. "It isn't far."

Several more steps, and the mound of a freshly dug grave came into view, half-hidden in a mist drifting in off the headlands.

"I want none of your contraband," Lark shrilled. "I know that's where you hide it—here in this graveyard! I saw the smugglers burying it here. It's sacrilege, burying stolen goods in consecrated ground while my poor father—"

"Precisely my thought," King said, pointing. "Look closely."

Lark took a halting step nearer the grave. King let go of her arm when she sank to her knees. She scarcely felt his hand fall away. Her trembling fingers traced the letters engraved on the headstone:

Malcolm Sebastian Eddington, Earl of Roxburgh, Beloved father of Lark Eddington Kingston, Countess Grayshire, R.I.P.

And at the top, the device of his office—a crowned raven.

"I didn't know the date of his birth, or . . . death," said King. "There wasn't time to research it and have the stone cut in time for the burial. You need only to supply it, and I shall summon the stonemason."

"Y-you did this . . . for me?" she murmured. "When . . . how? I don't understand."

"I sent Lee to London, with a letter for my solicitor there to obtain a writ so we could claim the body. It was accomplished easily enough, since he was buried outside the churchyard. Vicar Tim said words over the grave when he was laid to rest, but I thought you'd prefer to be here for a proper ceremony. Lee carried out my wishes during my absence. That's why I stopped at the vicarage. I wasn't sure of the exact location."

Lark embraced the headstone and sobbed her heart dry.

"Vicar Tim was of the same mind as we," King said, his voice soft and deep, riveting her with gooseflesh. "If we can bury pirate's plunder in consecrated ground, how can we deny the pirate—to put it rather indelicately, and I do beg your forgiveness. Vicar Tim is a good man, Lark, and so am I, if only you'll give me the chance to prove it."

Staggering to her feet, she threw her arms around his neck with little regard for his injured arm, and cried out when he stiffened.

"It's all right," he soothed, showering her face with kisses. "My God, just hold me!"

Lark searched his face to be sure, and he met her gaze, looking deep into her eyes, his own dilated black with desire.

"Don't ever leave me again, my love," he said. "I've been in hell."

Were those tears glistening in his eye? She looked away, and he raised her head to meet his lips. They were hot and dry. The fever hadn't left him, and her heart leapt at the thought of him fighting a duel in the morning. As though he'd read her thoughts, he held her away.

"Come," he said, leading her back to the waiting coupe, "we have a lot to talk about before morning."

Twenty-nine

*L*ark tried to dissuade him, but King would have none of it. They lay together in the vast four-poster in the master bedchamber at Grayshire Manor. Across the way a blazing fire in the hearth crackled, shooting sparks up the flue as now and then a burnt log fell. It was the only light, casting auburn shadows on their naked bodies.

"King, you're burning up," she murmured, feeling his brow. "There'll be plenty of time to—"

"Shhhh," he whispered, swallowing her words with a hungry mouth.

He lay on his back beside her. He was aroused, and when he guided her hand to his member, she thrilled at how it responded to her touch.

How magnificent he was! How lean and firm and well muscled his body. Every sinew in him replied to her strokes with a shudder, a quiver, a throb of delight, and she could only stare in wonderment as the member she caressed grew larger, more demanding with the slightest encouragement from her unskilled fingers. She wanted not to think of how unskilled by comparison to those of Hazel Helston, but that thought came unbidden. She pushed it back. He was in *her* arms, wasn't he—reacting to *her* touch, no matter how inept.

"Don't stop," King groaned, when those thoughts disturbed her rhythm. "No one has ever loved me so . . . wonderfully."

The man was a sorcerer! He had to be. He'd read her

mind, and was trying to reassure her. Either that or the fever had addled his brain far worse than she'd feared. Whichever came closest to the truth, whatever the cause, there was no denying the effect. He was malleable in her hands.

"Mount me," he whispered, "as you would straddle a horse."

Lark hesitated.

"Take me inside you . . . and ride," he groaned.

Lark hovered over him, uncertain, then did as he bade her, taking him slowly at first, letting him fill her. He groaned again, holding her down with his good hand. How it fit her waist. How easily it lifted her up and down, setting the rhythm of their frenzy.

Lark held her breath and bit into her lip. Shuddering waves of white-hot fire surged through her core as she moved atop him. When he engaged his wounded arm, and inched his fingers along the inside of her thigh until they touched her sex ever so lightly, she thought she would expire: It responded to his touch just as his sex had responded to her caress, a bonding so total it nearly stopped her heart—like something remembered from another lifetime, which didn't surprise her; she had already determined that they were soul mates eternal.

He cupped her breast with his hand, seeking the aching nipple grown tall and hard under his palm. She groaned as he moved his skilled fingers over first one dimpled tip and then the other, until she convulsed as he brought her to climax. Silky ripples of sensation coursing through her belly and thighs dulled her reason, reduced her to involuntary quivers. Excruciating ecstasy, indeed. He was the master of it. A quick intake of breath that caught in her throat was her only exclamation. It was her body that spoke.

King shifted his hand to her shoulder, holding her down as he reached deeper still, his thrusts gentle at first until her inner contractions had nearly subsided. It was no use; new ripples of icy-hot sensation became surging waves that broke over her soul, and he took her again and again, until at last he exploded inside her, emptying himself, filling her with the warm, pumping rush of his seed.

His groan was deep and resonant, channeled through a heaving breast. His skin was on fire, his eye glazed with fever, his body shuddering now with chills, his breath coming short for more than one reason, thought Lark. She never should have given in to him. They could have waited until he was stronger. They had the rest of their lives . . . or was that why he'd made love to her so desperately? *The duel.* She'd nearly forgotten in the heat of their passion. Was he afraid this might be their last—*his* last?

"Oh, my God, King, you're burning with fever," she breathed. "You've overreached yourself. You're out of bed too soon. I beg you, send word to Lee to postpone the duel. You're in no condition to—"

"Shhhh," he whispered. "Don't spoil this moment. Don't tarnish it with that bastard's image between us."

"Nothing can come between us," Lark murmured. *Nothing but death*, she couldn't help thinking. No—no! She wouldn't think it, couldn't think it. That might make it so. How could she have ever left this man? How could she have hoped to live without him? Nothing mattered but that they were together, never to be parted again; let thinking *that* make it so.

Settling herself beside him, she drew the counterpane up over them and held him close, her head on his heaving breast, and prayed her awakening hadn't come too late. Cold sweat beaded on his brow and glistened on his hot skin. Was the fever breaking? How could it be, when his body heat was scorching?

"King, you're burning up. You need something for the fever," she said.

He drew a tremulous breath and pulled her closer. "You're all the medicine I need," he murmured, fondling her gently. "When I thought I'd lost you . . ."

"King, I don't know if I can live in this world of yours, and that scares me."

"I told you, I've a plan," he said. "I never wanted this sort of life for myself, either, Lark. I thought I was well out of it, that losing an eye was enough to satisfy the Crown and give me an honorable retirement from active duty. I was looking forward to settling down . . . taking a more active part in the shipping business Lee has been managing for me for so long . . . traveling abroad on one of my vessels. I hardly have to work for a living, and I've always wanted to sail to far-off lands. I'll not lie to you. Whatever I do, the sea will play a part in it. I've got salt water in my veins. The sea is as much a part of me as the air I breathe—but not this. When I received that summons from the Admiralty I was beside myself. Privateering was the last occupation I wanted, yet I couldn't refuse. I had the ships, you see, and the Crown has the right to commandeer them. I'm going to transfer ownership of the fleet to Will Bowles first thing after the . . . first thing tomorrow—"

"Oh, King!" she cried. "You can't! You love those ships."

"No, hear me out," he said, pulling her close. "I love *you*. I'll still have access to those vessels. Will is my brother. If we want to sail around the world, we shall; let that be understood. But if I don't own them, the Crown cannot command me to man them, unless it pays me to outfit another craft, and why would it do that, when Will Bowles owns so many ready to sail? No. It's the only way. Will is itching to legitimize. This may just save him into the bargain. He's young and reckless. Going on as he is, his life is forfeit. It's only a matter of time. He shan't make old bones as things are. That's for certain. It's high time I passed on the torch. Let him deal with his smuggler brethren. I've had my fill."

"Can he do that? I mean, wouldn't he have to be in the Royal Navy?"

"No. Private citizens can be awarded a Letter of Marque—anybody with a seaworthy craft these days. But I have been toying with the idea of buying him a commission. He's got a lot of growing up to do, and the Navy might just be the place for him to do it. It whipped me into shape, I'll be bound."

"King, are you sure?" she pleaded. "It seems such a drastic sacrifice."

"We shan't be at war forever, my love. I didn't say I'd never own a ship again, just not *these* ships in *these* times. We have our whole lives ahead of us. Who knows what the future will bring."

"But such a sudden transfer, won't the Admiralty be suspicious?"

"Zephaniah Job is the advocate for the traders hereabouts. He stakes them, keeps their accounts, even provides legal counsel for them if needs must. He has a fleet of solicitors in his pocket that can handle the transaction seamlessly, I promise you. Besides, Father never left Will a legacy. That wasn't intentional, just poor foresight. I've always felt it was up to me to rectify that, and I'm prepared to move heaven and earth to do it. Will and I have always been close."

"Will Bowles is a very lucky young man," Lark observed.

"I'm the lucky one," said King. "But for Will, I'd be dead now. Without his quick thinking when I washed up at his feet on that beach with the spoils—pumping the water out of my lungs, and applying a tourniquet—I'd be out there in that bloody graveyard."

Lark didn't want to think about that. She shuddered, and King tightened his grip.

"I'm worried about that arm," she confessed, nuzzling against his chest. "It wants the surgeon's care."

"Frith is as deft as any surgeon," her husband returned. "He's cleaned and dressed it. There's no infection. I know what you're trying to do, and I love you for it, but this duel is a point of honor, Lark. I cannot back down from a challenge. It was deserved, and I shall see it through. I shan't need that arm to lay Westerfield low. It's not attached to my shooting hand."

"He does not deserve your honor," she argued. "You

should just have turned him over to the land guards. Your fever will put you at a disadvantage."

"Not if you slake it, my love," he murmured sultry-voiced.

Favoring his wounded arm, he eased himself up on his good elbow, and lowered his mouth to her breast, teasing the nipple erect against his silken tongue. Lark groaned, arching herself against him as his hand explored each curve and contour of her body as though memorizing every inch. Her breath caught in a gasp when he seized her hand and wrapped it around his aroused member.

"This is the only fever you need concern yourself with," he murmured against her ear, before he closed his hungry mouth over hers and eased himself inside her.

It was the wee hours before exhaustion lulled them to sleep in each other's arms. King succumbed first. Lark watched the firelight play on his still face, casting shadows, elongating his sweeping lashes, already longer than they had a right to be. What woman wouldn't envy them? She listened to his tremulous breathing as it sought a calmer level. She monitored the rapid rise and fall of his breast until it slowed, and the heart beneath her ear began to shift its hammering pace to something less frantic. Burying her fingers in the mat of soft, dark hair spread over his chest, she felt the shuddering vibration of his contentment. How he had loved her, again and again, depleted though he was.

When last they'd lain together, she'd dreaded the dawn. Now, she dreaded it even more. It was becoming a habit, only this time was worse. When he'd set out on the *Cormorant*, the odds were not nearly as slim as those facing him now in his altered state.

Damn the dawn!

As if to beat it back, Lark clung to her husband, and was eventually lulled to sleep by that beloved heartbeat. Dawn broke despite her, and when the first fish-gray streamers of morning light pressed up against the mullioned panes and woke her, the space beside her in the great four-poster was vacant.

Lark rose and dressed, but she elected not to go down to breakfast. She would have choked on any food, wondering what was happening at Colors Cove. Standing at the window, she stared out through the whitewashed glass at the thick milling fog, but there was no life in it—not a bird or woodland creature, and for the first time since she'd come to the Cornish coast, not a breath of wind was stirring.

If she knew the way to Colors Cove, she would be there. Was it over now? Was King on his way home . . . or was she a widow before she'd ever had the chance to be a wife? She was thinking on that when a light knock on the door sent her to answer. She threw it open hopefully, but it was Agnes on the threshold, teary-eyed and contrite.

"Do you hate me?" she sobbed.

Lark reached for her. "Of course I don't hate you, Agnes," she murmured, embracing her.

"I know I gave my word," Agnes mewed, "but his lordship was sure you'd gone to Yorkshire and set his mind to go there straightaway. I couldn't let him do it—not in his condition. My conscience wouldn't let me. He could barely stand up."

"As it turned out, it was a good thing you did tell them," said Lark, sinking down on the edge of the bed. "Westerfield was hiding in there for God alone knows how long. And now . . ."

"Oh, la, you mustn't worry," Agnes soothed. "His lordship can take care of himself. He's ten times stronger and cleverer than Westie is—even wounded. Believe me, I know. Didn't I spend three long years in the Marshalsea with that jackanapes? I was there when his lordship planted Westie a leveler, remember—right in the courtyard, laid him flat for manhandling you like he did. He challenged him then and there, told him the minute he got out to expect a call from his second. I told you all about it. Westie should have steered clear of Grayshire Manor—all of Cornwall, come to that."

"Oh my God, this duel is *my fault?*" Lark cried.

"Oh, la, no! Did you encourage the bounder? Of course not! Westie had that coming for a good long while, Lark. His lordship is a proper gentleman. He challenged Westie for his actions. He didn't even know you then."

"Still . . ."

"Never you mind. The bounder's getting his due. His lordship knows what he's about. Besides, Lee's with him. He's acting as his second. It'll be fine. You'll see. Who you should be worrying about, though, is her ladyship. She couldn't get up out of bed this morning. She looks dreadful, Lark. I'm afraid this last—the *Cormorant* going under, his lordship so low . . . and you leaving—may have taken its toll."

"I must go to her," Lark breathed, surging to her feet. "That is, if she'll even see me, after—"

"Oh, she'll see you," Agnes interrupted. "I think you're just what she needs right now."

"Does she know . . . about the duel?"

"She knows."

"Why on earth did you tell her?"

"We didn't. She overheard Lee talking to Frith and dragged it out of them. I was there. It wasn't pretty. I thought she'd swoon dead away, she was that overset."

"I shall go to her at once," Lark murmured. "But Agnes . . . if there's any word . . ."

"Don't you worry, I'll come straightaway."

Lark raced along the corridor, her feet scarcely touching the carpet. She didn't knock. Protocol be damned! She wouldn't risk being denied admittance—not now. Inside, the draperies were still drawn. Stepping quietly over the threshold, she let her eyes become accustomed to the dark. Across the room, the dowager lay heaped with quilts. How small she looked, how wizened and spare, and how utterly devoid of color. Beside the bed, her cane stood in a bracket fastening it to her nightstand. Shrouded in shadow, there was an air of finality about it, of defeat, and Lark's heart leapt. Was the woman even breathing?

"Come," said the dowager's feeble voice. "Sit beside me, daughter. Let me see your face."

"Shall I open the draperies, my lady?" Lark queried, coming nearer the bed.

"No," the dowager almost shrilled. "I don't care to see the light of day that may well take my son from me."

These were not the words Lark needed to hear. She had mustered all her strength to foster positive thoughts. How could she hope to reassure her mother-in-law when her own heart was gripped by fear?

"I won't have such talk!" Lark said. "King will soon return and scorn you for it."

"I've been a terrible mother," the dowager lamented, "a termagant of the first order. I drove him to that woman's home—to her society—no more than a hovel; it's falling down around her, and that, too, is my fault. All because of my jealous pride."

"Don't think of all that now."

"When, then?" the dowager flashed. "When should I think of it? When my son retreats there altogether, in his heart, if he even lives to?"

"That shan't happen, my lady."

"I saw what drew him. I saw what drew my husband. I cannot fault Basil's father . . . not really. I didn't really love him, Lark. Oh, in the beginning, yes, when I was starry-eyed and hopeful and very, very naïve, I suppose I did, but not for long, and yet I punished him for not loving me—played the long-suffering martyr all these years for naught, and it hurt Basil so deeply. I never really understood until I entered that cottage. I drove my husband into that woman's arms. God knows, I didn't want him, and he never wanted me—only what I could give him, an heir. Once I'd done that, my obligation was ended as I saw it. I should be grateful to Mattie Bowles for taking him off my hands. Instead I made *her* the villain. I saw the fear in her eyes—not only of me, but fear that I would carry out my threat and put her off that meager scrap of croft land. Now I may never get the chance to set things to rights. If Basil dies out on that strand today, I shall follow right after him. My heart won't stand it, Lark."

"Nonsense! Nothing is going to happen to him. I won't hear it!" They were the right words. Lark wished she believed them.

"They weren't going to tell me, the gudgeons! If they hadn't, and something did happen, the news would have killed me outright. Will you stay with me . . . until . . . ?"

"Of course," Lark murmured, "but only if you will eat something." She crossed the room and yanked the bellpull. "You aren't angry with me for—"

"No, I understood your motives, dear," the dowager interrupted, with a wave of her hand. "All of them—the jealousy, your disdain for the trade. How could I not, since they were my own? Surely you can see that. But I'm glad you've come to terms with them. It would have broken my heart to lose my daughter."

Thirty

The fog had rolled in thick and gray on the strand, the lapping waves scarcely visible beneath the blanket. Until the dawn breeze broke the spell, there hadn't been a puff of wind; now, awakened like a sleeping giant, the wind breathed deeply and began to blow.

King cursed under his breath. Nothing could be taken for granted in Cornwall. He would have to adjust his aim to allow for the savage gusts that now whipped the waves to froth creaming over the strand. There was one consolation. This wind would eventually chase the fog. At least he would be able to see what he was aiming at. That duels were outlawed mattered not a whit. Such occurrences were mild and commonplace compared with much of the rest that went on in that quarter.

Westerfield was late. Where the devil was the blighter? There was no chance that he might run, not with Will Bowles holding the reins. Leander Markham was setting out the brace of dueling pistols on a little folding table, and King stomped toward him.

"Where the devil are they?" he growled. "I want this over with before that wind becomes a full-fledged gale."

"Take an ease, King," Leander responded. "They'll be along. I expect Will's not finding it easy to locate a second for the gudgeon, considering who you are."

King began to pace along the beach. The tide was coming in, and lace-edged surf licked his polished Hessians. He'd gotten used to the pain in his wounded arm—a dull constant ache that gave him no peace awake or asleep without the laudanum that he dared not take. He needed his wits about him. He flexed his right hand, limbering the tendons, readying them for the hammer and the trigger his fingers would soon caress. He'd nearly reached the end of his tether when three shapes parted the ghostly fog—Westerfield, Will Bowles, and the seediest-looking sloven he had ever seen. He almost laughed. Was this the best they could do?

Will must have read his thoughts, because he answered them. "Sorry, King," he said. "There's not a man on the coast willing to stand against you on the dueling ground, except old Tim Bud here."

"*Zeus!*" King snapped. "Is he sober?"

"Don't think so."

"I'll get me pint?" Tim Bud urged. "Ya said I'd get me pint."

"You'll get your bloody pint, old man," said Will, "once it's done."

"This is hardly ethical, you know," said Leander, leaning close to King's ear. "He's hardly Westie's peer. Nobody would blame you if—"

"Not on your life!" King cut in, anger mouthing edged words. "Prop him up and let's have done."

"I'll referee," said Will, scooping up three sizable rocks from the berm. "Thirty paces?"

King nodded. "Set the markers," he charged.

Will did as he was bidden, setting one stone at the central point and pacing off the distance for the other two, though they were scarcely visible beneath the fog.

"All right, Westerfield," said Will, "you get first choice. Choose your weapon, and have your second load it."

"What, *him*? I think not," Westerfield blurted. "He wouldn't know which end to ram the ball into. I'll load it myself, if you don't mind."

"Suit yourself," said Will, "but be quick about it."

King watched Westerfield load the pistol, while Leander loaded his and handed it over.

"King," Will said, "according to the rules, I have to ask you . . . if he were to apologize—"

"Not a chance!" snarled Westerfield.

"You heard him," said King. "Get on with it."

"Back-to-back," Will charged, nodding to the center stone. Both duelists complied. "Walk to your markers and turn, but don't advance until I give the command."

"I'll get me pint no matter who goes down?" Tim Bud asked, tugging at Will's sleeve.

"Not if you don't get out of the firing line," Will growled. "Stand back, you drunken old sod!"

The old man staggered to one side as King and Westerfield reached their markers and turned.

King squinted toward his opponent. Fighting a duel with only one eye would be difficult on a clear day; trying to do so in a pea-soup fog and feverish was something else entirely. Nevertheless, he zeroed in on his target, noting that Will Bowles gave him ample time to make the adjustment.

"Advance, and fire at will!" his brother commanded at last.

Hard-packed wet sand crunched under King's feet as he paced toward the center stone marker hidden beneath the stubborn fog. The wind had chased the upper layer, but groundward along the strand the swirling mists were chest high. All at once Westerfield ducked beneath them out of King's view. Two shots rang out . . . after several moments, a third.

Both duelists fell.

Amplified by the fog, Leander's shouts and Will's curses echoed over the beach. King felt the tremor of heavy footfalls running over the sand beneath his face. He saw the distorted shape of Tim Bud staggering off at a pace he would have thought impossible for a drunken man . . . and then nothing.

* * *

The day was half-gone and still no word. Lark was beside herself. She hadn't left the dowager's side, but it was becoming more and more difficult to keep up the pretense. King should have been back by now. Leander should certainly have brought news despite the outcome long ago. With no sign of either of them, it didn't bode well.

Lark had managed to persuade the dowager to take a little broth, a bit of scone, and some fruit, a close eye upon the woman's trembling hands as she picked at the fare. She seemed so altered. It was painful to witness, and Lark couldn't help but fear that she had spoken truly when she'd said that she would follow after if anything happened to King. She looked about to expire.

"He isn't coming back," the dowager said, her grainy voice sounding like a death knell in the quiet. "The duel was over hours ago. If he were alive we would have had news. They don't know how to tell us." Shoving the tray aside, she burst into tears.

"Don't, my lady," Lark soothed. She set aside the book she'd been reading aloud, and went to her, laying a comforting hand on her shoulder. "We don't know that. I refuse to believe it."

"Colors Cove is a scant two-and-a-half miles away," the dowager pointed out. "Even if they were traveling afoot they would have been back by now, and they have horses, and the coupe."

Lark opened her mouth to speak, and froze. Raised voices echoing along the corridor outside sent her to the door. When she flung it wide, King stumbled over the threshold into her arms. Frith was at his side. Lark felt King's face, his chest, his torso, looking for the injury that kept him tethered to the valet. Across the way, the dowager raised her wrinkled hands to her mouth and sat bolt upright in the bed, sobbing softly.

"Let go of me, Frith!" King barked. "You're like a mother hen. I can stand on my own."

"My lord, please," the valet pleaded, "that boot's got to come off before your ankle swells so that we can't remove it."

"Your *ankle?*" Lark cried, looking down. The Hessian on King's right foot was scorched around a ragged hole.

"The blighter's aim was off, thank Providence," said King.

"The blighter was no gentleman," said Leander, who had finally reached them. "He ducked down in the fog and fired, like the coward he was. The bullet struck King in the ankle, and lodged in his boot. We've yet to evaluate the damage. That's what's got Frith here so overset. King fired back blind as he went down and hit Westerfield in the shoulder." He turned to King. "How you ever did, I'll never know," he said. "That fog was thick as porridge, and you landed on your bad arm."

"Oh, my God," Lark moaned, clasping King to her.

"That's not the half of it," Leander went on. "The coward wasn't through. While we went to King's aid, the blighter reloaded. He had dead aim to kill King when he was down. He shan't try that on anyone again. Will Bowles shot him dead. He saved King's life."

A dry sob escaped the dowager's lips at that. They all stared toward her.

"Mother? What are you doing abed in midafternoon?" said King. "Are you ailing?"

"Go to your mother," Lark whispered in his ear. "She's nearly expired from worry over you."

King turned to the valet. "Stop your infernal hovering!" he barked. "Go and draw my bath if you would be of use here. I'll join you directly, then you can have at this foot to your heart's content. Right now, I need a moment with my mother . . . and my wife."

Leander turned the valet aside, following him out, and Lark closed the door behind them. King limped to the bedside, sank down on the edge of it, and went into the dowager's outstretched arms. It was an awkward embrace that brought tears to Lark's eyes looking on, but it ended well. The dowager clasped King to her in a way—Lark suspected by King's reaction—that she had never done before; and he responded. Oh, how he responded.

Lark stood her ground, delighting in the scene, as the dowager reached to stroke his face with both her trembling hands.

"Are you really all right?" she asked her son. Even her voice had changed. Soft, and full of emotion, Lark hardly recognized it.

"I'm fine, Mother," he soothed. "At least I will be once I've gotten Frith off my back and had some time alone with my wife."

"Frith loves you, son. He takes everything you do to heart. Humor him, dear."

"I know," King chortled. "Now, I want you up and out of that bed."

She laid a finger across his lips, her misted eyes sparkling with unshed tears. "I'm so sorry, son," she murmured.

"For what?"

"For . . . everything," she replied. She reached for Lark's hand, and Lark went to her side. "Frith and this precious daughter you have given me aren't the only inmates in this old mausoleum who love you. We shall have a long talk . . . when you've rested. I shan't ask for your forgiveness, only for a chance to make amends however needs must. I love you, too, Basil . . . so very much."

Twilight darkened the master bedchamber early that night. Outside, the risen wind whistled about the pilasters, rattling the windowpanes in their casings. With the draperies drawn to keep out the drafts, the blazing hearth filled the room with radiant heat. It pulsed toward the vast four-poster where Lark and King sat propped with down pillows atop the counterpane, King with his wounded ankle resting on a satin bolster.

Across the room their dinner trays rested on the trestle table, the food long since devoured except for some fruit. Grapes and winter pears, succulent and ripe, perfumed the air.

"You're sure that isn't serious?" Lark said, nodding toward his bandaged ankle.

"I'd unbind Frith's handiwork and prove the point, if he wouldn't fly into alt over it," King said, through a dry chuckle. "It's just a graze, thanks to my bootmaker's skill and Westerfield's ineptitude. I will mend without the surgeon. I was more embarrassed than harmed that the blighter knocked me off my pins."

Lark bristled, vaulting upright, her diaphanous nightdress like a cloud around her. "I should fly into alt," she said. "Why didn't you come home and ease our hearts? We were nearly mad with worry. What took you so long?"

"We stopped in Polperro village on the way, to see Zephaniah Job regarding what we discussed."

"So soon?"

"There was no reason to wait, Lark. I shan't change my mind. The arrangements needed to be made before the ships go out again, and I knew once I got back here Frith would have me under house arrest until I mend. We had to pass right by the village. It seemed the most logical solution. The trade was the last thing that stood between us. I wanted it settled before I came to you again."

"And . . . is it?" She was almost afraid to ask. That he would make such a sacrifice for her was beyond imagining.

"As far as I'm concerned it is," he returned. "Oh, there'll be an audience with the Admiralty over it, of course, and a formal issuance of Will's Letter of Marque. Zephaniah's solicitors will fine-tune the details. Trust me, they're a clever lot. The upshot is, I'm out of it. Finally. Will is ecstatic. That was the first time I've ever seen him speechless, and we have a verbal agreement. Any time we want to sail the high seas, there'll be a ship at our disposal. I would ask, however, that you control those urges until peacetime."

Lark drew a ragged breath and snuggled down against his chest. He smelled of coconut soap, shaving paste, and contraband brandy. One couldn't have *everything*. Some things would never change. As long as Will Bowles was in command, she had no doubt that there would be plenty of brandy.

"King," she murmured, her eyes clouding. "Something strange happened in the dower house when Westerfield and I—"

"Don't think about that anymore," he interrupted. "All that is over, Lark."

"Yes, I know, but hear me out," she insisted. "When he had me tethered, his foot on my frock, a shaft of light spilled in at the window . . . just enough to pick out the fireplace tools in their bracket. They rattled, as if an unseen hand was shaking them . . . as though someone or some*thing* wanted me to take up that poker. I never would have noticed it otherwise. I was watching Westerfield's every move then."

King burst into laughter. "One of old Smythe's 'ghosties'?" he scoffed.

She awarded him a playful swat. "Don't laugh at me," she said. "There's been so much talk of Great-grandfather Basil's ghost . . . and you did take my father out of that dreadful common grave and give him peace in the churchyard. What if one of them was trying to help me? I'd like to think it."

"Then you go right ahead and dream up all the 'ghosties' you like, my love—so long as they're friendly, that is. I shouldn't want you wielding any pokers at me."

"There's scant danger of that," she said.

"Speaking of the dower house," he said, "I understand that you'd decided to camp there until you were sure you weren't with child. Shouldn't you be sure by now?"

"I . . . should."

"But you're not?"

"It may take awhile."

"Does that mean . . . ?"

"It means, my impatient husband, that you shall just have to wait a little longer to see."

King pulled her close in his arms, but when she reached for his lips, he denied her, a playful glint in his eye as he untied the silk ribbon that closed her nightdress. He slid it down over her shoulders until it barely covered her breasts, and traced the mole there with the tip of his finger.

"I used to wonder if this was real or one of those paste-on affairs ladies are so fond of. I must admit, I couldn't take my eyes off it."

"I noticed," she said.

"Mmmm. And you have no idea whether or not—"

"You will just have to be patient," she interrupted, laying a finger over his lips.

He kissed it gently. "Then, while I'm waiting," he murmured, "we may as well take up where we left off in the Roman bath."

"And where was that?" she wondered, captivated by his playful mood.

"Do you remember when I showed you new and delicious ways to enjoy the noble grape?"

How could she ever forget? Hot blood surged to her temples just thinking about it.

"That bunch of choice Burgundians over there on the table looks to be the perfect thing," he went on, his voice husky and deep.

"It . . . does, doesn't it?" she agreed. She could just imagine the color of her cheeks, judging from the heat they generated.

"I ordered them especially," he informed her, his deep voice resonating through her body as he pulled her closer. This time, he did take her lips, and kissed her deeply.

Lark moaned at the suddenness of his advance. White-hot needles pricked at her loins, and rendered her as weak as water. When he buried his hand in her hair, she was un-done, melting against him as he spread her nightshift wide, exposing her breasts to his touch.

"I'll tell you what," he murmured against her lips. "Why

don't you remove this ridiculous gown, and fetch that succulent bunch of Burgundians over there. I have a sudden insatiable craving for dessert."

Without hesitation, and with a shocking lack of embarrassment, she did exactly as he bade her.

EMILY BRYAN

BARING IT ALL

From the moment she saw the man on her doorstep, Lady Artemisia, Duchess of Southwycke, wanted him naked. For once, she'd have the perfect model for her latest painting. But as he bared each bit of delicious golden skin from his broad chest down to his—oh, my!—art became the last thing on her mind.

Trevelyn Deveridge was looking for information, not a job. Though if a brash, beautiful widow demanded he strip, he wasn't one to say no. Especially if it meant he could get closer to finding the true identity of an enigmatic international operative with ties to her family. But as the intrigue deepened and the seduction sweetened, Trev found he'd gone well beyond his original mission of...

DISTRACTING
the DUCHESS

AVAILABLE MARCH 2008!   ISBN 13: 978-0-8439-5870-6

To order a book or to request a catalog call:
1-800-481-9191
This book is also available at your local bookstore, or you can check out our Web site www.dorchesterpub.com where you can look up your favorite authors, read excerpts, or glance at our discussion forum to see what people have to say about your favorite books.

JENNIFER ASHLEY

Egan MacDonald was the one person Princess Zarabeth couldn't read. Yet even without being able hear his thoughts, she knew he was the most honorable, infuriating, and deliciously handsome man she'd ever met. And now her life was in his hands. Chased out of her native country by bitter betrayal and a bevy of assassins, Zarabeth found refuge at the remote MacDonald castle and a haven in Egan's embrace. She also found an ancient curse, a matchmaking nephew, a pair of debutants eager to drag her protector to the altar, and dark secrets in Egan's past. But even amid all the danger raged a desire too powerful to be denied....

Highlander Ever After

AVAILABLE APRIL 2008!

ISBN 13: 978-0-8439-6004-4